FATE'S SWEETEST CURSE

MIRRORS OF FATE BOOK 2

NICOLA VICTORY

Book Cover by The Book Brander at thebookbrander.com

Edited by Emily L. Henry at spottydogediting.com

First Edition 2025

Published by Violet Moon Press

Port Townsend, Washington

nicolavictory.com

For anyone who has ever dimmed their sparkle to be more palatable.
The world needs your unique light — let it shine.

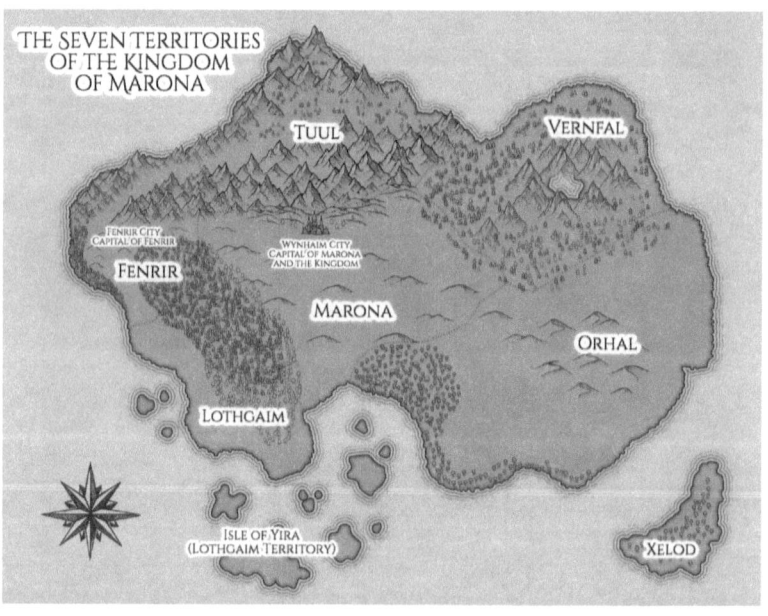

PROLOGUE: PEACH

HATTIE, ONE YEAR AGO

I t was raining the day I saw him for the second first time.

I was at Waldron's spring market, perusing a selection of potion ingredients. I had a jar of dried gardenia in one hand and powdered rose petal in the other, and when I looked up, there he was: standing under the canopy of an open-sided tent two down from mine, speaking with the local blacksmith.

Seeing him here in this tiny cottage town—far, far from home—was like seeing a ripe plum on a tree in winter: so out of place that I doubted my own eyes before my mind even considered the improbability of it being true.

Noble Asheren. *Here*, in Waldron-on-Wend.

"Looking for love, are we?" the herb merchant asked me, breaking through my trancelike shock.

I stared down at the jars in my hands. Ironic that I was—by sheer accident—holding two common ingredients in love potions. Hastily, I dropped them on the velvet-draped display table, the glasses thudding.

"I'll be right back," I told the merchant distractedly, stepping out into the street.

Rain freckled my face and soaked the hem of my dress, but I was impervious to the chilly spring haze as I made my way toward the blacksmith's tent. My mind pattered with all the reasons Noble could be here.

Had someone died? Was I in peril? Would there be another attempt on my life?

Yet no looming tragedy seemed to matter compared to the thrill of his unexpected presence. Since childhood, I'd been drawn to Noble by a desperate ache, instinctual as the urge to inhale after a long-held breath. For the past eight years, I had been underwater; now, I was swimming toward the surface, and *he* was my fresh air.

As I approached, the differences in his appearance since the last time I saw him became stark. For one, he was a *man* now. His lean frame from adolescence had filled out considerably, adult muscle adding rigidity to his shoulders and chest. His hands were crisscrossed with a myriad of tiny pale scars. A faded Oath tattoo ringed the base of his masculine throat. There were new worry lines beside his eyes, and I wondered if any of the creases had formed because of me.

The rest of him was painfully familiar. The same warm brown skin, with a chaotic cascade of black wavy hair that curled by his ears and nape. The same observant, spring-green gaze, made more cutting by his straight nose, wide jaw, and stern but full mouth. The same carefully trained gestures, graceful but restrained. A calm, chilly countenance that gave nothing away.

Fates help me. Eight years of distance had done nothing to quell my hopeless desire for Noble Asheren.

When I entered the blacksmith's tent, the men were still in conversation, and Noble's tone dropped to a lower register, maintaining a semblance of privacy in the cramped space. And that *voice*. It was raspier than I remembered—deeper. Silk draped over stone.

He didn't even glance in my direction. Was he pretending not to know me? Or did my childhood best friend truly not recognize me?

It didn't matter. The blacksmith was not one to ignore a customer. Breaking from their conversation, Richold swung his kind gray eyes in my direction. "Hattie, how are you, dear?"

I'd always liked Richold. He was a regular at the Pretty Possum Inn & Pub—my best friend Anya's establishment, where I lived and tended bar—and not once had he ever been impatient or rude. He was in his early fifties, silver streaking his light brown hair, and was desperately in love with Kara, the seamstress. The gossips in town had already concluded that Kara wasn't interested, but I was still rooting for him.

I knew a thing or two about unrequited love.

"Richold, nice to see you," I replied.

At the sound of my voice, Noble finally turned, a slow reangling of his torso in my direction. Every person in the Seven Territories possessed one magically heightened sense, and as a sight magician, Noble's proclivity for visual detail meant that he noticed *everything*—and therefore was rarely caught off guard.

He was now, though.

I saw it in the way the skin around his eyes tightened when he saw me—the strained look straight out of a childhood memory. His expression quaked—lips parting, brow furrowing, a brief slackening of his features, like his world was coming undone. Surprise, but also confusion, pain, regret. He drew back as if to see me more clearly, as if a slightly different perspective might explain my presence.

Then all his polite society experience kicked in and his features shifted into the perfect mix of casual curiosity and mild boredom. *Court face*, we used to call it.

It would've been unrealistic for him to sweep me into his arms—or acknowledge me at all. The last thing either of us needed was for the gossips of Waldron to catch on to our perilous history. Yet his flat, dispassionate expression still stung.

My heart began to riot in a manner I knew all too well. Noble wasn't the only one who'd received etiquette lessons, but my governess had never completely succeeded in training the expressiveness out of my face.

My emotional openness, paired with Noble's preternatural observation skills, meant that he was able to read me with annoying clarity.

Still, I tried my best to act casual. "And who is this?" I asked Richold.

"This is Noble. He's new in town," the blacksmith answered. "Noble, this is Hattie."

"Hello, Hattie." His confident drawl turned my insides to syrup.

But I recovered—*barely*. "Noble? That's a unique name."

I already knew that he'd been named after the first Knight of the Order of the Mighty, a legendary hero whose given name of *Nolan* had morphed into *Noble* over centuries of retellings. The Noble in Richold's tent had essentially been named after a mistake. He'd never said as much, but I had a feeling that had shaped much of his self-image growing up. He'd always had something to prove.

His wry amusement toward my comment was there and gone in a flash of teeth. "My parents thought themselves clever," he said, slow and low, giving nothing away.

Oblivious to our familiarity, Richold asked, "What can I help you with, dear?"

What I really needed was to learn why Noble was *here*, of all places. His blank stare gave me no clues. I glanced down at the array of axe heads on Richold's display table, trying to think of an excuse to get Noble alone. "Noble, did you, um, happen to arrive here on horseback?"

"Yes, last night."

Last night? Did Anya check him into the Possum? How had I not noticed him in the same Fates-damned building as me?

"Why, is...something wrong with my horse?" Noble prompted.

The leading question was just what I needed. "Yes," I said, settling into the charade. "Yes, perhaps? Is it a sorrel mare?"

"Indeed." Green eyes bored into mine as if to say, *You're terrible at this.* "What's wrong with her?"

"She's...loose."

"Loose?" he repeated dubiously.

"Loose," I confirmed. "I'll show you. Please excuse us, Richold."

The blacksmith glanced between us, forehead creased.

Noble unfolded the cloak that had been draped over his arm. "Mind if I visit the smithy later?"

Richold bobbed his head. "Please do. Good luck with your horse."

Unceremoniously, I lifted the hood of my cloak and stomped into the downpour, leading Noble away from the crowded market. When we reached the southern end of town, I glanced over my shoulder, making sure no one was watching. Then I lifted my skirts and stepped off the cobblestones onto an overgrown deer path.

We passed through the dreamy shelter of willow boughs, over fallen logs, through a tangle of wild rose bushes. Lush spring foliage caught at my cloak and snagged Noble's trousers, but he didn't question our path. He simply followed. Trusting me, even after all this time.

When the brush opened up again, we'd reached the old fishing dock that Anya and I liked to bask on in the summertime. It extended out over a wide, shallow stretch of the River Wend, its location unseen from the rest of town.

I walked down the length of the dock, then turned and rested my hands on my hips. Noble halted, facing me at a respectable distance. A gauzy gray haze of rain sheeted around us, hissing on the river's calm surface, shrouding us in privacy.

His smirk was knowing. "Sorrel mare?"

When we were kids, the private stable utilized by our families had housed a rather mean-spirited copper-colored mare named Sweetpea, who once took a chunk out of Noble's shoulder with her teeth. She and I had gotten along splendidly—she and Noble, not so much.

I folded my arms across my chest, too rattled and impatient for nostalgia. "What the *fuck* are you doing here, Noble?"

His indifferent mask fell away in an instant, revealing a pained expression underneath. "What am *I* doing here?" Noble asked miserably.
"What are *you* doing here?"

So, he hadn't come to Waldron for me. Could this really just be an
awful coincidence?

A knot formed in my throat. "I live here," I answered tightly.

"But you were married off to the mayor of *Poe*-on-Wend."

"I left."

A muscle in Noble's jaw ticked. "When?"

"About three months after I arrived."

He stared at me for a moment, then ran a hand through his rain-wet
waves, pushing them back—only for a few unruly strands to fall across
his forehead again. The prominent bulge in his throat bobbed, drawing
my attention to his Oath tattoo.

"You made it into the Order of the Mighty," I observed. "Congratulations. Your father must be so—"

"I was never worthy of Mighty Knighthood." He pointed at his neck.
"This is meaningless. I'm retired."

"So, you decided to retire...in Fenrir Territory? In *Waldron*?"

Noble took a step closer, staring down at me through the rain-soaked
tips of his hair. His pupils blew out his bright irises, making his eyes
appear almost black. "What?" he intoned, taunting and sarcastic. "Are
you not happy to see me?"

I lifted my chin. "You don't seem particularly happy to see *me*."

"I'm not."

It took all my willpower not to place my hands on his chest and shove
him off the dock.

"I am not happy to see you," Noble continued coolly, "toiling in
obscurity when you deserve better. I am not happy to see you hidden
away in some inconsequential town, when it's my fault, and—"

Without thinking, I reached out and gripped his forearm. "It *wasn't* your fault." The muscle beneath my palm flexed, ropey and hard; his lips pulled into a frown, and I let go. "It wasn't your fault," I repeated.

A streak of rainwater traced down the side of his face. The collar of his shirt was soaked through. His eyes searched mine and I wondered what he saw.

"I am not happy to see you because I am not *allowed* to see you," he said firmly. "I am not allowed to—" He broke off, eyes lifting to the heavy clouds. He shook his head as if to clear it of whatever he'd been about to say.

Hold you.

Want you.

That's what I *hoped* he'd been about to say. Yearning was an old, terrible habit of mine, apparently unbroken by time. Yet not only had Noble never wanted me in the way I'd wanted him—even if he did, we *couldn't.*

Be near you.

Interact with you.

That's probably what he'd meant to say.

"If you're not here for me, then why *are* you here?" I asked, trying to sound more curious than hurt. Familiarity was quickly being overtaken by long-buried grief, and I wasn't in the mood to dig it up.

"Better you not concern yourself with my goings on."

"How long are you staying?"

"As long as it takes."

I growled through my teeth. "Seriously? You barge into my life for the first time in eight years and you can't even tell me—"

"You aren't supposed to be here," Noble pointed out.

I stomped my foot. "I'm not supposed to be *anywhere.*"

His jaw ticked again—the only evidence that he felt any type of way about my outburst. "Look, Hattie, I'm not here to interfere with your life. Ignore me. Pretend you don't know me. We're supposed to be apart, so let's just...*be apart.*"

In true Noble Asheren fashion, his sentiment was completely logical and altogether infuriating. "So...what? We just live in the same small town and pretend we don't—after all we—" I broke off before my voice cracked.

"You and I both know it's safer that way. Not just for you, but..."

My lower lip quivered, and I caught it with my teeth, biting down to distract from the swell of anguish in my chest. I glanced out across the river, into the misty rain. A pair of swans bobbed on the calm surface, ghostlike in the haze.

Noble took another step closer. I could feel the heat radiating off of his body, steamy as a sudden break in a storm, like sunlight beaming down on wet cobblestones. Inexplicably, he reached up and grazed his thumb across my bottom lip, gently pulling it free of my canine.

We'd touched plenty of times in our youth—playful pokes, casual hugs—but *never* like this. The intimate, unbidden contact must've been from his shock at seeing me—mere evidence of our long-ago platonic affection. *Nothing more*, I told my hopeless heart, but still, it *throbbed.*

"It *is* nice to see you, Peach," Noble said, that cruel and lovely mouth biting into my old nickname like the fruit it represented. "Even if I'm not happy about it."

The reference took me back to summer mornings racing through the orchards, hot afternoons picnicking by the river, and sticky evenings sneaking Noble onto my balcony to snack on sugared peaches.

But those days were long gone. A faded dream.

His hand fell, and he turned away, walking back down the dock.

It took me several heartbeats to recover. To call after him. "Where are you staying?"

He swiveled. "The Pretty Porcupine?"

"Possum," I corrected. "You can't stay there."

"Why not?"

I met him at the base of the dock. "I live there. Tend bar there. It's my friend's place. You can't stay."

He regarded me like he was doing math in his head, calculating how I'd gone from the girl I'd been to the woman before him. "You're too talented to tend bar."

The comment was irrelevant. Insulting. "Oh, but being a random mayor's wife was just right?" I retorted. "Hosting tedious social gatherings only to get shoved and struck after everyone went home?"

"He *didn't*," Noble said darkly, scarred knuckles paling as his fists clenched.

"He did," I stated flatly. "At least here, I have safety. Autonomy. People who love me."

"Hattie—"

"The next time you want to compliment me, don't put down the one place that welcomed me when no one else would."

Noble's throat bobbed, and he nodded.

"And if you're going to live here," I went on, "let's get one thing straight: you don't know anything about me anymore. I'm a different person now."

He huffed a harsh, joyless laugh. "Keep telling yourself that."

"What's that supposed to mean?"

For a moment, he looked like he'd hedge—the younger version of him probably would have—but adult Noble was...maybe not *unrestrained*, but definitely *sharper*. Colder. "It means I can still read you like one of your cherished alchemy books. It's plain as day on that pretty face of yours: you still love me."

The taunting words hit like physical blows.

You.

Still.

Love.

Me.

My infatuation had never been a secret, but he'd been less of a prick about it when we were adolescents.

I forced a laugh, even though I felt like a bug trapped inside a small glass jar. "Seems you still think too highly of yourself."

His lips pulled into that smug smile, even as his eyes pinched. "You know that's not true, either." He invaded my personal space again. "Whatever fond memory you have of me," he murmured, "that boy is gone. Do us both a favor and forget him."

I scowled. "Happy to."

"Good girl." He stepped back, about to leave.

"I am *not* a girl anymore, Noble," I bit out.

His eyes dipped, taking in my figure with quick efficiency, before meeting mine again. "Clearly," he said, but his tone wasn't suggestive or sarcastic—it was thick, as if the fact pained him. "I'll see you around, Peach."

With that, he turned, abandoning me on the riverbank.

Only after he'd disappeared into the trees did I venture a breath. My tongue darted out, sweeping the same path Noble's thumb had traced on my lower lip, savoring the residue of him with my taste magic: salt, iron, leather, and the indescribably primal flavor of his skin.

It wasn't just my unresolved feelings for Noble that rattled me, but the collision of past and present. I might've insisted I was different now, but the truth was, even after eight years apart, Noble still understood me better than anyone else. Because he knew where I came from. Who I truly was.

After living a lie for so long, I'd forgotten what it felt like to be *known*. It was a painful relief, like working a knot in a muscle, a tension that unraveled into something tender.

A hot tear streaked down my cheek, mingling with the rainwater. How in the Fates was I supposed to live in the same town as the *one* person who knew the real me...and pretend we were strangers?

You will endure as you always have, I told myself. *You will endure because you must.*

By the time I returned to the Pretty Possum, Noble had vacated his room, and I'd shoved my heartache back into the cellar where I kept all my darkest and most painful secrets.

Where I kept the real me.

1

FAREWELL FOR NOW

HATTIE

D o you have everything you need?" Anya asked, adjusting my shawl before pulling me into a tight embrace.

From over her shoulder, I saw her partner, Idris, cross his arms. "I already loaded her trunk into the wagon," he said. "It was surprisingly heavy."

"Can't study herbal alchemy at the esteemed Collegium of Fenrir without my books." As Anya and I drew apart, I gripped her hands, squeezing. The midmorning sunlight was bright, making her red hair spark with copper. "And the real question is, do *you* have everything *you* need?"

I'd helped my best friend run the Pretty Possum Inn & Pub for going on nine years—ever since I showed up in the middle of the night as a bruised and frightened newlywed, half frozen to death—and while she pretended to only *tolerate* my concern, I knew that deep down, Anya appreciated someone looking out for her. Especially since *she* played that role for everyone else in our merry little town of Waldron-on-Wend.

This would be the first time I'd left Waldron since my harrowing arrival, and it wasn't just Anya's lack of assistance behind her bar that had me feeling anxious. Waldron was *home*. More so than anywhere else.

Anya scoffed. "I'm *fine*," she said. "I have Idris, and Martha already agreed to help me in the kitchen while you're gone."

"Are you telling me you don't need me *at all*?"

Anya reached up and tugged on a curl that had escaped the bun on my head, letting it spring into my face. "I'm *saying* that I'll manage without you while you pursue your dream. It's the least I can do."

"You've already done so much."

Anya dismissed my comment with a wave. "Don't start."

I glanced at the gathering crowd. Martha, the town baker, was gesticulating wildly at Hugh, the chandler, who'd arranged for me to travel with the wagoner who led his candle shipment. Around them, I spotted countless familiar faces—Farmers Timmons and Quinn, Vera the florist, even Richold—but not the face I continually sought.

Nearly the entire town had come to see me off, but Noble was nowhere to be found. *Not* that I expected him to come to my sendoff. For the past year, we'd succeeded at pretending we were strangers; me leaving was no reason to deviate.

I turned back to Anya. "Don't let Martha move anything."

She laughed. "You'll be gone for six months, I make no promises."

I tossed my hands in the air. "That's it! Idris, unload my trunk."

He came forward, folding me into a strong hug. "No turning back now, Hattie." His short beard tickled my cheek as he added in a faint whisper, "Don't worry, I'll look after her while you're gone."

"I heard that," Anya said.

"Of course," Idris and I said in unison, breaking apart.

"Ready?" the lead wagoner called.

We stood on the edge of town, right where Waldron's main cobblestone road ended. The modest caravan—three wagons in total, each with one driver and two horses—waited in the grass not far off, facing north.

"Almost!" I replied, dropping into a crouch to pet Anya's elderly wolfhound, Wicker. His pink tongue darted out, lapping at my cheek. "I'll miss you, too," I told him.

When I stood again, I surveyed the street, trying to soak up every detail. Quaint cottages were snuggled up in neat rows, edged with unruly flower boxes. The River Wend meandered through the middle of town, swans gliding along its calm surface and ducks bobbing butts-up for pondweed. The surrounding hills looked like a massive, rumpled quilt, patched with square crop plots and fields dotted with sheep and buttercups. The wind smelled of loam and livestock; the sun seemed to kiss every stone sweetly.

I loved Waldron in the spring. I'd never been to the capital city of Fenrir Territory, but I knew it wouldn't be as charming. Nothing was.

Hiking my satchel a little higher on my shoulder, I started toward the wagons, shaking hands, offering hugs, and speaking my farewells to everyone who'd come to witness my departure. Waldron was the closest I'd ever come to feeling a true sense of belonging, but the terrible truth was: no one here knew the complete me. The Hattie they knew was a carefully constructed portrait, where only the prettiest glimpses of a larger and more complicated painting were visible.

But that didn't mean my love for them wasn't real—that I wouldn't miss them all terribly.

When I approached the last wagon in the line, Idris was there to offer me a hand, helping me up. I took a seat on one of the numerous candle crates, setting my satchel on the floor by my feet, the vials inside it clinking. There were a few things did not wish to travel without: my herbology books, an arrangement of tinctures and potions, plenty of dresses, and copious snacks for the road.

Gripping the railing, I gave Anya my best, most optimistic smile, hoping she couldn't see the nervous anticipation I was feeling. "Wish me luck!"

Anya shook her head. "You don't need it."

"Pretty sure I do."

Apothecary apprenticeships were only a small fraction of the teachings that happened within the walls of Fenrir's Collegium. Folks from all over the Seven Territories of Marona traveled there with the hopes of one day becoming an Adept of the Order of Alchemy, the Arcane, or the Archives. And while I'd set my sights on a more modest and applicable apothecary license—with the sole intention of being able to legally practice healing alchemy for the folks in Waldron—I'd be studying alongside students of all calibers, from all corners of the kingdom.

I needed all the luck I could get.

But Anya wasn't having it. "I know you, Hattie. Luck or no, you're going to take them by storm."

I know you, Hattie.

Her words made my heart twist like a wrung-out bar rag.

While I'd never *lied* to Anya, but I'd never been entirely truthful, either. I'd omitted large swaths of my past from her—not only because I hadn't wanted to relive the events that led me to Waldron, but because my history was too dangerous to divulge, even to her. Anya had respected my caginess—never prying—and that had only made me feel worse about my inability to be completely honest.

So, while she *did* know me—from my favorite tea (chamomile) to my love of reading (mostly about herbs) to my teasing (but doting) sense of humor—she didn't know the labels of my identity. She *couldn't.* And no amount *I-lie-to-keep-people-safe* reasoning could assuage my guilt. Because when it came down to it, I was deceiving my best friend. I was living a lie.

I compensated by being as truthful about everything else as I could. Always sharing my honest opinion, always wearing my heart on my sleeve, always offering my friendliest and most social self. But deep down, I craved *real* connection, and in spite of what I hid from her, Anya was as close as I'd ever get. My safest place in a dangerous world.

Thinking about all this—how much I wanted to tell her and had to hold back, how much I loved her, how much I'd miss her—made my eyes well with tears. When one tracked down my face, I caught it with my tongue, my taste magic noting the quality of the salt.

"Oh, Hattie," Anya said, reaching over the railing of the wagon to give me one last squeeze. I tucked my face into her shoulder, feeling more tears wet the fabric of her dress. "At least they're not carting you off in a prisoner caravan."

At our last farewell, Anya had been in shackles, heading off to trial for a Fates-predicted crime she hadn't yet committed. Though she had eventually been absolved, her journey to the capital had been far more fraught than mine would be.

Hopefully.

I snorted and wiped my eyes. "I always love being reminded of watching my best friend being taken away like a criminal. That's comforting, thank you."

"You're welcome," Anya said, bouncing her eyebrows. "Your time in Fenrir will fly by. Just enjoy it."

I gave her my best bubbly smile. "I will." Then I met Idris's eyes again, inclining my head.

"I know that look," he said, scratching his beard. "I'll keep her safe."

Two nights ago, I'd caught a glimpse of a terribly diseased bobcat from my bedroom window, skirting the edge of the Western Wood. Its body had been deformed—stretched larger—with gnarled antlers pushing through its skull, spider-like legs protruding from its sides, and glowing red eyes.

A monster.

I'd never seen anything like it; I'd never *heard* of anything like it. It'd shaken me to the core, leaving me panicked and sweating.

Minutes after the horrifying sight, a visitor had arrived on the porch of the Pretty Possum with black blood dripping from her sword. Her arrival was eerily similar to how Anya and I had met Idris: a late-night intrusion, black saliva slicking his hand. He'd needed an apothecary, and I was the only person in town with any knowledge of purifying herbs. Our recent visitor, however, hadn't needed tinctures or salves—she'd come to deliver a warning.

After she left, Idris had confirmed that monsters were infringing on the towns of rural Fenrir with more frequency. He'd made me promise not to tell anyone about what I'd seen (I'd felt vindicated to learn I wasn't the only person with secrets). But still, the monster's presence was troubling, and while I would be useless against such a creature, that didn't stop me from worrying about Anya—and *all* of Waldron—in the meantime. I was glad Idris was around to look after everyone.

Anya only rolled her eyes, not one to be cowed—even by the implication of monsters. After all, she'd faced a few herself. "I'm plenty self-sufficient without you two."

"Yes, but—" I began.

"You don't have to be," Idris finished for me.

Anya gestured between us. "Had I known you two would form an alliance to smother me..."

"You love it," I said.

Idris chuckled and wrapped an arm around Anya's shoulders, tucking her close. To me, he said, "You be safe, too."

I gave him a nod. I'd packed a vial of Hylder tincture and one pot of salve—the same recipes I'd given Idris to stave off the infection of his nasty wound—just in case.

Anya snaked her arm around Idris's waist, leaning into his embrace. "This is supposed to be a *happy* sendoff," she told us, throwing a meaningful glance over her shoulder at the townsfolk forming a half-moon behind her. Raising her voice so the others could hear, she added, "We're so excited for you."

A chorus of "*Hear! Hear!*" filled the air, with folks calling out their hopes that the Fates would favor my travels, keep the roads safe and the weather mild.

Wicker plopped down at Anya's feet, his feathery tail swishing jubilantly. She patted his head, beaming up at me. "By the way, I slipped a birthday gift into your trunk; don't open it until the day!"

"You didn't have to—"

"You're not the only caretaker in this relationship," Anya teased.

My twenty-ninth birthday was four weeks from now. It saddened me that I wouldn't get to celebrate the milestone in the usual, over-the-top Waldron fashion, but it was just like Anya to do something special for me, anyhow.

Tears welled again. "I love you."

"I love you, too, friend!"

A sharp whistle pierced the air. One of the horses let out a startled whinny.

Then we were moving, the axles of my wagon creaking as the horses picked up speed. I sat a little taller on my crate, waving at the friends and neighbors I was (temporarily) leaving behind.

"Farewell!" I yelled.

"For now!" the crowd answered—a customary goodbye in Waldron.

The horses' hooves and wagon wheels kicked up a cloud of dust, obscuring my vision of the congregation. Then it cleared, and—

I saw him.

Noble, apart from the rest, leaning against the trunk of the oak tree that bordered the edge of downtown. His arms were crossed, his cheeks shaded with day-old stubble. The black waves of his hair were pushed away from his forehead, showing off his strong jawline and long neck. As always, his expression was painfully unreadable, but when his green eyes collided with mine, our gazes held for a fleeting, desperate moment.

A memory took shape, painful and panicked. Suddenly we were nine years younger: him, hiding behind the willow tree in the courtyard of my childhood home, and me, peering helplessly out the window of a midnight carriage as I was whisked away, never to return.

Except, this time, I *would* return. I was older now, wiser, and I wouldn't let what I'd built in Waldron slip so easily through my fingers.

The wagon lurched, breaking our tense stares. I gripped the railing, holding on as I lifted my gaze to Noble again—but he was no longer there.

"Safe travels!" Anya called.

Wicker howled, setting off other dogs in town, which in turn set off all the citizens again, hooting and cheering and wishing me well. I waved enthusiastically, grinning from ear to ear, even as my heart twisted. I was traveling to the capital to realize my lifelong dream of becoming an apothecary—an herbal alchemist—but that didn't mean I wouldn't miss Waldron sorely while I was gone.

Then again, at least I wouldn't have to worry about seeing Noble around every corner. Avoiding the object of my unrequited love was certainly an upside to this adventure.

2

CURSE

NOBLE

Noble let out a guttural, throat-tearing growl and fell forward onto his hands and knees. Pain seared his fingertips as his nails elongated, sharpening into charcoal-black claws. His temples ached with a pulsing, budding pressure. When he reached up with one hand, he felt the knob of a horn growing from his skull, threatening to split through the stretched skin. His eyes felt like hot coals inside their sockets.

A woman with golden curls spilling down her back was walking down the forest path ahead of him, barefoot. Her ivory dress glowed white in the moonlight; he could see the silhouettes of her slender legs veiled by the thin fabric. At the sound of Noble's next pained growl, she turned, her kind face distorting into an expression of wide-eyed horror.

A foreign and grotesque instinct welled up inside Noble, clouding his logic and sense of self. He crawled forward on the dirt, snarling. He wanted to pounce. To bite. To shred. To—

Noble woke suddenly, shoving off the mattress into an upright position. His bare chest was slicked with sweat, rising and falling in quick, panicked pants. With his nightmare still clinging to his mind, he looked down at his hands, half expecting them to be claw-tipped. They were flecked with pale scars from years of knighthood and metalworking, with veins that were a little too pronounced—but otherwise they were fine.

Just fine.

Noble sighed heavily, then stood, padding over to the front door of his tiny guesthouse on the edge of Waldron-on-Wend. Hinges squeaked.

A crisp spring wind gusted in, smelling of pine and pollen. The sky was a deep cobalt stretching over the jagged treetops of the Western Wood. The Fates had gifted every person on the continent with a drop of magic, a single heightened sense; his gift was sight, and his magic—semi-nocturnal and incredibly keen, even from a distance—spotted no lurking threats in the underbrush.

Another chill swept over his naked form, but he embraced its bite. It made him feel alive. *Human.*

The nightmares used to be few and far between, but their frequency had increased as of late, the images and emotions becoming more vivid. He'd been living in Waldron for a full year, studying with Richold for eight to ten hours per day, six days per week, and what had his efforts amounted to? *Fuck all.*

Noble lingered in the doorway a moment longer, then shuffled back inside. Crouching beside the bed, he slid out a shallow basket. Inside it were twelve identical vials. All empty except for one.

"Shit," he grumbled, holding the final vial up to the moonlight. The glass was indigo, making the syrupy plum-colored liquid inside appear black. Noble removed the cork with an unceremonious *pop*, drank a third of the sweet and botanical tincture, then replaced the cork and shoved his shame back under the bed.

By his estimate, he had three weeks until he needed to replenish, which was just barely enough time to get to Fenrir City to visit his alchemist.

Noble *really* didn't want to travel to Fenrir City.

Not because of the inconvenience—though it *was* inconvenient—but because of Hattie. She'd started her apothecary apprenticeship in the capital barely a month ago, and while it was unlikely that he would run into her during a quick visit to the alchemist who supplied him with his tinctures, he felt guilty for constantly haunting Hattie's steps like a Fates-damned shadow.

The past year in Waldron had been hard enough.

In that time, they hadn't spoken more than a few scant words to each other—but for Noble, encountering his childhood obsession around every corner, continually witness to her radiance, had been a constant punishment. Hattie had always been a beam of sunshine in his otherwise shaded existence.

No matter how forcefully his parents and tutors had engrained in him the importance of pushing her away—no matter how dangerous their shared history and how wretched his present affliction—he'd never found it *easy* to feign disinterest.

It *was* necessary, though. They might've grown up in the same castle, but they were not of the same pedigree, and where Hattie came from, that mattered. *Greatly.* Her identity mattered, too. So much so that she'd been stripped of her name and married off to a lesser-born brute before rumors of her true parentage spread.

It's why he'd been horrified to find her here in Waldron, why—on the day of their first encounter—he'd taunted her with the affection she didn't realize was mutual. What he'd *wanted* to do was tug her into his arms and crush her against his body, soak up all her warmth after an eight-year winter without her presence—but he couldn't. As the lesser born of the two of them, it had always been up to him to keep her at arm's length. So, he pretended to think nothing of her desire—even though, in truth, it was *everything*.

His callousness that day had had its desired effect: for the first three months of his time in Waldron, Hattie had ignored him (with a stubborn haughtiness that was, in all honesty, a turn-on).

Summer changed their chilly standoff.

When Noble could no longer deny Richold's kindhearted offers for a drink at the Possum after their long days at the forge, he'd had no choice but to break a rule and enter Hattie's domain. His appreciative groan when he'd tried her signature concoctail—an exquisite blend of liquor, syrup, and bitters—hadn't helped matters. Between moments of forced congeniality to keep up appearances as veritable strangers, she'd glared at Noble with a mix of surprise and hurt and vengeance in her oceanic blue eyes.

Then she'd *flirted* with him.

Mercilessly.

Hattie was not one to balk at her own emotions, and so—just as she had in their childhood—she'd weaponized them against him. A teasing, frisky, unceasing barrage of stolen glances and suggestive quips.

You still love me, he'd said.

What a major inconvenience for you, her actions seemed to retort.

It was maddening. Amusing. Torturous.

The rest of their year had unfolded much the same, with Hattie at turns icy and sweet. Noble didn't know what he hated more: the agony of having to rebuke her playfulness, or the jealousy he felt whenever she gave him the cold shoulder in favor of other townsfolk (if he had to watch her dance with another moon-eyed fool at another festival he'd combust).

But Noble remained stalwart in his convictions. If someone so much as *observed* a moment of ease between them, the gossips in town would spread the news like sparks on the wind. Noble had already ruined Hattie's life with one wildfire of gossip; he'd never make the same mistake again. For her safety, no one could ever know how they knew each other.

So, he'd been glad when she left Waldron for her apprenticeship—not just because he delighted in her realizing a lifelong dream of studying with the Order of Alchemy, but because, for several blissful weeks, he hadn't been tormented with the push and pull of *wanting* to see her and *needing* to avoid her.

And now—*Fates help him*—now he had to follow her to Fenrir. The vials should've lasted him longer—another reason to consult his alchemist in the city.

Noble scrubbed a hand over his stubbled jaw. Dawn hadn't yet broken, but there was no way he'd get back to sleep now.

Not bothering to get dressed, he retrieved a heel of sourdough and a jar of preserves from the pantry, then plunked down at his two-person dining table. He tore off a hunk of hard crust, dipped it into the jar, and ate. The taste of peaches exploded on his tongue, making him sigh.

A year. A whole *year* of studying with one of the last Gildium artisans in the kingdom, and Noble still hadn't gotten any closer to alchemizing the magical metal and finding a proper cure for his curse. His letters to the Adept of Alchemy who'd sent him here were punctuated with apology. Waldron, itself, had been lovely—a veritable paradise of pastoral peace and charm—but his time here had been marred by disappointment. Noble was no stranger to failure; his whole life had been defined by it. But the waning of efficacy of his tincture—the very thing keeping him from becoming a literal monster—scared him.

And he was right to be scared.

Fear is your friend, the Adept of the Order of the Arcane had told him when he underwent his change seven years ago. *Fear reminds you of what you value. Fear tethers you to your humanity.*

Noble dipped another piece of sourdough into the peach preserves and bit into the soft flesh of the bread. He licked the sweetness off his bottom lip, an ache opening up inside him that felt worryingly similar to yearning.

And what of love? he'd asked the adept through gritted teeth.

Love? the adept repeated. *Love should no longer be in your vocabulary.*

A LETTER

POSTED FROM: ANYA ALVARA, PRETTY POSSUM
INN & PUB, WALDRON-ON-WEND, FENRIR T.

Dear Hattie,

In the spirit of honest correspondence, I should admit that Martha already rearranged your baking supplies. Not to worry, we can put it all back when you return.

What else is new? It's Waldron, so, not much. I am proud to report that all the herbs in your garden remain alive. The logistics for Illian's wedding are coming together nicely. There are ducklings, cygnets, and goslings all over town—I'm sorry you're missing the mass hatching, I know you love watching them waddle.

No significant gossip, although I did overhear Richold and Kara laughing rather flirtatiously together at the market the other day. Martha and Vera are still convinced there's nothing between them, but I sensed something. Perhaps your romanticism has rubbed off on me. I suspect Idris's influence has had an effect on my belief in love, too.

Speaking of love, I haven't seen your crush in days. I know he's handsome, but why a social butterfly such as yourself would pine after such a recluse, I'll never understand. Do opposites ever really attract?

Anyway, I miss you sorely—sass and all. Are your fellow classmates impressed by your considerable wit yet?

Love and hugs,

Anya

P.S. Send me the recipe for your blackberry drinking vinegar, would you? Vera has been requesting it and I can't find any in the pantry.

3

APPRENTICE

HATTIE

Y our drinks are so much better than these, Hattie," Uriel said, frowning at her glass of brandywine and bitters.

"She's right, you have a *gift*," Sani slurred.

I pursed my lips in a proud little smile, even as I waved my hand to clear away my new friends' compliments.

We were seated around a narrow table in the back corner of Fenrir's Charm, the tavern that adepts frequented. Across the street, a raucous clamor of metal and voices came from Fenrir's Ire, the tavern where knights spent their off time. If I had learned anything in the past two months as an apprentice at the Collegium, it was the willful disconnect between the academic Orders and the weapon-wielding Orders.

"You just like my concoctails because they're free," I said.

Uriel threw back the rest of the golden liquid. "That certainly does not hurt."

In my first week living at the Collegium, I'd made my signature "concoctions to avail merriment" for my new roommates: mixtures of spirits, citrus, herbal bitters, and syrup. While winning friends with alcohol wasn't the most *genuine* tactic, it did promote bonding. It took only one late night of giggle fits and tales from our trips here for our friendship to blossom (Sani, a scent magician, had traveled from Lothgaim, while Uriel, a touch magician, hailed all the way from central Tuul). Amidst the uncertainty of moving to a strange city and the sudden rigor of my studies, their friendship made my homesickness for Waldron tolerable.

I pointed a thumb over my shoulder, toward the overcrowded room. "I'm going to mingle. Want to come?"

Sani hiccupped, eyes going wide.

"Why would we do that?" Uriel asked.

"Because it's why we're here?"

Fenrir's Charm was currently filled to the brim with professors and apprentices like ourselves for an official gathering put on by the academic Orders. The event was meant to give students the chance to make connections, but the three of us had been rooted in our corner all night.

Unlike knights—who, aside from the Mighty, usually received the bulk of their training *after* joining their Order—adepts earned their roles with vast amounts of studying and testing. Even so, only about one in thirty apprentices managed to earn an Adept Oath and access the exclusive knowledge, prestige, and power that entailed.

I was not here for prestige or power; while it would take me only six months to receive my apothecary license, Uriel and Sani's pursuits of adepthood—with the Order of the Arcane and Archives, respectively—would take years. Gaining a mentor would greatly increase their chances of succeeding.

But Uriel scoffed. "Mingling will not make me a better adept."

"Connections could help you gain a better mentorship, though," I pointed out.

Sani bobbed her head. "Hattie has a point."

Uriel lifted her chin, the hoop in her left nostril flashing in the orange glow of the surrounding sconces. "I do not see *you* mingling," she said, pinning Sani with a pointed glare. With her shaved head, piercings, and persistent smirk, Uriel was by no means *approachable*—but she was unapologetically herself, which I admired. "Besides," she added tartly, "my merit is not predicated on my friendliness."

"You should thank the Fates for that," Sani quipped.

Uriel gave her a playful shove that had Sani teetering on her stool.

"What about you, Sani?" I asked. "Want to come?"

She wrinkled her nose. "In truth, I'd rather be reading."

"We *know*," Uriel quipped.

All three of us giggled.

Sani was Uriel's opposite, with cautious eyes and birdlike features. While Uriel could pass as a knight if only she carried a sword, Sani looked just as delicate and bookish as the archivists she idolized.

"Well, unlike you two, I'm feeling social," I said, tossing back the last of my cider—a Maronan brew, too sweet for my taste—before hopping off my stool. I didn't need a mentor to receive an apothecary license, but I *was* here to learn.

Uriel tipped her empty glass in my direction, as if to say, *Suit yourself.*

"Have fun," Sani sang in a teasing lilt, sounding content to watch from her quiet corner.

I flashed them a cheeky grin, then turned, trying not to lose my nerve as I wound my way through the crowded pub in search of a conversation to join.

I might've read every book on alchemy I could get my hands on, had been studying herbs since I was a girl, and knew enough magic weaving to turn tinctures into potions, but compared to my fellow classmates—all much younger than me, who'd already mastered techniques I'd only read about—I felt out of place.

Extremely grateful, enthusiastic, intimidated—and out of place.

My self-doubt was probably a remnant of an adolescence filled with guardians, governesses, and tutors all telling me that alchemy was an improper trade for someone of my lineage. No amount of time, distance, or self-awareness had dispelled the constant and unshakable cloud cast by those long-ago voices telling me all the things I wasn't allowed to love.

Herbology.

Noble.

Myself.

I tried to silence the constant chorus of inner naysayers with humor and warmth, but no matter how friendly or funny or lighthearted I acted on the outside, there was still a part of me that felt wretched, small, and unwelcome.

No more, I told myself, resisting the oncoming swell of self-pity. I might not've been able to be completely honest about my upbringing, but no one was keeping me from becoming an apothecary anymore.

A barmaid breezed past me, and I stepped out of her path—only to narrowly miss a student carrying two pints in the opposite direction. Fenrir's Charm was filled with a cacophony of laughter and debate, with clusters of conversationalists standing shoulder-to-shoulder in the cavernous space. I paused by a wooden column, feeling my cheeks heat.

Great. I had a propensity for blushing whenever I felt anything other than calm. My pale skin and overabundance of dark freckles was a trademark of my mother's family. She'd died in childbirth, but my aunt—who'd raised me in the absence of my father, whom I'd never met—was proof enough of the claim. Every woman in my matriarchal line appeared constantly flustered.

Not that *flustered* was an incorrect descriptor of me in this particular instance. I'd just rather my professors not *see* the extent of my nervousness painted on my cheeks.

Back at the Pretty Possum, I knew how to own a busy room—how to float confidently from table to table, take orders, make drinks, flirt for tips, and keep up with countless conversations. Having been born into a world where connections were the third-most important currency after bloodline and deep coffers, I'd been a master at navigating busy shindigs since I learned to talk.

But this was different.

The people in this room hadn't been born into prominence like those who'd surrounded me in adolescence, nor were they friendly small-town folk enjoying a well-earned supper at the end of a long workday. The people in this room were here because they were among the most intelligent in all the Seven Territories.

My rusty court etiquette and barkeep charm probably wasn't enough to impress an adept, but I had to at least *try* to fit in. Where I lacked Uriel's self-assuredness and Sani's encyclopedic knowledge, I would have to make up for with earnest participation.

Mustering up a false air of easy confidence, I perused the room, half expecting to see Noble lurking at a table in a dark corner. After a year of living in the same town as him, I'd fallen into the habit of seeking him out, caught between wanting to know where he was so I could avoid him and simply...wanting to know that he was near. He might've been the one with sight magic, but it was my eyes that had attuned to him, growing sensitive to his movements as the months went by.

Of course, Noble was *not* in Fenrir City.

He was still in Waldron.

So why was I still looking for him in every crowded pub, down every side street, among the tents of every weekend market?

Because you're a hopeless sap, Hattie, that's why.

I rolled my shoulders back, forcing Noble from my mind, and refocused on tonight's objective. When I spotted a tall, svelte blonde at the opposite end of the room, I made my way over to the circle of apprentices surrounding her.

Phina Farkept looked particularly professorial in a pair of brown trousers and a matching waistcoat. Her hair was cropped close to her head, accentuating her strong jaw, expressive mouth, and youthful skin. As a skilled herbologist, she'd looked after Anya and Idris after their harrowing journey into the Western Wood last autumn—when Anya had shared that particular detail with me, I'd *squealed*.

In the alchemy world, Phina was a phenom.

Though she was not much older than I was, she had earned her Adept Oath in her early twenties and was now more accomplished than half the other professors at the Collegium—a fact I found impossibly impressive.

Phina also happened to be an expert in my favorite subject. The way she spoke of even the most common herbs was a direct reflection of my own feelings: reverence, passion, excitement. It didn't hurt that we had taste magic in common, too, so her methods and limitations for imbuing tinctures with magic were similar to my own.

I'd also already read all her books.

"What about the intersection between metal alchemy and herbal alchemy?" a young woman with stringy shoulder-length hair asked Phina.

"What about it? They're separate fields," the man beside her cut in. I recognized him from my mathematics class, an opinionated metalworking apprentice with a square head, torso, and personality.

The woman met his scowl with one of her own. "I know a Mirror Knight who says—"

"Oh, here we go," the man interrupted. "Mirrors this, Mirrors that. Don't waste Professor Farkept's time."

"I believe professor Farkept can manage her own time without your input," another young woman interjected.

The man glowered but didn't continue.

Phina—who'd been listening with an arched brow—extended a hand in the first woman's direction. "Please continue, Gillen."

Gillen tucked her hair behind her ears. "I heard a theory that it was the algae in the water interacting with the Gildium that caused the Mirrors' creation."

"That is one theory, yes," Phina said, glancing around at the other students. "Though over the years many adepts have endeavored to theorize the exact conditions that created the Mirrors of Fate."

The Mirrors of Fortune and Death were famed relics in Fenrir.

Every year, a collection of knights took the two seven-foot-tall Mirrors on a tour of the territory to allow citizens to gaze into the magical reflections and glimpse their Fated futures. The Mirrors were created seven hundred years ago, when ornate Gildium frames had fallen into a magical pool called the Well of Fate, located somewhere in the treacherous geothermal flats south of the Bone Mountains.

Most particulars had been lost to history. The only reason I knew as much as I did was because Anya and Idris had ventured there and had returned to Waldron...*changed.*

But even my best friend had been unwilling to share with me exactly what had happened at the pool. *The less you know, the safer you are,* Anya had told me late one night, huddled under the silent shroud of her sound magic. *Knowing too much almost got me killed, Hattie, and I couldn't bear to put you in danger.*

If Anya only knew how well I understood the importance of keeping dangerous secrets.

Still, it seemed strange that there were apprentices asking about the Mirrors' creation so soon after Anya visited the location of their inception. Had word gotten out? Or were the Mirrors simply a common topic of debate in Fenrir City, given their mysterious power?

When Phina spoke again, her voice took on the resonant quality she used in class: measured, curious, authoritative. "What you need to understand here is the bias among adepts," Phina said to the group. "Ask an archivist, and they'll cite only the *known* history of the Mirrors—dismissing all else as conjecture. Ask an Adept of the Arcane, and they'll insist it was magic weavers who wove power into the Mirrors in much the same way that their Order weaves Oath magic. Ask an Adept of Alchemy, and they'll insist..." Phina trailed off, eyes sweeping across the crowd expectantly.

Apprentices were quick to finish her sentence: "Alchemy."

"What *all* adepts lack is irrefutable proof," Phina concluded. "The Mirrors are an enduring mystery. Best not to try to solve it in your first year at the Collegium." She winked, and a few students chuckled.

"But you're trying to solve it, aren't you?" Gillen asked. "Is magical water not a part of your study?"

Phina appeared amused by the bold question. She lifted a shoulder, feigning ignorance about the topic of her confidential research—a program which the Lord of Fenrir himself was a benefactor. "You know, I really couldn't say."

Others in our circle began talking over one another, jumping in with more questions, but a commotion from the front of the pub stole my attention. A pair of knights were arguing outside again, and—*no*, not outside, they were coming in through the front door.

And heading straight for *me*.

4

FATELESS

HATTIE

The knights were broad, male, and fitted in extravagant gold armor. One had an elegant longbow strapped to his back, while the other's head was framed by exquisite twin shortsword hilts protruding from scabbards along his shoulder blades. While I did not recognize them personally, their finery was that of the esteemed Order of the Mighty, the most trusted and highly trained knights in the kingdom, loyal to not only the ruler of their respective territory but to the entire realm.

Had someone told the Mighty that I was here? Noble's father was one of the most lauded Mighty Knights in the kingdom; after the attempt on my life nine years ago, he'd orchestrated my clandestine escape to Poe-on-Wend. Were these men loyal to his leadership? Had I been discovered?

When I'd applied for study at the Collegium, I'd used the same false surname I'd chosen the night I met Anya: Mund. I told myself that as long as I stuck to my story—that I was an anonymous woman from an inconsequential small town in rural Fenrir—everything would be fine, but the truth was, it was dangerous for me to be here. I'd *known* it was a risk to have my name—even a fake one—recorded for my enrollment, but—

Wait.

A third knight followed on their heels, inconspicuous by comparison—but when my attention found her, a different sort of fear gripped me. Black armor. Doe-eyes. A white scar across her upper lip. A menacing swagger. She was confident, lethal. The men at her sides might've been gloriously intimidating, but intimidation implied a hypothetical. A peaceable solution.

There was nothing hypothetical about Mariana's potential for violence.

Memory took me back to the Possum, her voice interrupting the stillness of midnight. Black blood on her sword. A scowl on her angular face. I'd been somewhat preoccupied with my lingering distress over seeing a Fates-cursed *monster* so close to the inn, but Mariana had seemed unperturbed by that.

She'd come to confront Anya and Idris about their blank visions in the Mirrors of Fate.

Ever since my friends' trip to the Well, the Mirrors of Fortune and Death had shown them a tumultuous grayness, like an overcast sky. Blank, untold futures. Mariana had warned us about more individuals like them, but she hadn't explained *why*—just that we ought not trust them.

I might have an idea, I'd told Anya and Idris once Mariana had left. What if Mariana had been talking about Noble?

I'd seen it myself, six months ago, at Waldron's Fate Ceremony. He'd been among the first to look into the Mirrors, early enough in the procession that no one from town was really paying attention. Noble was a recluse, after all—curious as the gossips in town could be, he'd proven himself uninteresting, and therefore his blank Fate had gone unnoticed.

Except by me.

Could Noble have also visited the Well of Fate? Anya and Idris had quickly dismissed that theory, as the path was treacherous, and its secrets were not widely known. Besides, even historically, none of those who visited the Well had come away with *blank* Fates—at most, just *altered* Fates. Anya and Idris had no guess as to why *their* futures had been different—except for the presence of monsters. According to Idris, close proximity to monsters could warp one's Fate. Perhaps the monsters lurking around the pool had changed its effect?

We'd discussed the matter at length, deep into the night, only to come away with more questions than answers. Ultimately, neither Anya nor Idris had much to say about the implications of Mariana's warning. Not because they were being secretive, but because they genuinely didn't understand the forces of the Mirrors. No one did.

Still, I'd wondered: what if Noble could tell us what Mariana had not?

I'd tried asking him about it, once—but he'd coolly evaded me, offering nothing. And seeing as we'd agreed to avoid one another, my determination to confront him again—to force an answer from him—eventually waned. Mariana's warning had been vague, and Anya and Idris had stressed that the less we pried into matters that concerned her, the better. After all, Mariana was a knight of a secret Order. I was not supposed to know about her charge—and technically, I didn't—but I had an idea...

And that idea disturbed me.

But now...now that she was here in Fenrir's Charm, heading straight toward me...something must be wrong. My heart dropped like a stone into my stomach, a sudden panic rippling through me, even as my curiosity stirred. As the trio of knights neared, my muscles tensed, bracing for the inevitable threat.

But they weren't walking toward *me*, I realized.

They were walking toward—

"What's the meaning of this?" Phina asked, folding her arms across her chest, her eyebrow arching ever higher—unperturbed.

A few nearby students shrunk away from the professor. I should've done the same, but I was rooted in place, hovering on the edge of their congregation, eyeing Mariana with a mix of surprise and dubiousness. When her gaze flicked in my direction, her eyes widened with recognition—then continued their shrewd perusal of the room.

"We have a problem," the man with the shortswords said.

"Have you gotten lost on your way to the Ire?" Phina asked.

The man with the longbow huffed what might've been a laugh, but the others remained tense, watchful, unamused.

Phina's lips quirked. "Care to elucidate? Or would you like me to start guessing?"

"Not here." Mariana's hand tightened around the pommel of the sword at her hip. The movement caught my attention, and I noticed a black smear across her wrist bone.

When my gaze shifted to her dark eyes again, they'd narrowed on me, and I glanced away—back to Phina, wondering what she would do.

The professor's wry expression shifted into something sharper—then she assumed a look of bored inconvenience. "Fine, fine," she said with a wave of her hand, then turned on a heel.

I watched as my professor followed the knights out of the warm glow of the pub's sconces and into the moonlit night. Mere moments after the door snicked behind them, the chatter in Fenrir's Charm—which had diminished considerably with the unwelcome newcomers—returned in full force.

"What was that about?" Uriel asked, suddenly by my side.

"No idea," I said, even though my mind was racing at a pace that matched my galloping pulse.

"Huh. Well." Uriel jerked her chin in the direction of the bar. "I am getting another drink—want one? Sani is cut off. She cannot hold her liquor for shit."

"I think I'm going to retire," I replied, glancing at the door again. "I'll see you at the dorm in a bit?"

"Tired from all the mingling?" Uriel asked with a smirk. "If we do not return before midnight, assume Sani is emptying her stomach in the street, and I am holding her hair."

"She's not *that* drunk, is she? She seemed fine when I left the table."

"Snuck up on her," Uriel said, already walking backward toward the bar. "Apparently books did not teach her how to pace herself!"

I laughed, waved, waited for Uriel to disappear into the crowd—then I darted out the door after my professor.

5
TINCTURE
HATTIE

A shocking chill swept over my pub-warmed skin as I stepped out of Fenrir's Charm and into the night. Across the way, a jaunty chorus of deep voices were spilling out of Fenrir's Ire, the tune obscured by drunken enthusiasm. A few off-duty knights loitered on the cobblestones outside the pub, their hot breaths curling around their faces. Otherwise, the street was empty.

Except for the foursome turning briskly down an alley to my left.

I lifted my skirts and hurried after them, the bare skin of my arms puckering. Even in spring, frost still clung to Fenrir City with cold claws. The metropolis had been built into the base of Mount Shield in five massive steps, and the elevation paired with the icy fog that spilled down from the mountain's snow-capped peak made the territory's capital much colder than the southern towns clustered along the Wend.

And I'd foolishly left my cloak at our table back at the Charm.

My curiosity superseded the chill. As I neared the mouth of the side street, I slowed. Wooden crates and empty casks were piled off to one side, remnants of past nights at the nearby pubs. I crouched behind them, listening intently to the hushed voices that congregated midway down the alley.

A fifth figure had joined Phina, Mariana, and the two Mighty Knights. The newcomer was male, based on the height and build that filled out his slate-gray cloak. His hood and the shadows of the surrounding buildings obscured his face from the shard of moonlight that cut down onto the narrow street. His size made him look like another knight, but without a closer look for an Oath tattoo, I couldn't say for certain.

Not that this was any of my business.

There were many reasons I ought not eavesdrop and risk getting caught: the possible wrath of highly skilled and vicious knights, the potential to lose my place at the Collegium for meddling in an esteemed adept's affairs, the moral ambiguity of sticking my nose where it didn't belong, to name a few.

But I couldn't help myself.

Not when Mariana was here so soon after her visit to the Possum. Not when Phina was involved in some kind of alchemical research (possibly) involving the Well of Fate. Not when people I loved could be caught in the crosshairs.

Pure nosiness was also a factor. My aunt used to say that my insatiable curiosity was my greatest asset and my most calamitous weakness, and she was not wrong.

Crouched behind an old barrel, peering through the slats of a large crate resting beside it, my knees ached, and my toes went tingly from a lack of circulation—yet I leaned forward, straining to listen. Voices faded in and out with the interruptions of city noise and the undulations of whispered conversation.

"—didn't expect you for another six months, at least," Phina was saying.

"None of us did," Mariana added.

"—the efficacy of the tincture—" A cold wind whispered through the alley, taking the rest of Phina's sentence with it. "—symptoms have accelerated?"

The hooded figure nodded.

A sharp swear from Phina. "Any new symptoms?"

He shook his head.

She continued, but all I caught was the end of her next question, again aimed at the newcomer: "—progress in your studies?"

His voice was a landslide, rumbly and raspy in a way that was both familiar and foreign. "Inconclusive."

My knees were beginning to throb. I shifted, boots grinding against the cobblestones. I tried to rub some heat back into my numb upper arms. I'd worn a short-sleeved dress to avoid overheating in the crowded Charm, but out here, my fingertips were beginning to numb. I really should've grabbed my cloak, but—

The Mighty Knight with the fancy swords took a step closer to the figure. The edge in his tone was unmistakable. "So, the experiment failed?" From my angle, I saw his palm brush the leather-wrapped hilt of a dagger strapped to his belt.

Mariana saw it, too. She rolled her eyes like he was the epitome of irritating. "Back the fuck off, Faren," she said. "You have no authority in this matter."

"I have more authority than *you*."

They began talking over one another, arguing full force, with no apparent concern for their loudness. Faren held his arms out wide, looming; he had at least a foot of height and sixty pounds of muscle on Mariana, but she invaded his personal space, jabbing a finger against his gold-plated chest. To anyone else on the street, the shouting probably sounded like any other night outside the Ire.

While they bickered, the hooded figure raised a hand to his mouth and descended into a fit of coughing—no, *convulsing*. He doubled over, body shaking like he might vomit. The Mighty Knight with the longbow took a concerned step forward, but it was Phina who rested her hand on the newcomer's shoulder, her delicate fingers gripping firmly.

"Look at him and tell me this isn't a failure," Faren shouted.

Mariana turned to Phina. "He needs Hylder. *Quickly*."

"He needs more than Hylder," Faren spat. "He needs—"

A blur of silver flashed white in the moonlight. Bodies collided—a lunge and a block. A gasp gusted out of me, unnoticed in the sudden melee, the clash of knights and steel. Then Faren's back hit the street. Mariana's boot pressed firmly against the base of his neck and her sword angled against the underside of his chin.

"I *said*, back the fuck off," she snarled.

Mere feet away, the second Mighty Knight aimed an arrow directly at Mariana, but she was unafraid. Whatever Order she belonged to, she did not fear the Mighty as most did. Threatening as she was, I couldn't help but admire her tenacity. Her self-sufficiency. Her lack of fear.

"Is this what you do in your Orders? Stab first, ask questions later?" Phina's harsh tone bounced off the walls of the alleyway.

She was gripping the hooded figure's bicep with one hand and rubbing his back with the other—not soothingly, but roughly, like she was trying to warm him up. He was still leaning forward, hands braced on knees, hooded head bowed. His body shook, but it didn't look like the persistent shivers of a chill. He looked like he was still coughing—*hacking*—but he was soundless. Was it pain? Adrenaline? I couldn't tell with his face obscured.

When the knights did not immediately break their standoff, Phina stomped her foot. "*Fucking Fates*, stand down, you childish brutes."

The bowstring groaned as the Mighty Knight lowered the arrow pointed at Mariana. She, in turn, lifted her sword away from Faren's neck—but not without purposefully nicking his chin. When she lifted her boot from his clavicle, he twisted to the side, leaning on one elbow to wheeze a couple deep breaths.

As the near violence among the knights dissipated, the details of their conversation finally permeated my thoughts enough to stick.

Hylder.

It was a common botanical in medicine. Great for healing, immunity, and purification. Apothecaries often included it in potions for protection, but there were historical records of alchemists also using it to purge evil.

This past autumn, when Idris had arrived at the Pretty Possum with a nasty wound on his hand—the puncture oozing black sludge—he'd requested I treat it with Hylder. Ever since—and *especially* after seeing the monstrously diseased bobcat outside the Possum—I'd carried a small vial of the tincture with me at all times.

So, when the newcomer began to shudder and cough for real this time, and Mariana again demanded for Phina to give him Hylder as soon as possible, and Phina apologized for not having any on her person, I didn't think.

I simply stepped out from behind the crates.

6

THEORIES

HATTIE

I have Hylder," I said, procuring the heart-shaped vial from a pocket in my dress.

"We'll have to get him to the Collegium," Phina was telling the others.

"Is there time?" Mariana asked.

"I have Hylder," I called out, louder this time.

The lot of them turned toward me. Phina's brow furrowed. Faren's temple pulsed. Mariana smirked with menacing amusement. The Mighty Knight with the longbow brushed a finger over the fletching of his arrow, which was still nocked—but he didn't take aim. *Yet.*

Quivering a little, I lifted the vial higher with one hand and showed them my other palm, too, just to prove I wasn't a threat. "You said he needs Hylder?" I inquired, jutting my chin in the direction of the newcomer.

His attention was on me—sharp. Underneath the shadow of his hood, I still couldn't make out his face; but the gaping neckline of his shirt revealed a triangle of bare sternum, dark skin. He'd gone stone-still, fists clenched at his sides.

Mariana was the first to break the tense silence. Her laugh was a single, mirthless breath. "Of course, *you* carry Hylder." She held out a summoning hand, making a grabbing motion. "Don't be shy. Give it here."

I walked down the narrow street, keeping my head held high as I approached the group. The Mighty Knights shifted on their feet. The hooded figure turned fully away, facing the opposite end of the alley with his back to me, coughing again. Phina took a tentative step closer to me, retrieving the vial from my fingers, even as I kept my eyes trained on Mariana.

Her lip curled. "Had a feeling I'd see you again, barkeep."

Anya's words echoed in my head: *The less you know, the safer you are.*

I gave Mariana my most winning smile. "Had I known that you, too, were traveling to Fenrir from Waldron, I would've suggested we ride together." I kept my tone bright and convivial, even as my heart pounded. "Could've been fun: telling stories around the campfire, singing merry tunes, frolicking in country meadows."

All three Knights' scowls deepened. Phina's mouth twisted with not-quite amusement.

Maybe revealing myself had been a bad idea.

But then Mariana *laughed*, the sound both musical and harsh. "You're funny."

With the tension mostly broken, I looked to Phina again. As my professor, she was the closest thing to an authority figure in this situation.

Only...she was staring down at the label on my vial. "You made this?" she asked.

"I did."

"Tincture?"

"Yes."

"Next time, add a *T* to the bottom right corner of your label," she said somewhat absentmindedly, as if teaching was second nature. "Standard notation."

"Alright."

Without another word, Phina uncorked the tincture and sprinkled a drop onto her tongue. She opened and closed her mouth, tasting, assessing. When she appeared satisfied with the quality of my work, she approached the hooded man, placing a hand on his back again as she offered him my vial. He did not hesitate; he tipped it back. The liquid burbled within the curvature of the glass as he drank it down.

Silence spread, as if everyone was waiting to see if any adverse effects occurred. To my relief, the figure's shivers diminished, and a rough sigh slipped out of him. Pride budded in my sternum. Though he was a stranger—he still faced away from me, preserving his anonymity—I was happy to see in the slight relaxation of his shoulders that I'd helped ease his discomfort.

"Escort him to my quarters," Phina told the knights. "I need a moment with the apprentice."

The knights did not question Phina's demand. Faren started toward the opposite end of the alley in a huff. The archer lowered his bow, slid the un-shot arrow back into his quiver, and followed. Mariana spared me one last lingering glance, as if trying to make sense of me—then gripped the hooded figure's arm, leading him away.

Only after they'd disappeared around the corner did Phina turn back to me. Her mouth was pursed, concern scrunching her youthful face. Or maybe that was anger. I couldn't tell. My teeth were beginning to chatter from both cold and adrenaline.

"Hylder," my professor said. "What do you know of it?"

I didn't expect a quiz. I cleared my throat, cleared my mind, and relaxed into my knowledge of herbs—the safest place in my memory. "It's a healing botanical that—"

"No," Phina interrupted. "What do you *know* of it?"

The word was loaded. I stiffened.

The less you know, the safer you are.

Seeing my hesitation, Phina took a step closer, trying a different tactic. "Remind me your name?"

"Hattie Mund," I said. "I'm a pupil in your herbology class."

"I recognize you," Phina said, flashing me an encouraging smile. "Listen, Hattie. It's important that you are honest with me right now. Why were you carrying a Hylder tincture on your person?"

I suddenly felt like I was in *way* over my head. I was here to earn an apothecary license, not meddle with secret Order business between adepts and knights. But with the way Phina was staring at me, arms crossed—I couldn't evade the question. I respected her too much to lie.

"Mariana had a spot of black blood on her wrist," I said, watching Phina's features closely.

Judging by the way she flinched, Phina got my hint. "How do you know it was blood?"

"I suppose it could've been saliva." I shrugged. "It's not the first time I've seen a knight of an unknown Order with—"

Phina swore, cutting me off. She tipped her head back, glancing at the starlit sky as if she were praying to the Fates. When she leveled her eyes on me again, they were filled with intensity. "How do you know Mariana?"

"We have a mutual acquaintance."

That seemed to surprise her. "Who?"

"Idris Togren."

A grin flashed across Phina's face, bright as the strobe of lightning, there and gone so quickly that I wondered if I'd imagined it. "He's a friend of mine, too."

"I know." Idris was close friends with Phina's older brother; it's how she'd been roped into healing him and Anya last fall.

Phina's face grew serious again. "What do you know of his former duty?"

"Very little," I replied honestly. Phina sagged with relief, but it was short lived when I added, "Though I have my theories."

Phina wiped a palm over the lower half of her face. As she did, her sleeve slipped down her arm, revealing the ring of black ink that encircled her right wrist. It was the Oath tattoo of all adepts, not dissimilar from the tattoos that knights wore around their necks—proof of the magical thread that tethered all Order members to the binding magic of their Oaths.

Idris had once referred to his old Oath as a leash.

In addition to the ring around her wrist, there were tattoos on her fingers—odd symbols that looked like an alphabet in another language. They, too, were magical, each representing another level of clearance within the hierarchy of adepts. Based on her countless markings, Phina kept *many* adept secrets.

And I was certain I'd just stumbled into one of them.

A slippery sense of dread slid through my chest. "Am I...am I in trouble?"

Phina's eyes cut to mine again. All warmth had left them, like sunlight disappearing behind storm clouds. Her expression became thunderous, foreboding.

Fearing I was about to be expelled, I went on talking. "I know I shouldn't've followed you. It's just that, well, I've wanted to be an apothecary for so long, and I—" I shook my head, well aware that I was rambling but unable to stop. "I just respect you so much, and when I saw Mariana in the Charm, I was curious, but also concerned you were—I mean—I didn't—" *Fates, rein it in, Hattie.* "Did I do the wrong thing by offering the Hylder? It seemed like he needed help, but—"

"It's cold," Phina mercifully interrupted, gesturing at my bare arms. "And late."

"Professor Farkept, I—"

"Say nothing of what you overheard tonight."

I tensed. "I won't."

"You put yourself, me, and countless others at risk."

"I'm—" I swallowed. "I'm sorry."

"Go directly to your dorm," Phina ordered. "No detours."

I could've kept my mouth shut after that. I *should've*. But my self-control was no match against my curiosity.

When I was growing up, so much of the world and the truth had been kept from me. After years of being denied answers—of keeping my own secrets—I'd developed a hypersensitivity to that which was hidden, and an insatiable desire to uncover it.

Black blood. Hylder. The Well of Fate. Could they all be related, somehow?

I couldn't help myself. "Your research. It has something to do with monsters, doesn't it?"

Phina blanched, too shocked by my question to hide the answer on her face. The confirmation.

"Hylder is a purification herb." I shook my head, my forehead furrowing. The hooded figure tonight didn't look like a monster, but if Mariana knew them... Perhaps they'd been bitten? Perhaps...the monstrousness was an affliction of some kind? That would certainly explain the bobcat. Which meant: "It's a curse. You're studying curses."

Phina clenched her teeth, jaw bulging. "Go. *Now*."

I was prying. I was asking too much. I *idolized* Phina, I should've respected the secrets of her Oath-protected research, but—

I took a step closer, too horrified and intrigued to stop. "I'm right, aren't I?"

Phina glanced around as if we were at risk of being overheard, the whites of her eyes flashing wildly. Then she gripped my shoulders, squeezing until she'd no doubt leave bruises on my skin. Her voice came out as a breathy whisper, strained with warning. "Say anything more, and I won't be able to protect you."

A chill cascaded down my spine. Her words were eerily similar to what Noble's father had said to me the night I was sent away. I bit my lips together and nodded.

Phina gave my shoulders a rough shake. "Do you understand?"

"I understand."

She let go. Nodded. Jerked her head in an obvious dismissal.

So, I did as she asked. I walked purposefully down the alleyway, leaving Phina behind, my mind racing with theories and assumptions, half-truths and countless more questions—even as I dreaded all the possible answers.

7

AFFLICTION

NOBLE

That was close, Noble thought bitterly as he paced the woven rug in Phina's chambers.

His last week on the road to Fenrir City had been rough, filled with nightmares and disturbing urges that had left him so ragged that for the final two nights of his travels, he'd eschewed sleep altogether.

Upon his arrival in the capital, he'd immediately sought Phina for more tincture, but the curse had almost caught up to him. Thank the Fates he'd stumbled upon Mariana, who knew of his affliction and where Phina could be found. Thank the Fates that when Phina didn't have any Hylder on her person, Hattie had been nearby—carrying *exactly* what he needed.

Hattie's unexpected preparedness was perplexing—*concerning*—but for tonight, he was grateful. He didn't want to consider what might've happened if even another ten minutes had passed without it.

But *fuck*, that had been close.

At first, when his sight magic had snagged on the pretty blue of her dress shifting behind the slats of a stack of old crates, he'd thought she was a drunk Collegium student semi-passed-out in the alley. Nonthreatening. Then she'd revealed herself with that bottle of his temporary cure, and within the depths of his sleep-starved brain, a different sort of panic had clutched him. He hadn't turned his back to her to spare her of the dangers of his secret—though that was a worthwhile reason not to tell her. No, he'd hidden his face because, selfishly, he didn't want her to think differently of him. He didn't want—

Fates, he didn't want *any* of this.

"You recognized her," Phina observed. "The apprentice. Hattie."

She was leaning against the doorjamb, watching patiently as he walked off the excess adrenaline. He'd been awake for the past thirty-six hours, yet he felt hot as a spark burning through paper.

"From Waldron." Not a lie, but not the barest truth, either.

"Small towns," Phina muttered with a scoff, pushing off from the wall. "Drink?" Without waiting for his answer, Phina strode over to a wheeled cart that was crowded with crystal decanters.

"Any idea why she followed you?" Noble asked.

Phina lifted a shoulder. "She's a...gregarious apprentice."

"She's in your class?" Suddenly he had to know: "Is she any good?" She *had* to be.

How many afternoons of his adolescence had Noble spent trying not to stare at Hattie as she poured over encyclopedias and compendiums in her family's private library? While she'd memorized the names and properties of healing herbs, Noble had memorized the pattern of deep brown freckles on the side of her creamy neck. He used to peek at her from behind the pages of a novel and watch helplessly as she tipped her head to one side while reading, or scrunched her pert nose while taking notes, or licked her plump bottom lip in thought.

If Hattie had retained even half as much of the books as Noble had of her mannerisms back then, she must've been an excellent student.

Of course, Phina was oblivious to his bias—and, if he could help it, she'd remain that way. Noble reported to Phina for his Gildium studies, he respected her deeply, owed his *life* to her—but the safe-keeping of Hattie's secret superseded all else.

Phina hefted a decanter, removed the stopper, and sniffed. "Thankfully for you, she's smart enough to properly balance a Hylder tincture."

There was no context in which he could ask follow-up questions without giving away how much he cared about Hattie's ambitions, so he continued pacing.

"How do you feel?" Phina prompted.

How *did* he feel?

Noble rubbed the back of his neck, assessing his inner state. Waning panic. Antsy exhaustion. Blessed *calm*.

In fact, he was calmer than he'd felt in *months*. Was it possible that Hattie's tincture was more effective, somehow? No, that had to be his bias again.

"I feel like shit," he answered honestly. "But also like myself."

The remark made Phina snort, but it didn't entirely ease the tension in her forehead. Something else must've been troubling her. But as she busied herself with selecting a decanter, it was clear to Noble that she wasn't in the mood to discuss it. At least, not yet. So, rather than prying, Noble looked around the ornate room.

Last he was in Fenrir, Noble had visited Phina's home, a quaint but welcoming cottage on the outskirts of the city. Her Collegium chambers were neither quaint nor welcoming. Floor-to-ceiling bookshelves were overstuffed with dusty tomes in shades of moss green, rusty orange, and faded brown. There was an imposing writing desk, a bed in the corner that looked like an afterthought. Heavy velvet curtains framing a lone window. No wonder Phina seemed so subdued compared to the last time he saw her, with new shadows under her eyes. The stodgy accommodations were obviously stifling.

The music of liquid filling cups had Noble turning back toward his host. "Have you always had onsite chambers?"

Phina chuckled, but the sound wasn't jovial. "I was awarded numerous unwanted luxuries when Lord Haron took interest in my research," she said. "For a while, I went back and forth to the cottage, determined to retain a sense of—I don't know, independence? self?—but the late nights eventually caught up to me. I haven't been home in months."

"Well, the look suits you."

"No, it doesn't."

A chuckle. "You're right. I was just being polite."

Phina handed him a cup of what smelled like brandy. "What *suits* me is having funding for my research. The rest is just..." She waved a hand, dismissive, then gestured for Noble to sit in one of the upholstered reading chairs by the window.

Reminded of why he was here, he resumed pacing instead. "Is it safe for me to imbibe after...?"

Phina settled into her seat and crossed one leg over the other. "You seemed like you needed a drink."

That was permission enough. The brandy was a sweet burn on the back of his palate as he continued his travels back and forth across the rug.

"You're lucky Hattie had what you needed tonight."

His steps faltered; he covered it up with another sip of brandy. "Jumping right into it, are we?"

"I thought we'd undergone sufficient preamble, but I'll endure more small talk if you prefer?"

"No. Continue."

"So, do you know why?"

Between the sleepless nights and the come down from tonight's adrenaline, he didn't follow. "Why what?"

"Why she had what you needed?"

"I don't." He rolled his neck; when normally he felt like a coiled spring, he currently felt more like a pile of unspooled ribbon, loose and silken. "Whatever she gave me was..." He did another internal assessment, feeling for the ever-present curse in the back of his mind and finding it especially subdued. "It was effective, Phina. More so than the last batch. Do you know—"

"I didn't have time for proper analysis with you writhing in an alley, but yes, I noticed her tincture was strong."

He had no idea what to make of that.

"She mentioned a knight who recently retired in Waldron," Phina continued. "Do you know an Idris Togren?"

Noble shrugged. "I keep to myself."

"Not what I asked."

"He's in love with the innkeeper. Hattie's employer."

Phina's cheeks tightened, a barely imperceptible shift. "Hattie works for Idris's lover?"

He nodded.

"*Hm.*"

"What?"

"I'm afraid she knows more than she ought to about"—Phina gestured at his general state of wretched being—"you know."

"Monsters," Noble supplied flatly.

Phina stared into her cup for a moment. "She knows Mariana, too. Do you think it's possible she's aware of the existence of the Order of the Valiant? Their purpose?"

The Valiant were one of Lord Haron's covert Orders, in which skilled criminals were offered knighthood as an alternative to the dungeons. The Valiant's sole duty was to protect the realm from horrendous monsters called Morta, along with any poor souls afflicted with the poison of a Morta's bite—usually animals. Noble's former Order had caused him to encounter many Valiant Knights over the years.

He tossed back the rest of his brandy and set the empty cup on a side table. "Ask Mariana. The leakage of her Order's secrets is *her* problem, not mine."

"I'm afraid you are mistaken." Phina uncrossed her legs and rested her forearms on her knees. "Whether you like it or not, you're *in this*. From the moment you agreed to partake in my research—"

"Your research is the only thing keeping me—"

"—you gave up your right to decide what is and is not your problem. At least when it comes to my work."

Talk of her research had his mind pivoting to the particulars. He'd been in Waldron for a year, and due to the clandestine nature of Phina's work, her letters to him had been few—and vague. "Have you learned anything new?" he asked. "Any luck?"

"A good alchemist does not rely on luck," Phina replied tartly. "But no. No answers yet."

He would've been devastated if he hadn't expected that response. "New insights, then?"

"Depends on *your* research." She took a quick sip of her brandy. "What have you learned in Waldron?"

"Not enough," Noble grumbled. "The resources there are...lacking."

"Perhaps it's time to apply your newfound knowledge here, in my lab, with my resources."

"I'd rather not stay, Phina."

"You might not have a choice, Noble." She sat back, tattooed fingers laced around her cup. "But don't think I didn't notice the way you evaded my question. Do you think it's possible Hattie knows why the Order of the Valiant exists?"

Noble balled his fists, suddenly furious that Hattie had been dragged into the fucked-up machinations currently transpiring between the knights and adepts of Fenrir.

He resumed pacing. "I don't know, Phina," he said, annoyance in his tone. "As far as I'm concerned, Hattie is just an innocent barkeep from an inconsequential small town on the Wend."

"Waldron," Phina said, setting her drink aside. "The same small town where you've resided for the past year. The same small town where one of the last true Gildium artisans retired. The same small town where Idris Tog—"

"I get it," Noble interrupted.

"Do you?" Phina asked, gripping the upholstered arms of her chair. "Because I don't."

He shrugged. "What do you want me to say? That I recognized Hattie? Sure. I've seen her around plenty. But as for what she knows and does not know, I am in the dark as much as you are."

"She knows nothing of your intentions?"

"Nothing." Of that, he was certain. He'd made sure of it.

Phina nodded, accepting his words. "Well. She is, unfortunately, more aware of the secrets that the Valiant protect than she ought to be, which puts her in danger."

Noble ran a palm over his jaw and glanced away, trying to get ahold of the emotions on his face before—

"You care for her." It was not a question.

When he faced Phina again, he made sure to make his expression hard. He was well practiced at concealing his fondness for Hattie. "I care for any innocent who is unnecessarily swept up in Lord Haron's dealings."

"Nice to know you care about me, then, too," Phina quipped.

Did she truly see herself that way? Caught in the Lord's scheming because of her expertise? To anyone outside the situation, Phina seemed fortunate to have been chosen for patronage by the Lord—but maybe Phina didn't have as much autonomy as she let on.

"What do you plan to do about her?" Noble asked.

"The only thing I *can* do, without raising suspicion," Phina said. "I have to bring her into the fold."

A LETTER

Dear Anya,

"Do opposites attract"—really? Have you MET Idris?

Thank you for the update from home. I admit I've been quite home-sick—about the ducklings and everyone else. It's lovely to hear that Richold and Kara are getting on—and I can't wait to hear all about Illian's wedding. As you know, I love Waldron weddings. Perhaps yours will be next? (Hint, hint!).

Whatever Martha's done to my kitchen, please put everything back BE-FORE I return; I do not wish to witness the insult of her "improvements." And please thank Idris for lending his green thumb to my herb garden—if they're still alive under your care, he must've intervened somehow!

~~*Also, what happened when you visited the Well of Fate?*~~

~~*What do you know about Mariana's Order?*~~

~~*Something happened here involving Hylder that I*~~

The vinegar recipe is on the back of this letter; be careful with your ratios.

Your sassy friend,

Hattie

8

LOVE POTION

HATTIE

W hat's imperative for you to understand," Professor Farkept said, striding across the length of the platform at the front of her classroom, "is that alchemy is not *willed* into existence with your magic, it is *woven* through a delicate process of mental knot-tying." She scribbled a formula onto the pale slab of slate mounted on the wall behind her, charcoal squeaking. "Every material in existence possesses the potential to be woven with magic, but herbs are unique. Any guess as to why?"

My pencil paused above my notebook paper, and I tucked my chin, waiting for my professor's expectant gaze to sweep over me—and past me.

Sunlight slanted through the swirling tracery of the arched windows that lined one wall of the classroom. Instead of theater seats, Phina's herbology class consisted of five rows of narrow lab benches. Glass vials, jugs of liquid, bundles of dried herbs, and jars of powder were arranged in neat, identical clusters before each student.

Today, I'd chosen a stool in the back.

I hadn't heard from or interacted with Phina since the incident in the alley two nights ago, but I still wasn't fully convinced I wouldn't be dismissed for what I'd uncovered about her research. I'd concluded it was best to keep my head down.

"Yes, Poppy?" Phina called, pointing to a young brunette seated up front, right beside Sani and Uriel—in my usual spot.

"They're alive?" the apprentice asked.

"Precisely. Herbs are unique because they're alive."

Phina drew two rectangles on the slate, one with a fringe of hair-like lines and one without. Then she drew the rough outline of a person with a squiggle emanating from their outstretched hand—magic.

A person's innate sensory magic wasn't just a heightened ability to see in the dark or smell pheromones—magic was a thread of potent energy, something a trained practitioner could manipulate. *Wield.*

"When an alchemist imbues an inanimate object—like a metal—with magic, that process is known as *binding*," Phina continued.

The charcoal screeched as she dragged it from the person to the plain rectangle, circling it to demonstrate the binding.

"But when you work with something living, like a plant—especially a magically potent plant, which we call herbs—you are weaving your threads of magic with the herb's threads of magic in a process known as *braiding*."

With confident, practiced detail, Phina drew a line to the fringed rectangle this time, looping the charcoal in a braid-like pattern.

I copied her drawing in my notebook.

"While arcane magic comes solely from the wielder, alchemy is the blending of magic between the alchemist and a material."

None of this was new to me. By the time I was fifteen, I'd memorized all the salient points in the five-hundred-page unabridged volume of *Fundamental Principles of Herbal Alchemy*—but Phina's description was far more eloquent.

"Whether you're an apothecary, an un-Oathed alchemist, or you want to become an adept one day, it's essential that you not only *intuit* this process, but visualize it, *feel* it within your sensory magic. After all, your innate sensory magic is..." She spread her arms invitingly.

"...the thread from which all other magic is woven," the class answered in unison.

Phina smiled, clearly pleased with her students' retention. Then she dropped her nub of charcoal onto her desk and pointed a black-smudged fingertip toward our workbenches. "Today, we're going to practice alchemizing a simple gardenia tincture into a love potion."

Papers rustled and stools squeaked as apprentices began preparing their materials.

Though I'd read about alchemy extensively, I didn't possess much hands-on practice. Proper ingredients were hard to come by in a small town like Waldron, and because I couldn't legally charge for my offerings without a license, it was expensive to experiment. Even when I was a girl, and I'd had practically *all* the resources in the kingdom at my fingertips, I hadn't been *allowed* to make potions. *Nobility don't* become *alchemists,* my aunt had chided me on numerous occasions, *they* employ *alchemists.*

Such limitations were why this was my favorite part of class.

Excitedly, I retrieved a glass pitcher and gathered the ingredients for the simple tincture that would serve as my base. The classroom fell away as I worked, becoming a soft blur in my periphery.

With a mortar and pestle, I ground dried gardenia petals into a fine powder. Next, I added a sassy dash of cinnamon, which wasn't required, but would provide a spark of lust to the affectionate sweetness of the gardenia. I sprinkled a few drops of rose water for desire and longing, and worked the ingredients together into a paste, thinning it with clear distilled alcohol. Finally, I poured the slurry into my pitcher and used a quartz spoon to stir in more alcohol until the tincture was a thin, slightly viscous swirl of pale pink.

I watched it whirl in the glass for a few seconds, then dribbled a couple drops of the tincture onto my tongue. My taste magic immediately lit up. Botanical, bitter, with notes of a floral sweetness—almost creamy in quality. The balance was slightly off—too much rose water—but I didn't want to waste ingredients, so I continued.

With my taste magic still sparking across my tongue, I gave the tincture another swirl. When it came to alchemy or arcane weaving, it didn't matter where one's magic originated—sight, smell, taste, touch, hearing—it was one's *intent* that made the difference.

I closed my eyes, practicing channeling my magic into the tincture. When it reached the liquid, the floral flavor hit the back of my palate—no tasting required—and a tingly sensation traveled over my skin.

It was exhilarating. *Distracting*.

I clenched my teeth, trying to concentrate. Weaving magical threads was kind of like mental crochet—it was tough to keep track of all the loops. Using the quartz spoon like a crochet hook, I stirred the liquid in precise circles. There were hundreds of alchemical knots to master, but today, I practiced the most basic weave: a square knot.

When I felt my work was done, I relaxed my magic with dizzying relief, and opened my eyes to see...

A pleased, joyful smile stretched across my lips.

The liquid in the pitcher was no longer a dull pink, but vibrant and shimmery, as if I'd imbued it with moonlight. Though I'd made plenty of simple potions like this over the years, none were so finely tuned. A deep sense of pride unfurled in me like an opening blossom.

Last autumn, when I'd gazed into the Mirror of Fortune at Waldron's Fate Ceremony, it had shown me a workbench similar to this one. My hands—deft and without hesitation—alchemizing a potion of some kind. The Mirror of Death had depicted my usual vague but peaceful end by old age. While I'd hoped for a more romantic future—a sign, *any* sign that I wouldn't die alone—my visions in the Mirrors made sense.

This blend of knowledge and magic and skill—this *alchemy*—*did* bring me a sense of Fortune. Of profound purpose. Unmatched by even the love that the potion I'd just created could induce. As I stared into the pitcher of swirling liquid, I had the overwhelming sense that this was what I was meant to be doing.

I glanced around the rest of class.

Phina was walking slowly between the rows of students, assessing potions, asking questions, offering suggestions. There would be no avoiding her when she reached my station, but for now, I refocused on my work, jotting down notes on areas I could improve: less rose water, perhaps grinding the petals into a finer powder for a better consistency, and was the viscosity too thin?

Of course, what mattered most was that the potion was effective.

Lifting my spoon, I tasted a couple drops, seeing if I could judge its efficacy. Love potions weren't strong enough to sway just *anyone* into loving another—they worked best on individuals who already harbored a faint attraction or interest. Among arranged marriages, couples were traditionally given love potions to spark affection in otherwise reluctant hearts.

I'd been forced to take one for my own arranged marriage, and it'd had no effect; the mayor of Poe-on-Wend, Corvin, had been a vile man from the start, and with nothing but fear and disgust in my heart, the potion had nothing to latch onto. Next year, my beloved cousin Raina—with whom I'd been raised—would take her own love potion on her wedding day. I wondered how she felt about the prospect if it would prove effective. For the sake of her happiness, I hoped it did.

I flattened my tongue against the roof of my mouth, coating my taste buds with the familiar flavors. A potion like this was meant to be mild. Almost imperceptible, when taken in the scant quantity I'd just ingested.

But what I tasted was...not mild.

The liquid was floral and bitter, just as the original tincture had been, but more complex now that I'd imbued it with power. I was reminded of not just gardenias, but an entire garden: sun-warmed flagstones, bees buzzing, the welcoming humidity of morning dew evaporating off greenery.

A warming sensation followed, traveling down my throat and pooling in the bowl of my belly. It felt like molten honey dribbling through my core, deliciously sticky. I closed my eyes, and through a haze of sunlit fog, I *saw* someone else in the garden behind my eyelids.

He faced away from me, a white shirt clinging to the hard ridges of his back. When he glanced over his shoulder at me, green eyes appraised me, sparking with an unspoken dare. His jaw was sharp enough to cut me open, and for him, I'd happily bleed. Suddenly, my dress felt too tight across my chest; I had the immediate urge to tear it off and offer myself to him like an unwrapped gift.

"What do you think you're doing?"

My eyes snapped open.

I was back in the classroom. Phina stood in front of my workbench, frowning.

"I..."

"Did you sample your potion?"

I swayed on my feet. Swallowed thickly. My cheeks were aflame, but that was nothing compared to the heat still radiating through my core.

"Hattie." Phina's tone was sharp.

"Just a few drops," I answered quickly, "to assess the quality."

Brown eyes narrowed, then dropped to my pitcher. Phina dipped her ornate quartz spoon into the liquid and gave it a swirl. When she looked at me again, a hint of amusement sparkled in her otherwise scolding expression.

"What did you find in your assessment?" she asked slowly—wryly.

I cleared my throat, unable to get Noble out of my mind. "Effective."

A single *ha* escaped Phina's lips—seeming to surprise even her. "Elaborate, please."

With the magical effects of the potion fading, I slid my tongue into the pockets of my mouth, tasting the remnants of the ingredients with more acuity. "For a client seeking to spark lust, this would be..." My face was *flaming*. "I think I added too much cinnamon."

Another laugh. "Indeed, you did. Also, too much rose water, but I suspect you already tasted that?"

"Not enough gardenia?" I guessed.

"Your ratios are certainly off, but better to lessen the complimentary ingredients than to create more volume," Phina said. "Tell me what else you noticed. What of the magic?"

I lifted the spoon to try another taste—suss out the elements with less *distraction*—but Phina tutted.

"Do not use your sense of taste as a crutch, Hattie." She lifted her chin encouragingly. "Use your *mind*."

"Ugh," I groaned, pinching my eyes shut to *sense* instead of *taste*.

I was back in the garden, but this time, I wasn't *feeling* the emotions but *witnessing* them. It was the difference between being *in* a garden versus viewing a painting of it. And what I saw...

I dropped concentration before I gave myself a headache. "There's too much longing," I said to Phina. "A sense of distance and sorrow mixed in with the lust and affection." My forehead scrunched. "Could that be the cinnamon?"

Phina lifted a finger and tapped the air as if I were onto something.

Returning to the head of the class, she raised her voice to address the group. "Hattie has reminded me of an important component of alchemy that I'd like everyone to hear."

Glasses clinked, notebook papers rustled, and stools groaned as students set down their tools and gave their professor their full attention.

"Magic comes from *you*," Phina emphasized. "Your desires, fears, intentions, unmet needs. All of these can alter the nature of the threads you weave into a material. Which means if you've just had your heart broken, or you're experiencing unrequited love," Phina's eyes flicked—mortifyingly—right to me, "it's possible for you to inject some of that emotional signature into what you create. Contamination is not entirely avoidable; it's a symptom of being your own primary source of power: a flawed human being. It's important for you to meter your emotions when you weave, lest you imbue your potions with your own emotional residue."

If my face had been aflame before, it was ashen now. Had I really imbued my own heartache into a love potion? Had Phina truly *felt* it?

How *humiliating*.

Sani raised her hand. "How does one limit one's emotions while weaving? Are there practical tactics we can employ?"

As Phina described meditative practices and deep breathing techniques, I winced with shame. Since girlhood, I'd always *felt* deeply. Pining when I should've been coy. Flaring with anger when I should've been demure. Aching with longing when I should've moved on.

Anya pinned me as a romantic because I rooted for budding attraction, swooned at sappy stories of professed love, and encouraged my neighbors to *just go for it* (even when I, myself, never had any luck with grand gestures). She found my romanticism charming, but I mostly found it painful.

When Noble had arrived in Waldron, I'd tried to ignore him as he ignored me. Then he came to the Possum with Richold, and it was impossible not to give into my emotions—to ogle and flirt and *taunt* him with my affection. By the time he and Richold had paid for their drinks and left, a permanent teasing grin had affixed itself to Anya's face.

"Fates, Hattie, I've never seen you like this," she'd said, bumping me with her hip.

I'd dabbled with a few courtships during my time in Waldron, but nothing ever felt right. No one had ever compared to the boy I'd loved in my youth.

"You're blushing so furiously you look sunburnt," she'd added.

The delicate skin underneath my eyes had certainly stung like a burn. "Just flustered, is all," I'd replied, forcing an eager smile. "He's handsome, isn't he?"

My best friend had shrugged. "I like my men a little more rugged."

For the next year, I'd done my best to minimize my pining glances around Hugh, Martha, and the other gossips in town, but with Anya... Well, if I couldn't be honest with Anya about my past, I could at least be honest with her about my emotions. I wasn't great at pretending with those, anyhow.

But now, for the sake of my studies, I had to repress them even *more*? I didn't see how that was possible.

Thankfully, Phina's lecture was interrupted by the ringing of the clocktower bells, announcing the end of the day. Students began packing up their things, chatting and laughing, while a pair of mentees entered through a side door to clean the workbenches.

Tucking my notebook under my arm, I hurried toward the exit, catching up to Uriel and Sani. I was eager to escape with them into a balmy spring afternoon of reading under the big oak in the courtyard and drinking cheap wine. Most importantly, I wanted to get far away from the ever-growing discomfort of embarrassing myself in front of my academic idol—and my lingering unease after confronting her in the alley.

"Hattie."

When I turned, my professor's arms were folded across her chest. The plain burgundy tunic she wore brought out the amber flecks in her eyes, which currently felt like hot embers pressing into my skin.

"Do you have a moment?"

When just a week ago I would've loved to have a one-on-one chat with Professor Farkept, I now dreaded the notion. Was this *it*? Was I about to be dismissed from the Collegium for what I'd done? "I, uh.

Um." I scrambled for an excuse, *any* excuse, that might keep me from the impending conversation.

"We'll meet you outside," Sani said.

My gaze swung to hers, then Uriel's, latching onto them with wide-eyed terror in the hopes they'd get the hint and help me out of this. But I was met with two grins that—*Fates*, were they mistaking my panic for excitement?

Phina extended her arm, gesturing at the door directly across the hall. "Let's go to my office, shall we?"

9
OPPORTUNITY

HATTIE

P rofessor Farkept clasped her hands and rested her forearms atop her heavy wooden desk. "Do you know why you're here, Hattie?"

Seated across from my professor, I felt crowded on all sides by the bookshelves that lined the walls of the cluttered space. Dread swirled through my stomach, acidic. "I...can't say that I do."

The curtains were drawn, casting the room in darkness; surrounded by formidable, oppressive furniture, Phina appeared almost as out of place as I felt. I knew from the backs of her books that she'd grown up here in the city, often visiting Castle Might. Her parents were Fenriran aristocrats of some kind, her brother a prominent knight. But if I had to wager a guess as to where she felt *most* at home, it wouldn't be in a room like this, but the countryside somewhere, collecting herbs in a big basket, a summer breeze ruffling the ends of her hair.

Had Phina resented growing up among nobility, as I had? Had her guardians discouraged her studies in alchemy, as mine had? I'd traveled to Waldron at first out of necessity, but there was something about the fresh country air—green, earthy, vibrant—that lent itself to alchemy.

"Please don't dismiss me from the program," I blurted, gripping the smooth wooden arms of my chair. "I know I shouldn't've eavesdropped the other night, but studying here means *everything* to me."

"Hattie," Phina said patiently, ending on a chuckle. "You're not being dismissed. Quite the opposite actually."

Still gripping the arms of my chair, I sat back just an inch, regarding her. "The opposite?"

"I'd like for you to join my team of research apprentices."

The offer was a high honor, a rare opportunity.

I found it suspicious. "I...don't understand."

"The offer? Or what it entails?"

"Why offer it to *me*?" I narrowed my eyes at her. "Is this because I'm friends with Idris?"

"No."

"Then *why*?" I asked, incredulous.

"Why not?"

I could think of many reasons why not. I started with: "Because I can't alchemize even a basic love potion. Don't you want an advanced apprentice? Someone who's more—"

"Are you questioning my judgement?"

I stared at her, horrified.

Phina's elbows were still on her desk, and when she leaned forward, the wood groaned. "What's the difference between you and your fellow pupils?"

I huffed. "I'm older."

"What about the way you alchemize?"

I scoffed. "I'm messier."

"You're *scrappier*," she amended. "Intuitive. Mindful of waste. You're also aware of your shortcomings, whereas most of your classmates are not."

I thought of Sani and Uriel and how hard they tried—how talented they were—and frowned.

Phina gave me a shrewd look. "Of all the students in my class today, your potion was the most polished, effective, and viable. Shaky on the details, but you're learning. That's normal. You'll improve with practice." Phina's lips quirked. "Your biggest flaw is that you lack confidence.

You have a keen instinct, but for some reason you don't always listen to it. Why is that?"

I glanced away, my attention landing on the green spine of a book with a gold-foiled title: *Herbs*. For the first twenty years of my life, I was taught that my instincts were not to be trusted. That becoming an apothecary was a dream, not reality, and that dreams were for little girls, not responsible noblewomen.

And though I was *free* from those old expectations, the training and beliefs were still imbedded in my skin like splinters, deep, painful, and impossible to pull out.

"I don't know," I replied thickly, trying to force the emotion out of my throat.

"I think you do."

My palms were clammy, slick. I slid them across the tops of my thighs, rubbing them slowly over the front of my dress. "I'm not here to become an adept," I argued. "I'm only here for a few months, to get my apothecary license."

"You can be an apprentice on my team and still pursue your license," Phina assured me. "But let me ask a different question, Hattie: Do you *want* to participate in my research?"

The only thing publicly known about her research was that one minute, Phina Farkept was just another young professor, and the next, she was being given permanent residence at the Collegium and heading a research program funded by Lord Haron himself. A veritable coup within academic circles. Unknown as Phina's research was, it was *still* the talk of the city.

Of course, I was curious. *Of course*, I wanted to participate. Not just because Phina was my herbology idol—but because her research was highly covert. Which meant it must've been highly important. *Groundbreaking*.

"It would be an honor," I answered, sitting forward. "I've read all your books. My first copy of *An Herbologist's Guide to Tinctures* became so worn that the binding literally fell apart; I had to buy another. Absolutely brilliant, the way you break things down so succinctly. Same with your compendiums. I know *Gamin's Compendia* are considered the definitive source, but yours are far more intuitive. I even read your pamphlet theorizing the fertile properties of Fenriran water—which was fascinating, by the way, although I'll admit I didn't fully understand the alchemical principles you cited. I only wish you'd started publishing a decade earlier, but"—I snorted at the foolishness of my own comment—"you were a teenager then, same as me."

"It was just a question, Hattie, I wasn't vying for flattery."

"Not flattery," I said with a quick shake of my head. "I'm being genuine."

A smile crinkled her eyes—then she sat back, her expression turning thoughtful. Serious. "You were not incorrect the other night." Her careful phrasing was no doubt due to her Oath, which probably prevented her from speaking freely about her research in mixed company. "Does that scare you?"

Monsters. Her research was about monsters.

I should've been scared—*terrified*. But instead, my curiosity was stirring, a hound locking onto a scent—insatiable. "No," I answered. "It doesn't."

Phina stroked her jaw with a tattooed finger. "It should."

"Are you inviting me into your program because I know too much?"

"I'm inviting you into the program," she said, "because your Hylder tincture was stronger than mine."

I laughed. "That's impossible."

"I am not a paragon, Hattie. Yours was better."

I shook my head, dumbstruck. I was a decent amateur alchemist by Waldron's standards, but compared to an adept of the Order of Alchemy? "How is that possible?"

"I'm not sure," she said, "that's why I want you in my lab."

I thought of the hooded figure in the alley, coughing and convulsing. My heart twisted. "Your friend. Are they improved?"

"Yes, and grateful for your help."

I was glad to hear it. But— "There wasn't anything special about my tincture," I insisted.

"I'm telling you there is."

I slumped back in my chair, shaking my head in disbelief.

Phina clasped her hands and squared her shoulders, back to her professorial posture. "What is your goal here, Hattie?"

"To receive my apothecary license," I replied.

"Why?"

I glanced away again, back to the green book titled *Herbs*.

My interest in herbal alchemy came from a fascination with the healers who frequented my childhood home. My cousin Raina had been a sickly girl, and apothecaries had come from all over the Seven Territories to solve the mystery of her illness. Not only were they enigmatic—shuffling in through the servant's door with their moss-green robes, tattooed hands, and cases filled with countless clinking bottles—they'd saved Raina's life.

To me, Raina's healers were as miraculous as the Fates themselves. To heal someone I loved with herbs—*that* was awe-inspiring. I wanted to know all their secrets.

As Raina's illness diminished, the two of us emulated her healers by playing "apothecary" in the kitchens and greenhouses, mixing cooking herbs with dirt, water, sometimes even wine if we could get our hands on it (Raina's father put an end to that when we got into a particularly valuable vintage gifted to him by the Lord of Lothgaim). The "potions" of our childhood did not hold any real power, but *we* felt powerful making them—and therein lay my growing passion.

As Raina's interests pivoted toward music and the horse stables, my obsession with herbs only increased as I spent more days in the gardens and our home library, learning all I could about medicine, plants, and magic. Around that same time, my uncle promoted a lesser-born knight to lead his personal guard, whose son—when he wasn't training to become a knight, himself—also enjoyed reading. Those peaceful afternoons with Noble in the library—along with heart-thumping rides with Raina—remained among my most cherished memories from growing up.

And no matter where my life took me, I could always find safety within the laws and properties of plants and magic. Herbs didn't care who I was, where I came from, or my status; as an aspiring apothecary, my identity was measured only by my skill.

I'd always wanted to be an apothecary, but my enrollment at the Collegium wasn't *just* about taking my license back to Waldron—it was about the personal liberation of finally living the life *I* chose.

"I feel most like myself when I'm alchemizing," I amended. "I want to use that passion to help people. *Heal* people."

The left corner of her mouth lifted. "Your talent with Hylder could help a lot of people."

A buoy of hope bobbed at the top of my chest—even as a sense of foreboding slithered in my gut. "Are a lot of people at risk?"

"I'm afraid I can't divulge more until you join my team." Her smile broadened with a blend of encouragement and challenge. "So, what do you say?"

10

No

Distractions

Noble

"Again," General Kalden Asheren barked on the morning of his son's sixteenth birthday.

Noble reset his stance in the training yard, hefting his practice sword. His shoulder shook with strain. Sweat was trickling into his eyes, making them blur and sting with salt. Hot blisters on his fingers and palm threatened to pop under his weapon's weight.

His father lifted his own training sword with ease and leveled it toward Noble's, crossing the dull blades—the customary starting stance among Mighty Knights. Compared to his six-foot-six oak tree of a father, sixteen-year-old Noble was a mere sapling. It was times like this—staring down the length of Kalden's practice weapon—that Noble both feared and revered his father.

"Fate, Fortune, Death," they recited in unison, beginning again.

Kalden's blows juddered up through the steel of Noble's shortsword, rattling the tired joints in his right arm. Noble gritted his teeth, ignoring the pain, shoving it down into the pit of his stomach. He parried the strikes—barely—as he focused on his footwork, making quick, calculated steps around his father.

"Your advantage, Noble! Use your advantage!" Kalden ordered.

Spring sunlight glared off the pale, dusty earth of the training yard, making Noble squint—but he did as he was told, tracking his father's movements with his preternatural eyesight. The shift of muscle beneath his father's shirt told Noble that he would swipe horizontally; Noble deflected it by side-stepping. His father's eyes tracked to his next target—Noble's sword wielding arm—and Noble's observation saved him a bruise to the cap of his right shoulder.

"That's it!"

It was as close to praise as Noble ever got.

But as he shuffled his feet, lunging to strike his father's left thigh, his boots kicked up a nasty cloud of grit. Caught up in the fancy maneuver, Noble inhaled when he should've exhaled, not only robbing him of extra power from his core, but also causing him to choke, stupidly, on the plume of his own dust. Without air, he became disoriented—and his father struck him squarely in the oblique.

Pain lanced through Noble's stomach, and he went down, landing on his side. His father loomed, the shadow of his presence blotting out the sun; he leveled the dull tip of his sword at Noble's throat.

"You're distracted," his father scolded.

"It's my *birthday*," Noble complained.

He had plans with Hattie later; they were going to pack a picnic of chocolate pastries and preserved peaches and eat by the river—maybe go for a dip if the afternoon was warm enough. They'd meant to do all that on *her* birthday last week, but it'd rained all day, and they'd ended up playing cards in the solarium with Raina.

"Training does not stop for birthdays, Noble," his father stated tersely—then held out a hand to help him up.

Noble brushed the dirt off his pants, then reset his stance. They went again, blows and blocks screaming through his right arm to the point that he switched his sword to his left hand. The dexterity seemed to please his father, winning Noble a slight squint of approval. His father rarely smiled—not, except, for in the presence of his wife, Noble's mother. Smiling at Helena was the only time Kalden looked *soft*.

Noble, on the other hand, was quick to smile, laugh, *emote*—at least, when he was allowed. In the past four years of living at Castle Wynhaim, he'd taken countless court etiquette classes, the tutors seemingly *determined* to wrestle the playfulness out of Noble, Hattie, Raina, and Raina's older brother, Torin. Noble might've had the same straight nose, defined jaw, and full mouth of his father, but he hoped he never lost his ability to smile for real—propriety be damned.

"You think Mighty Knights skip training on their birthdays?" Noble's father continued, forcing Noble back with a quick series of lunges, their feet scuffing quickly over the dirt.

"No," Noble grunted.

"Do you think your namesake took a day off in the midst of the Battle of East Hammer?"

Kalden loved bringing up Noble the Mighty of Fenrir, the first Knight of the Order of the Mighty, who joined Marona's army to help win the War of Wraiths some six-hundred years ago. Kalden didn't seem to care that Noble the Mighty's actual name had been *Nolan*; he cared more about who Nolan had become—his status and deeds.

The Order of the Mighty meant everything to Kalden Asheren. He'd built himself up from nothing, rising through the ranks and bringing honor and status to his family through the glory of his charge. He wanted nothing more than for his son to follow in his footsteps one day. To become a Mighty Knight of Marona, personal guard to—

"*Focus*, Noble, for Fate's sake!" his father demanded.

Noble was knocked on his ass again, sending an aching jolt up his tailbone.

After that, he *did* focus. He forced thoughts of his birthday and the pressure of his father's expectations into the pit in his stomach with the superficial pain and focused on the fight. Sunlight beating down. Grit beneath his boots. The tear of his muscle fibers as new strength was built.

He kept his eyes on his father's imposing form: pitch-black hair braided back against his scalp, tree-trunk arms and legs, persistent scowl. Kalden was harsh but admirably fierce. Loyal. If Noble grew up to be half the man that Kalden Asheren was, he would know he'd grown up to be a good man.

But that didn't mean he wanted to *be* Kalden.

Strike, block, step, repeat. Strike, block, step, repeat. Noble lost track of time as he trained, everything else blurring into the background until he became nothing but sweat, steel, and calculated movement.

That is, until a fluttering of white caught his peripheral attention.

A long balcony walkway overlooked this part of the castle grounds; under the shadow of its overhang, Hattie leaned against a support beam, arms folded. Even from halfway across the training yard, her blue eyes were arresting.

Noble allowed himself only a moment to look, but his sight magic soaked in every detail. Blonde hair spun up into bun. Pale cheeks flushed raspberry and dusted with dark freckles. Long throat leading to the jut of prominent clavicles. A plain, shapeless white dress draped over her lithe form. Her mouth: wry.

When Noble was younger, his father had remarked that it was *advantageous* for Noble to befriend children of higher birth; but the older Noble got, the less Kalden approved of his friendship with Hattie. *You might be the same age, but you come from different worlds*, Kalden liked to remind him. *It is your responsibility to maintain propriety, lest you ruin her prospects and destroy your reputation.* The social hierarchy was archaic, but at Castle Wynhaim, it mattered greatly.

The problem was: Noble's sixteen-year-old body worked independently of his brain. His heart had beat only for Hattie since the moment he laid eyes on her, and through puberty—his and hers—the constant pulse of his affection for her had developed into a feverish thudding.

Even now, as he turned his attention back to this endless sparring session, Noble could think only of their afternoon ahead. Her laugh: filling the small meadow of their secluded grove by the river, sunshine beaming through the budding alder trees. Her mouth: slipping a peach slice past her teeth, talking circles around him. Her body: slicing into the water like a dagger into his chest.

His whole body hurt with sore muscles and bruises, yet suddenly it was his heart that ached the most. Because not only were his growing romantic feelings for Hattie socially inappropriate, they were a distraction from what his father saw as Noble's predestined purpose: Mighty Knighthood. The most direct path to status, security, and prestige for Noble and the legacy of their family.

With a grunt, he swung his shortsword down, blocking another one of his father's brutal hits. Hattie's presence revived Noble's energy, and he worked his way forward in an onslaught until finally his father deflected and swung for Noble's neck. Kalden stopped the blunt blade a hair's width away from Noble's pulse-point.

Noble's cheeks flamed. Losing in front of Hattie embarrassed him, but his father's pleased little squint had returned, and Noble was relieved to see the pride in his father's expression—the possible end of this training session.

But then Kalden's gaze flicked to Hattie, no doubt spotting the hope and expectation on her face—the implication of plans made. Noble saw the moment his father decided to ruin his birthday. A quick pulse of a stony jaw.

With a frown, Kalden looked back at his son and said, "We'll rest for a quarter hour, then continue."

The sun had risen considerably since Noble had been in the training yard. "It's been nearly three hours," Noble protested.

"And your form still isn't right."

Noble dropped his sword in the dirt. In his mind's eye, he saw the promise of a fun and relaxing afternoon slipping away like a mirage. As he approached Hattie, he tried to keep the dismay from his face, assuming a confident saunter, donning a cocky grin like armor to defend himself against her disappointment and his own.

He breezed past where she leaned against the beam, going for a small table by the weapons rack that held a jug of water. Ladling himself a cup, he drank deep, feeling Hattie's attention on him and pretending he didn't. He wanted to give himself a moment before he let her down.

"Ready?" Hattie asked hopefully.

Noble set his cup aside. "Can't make it. More training."

Hattie laughed—but when he didn't join in, her face fell. "Wait, really?"

He wiped his brow on the hem of his shirt, blotting the sweat. "Yeah."

The thought of continuing his training session made him want to cry; missing his birthday outing with Hattie made him want to rage. Yet there was nothing he could do. He was failing his father by not being a better fighter, failing Hattie with ruined plans, and failing himself by not being good enough for either of them.

Noble glanced past Hattie, trying to think of what he could say to ease her disappointment. The sight of a newcomer approaching from behind her had his stomach sinking further.

Bulky, blond, with cruel eyes and a conniving personality, Brendan Harrow was older than Noble by two years. He was of noble blood—the child of a former Lord—and having lost his father shortly before the arrival of the Asheren family at Castle Wynhaim, he *revered* Kalden in a way that compounded Kalden's disappointment in his own son.

Noble had recently overheard a pair of governesses whispering about the possibility of Brendan's eventual match with Hattie. Just two weeks ago, she and Noble had been snacking on a spread of cured meats and hard cheeses in the library—her favorite pastime, and therefore, his, too—and she'd mentioned offhand how much she detested Brendan: *I'll have to marry a nobleman someday, but* Fates, *please let it not be* him.

Noble hadn't known what to say, so he'd said nothing.

"But I've been looking forward to this all morning—all week," Hattie was saying, oblivious to Brendan's approach. "I baked the pastries fresh—extra chocolate and all."

His heart squeezed. "Tomorrow, maybe?"

"What's tomorrow?" Brendan asked, sidling up to Hattie.

She flinched at his sudden nearness—an almost imperceivable twitch, but it was obvious to Noble. "Nothing," she said, blinking rapidly.

Brendan rested a hand on her shoulder. "Has Noble hurt your feelings?"

Hattie shook her head, shrinking away from his touch. Thankfully, Brendan had the self-awareness to let go—saving Noble from having to break his fingers.

Noble crossed his arms over his chest. "This is a private conversation."

"Brendan," Kalden called cheerfully from the center of the training area. "Have you come to join us?"

Brendan swiveled toward the Mighty Knight. "If you'll have me!"

Kalden met Brendan with a chummy clap on his back. "Perhaps you can train some sense into my son, here," he said on a laugh.

Noble offered Hattie a sheepish smile. "I *am* sorry," he murmured.

"Me, too," she said in a warbling voice, and Noble wondered if she knew that this wasn't his doing, but his father's—wielding disappointment against Noble in the name of discipline and hurting Hattie in the process.

It made Noble irrationally angry, which would no doubt make him a better fighter against Brendan when his short break was up.

"Tomorrow," he stated firmly, desperate for it to be so.

"Tomorrow," she agreed. Then she brushed an errant curl off her forehead, assuming a haughty posture. "Or perhaps I'll just go today," she taunted, "on my own. I'll eat all your chocolate pastries myself, so they don't go to waste."

"You *wouldn't*," he said, thrilled to be teased by her. She wouldn't make jokes if she were truly devastated, right?

"I would," she said, already backing away down the open corridor. "You won't know what you're missing, Noble Asheren." She turned, skipping away, her dress billowing like sheets on a clothesline, like summer cumulus clouds, like the ballooning of his lungs.

"Trust me," he muttered after she'd disappeared around the corner, "I do."

"Whatever it is you're thinking—don't," Kalden said, arriving at Noble's side.

Noble glanced over his shoulder at Brendan, who was swinging a practice sword in the center of the training ring, warming up with unnecessary flare.

When Noble faced his father again, he assumed a mask of indifference. "I don't know what you're talking about."

"Good."

Frustration welled up in Noble, but he swallowed it like bitter bile. "Let's resume," he grumbled, brushing past his father and heading toward his nemesis for a brutal afternoon of pointless sparring.

Nearly thirteen years had passed since that day, and Noble—adult Noble—was still exercising the same restraint. Swallowing the same frustration.

Alone in his room at the Royal Inn of Fenrir—his home for the foreseeable future—Noble ducked under the surface of his bath. At this very moment, Phina was probably inviting Hattie onto her research team. When Hattie agreed—and he knew she would—Noble would once again be caught between wanting to tell her how he felt and stifling his emotions for the sake of her safety and future. Only this time, he wouldn't have Kalden to break their constant tension. This time, the distractions of Waldron wouldn't keep them apart. Forced to work together in Phina's lab, they'd be unable to avoid each other. They'd *have* to interact.

Noble really ought not look forward to it as much as he did.

He surfaced, wiping the water from his eyes.

At least in such close proximity, he would be able to look out for her—keep her safe from the perils of working on a project as volatile as Phina's research. Then again, it was possible that the most dangerous thing to Hattie was, in fact, *him*.

11

RISK

HATTIE

You're kidding," Sani shrieked, clapping her hands. "You're *kidding*!"

A trio of students walking along the edge of the lawn glanced curiously in our direction.

Uriel, Sani, and I were seated on a wool blanket beneath the oak tree in the center of the interior courtyard at Inver College, where we lived and studied. The Collegium was essentially its own city within Fenrir's capital, comprised of fifteen college buildings—which housed classrooms, offices, dormitories, and enclosed outdoor spaces like this one—as well as seven libraries, and three highly secure research centers. All the structures were stunningly built and fastidiously maintained, with grounds that rivaled even the most splendid royal gardens.

Snacking on bread, cheese, and olives under the oak tree at Inver was my favorite non-alchemy-related pastime at the Collegium—but it didn't quell today's uneasiness after my meeting with Phina.

I tucked a stray curl behind my ear. "I know I should be happy, but—"

"You are not," Uriel cut in. "Why?"

Sani reclined on one elbow to reach a piece of cheese. "Is it your new Oath?"

Oaths of Allegiance were a common practice at the Collegium—especially when it came to covert research. Because no magic was strong enough to tie someone's tongue completely, apprentices took Oaths of Allegiance as a way of officially binding them to the studies they served, discouraging disloyalty, and diminishing the spread of sensitive information.

Unlike the powerful Oaths of adepts and knights—which were taken before rulers and recorded in magical Oath Ledgers by arcane magicians called ledgermasters—Oaths of Allegiance were minor. The moment I'd said *yes* to Phina's offer, she'd had me recite my Oath right there in her office and had recorded it in her Research Ledger herself. Aside from the faint tattoo that'd formed around my right wrist, I felt wholly the same—*unchanged*.

Even so, I had to be cautious about what I told my friends about the program; I didn't want to inadvertently break my Oath and end up with my name recorded in Phina's ledger as a dissenter. I chose my words carefully as I elaborated. "Remember our night of non-mingling at the Charm?"

Sani chewed her cheese, looking queasy. "Of the little I remember," she said, "I wish I didn't." She wrinkled her nose as if she could still smell the vomit with her scent magic.

Uriel cringed. "You and me both."

Sani threw an olive at Uriel's face, which she caught in her mouth with impressive coordination.

"Well, after those knights came to talk to Professor Farkept..." I trailed off, wincing. "I followed them."

"You *what*?" Sani asked at the same time Uriel wondered, "Were you caught?"

I shoved a piece of bread in my mouth, chewed, swallowed. It seemed dangerous to divulge that I recognized Mariana, so I left that out. "I was curious, I guess? And I wasn't caught, I made myself known."

"*Why*?" my friends enunciated in unison.

"They were talking to someone who seemed...afflicted. Maybe a sickness, or...I don't know." I shuddered, thinking about the implications of that night. Was the hooded figure a knight in Mariana's Order who'd been bitten? "They needed a medicinal tincture that I happened to have on my person, so I offered it to them."

"What kind of tincture?" Sani asked.

I glanced down at the Oath tattoo that ringed my wrist. "I shouldn't say. But part of the reason I was invited into the program was because of what I learned that night." I still wasn't convinced that my Hylder tincture had been more effective than Phina's (and effective at *what*, exactly?). "I guess I feel like I didn't truly earn my place."

Uriel brushed the breadcrumbs off her trousers. "Professor Farkept would not invite a liability into her lab." She tucked her legs and leaned forward. "Even if you overheard something, she must see *some* potential in you."

I nodded reluctantly, eyes floating up to the splay of leaves above our heads and the periwinkle sky beyond the canopy. Phina had said the same thing, but the problem was, I still didn't fully believe my professor's praise.

"She's right," Sani said. "It's a prestigious and highly secretive program. She wouldn't invite you into it without serious consideration."

"And *part* of what she considered was the intelligence I overhead." I sighed. "I'm sorry, I know I shouldn't complain. It just feels suspicious, is all."

Sani hummed thoughtfully, pursing her lips.

"What?" I prompted.

Sani pushed off her elbow and swiveled, so that she sat on her knees. "I don't want this to make you more anxious than you already are, but—" Her voice was a whisper when she continued. "My history class has been studying the transparency of knowledge and the weaponization of magic during the kingdom's early inception. Back before Fenrir was absorbed as a territory under Marona's rule, many of the local artisans and adepts here chose to obfuscate their research to prevent it from being developed by neighboring territories first." Sani's eyes widened meaningfully.

"We are not following," Uriel said flatly.

Sani let out an impatient groan. "Basically, alchemical and arcane research became highly valuable—a way for territories to seize a militaristic advantage. If a territory had alchemical or arcane power that Marona *didn't* possess, they could use that magic against their would-be conqueror."

"Why would this history lesson concern me?" I asked.

Sani fixed me with an almost manic stare, a mauve flush tinging her deep brown cheeks. Foreboding context aside, I loved it when she got intense about history. It's how I felt about herbs.

"Imagine you're a wartime adept working on a secret research project that could alter the course of the conflict. What would you fear most?" Sani asked.

"My notes getting stolen by the enemy?" I guessed.

"Assassination," Uriel replied.

A familiar pang of fear dropped into my stomach like a stone in a well, echoing through me.

Sani pointed at Uriel, pleased. "When it comes to high-level research, it's not just the *notes* that are valuable—it's the adept who's skilled enough to actually *perform* the magic. The Seven Territories have a long history of secret research projects and targeted assassinations of prominent adepts. Kidnappings, too."

Knowing too much almost got me killed, Hattie, Anya had said.

I couldn't help but feel windswept by Sani's words.

I let out a nervous puff of breath, my appetite gone. "You're telling me that joining Phina's program could put me at risk of being kidnapped or *murdered*?"

All this talk of politics was...too *close*. Suddenly, I wasn't just worried about the program itself, but how my involvement could call attention to my identity.

"*Pah*," Uriel grunted dismissively. "You have been reading too much, Sani. While the dramas of history are exciting, the past is not destined to repeat. We are not in a war; therefore, the adepts of today are not harboring war secrets. There has not been any meaningful conflict among the territories for hundreds of years."

She was right. King Braven had made sure of it—with Oaths and unifying arranged marriages and constant diplomatic tending.

Sani frowned. "But why else would Phina's research be kept secret?"

"Trade advantage? Public safety? Integrity of study?"

I would've believed Uriel's less-frightening suggestions if it weren't for what I'd witnessed in the alley. The involvement of knights that evening did seem rather...*political*.

Uriel swung her attention back to me. "Do not let Sani's warmongering sour your triumph."

"Hattie," Sani said apologetically. "I wasn't trying to discourage you. I'm happy for you!"

I grabbed an olive and a piece of cheese, weighing them as if my hands were scales. "Political conspiracy or boring research project?" I ate both bites and forced a smile. "I'll find out soon enough."

Uriel kicked her legs out, crossing them at the ankles. "If you are murdered, I promise to avenge you."

"Then I pity my murderer." The comment earned me a wide and wicked grin from Uriel, but Sani was still watching me with a hint of concern.

I poked her thigh, and she snapped out of whatever was troubling her and returned my smile. The conversation meandered to other topics from there, Sani's expression easing as we joked and laughed. But a sense of foreboding was forming behind my ribs, hard and jagged as crystal.

The last time I'd felt like this—had entertained concerns of political scheming and a threat on my life—I *had* become a target. In response, my uncle hurriedly married me off; the best way to protect me from the scandal of my parentage—long-buried, freshly uncovered—was to strip me of any connection to my family.

In addition to Oath Ledgers, there were Census Ledgers, too: records of births, marriages, and deaths for every territory. Sending me all the way to Fenrir to take the name of a no-name mayor in a no-name town had effectively erased my true identity.

But it had also taken away my personhood. My sense of self.

I had not even been permitted to write to Raina, Noble, or my guardians. And while I'd grown up at court *knowing* that I'd eventually have to marry a random nobleman, having it rushed—having it be to someone unvetted and *vile* and violent—was terrifying.

Painful.

Lonely.

Mustering the courage to escape to Waldron and knock on Anya's door was the greatest thing I'd ever done for myself, and up until this moment, I'd thought that realizing my alchemy dreams at the Collegium was the second greatest. But now, Sani's warning and the resurgence of that familiar sense of foreboding was hard to ignore.

Because the last time I'd felt like this, I'd been right to be afraid.

Fates, what had I gotten myself into?

A Note

Included with Hattie's Birthday Gift

Dear Hattie,

Happy twenty-ninth birthday!

I purchased this necklace for you at last year's Astrophel Festival and have been saving it for this occasion. Now you can carry a piece of Waldron with you everywhere you go (the vial is filled with water from the Wend).

Wishing you a fortuitous final year of unfixed Fate!

Love and hugs,

Anya

A Letter

Dear Anya,

I just opened my birthday gift! How thoughtful of you to know I'd want a piece of home while I'm here. I love it. (The vial looks familiar; I must've been admiring it during the festival—what a lovely coincidence!).

Also, some exciting news: Phina Farkept was impressed by a Hylder tincture I brought from home and has invited me to join her research team! I wish I could tell you more, but I had to take an Oath of Allegiance, and besides, I don't yet know all the details. Even so, I'm proud of myself for catching her attention, excited about the opportunity, and also immensely nervous for numerous reasons I won't belabor here.

I keep asking myself, "What would Anya say?" and I come up blank. What do you say?

I miss your hugs. Give Wicker a smooch for me.

Hattie

P.S. Remember when Corvin sent records of our divorce? Do you remember if

12

REUNION

HATTIE

I promise I'll stay out of your way," I said, hefting my basket of ingredients a little higher. "I brought my own supplies and everything."

Cook Tillen—the kitchen master for Inver College—folded her arms across her ample chest. "What did you say your name was?"

"Hattie," I replied. "I'm an apprentice of—"

"Apprentices are not permitted in the kitchens."

Lavender pre-dawn light filtered in through the venting windows that lined the ceiling, spilling onto the bare surfaces of the butcher-block tables. At this Fates-forsaken hour, Cook Tillen and I were the only two people here.

"You won't even know I'm—"

"No. Apprentices."

My fingers lifted to my chest, where Anya's birthday gift was tucked inside the front of my dress, between my breasts: a necklace with a tiny teardrop vial as the pendent. I lifted my chin a little higher. "Even on my birthday?"

It wasn't *exactly* a lie. My birthday had been yesterday.

I hadn't made a fuss about the milestone, instead opting for a quiet night studying and snacking with my friends. Aside from the fact that no celebration could top a Waldron celebration—especially one organized by Anya—my logic was this: if I downplayed the significance of my age, perhaps the year would pass uneventfully.

Twenty-nine *was* a momentous year, after all.

In adolescence and young adulthood, one's Fate was considered malleable, which meant that if the Mirror of Fortune or the Mirror of Death predicted an undesirable future, the outcome could be avoided. After thirty, however, one's Fate became "fixed." Unchanging.

Whether a person *wanted* their future to change or remain the same, the twenty-ninth year was crucial. It was the last chance to point one's life in a better direction—or hold on tight to a desirable Fate.

My visions in the Mirrors of Fortune and Death had been favorable, so I couldn't wait to turn thirty and be done with the uncertainty. The fact that I was joining Phina's research team in my final unfixed year, however, was...worrying.

It's why I'd come to the kitchens. To take my mind off of my self-doubt, Sani's tales of politically driven assassinations, and my fear of my own turbulent past repeating itself. And to partake in a treasured birthday tradition.

I forced a smile, hoping Cook Tillen would see my request for what it was: genuine, if a little desperate.

Cook Tillen made a show of assessing me, from my curly hair pinned into a bun, to my basket, to the hem of my simple blue dress that dusted the stone floor. "You want to bake on your birthday?" she finally asked. "Why?"

I glanced at the sacks of flour, sugar, and lemons in my basket, which was growing heavier with each second we stood here arguing in the doorway. "It reminds me of home."

When I was a girl, the castle's kitchen master—Cook Zina—made me lemon cookies every year. Their flavor was bright and citrusy, not too sweet. On the morning of my eighth birthday, I decided it wasn't enough just to eat them—I wanted to learn the recipe. Zina was kind enough to teach me her secrets.

The rosemary she sprinkled into the batter for fragrant complexity.

How to zest the lemons without adding any bitter pith.

The duck egg she incorporated for richness.

As we dusted the cookies with sugar, Zina told me the recipe had been my mother's favorite, too. It'd brought me joy to have something in common with the woman who'd given me life, but whom I'd never met. My aunt and uncle had raised me as their own, and therefore I rarely felt my mother's absence, but those occasional reminders of her—a connection across time—still warmed my heart.

Besides, the cookies really were delicious.

Every year thereafter—until Zina retired—we made my birthday cookies together. There were few traditions I'd taken with me when I was forced to leave home—but that recipe was one of them.

I squared my shoulders at Cook Tillen. "What if I baked a batch for you, too?"

———— ❀ ————

Two hours later, my basket laden with cookies, I made my way down Adept's Walk—the wide road that bisected campus—to report for my first day as an apprentice on Phina Farkept's research team.

The Walk was abustle with professors and students heading to and from classes, libraries, research buildings, and the many shops that lined the street: apothecaries, chandleries, bakeries, jewelers, saddleries, and more. Colorful flags hung on crisscrossing lines above the road, snapping in the wind; gangs of pigeons and crows patrolled for dropped morsels.

The street could've easily been one in Wynhaim City. The pollen-scented breeze reminded me of the winds that whipped up from the grasslands of my home territory. The taste of mineral grit and smoke in the air was reminiscent of the Maronan turnips I refused to eat as a child. I heard Raina's laugh drifting through the clamor of clopping horseshoes.

Maybe it was because I'd spent the morning making lemon cookies, but nostalgia pulled through my heart like spun sugar, sweet at first, but quick to turn brittle. I shook my head, trying to clear it of the cloying memories. Wistfulness would only sadden me. Distract me from who I was now—who I *could* be.

Someone who made a difference. *An apothecary.*

Lifting my chin, I picked up my pace.

The building containing Phina's lab was just as magnificent as the rest of the Collegium's campus—pointy spires, decorative carvings, regal archways—with one unique, standout feature: a massive rose window above the entrance. Colored glass had been fitted into the gaps of intricate stone tracery, forming a wheel of symmetrical loops resembling the most common knots used in alchemy. Because of the window, the building had been named the Alchemist's Oculus, which everyone shortened to the Ocs.

Aside from the regal, arched entrance, the majority of the structure was surrounded by a forty-foot-high circumferential wall, guarded by knights. It was the most secure, secretive building at the Collegium; most apprentices would never step foot inside. So, as I walked through the heavy double doors, I felt an overwhelming sense of pride, curiosity, excitement, and nervousness. There was no turning back now—and in spite of my apprehensions, I didn't want to.

A steward welcomed me as I stepped into the dark foyer. Beyond the tunnel-like entryway was a vaulted atrium, with doors and hallways on the far end leading deeper inside; sunlight streamed through the stained glass, casting patches of blue, green, and pink onto the white tile. Between here and there, strange symbols—arcane lettering—marked the wooden threshold.

"Name?" the steward asked, standing up from her small desk.

My voice came out squeakier than I intended. "Hattie Mund."

"Oath?"

I lifted my arm, showing her my tattoo.

She jutted her chin at my satchel and basket. "Your things."

I placed them on the desk, allowing her to rummage through every pocket, flip through my notebook, and examine the vials (including my monthly anti-pregnancy tincture—mostly pointless, as of late—plus a potion for headaches).

"I don't have any weapons, if that's what you're worried about," I said. A pair of knights loitered at the other end of the foyer, casual and at ease, making small talk with each other.

The steward wordlessly replaced the vials, then inspected the basket, lifting the tea towel to reveal the cookies. Their toasted yellow tops glittered with sugar.

"You can have one if you'd like," I offered.

The steward dropped the towel, covering them again. "You can't take these inside."

"I can't bring cookies with me?"

"No food in the labs."

"Truly?"

Her lips pressed into a disapproving frown.

"They're not all for *me*," I insisted. "They're for my professor. Her team. As a thank you." They might've been birthday cookies, but I hadn't planned on eating them all myself.

"Thank your professor another way," the steward said, lifting the basket and setting it behind her desk.

I flashed the steward a teasing grin. "I think you just want the cookies for yourself."

The pair of knights—who'd paused their conversation to watch the scene unfold—chuckled.

With a scowl, the steward lifted a forest-green scarf from a hook on the wall behind her and held it out to me. I took the silken material, not entirely understanding, but getting the sense that this was my cue to continue into the building. With a reluctant smile, I shouldered my satchel and started toward the atrium.

"*Ah, ah, ah,*" the steward scolded. "Put it on." She gestured to her eyes.

I stared down at the scarf in my hand.

One of the knights—female, mid-thirties, and taller than her stocky male partner by a good foot—stepped closer, offering me a kind smile. "First day?"

I nodded.

"The blindfold is protocol for all first- and second-year apprentices," she said. "My name's Willa. I'll escort you."

Sparing the knight a longer look—pretty eyes and masculine features, hair pinned into a bun at her nape, burgundy tunic, leather armor, a dagger and a set of keys dangling from her belt—I then fitted the silk fabric over my eyes and tied it behind my head. When I was done, gentle fingers grasped my upper arm and led me forward.

My Oath tattoo tingled as we passed from the dark foyer into the bright atrium. I couldn't see anything through the tight weave of the silk, but the light that leaked through changed in quality as we crossed the sun-soaked tiles and turned—presumably—down one of the many passageways.

"What kind of cookies did you make?" Willa asked after a while.

"Lemon," I replied. "I make them for my birthday every year."

"It's your birthday?"

"Yesterday," I replied. "Twenty-nine."

Willa let out a low whistle, guiding me around a corner. "Fortuitous."

"Indeed."

For a few seconds, the only sound was the echo of our shoes on stone.

"I love lemon," Willa piped up, giving my arm a slight squeeze. "Let's hope Zorin hasn't eaten them all by the time I get back."

I chuckled. "Is that why she seemed to take offense when I suggested she wanted them for herself?"

"Oh, *definitely*."

We walked for a few minutes in silence, the footsteps of other passers-by nearing and disappearing. Light and shadow crossed my blindfold at intervals as we continued past narrow windows.

"If I've already taken an Oath, why the blindfold?" I asked. "It's not like I'll betray the location of the lab."

"It's for your protection, too," Willa said. "Fenrir has a long history of foreign spies attempting to infiltrate the Oculus and other classified areas of the Collegium. Having fewer individuals know the layout of the labs assists in continued security."

Suddenly Sani's talk of political conspiracies seemed a lot more...*real*.

"Not to worry," Willa continued. "Nowadays, the blindfolds are more of a tradition than an actual precaution. Aside from the occasional burglary, no one has attempted to break into a lab in over a century."

"Burglaries, really?"

"We had one just last week." Willa sounded entirely unbothered. "Such things occur in cities all the time."

We reached a set of shallow steps—just three in total, but Willa had to patently guide me as I toed their edges, sightlessly fumbling my way down. Once I was on flat ground again, we walked another ten strides, then halted.

"Willa," a gravelly male voice greeted.

"I'm here with Hattie Mund," Willa announced.

There was a loud click, followed by hinges squeaking.

Willa ushered me forward. Fresh, fragrant air gusted over my face, and the color of the blindfold paled again, suggesting we were...outside?

"You can take it off, now," Willa said, releasing my arm.

I slid the blindfold up my forehead and off, tucking it in my pocket as I blinked in the sudden brightness.

We stood at the edge of a huge indoor garden.

Past the cave-like entrance, the lab's ceiling was a massive dome made of sectioned glass, sunlight beaming through panels that reached three stories high. The lower windows had been propped open, letting in a cool breeze that ruffled my hair. Straight ahead were rows upon rows of raised garden beds, overflowing with lush vegetation—rosemary, mint, sage, thyme, and countless flowers—that painted the air with fragrance. Interspersed between the beds were narrow lab benches similar to the ones in our herbology classroom, with supply carts parked on the flagstone walkways that crisscrossed the garden in a neat grid. Trees and shrubs—all in bloom—grew along the garden's circumference, insulating us from the sounds of the city. Bees, butterflies, and birds fluttered in amongst the foliage.

It was as if the Fates had bottled a piece of lush countryside and deposited it here in the heart of the capital. A true testament to Lord Haron's stake in Phina's research.

All throughout the space, apprentices were conducting experiments at the benches, pruning plants, and studying in a sheltered alcove off to my right. To my left was a wide archway that led to a forge and metalworking area, along with a wooden staircase that climbed to a mezzanine overlooking the entire lab. As I craned my neck toward the balcony, I caught a glimpse of Phina standing at the railing, talking to—

I squinted.

Squinted *harder*, seething with disbelief at who I saw.

"Hattie, welcome!" Phina called, beckoning me from the balcony. "Come up, come up."

I glanced at Willa, who offered a quick smile. "You'll need an escort to lead you out, either a knight or one of your lab mates with proper clearance. To summon me, pull that"—she pointed at one of three cords hanging from the ceiling by the entrance—"and it'll ring the bell in the atrium." She paused, waiting for my acknowledgment.

Belatedly, I nodded. "Understood."

"I'm off to procure a cookie—if there are any left," she said, eyebrows bouncing. "Have fun!"

The heavy wooden doors groaned as she closed me inside the lab. It wasn't until they juddered shut that I went to the stairs, fists balled, taking the steps heavily. When I reached the top, I felt like I was the victim of an elaborate prank.

Because standing beside my professor was an infuriatingly handsome man, with captivating green eyes and a smirk that boiled my blood. A man who was *supposed* to be in Waldron. Far away from here.

As I walked up, Noble swiveled away from Phina to face me, his chiseled features morphing into cool impassivity.

Fury flared in my chest like a bonfire, as if to warm me against his chill. How *dare* he interfere with this once-in-a-lifetime opportunity? My long-ignored dreams coming true? How dare he exist in my presence when I was not allowed to *want* his company? When wanting him was part of the reason I'd had to go into hiding in the first place?

He'd haunted my steps in Waldron for an entire *year*. I was not interested in having him haunt my steps here, too.

Fingernails biting into my palms, I stomped the rest of the way up to Noble. "What in all the Seven Territories is going on?"

Phina's forehead creased at my sharp tone—then her attention cut to Noble, questioning.

His face remained controlled, blank. Fuel to my fire.

My professor, my idol, regarded me again, slipping into smooth congeniality. "Hattie, this is Noble. He's one of my researchers."

13

DETAILS

NOBLE

Noble loved the look of Hattie angry. Always had.

When they were young, he used to rile her up on purpose—a teasing comment, a playful shove—just to spot the unique shade of raspberry-pink that would sweep across her fair cheeks. It was times like those that Noble felt lucky to possess sight magic, so he could catalogue the exact hue of her exasperation. To see her unique beauty in heightened detail was a gift that he'd never taken for granted, not even when he was sixteen. *Especially* then.

Of course, back then, she usually shoved him back. Scolded him with a whiny *Noooble!* Descended into lilting laughter.

But Hattie wasn't laughing now. Nor was her blush the color of raspberries.

Her current expression was elemental: pure ice in her blue eyes, a wildfire blazing across her face. Her freckles might as well have been sparks drifting on a hot wind. Her mouth—a deliciously deep mauve speckled with a few of those sparks—was screwed up in the prettiest scowl he'd ever seen. He felt both chilled and heated by her presence, a hum in the air between them like imminent lightning.

He was a bastard for enjoying her rage, but they'd both grown up in such a *controlled* setting that, to him, her expressiveness had been pure rebellion. No matter how hard her family tried to train the emotion out of her, no matter how hard Hattie had tried to hide her feelings in mixed company, she was still the most emotionally honest person Noble had ever met. And in a life ruled by decorum and lies, it was refreshing to witness the range of her feeling. After all, the uncontainable version of her was the purest version of her. It didn't matter that the more she emoted, the more Noble had to rein his true feelings in; the burden of holding it together for the both of them had always been worth it to him, just to see her be herself.

"How are you *here*?" Hattie exclaimed, touching her temple as if his presence pained her (*It probably did*, he thought bitterly). "This has to be a cruel joke organized by the Fates themselves."

"If only," Noble muttered.

Phina shifted her weight, eyeing the two of them. "Am I missing—"

"You're an herbal alchemist?" Hattie was shrill, fuming, as if he'd stolen something that was meant to be hers. "How is that *possible*?"

"Metalworker, actually," Noble corrected, folding his arms across his chest.

Hattie's eyes tracked the movement, lingering on his biceps.

It was a stark reminder of the tenuousness of their reunion. The last thing they needed was Phina—or anyone else—catching on to their...familiarity. Noble's father's reputation spanned the continent; connecting Hattie to Noble's family could lead someone to deduce her true identity, and that wouldn't just put Hattie at risk, it would endanger Raina's future, too.

Thankfully, Hattie was too angry to linger on whatever remnants of ill-advised attraction she still felt for him. "Your Oath tattoo implies you're a knight, not an adept," she stated, jutting her chin in the direction of the faded black ring around his neck.

"Retired knight."

"And which Order was that again?"

"Nice try."

She scowled.

He couldn't tell Hattie his former Order even if he wanted to—and besides, that was off topic. Sort of.

"I'm not an adept, either." He lifted his wrist, showing off his Oath of Allegiance tattoo, which was thinner and more faded in color than the mark of an Adept Oath. "I'm just here to utilize the forge."

"You're as much a part of my team as anyone else," Phina said, gesturing to the sprawling lab below, before regarding Hattie again. "Noble is our lead metal alchemist on this project, just returning from a year-long apprenticeship in Waldron—though I take it you know him better than he let on?"

"It was my job to keep to myself," Noble reminded them both coolly.

For a moment, Hattie looked...*caught*. "We don't know each other *that* well." Her eyes flicked to his, narrowed. Then she rested her fists on her hips. "He probably downplayed our familiarity because he was embarrassed to admit that he never tipped his barkeep."

A small, surprised cough burst out of him at her blatant lie, but rather than defending himself, he shrugged. "You got me."

Phina watched the exchange carefully, as if she were trying to make sense of his and Hattie's dynamic.

Good luck with that.

"I always forget how insular small towns can be," Phina remarked finally.

"That's one way to put it," Noble mumbled.

Hattie's arms fell to her sides, limp. "Why didn't you tell me, Noble?"

Her anger was dissipating, leaving behind an ashen pallor. She was hurt, he realized. More hurt than a stranger ought to be about another stranger's secrets—but when it came to their friendship, she'd always been a terrible actress.

Noble itched to comfort her, tell her *everything*, but he had to keep up the chilly act. Keep her at arm's length. He clenched his molars, assuming a stern expression. "Wasn't my place."

"He was under strict orders," Phina added. "No one outside the program was permitted to know why he was in Waldron."

"Is Richold part of the program, too?" Hattie asked. "Is that why you were studying with him?"

"Richold believes I'm an enthusiast, nothing more." Noble spared a glance in Phina's direction. When she offered a small nod, he went on. "I went to Waldron to learn his techniques for working with Gildium, which is a rare metal that—"

"—was used to forge the Mirrors of Fate," Hattie finished for him.

Phina arched a brow, but Hattie's knowledge didn't surprise Noble. She'd always been too clever for her own good. And given her closeness to Anya and Idris...who knew what they'd told her?

"But I thought this study was about Hylder?" Hattie asked her professor.

Noble's jaw ticked. Phina had requested he not divulge that he was the one Hattie had helped in the alley; she didn't want Hattie to know the extent of his involvement in this program—his *dependency* on it.

Selfishly, he didn't want Hattie to know his shame, either. Though he had no right to her affection—and couldn't act on his own desires without endangering her—he did take pleasure in knowing she cared. That their friendship had...*meant* something—and still did, even if only in hindsight.

But if Hattie learned the truth, she'd be sure to change her mind about him.

Thankfully, all that was moot. His Oath—even in retirement—prevented his honesty, regardless of what any of them wanted.

"There are many parts to the study, Hattie," Phina clarified, "but Gildium and Hylder are our two primary areas of interest."

With an air of suspicion, Hattie took in her surroundings. First, the gardens beyond the balcony, an impressive expanse of green vegetation and golden light. Next, the high structure of the glass dome, its window panels providing a temperate climate in defiance of Fenrir's natural chill. Finally, the back wall of the mezzanine, where clear jars of liquid of various hues—from crystalline turquoise to opaque algae-green—had been arranged in neat rows on open storage shelves.

A vertical line formed between Hattie's eyebrows. Noble knew that look—not anger this time, but consideration. Curiosity. It was the same expression Hattie got when they used to read together in the castle library, and she happened upon a passage she didn't quite understand. The musculature in her forehead shifted, a slight furrowing that signaled to Noble that she was turning something over in her mind—pondering an idea from various angles.

When Hattie faced Noble and Phina again, her expression was purely academic. "I understand Hylder—but what does Gildium have to do with monsters?"

Noble had not expected *that*. He blanched.

Phina, on the other hand, chuckled. She extended an arm, gesturing for Hattie to walk with her. As the two women took the stairs side-by-side, Noble followed.

"The primary intent of this study is to bind Hylder to Gildium," Phina explained.

Hattie—her anger fully forgotten—glanced over her shoulder at Noble with a mix of disbelief and excitement. It reminded him of the glances they shared as adolescents, across dining tables and ballrooms, wide-eyed and filled with meaning.

This glance said, *Are you hearing this?*

Unable to help himself, he offered a faint smile. *Just you wait.*

"*Your* role, however, is Hylder," Phina went on. "We'll start by having you compare your tincture to mine. Note the variations. Experiment with different sources. And you'll assist the other researchers with notation and organization."

Hattie was quiet for a few steps. Absorbing.

Noble focused on the back of her elegant neck. A couple ringlets had come loose from her bun and bounced with her buoyant gait. Her hair was a blend of wheat and gold threaded with individual strands of strawberry blonde. He knew from brief, platonic touches in youth that her curls were silky-soft.

"Purification and containment," Hattie mused aloud—then looked sharply up at Phina. "You're seeking some kind of cure, aren't you?"

Noble all but stumbled, but Phina took Hattie's realization in stride, giving nothing away. "The true purpose of my research is not your concern." Phina's Oath prevented her from divulging everything to her apprentices, but Hattie was smart, persistent, and not easily deterred.

Hattie glanced over her shoulder at Noble again, beaming. This glance said, *I can't believe I'm a part of a* real *study.*

All he could offer was a tight-lipped frown. He was happy for her—so *miserably* happy to see her realizing her dream—but he was also dismayed. By her nearness. The dangers. The incomprehensible risks of Hattie being a part of *this* research in particular.

"But metal and herbs can't be bound—can they?" Hattie asked as she and Phina reached the base of the stairs. "Metal doesn't possess the open alchemical threads of herbs."

"Most metals don't, no," Phina said. "But Gildium is different. It's what the artisans refer to as a *living* metal."

A faint ringing was beginning to fill Noble's ears.

The more excited Hattie became about what Phina was involving her in, the more Noble began to fear for her safety. There was considerable danger in being a part of Phina's research, not just because programs such as this were historically fraught, and this one was being funded by a lord who was known for shady politics, but because they were fiddling with materials they didn't fully understand. Tinkering with the wills of the Fates. Altering the laws of nature.

Fear tethers you to your humanity.

Noble halted, gripping the banister.

In the midst of his disquiet, Hattie had asked another question—one he didn't hear—and Phina was now elaborating. "That's where the research gets interesting..."

The women didn't notice that they'd lost him; they disappeared into the reading alcove, discussing the details of the study. Meanwhile, Noble stood there, sweating.

He'd only meant to visit the capital for a couple days—just long enough to get more tincture—but somehow the combination of its waning efficacy and his need for better resources for Gildium experiments had resulted in Noble agreeing to work in Phina's lab indefinitely...alongside the *one* woman he ought not engage.

Had he known what was waiting for him in the city, he might not have left Waldron—just tied himself to the bed in his tiny cottage and allowed the change to overcome him, consume him. At least if he *became* a monster, his external appearance would match how wretched he felt on the inside.

Noble gave his head a shake, trying to clear away his dark thoughts. He stared down at his hand gripping the banister, the little scars of hard labor and his former Order on his hands. His knuckles grew pale as he gripped the wood, holding on as if his life depended on it.

He should *not* have let Hattie join this program. He should've tried harder to dissuade Phina from including her. It was too dangerous for her, and his presence only made that worse. And yet.

And yet.

Studying here was her dream.

And that dream...that dream had facilitated the most effective tincture he'd consumed in *months*—the first flicker of hope. He felt caught between his urge to keep Hattie safe and see her thrive. To be *near* her and leave her well alone.

With a sigh, Noble glanced around. Throughout the lab, apprentices were cultivating the materials that would one day set him free—hopefully. And he was a part of it. That, too, gave him purpose.

Which reminded him: what was his task for today?

The same thing as always, he told himself. *The forge.*

He swiveled, heading to the spacious workshop that Phina had set up just for him. There was nothing like metalworking to force him to focus on lesser concerns. Heat. Consistency. Alchemy. The process of tempering Gildium left no room for Noble to fret about the secrets Phina was telling Hattie, the dangers she was about to be exposed to, and his own culpability in it all.

But as Noble dove into his thankless task of trying and failing to work Gildium into submission, the fretful feeling remained. His heart was a cracked egg, dripping slimy yolk into the pit of his stomach, reminding him that no matter how hard he tried to get over his childhood obsession—his forbidden love—he could never truly escape her or the ways he let her down.

His future might've been unknown according to the Mirrors, but it seemed the Fates were determined to bring him and Hattie together—no matter how disastrous their reunion might prove to be.

14

RULES

NOBLE

By the time Noble looked up from the hot maw of his forge and the endless process of heat, hammer, quench, temper, alchemize, the lab was dark. Lanterns cast orbs of sunset-orange throughout the gardens and alcoves, and beyond the glass-paneled roof, stars twinkled in a sea of indigo. As usual, Noble was last in the lab—or so he thought, until he heard the soft *shush* of a page turning.

Wiping his filthy hands on a rag and his brow on his rolled-up shirt-sleeve, Noble sauntered over to the reading area, where only one other researcher remained.

Hattie was curled up in an upholstered chair, her legs tucked underneath the blue cascade of her dress. A thick journal was splayed across her lap, and she trailed her index finger along the pages as she read, oblivious to his presence. The vertical line between her eyebrows was back, along with her customary head tilt. More curls had sprung loose from her bun, her hair barely held together after hours of studying. What Noble wouldn't give to pull out the pins and sink his fingers into that softness, tug her head back and bring his mouth to hers.

For all their mutual pining over the years, they'd only ever kissed once, on a playful dare from Raina, when they were fourteen—a dry peck that had roused more feeling in his chest than any of the women he'd bedded in adulthood. Hattie—all blue eyes and flushed cheeks—had licked her freckled bottom lip after their kiss, blurted out a quick gasp of a laugh.

To this day, Noble wondered what flavors she'd perceived with her magic. Whether she'd liked the taste of him.

Forcing the memory from his mind, Noble leaned casually against the archway of the alcove. "You're here late."

When Hattie looked up, she was bleary-eyed. A pleasant smile formed automatically—then vanished. "What time is it?"

He stole a quick glance at the sky. "An hour past sundown."

"I forgot you could do that."

Given his sensitivity to color and light, he had a knack for telling time after nightfall, simply by the hue of the dark. Unable to help himself, Noble lowered his stern veneer—just a little. "Does it still impress you like it used to?"

Hattie snorted. "Hardly."

"I think it does."

"It most certainly does not."

"You've always been a terrible liar."

"And you've always been terribly *annoying*."

A pause spread as their childish bickering subsided.

This was the first time they had any privacy since their fraught reunion in Waldron—but just because they were *alone* didn't mean they were free of risk. As Noble had learned from childhood, it was moments like this that held the most potential for disaster. Not only because they could get caught being overly familiar, but because every time he was alone with her, his emotional fortitude eroded another inch.

It was easier to stay away.

"You've been reading a long time," he remarked.

Her candle had melted into a messy pile in its dish; the weak, flickering flame gilded the side of her face in gold.

"There's so much to absorb. It's dizzying." Hattie closed the journal and set it on a side table. "Are we the last ones here?"

"Yes."

The crease of her mouth twitched with an emotion that his eyes—keen as they were—couldn't quite interpret.

Then she frowned. "I'm still mad at you."

"Are you?"

"Furious, actually."

"Oh, good."

"*Ugh. No*, Noble. You're not allowed to enjoy my anger."

"Why not?"

Hattie unfolded her legs and rose to her feet. "You shouldn't be here."

"Phina would say otherwise."

"Phina can't know about us."

On that point, he agreed. "I know."

"This is so...*vexing*," Hattie grumbled. "I'm so angry you're here."

Noble bounced his eyebrows, teasing. "I *know*."

She shook her head—begrudgingly amused, exasperated. An aching, boyish part of him wanted to hold onto this feeling—this pulse of nostalgia beating between them like a heart.

That boy is dead, Noble told himself. He had to be an adult about this.

Hattie clearly agreed. "How in the *Fates* are we supposed to work in a research lab together?" she asked, taking a step closer—close enough that he could smell her. Rosemary and citrus.

"This doesn't have to be difficult," he said, serious. "As far as Phina is concerned, we know each other from Waldron. Your bad-tipper comment easily explains our animosity."

"But how are *we* supposed to..." Hattie trailed off, shaking her head again. "We could barely do it in Waldron."

"We did fine in Waldron."

"No thanks to me," she said, voice wobbling.

That wasn't like her. Normally, Hattie was all quips and sass with him—not near tears.

In Waldron, Hattie's humor, confidence, and sense of belonging had been evident—proof that despite her hurried exit from Castle Wynhaim and forced estrangement from everyone who resided there, she was better off. But now Noble wondered if those qualities were more akin to lilies on a lake, distracting from her murkier depths.

That night he watched the carriage take her away, he'd seen the panic plain on her face. How frightening it must've been to travel to a strange territory, sleep in a stranger's bed. How incredibly strong she must've been to endure her husband's abuse and find a way to escape. How difficult it must've been to start over—all while harboring a massive secret, alone.

Was it possible that Hattie's spitfire attitude was similar to the taciturn mask he wore, himself? Seeing the slight sheen in her eyes now, he wondered if he'd somehow missed the pain underneath her fury.

Noble took a tentative step closer, moving into her personal space. He touched her arm, just beneath the ruffled edge of her short sleeve, and her skin was—*Fates*—it was smooth. Soft. Chilled slightly from the evening breeze that trickled through the open windows in the garden. A sigh slipped out of her pursed lips, tickling the hair on his chest, where his collar gaped.

When she looked into his eyes again, her gaze was heavy. "I'm not sure I can stand it, Noble."

He let his hand drop. "Don't let my being here ruin this for you. This is your dream."

"And somehow you got to it first," she said bitterly.

"Look. If I could leave—trust me—I would, but I'm too enmeshed." He raked his fingers through his sweat-soaked hair. "We just need some ground rules."

A humorless huff. "Because that's what we need: more rules."

He lifted his chin in a cocky tilt. "Would you prefer I ignore the rules already established?" he teased. "Would you prefer I...do the opposite?"

He meant to distract her from her somber mood. He expected her to chasten to or scoff at his suggestive comment, but apparently this new Hattie—Hattie the grown woman—was not as susceptible to Noble's childish goading.

Her eyes narrowed with irritation. In direct defiance of her tears, she clasped her hands in front of her chest, taking on a sarcastic tone. "Oh, *please*, would you break the rules for me, Noble?" she begged mockingly. "Put me out of my twelve-year misery and throw caution to the wind, *finally*!"

Ever since he was a boy, he'd been made well aware of his lesser status and the forbidden-ness of the noble girl he fancied; he'd been forced into the responsibility of shirking her advances, allowing her to believe that when he teased her, there were no hidden meanings or veiled honesties. But every flush and grumble on her part was proof that he wasn't alone in his craving. That she was just as hopeless to their connection as he was.

Her sarcasm, however...that *stung*.

But at least she was no longer crying.

"Whether we like it or not," Noble said, no longer amused, "we're about to spend countless hours trapped in his lab together. I suggest we provide some structure to this lie we have to uphold. You don't want word getting back to your uncle, do you? That his problem niece escaped from her cage in Poe-on-Wend?" He invaded her personal space again. "The *moment* word gets out about who you are, we're both—"

She held up a hand, halting his cruel speech. Pivoting away from Noble, Hattie faced the row bookcases lining the wall. She scratched her nails over her head, then—sighing exasperatedly—she tugged out the pins and let her lush locks spill down her back. She continued scratching her scalp, shaking out her curls until they frizzed in a mass around her shoulders.

When she faced Noble again, she looked—

His throat bobbed, thick with arresting desire.

—she looked *undone.*

Oh, please, would you break the rules for me, Noble? Her mocking plea had teeth; the echo of it bit down, puncturing his mind. Remove the sarcasm, and that phrase was everything he'd ever wanted.

Hattie—a goddess with a gold halo—pinned him with a harsh glare. "Rule number one: we don't converse."

Noble swallowed again. Nodded.

"We don't even look at each other. We each pretend the other doesn't exist."

"Fine," he agreed tightly. "Good."

"The only acceptable interactions are those required by research," she continued. "For example, if I have a question about Gildium."

"Makes sense."

She folded her arms across her bodice. "I am *not* planning on having any questions about Gildium."

"Of course not."

"Rule number two," Hattie said, beginning to pace. "We avoid overlap in the lab."

"I work long days here, Hattie."

"And I have class," she said. "I'll be here in the late afternoons and evenings. At least at first, according to Phina. When I arrive, you leave."

That, he didn't like. But she was only being practical.

Because it was no secret who Noble's father was—where Noble had grown up—it was not uncommon for folks to ask if he'd still been living at the castle when the murder attempt happened. If he knew the girl who'd been sent away. If the rumors about her had been true. Minimizing contact with Hattie would also minimize the likelihood of someone learning that *she* was that girl.

"I'll do my best," he said, "but I won't interrupt important work just to avoid you."

"That's fair," Hattie conceded.

"Rule number three," Noble said. "Court faces."

Hattie stopped pacing.

Court faces had been Hattie's aunt's way of reminding Hattie, Noble, and Raina of their etiquette training. *Manners, please*, she'd scold. *Use your court faces!* Of course, her insistence always resulted in the trio pulling funny expressions—tongues out, eyes crossed, noses wrinkled—and breaking into giggles.

If the memory warmed Hattie, she didn't show it. "Agreed."

"Do you think you can manage that?" he challenged.

"Of course, I can."

His frustration flared, words coming out unbidden. "You didn't in Waldron."

"I—excuse me?"

"You put all the burden on me."

"Yeah, well, you deserved it," Hattie replied tartly. "Besides, you love to be the martyr."

Noble clenched his jaw hard enough to crumble stone. He might've had a knack for getting under Hattie's skin, but where his quips needled, hers sliced to the bone.

"I agree to court faces," she continued, "if you agree not to bring up the past—even in private. It's too..." She didn't finish her thought.

"Rule number four: no nostalgia," Noble confirmed.

Hattie wavered. "Unless..." She worried her lip. "Unless it's an emergency."

"What constitutes an emergency?"

"Being found out," Hattie supplied, "or threat of death?"

"Understood."

"I think that about covers it for now." She held out her hand. "Are we in agreement?"

Reluctantly, he took her hand in his. Her fingers were long and graceful—too delicate for his calloused palms—but he held on anyway, savoring the touch like it was the entire world he held. Inside the blue rings of her irises, the black orbs of her pupils reflected the twinkling stars shining through the glass dome of the lab, an entire galaxy contained in her gaze.

For a moment, the Fates themselves seemed to cease breathing.

Unbidden, Noble's attention sank to her mouth. Her lips were a rich mauve that deepened toward the center, where the tissue was tender and beckoning. Twelve dark freckles dotted her pout, perfect imperfections. Sensing his stare, her tongue traced the same path as his vision, wetting the blooming bud of her bottom lip.

They were still tethered by their hands, arms bobbing slowly up and down with their handshake agreement, their silly attempt at control.

"I thought of another rule," Hattie croaked, her fingers still enveloped in his. "No touching."

"Rule number five," he murmured. "No touching."

Hattie's gaze sank to their joined hands. "When do the rules start, exactly?" she asked thickly.

"I suppose as soon as we've finished shaking on it," he replied.

"*Hm.*" The left corner of her mouth pulled downward. It was an expression of resolve, but also something worse: Hattie *dimmed*. The change was minute, but he saw it. He hated it.

Noble thought again of her harrowing journey to this moment, guilt flooding him as he recalled all the ways he'd been cold to a woman who only ever deserved warmth. It might've been responsible of him to constantly push her away, but it was also *cruel*.

She deserved a brief moment of comfort. Maybe they both did. Maybe—before the warmth between them slipped behind winter clouds once again—they could spare one Fates-damned minute to simply *bask*.

When Hattie's fingers stiffened in his grasp, about to pull free, Noble squeezed tighter—then tugged her directly into his arms, against his chest, a soft *ooph* escaping her lips as they collided in an embrace that was nine years in the making.

15

HOLD ON

HATTIE

E nveloped in Noble's smoky cedar scent—comforted but bemused by the unexpected contact—I was transported back to the very beginning.

It was snowing the day I saw him for the first time.

A flurry of small flakes was fluttering onto the grass of the inner bailey at Castle Wynhaim. The ancient willow in the center of the courtyard swayed its frosty boughs, glittering like the arms of a crystal chandelier. I leaned halfway out an open upstairs window of the keep, curiosity keeping my hands firmly planted on the stone sill; snowflakes blew inside on a frigid wind, dusting the shoulders of my dressing gown and the hallway carpet.

Down below, a team of chocolate- and chestnut-brown horses were trotting through the barbican gate into the barren yard, stark against the backdrop of accumulating white. They pulled a carriage that was not as ornate as our usual guests', but still quite fine, with curtained windows and gold-painted trim. An army of guards and servants streamed out of the castle to greet the newcomers, their cloaks billowing behind them. A reedy male servant stepped out of the carriage first, followed by a huge bull of a man. He took one swiveling perusal of the yard, then turned, offering a hand to a woman, who climbed out next. The couple wore plain gray cloaks lined with fur, their style consistent with their carriage: well-made, but understated.

Releasing his wife's hand, the patriarch of the family began gesturing, speaking—to his servant, to the staff, to the guards. Wynhaim Castle had been built beside a great river atop a high plateau; the back of the keep was shrugged up against the crest of a waterfall, and over the constant roar of whitewater, I heard nothing of the scene unfolding below.

Snowflakes were catching in my eyelashes, melting on my cheeks like cold kisses. I flicked my tongue out, tasting their mineral quality, their flavor reminding me of the spray that rose off the falls. My skin was beginning to chill, my dressing gown not enough to insulate me against the wintry air. I lifted my arms to the windowpane, about to slide it down, when one more figure emerged from the carriage.

A boy of about eleven, same as me.

He shared the warm brown skin and stern bone structure of his father, and the black wavy hair and keen watchfulness of his mother. While his parents continued to direct the staff, the boy surveyed the yard, eyes trailing over the marble statues, the empty fountains, and the magnificent weeping willow around which everything else in the bailey had been built.

Then his gaze found me.

He smiled, a slow reveal of teeth.

I lifted my hand to wave.

He waved back.

I opened my mouth to call down to him, to tell him to *wait one moment* so I could descend the stairs and introduce myself properly—*a new friend!*—but I was cut off by footsteps in the hallway.

"Hattie, what are you doing? You'll catch a chill." Loreena, my governess, rushed over to the window and yanked it shut. Her lips curved into a grin that defied the stern set of her jaw and her perpetually shrewd gaze. "You're not even dressed," she tutted. "Come, let's get you ready for breakfast. Perhaps some hot tea to chase away the chill?"

Without giving me time to protest, Loreena ushered me away from the window and the boy—but by then, my curiosity had already gotten the better of me.

It was not love at first sight—just the piqued interest of a sheltered noble girl who was mostly isolated from other children (at least, other children to whom she was not related). Love came later, like the slow growth of a tree, developing over countless meals, days spent frolicking innocently throughout the castle grounds, taking long walks along the river, and reading together in the library. Each thoughtful conversation, playful shove, fit of laughter, casual embrace—these made up the leaves, boughs, and sweet fruit of our friendship.

By the time I realized I was *in love* with Noble, our roots were too strong to ignore. We already had inside jokes. I'd already learned his greatest fear (failure) and favorite type of pastry (chocolate); he'd already learned my favorite season (spring) and my most ticklish spot (neck). And I already knew what his skin felt like—holding my hand as he led me down the hall, the brush of his fingers against my knee to get my attention, his teasing elbow in my side. Back then, the meaninglessness of his touch was made all the more meaningful by how easily he gave it to me.

Then I ruined it.

"Hattie, please don't," Noble had said when I finally mustered up the courage to admit how I felt.

We were seventeen, standing on Fate's Landing, the bridge that over-looked the three-hundred-foot drop of Wynhaim Falls.

"You shouldn't," he'd said. "You can't."

I remember looking out across the city, laid out on the banks of the river far below. I remember staring down at the frothing spray of the water just beyond the marble balustrade of the bridge, transfixed by the mist that obscured the bottom of the deadly cascade. Noble's rejection hadn't made me want to jump, but it *had* made me consider pain; how *physical* it felt to have my heart broken. How breaking it on the sharp rocks below probably would have hurt less than those simple words.

Please don't. You shouldn't. You can't.

What I wouldn't give to relive the years leading up to that moment, though. Not carefree, per-se, but easier, because of what remained unsaid.

Perhaps it was his gift of heightened vision, but Noble had always been incredibly observant, attentive, thoughtful. He knew when I was happy, knew when I was sad, knew when I was faking calm. Even after he rejected me on Fate's Landing, I'd still felt *appreciated* in his presence. Cherished. Like he *saw* me and respected me, even if he didn't feel the same way. Even if it hurt sometimes.

Standing in Phina's empty lab, folded into Noble's unexpected embrace, I felt the unfurling of time like the ruthlessness of the falls. From laughter to heartbreak, each moment we'd shared was like a single droplet, their sum an elemental force. Nestled against his solid chest, I allowed remembrance to pummel me like water, cleansing me with the fluid pleasure of memory. Of buoyant surrender.

It wasn't like him to hold me like this. Had he spotted the sorrow I'd tried to hide on my face? Had he *sensed* my desperate need for comfort? Secrets were lonely things—but they could also bind people together. Was that what this was? An acknowledgement of our terrible shared predicament?

The moment we let go, our agreement would start, and there would be no more speaking, touching, or reminiscing. The thought had me fisting the fabric of his shirt, pressing the soft curves of my body against the hard planes of his, seeking *more*. In answer, one of his arms tightened around my waist. His other hand slid up my spine to cup the back of my head, fingers sliding into my hair, holding my face against his sternum.

Seconds passed, my limbs going boneless in his brutally strong embrace. Never in my life had I been held so reverently, protectively; it made me wonder how I'd *ever* stood up on my own. As I rocked with the tidal rhythm of his breaths, I wanted to weep from sheer relief.

But the hug couldn't last forever.

And it was *just* a hug, after all.

Soaked with longing and self-consciousness, I stirred against him. His arm slackened, and his hand slid from my nape, and we broke apart. I felt like I'd been tumbled by river rapids, battered against stone, half-drowned and disoriented.

Rule number four: no nostalgia. Rule number five: no touching.

This was why.

Stepping back, I regarded Noble in the dim light of the library, searching for a clue as to why he'd initiated the contact. His face was mottled with a deep blush, cheekbones tinged purple; his mouth—which usually defaulted in a confident slant—was parted, breathless; but his eyes were hard. Unyielding.

What the expression meant, I couldn't say. He always knew how to obscure his true feelings, and this was the perfect example.

Noble wiped a hand over his jaw and cleared his throat. "We should go."

"I'll ring for someone to escort me."

"I can do it," he said.

Me, blindfolded? Him, guiding me down unknown halls? "I'd rather you not."

A nod. "Right."

I brushed past him out of the alcove and yanked the cord by the entrance door. We waited in silence, him leaning against the wall and me standing with my arms folded, facing the moonlit lab. A cool breeze slithered through the gaps in the windows; as it ruffled the stems of the herbs, it took on a fragrant perfume. I filled my lungs with the herbaceous air, tasting its sweetness, trying to find my emotional footing.

When steps echoed in the hall, I turned back to Noble. He was watching me, green eyes keen and catlike in the dim foyer.

"I'll...see you around?" I said.

He dipped his chin. "Hopefully not much, right?"

"Rule two. Right."

He pushed off the wall. "I *am* happy for you, you know."

"Thank you."

"I know you'll make the most of it."

I thought of those long afternoons in the library when we were young, eating snacks and reading in mostly companionable silence. "I will," I said, "so long as you don't distract me by pelting me with chunks of bread."

His eyes crinkled. "That was *one* time, fourteen years ago."

"I'm adding it to the rules," I said. "No throwing food."

"Not sure I can agree to that."

We both smiled; then our smiles faded. I fished the blindfold out of my pocket and ran the fabric through my fingers, just to have something to do with my hands.

"*Fifteen* years ago," Noble mused, correcting his estimate. "Happy birthday, by the way."

I glanced up. "You remembered."

"You're hard to forget."

Willa's voice echoed in the hall outside, greeting the guard.

I lifted the silk scarf toward my eyes. "Well, I'm pretty sure we already broke rule number four, but happy birthday to you, too."

"Big year," he remarked.

Noble's birthday was in a few days. Twenty-nine. Just like me.

I paused. Lowered the scarf. Met his gaze. Without considering my words, I asked, "Do you think your Fate will become fixed when you turn thirty, even though it's blank?"

Noble's eyes widened. I'd caught him off guard with my question—I think I'd caught myself off guard, too. Back in Waldron, I never did get the chance to confront him about his blank visions in the Mirrors of Fate.

Don't trust anyone who doesn't show a future, Mariana had warned us.

No matter the awkwardness between Noble and myself, I would never not trust him. But seeing him here...why *was* he here? How had he met Phina? Why had she involved him in the study?

Idris and Anya had created their blank futures by entering the Well of Fate—an extremely dangerous journey that had almost gotten them killed by monsters. I couldn't imagine Noble—or anyone—braving such foes unless forced. Idris had all but dismissed the theory that Noble could've gone to the Well. Which meant that blank Fates had other causes, too.

Did his Fate have relevance to this study? I would've thought it unrelated if it weren't for seeing Mariana in that alley.

Noble took a step toward me. "Hattie, have you told *anyone* about—"

The door to the lab opened, and Willa stepped through, a broad and easy smile on her friendly face. "You rang?"

With Willa's entrance, our thread of conversation was severed. Considering our new rules, I wasn't sure we'd get another chance to discuss the mystery. And based on the way he was still staring at me, he didn't want me knowing any more than I already did.

Which, of course, just made me want to pry *more*.

"Did you have a fruitful first day?" Willa asked me, either oblivious or impervious to the awkwardness between Noble and myself.

I hiked my satchel higher onto my shoulder and—sparing Noble one final glance—placed the blindfold over my eyes. "I did," I replied, offering my elbow to my escort.

"Those lemon cookies were excellent, by the way," Willa informed me. "Did you add a hint of rosemary?"

"Someone must have taste magic."

"Close," Willa said. "Scent magic."

"I'm glad you enjoyed them," I said, ignoring the watery ache that spread through my chest as the knight led me out of the lab, leaving Noble behind.

16

CURSED
THINGS

HATTIE

H attie, a moment?"

Seated at a study table in the library alcove, I looked up from the messy spread of notebooks, diagrams, and dense tomes before me, to find Phina standing in the doorway. Though I had been brought on to work with Hylder, much of my time at the Ocs had been spent doing grunt work: cleaning, garden chores, tedious data compilation, and mind-numbing annotation. I scribbled an observation into the summary of research I had been tasked to compile, then set down my quill.

"Of course," I replied.

Phina took the empty chair to my right. "How's cataloguing?"

I let out a long sigh. "Tedious, but interesting."

Phina chuckled. "Welcome to the world of research."

"I'm loving every moment."

It was the truth.

The past month had been a blur of apothecary classes, tension headaches, and so much reading that my eyes felt constantly like they were filled with sand. Though Sani's warning about conspiracies and murders was concerning, getting to see Phina and her advanced apprentices' notes up close—to compile, organize, and search for patterns—was a privilege. Even when I returned to my dorm late at night and collapsed onto my tiny bed, there was pride and joy in my exhaustion.

Of all the Seven Territories of the Kingdom of Marona, Fenrir was renowned for magic. All territories had knights and adepts—some Orders, like the Mighty and the Arcane, spanned all borders, while others were specific to their territory—but as the birthplace of Oaths, Fenrir had become the kingdom's authority on *learned* magic. Folks came from all over the continent to study here. I thought about the magnitude of the Collegium's reputation every time I entered the Ocs, donned my blindfold, and found myself in Phina's lab.

"And your Hylder practice?" Phina asked.

I winced. "Inconclusive."

In addition to the grunt work, Phina had tasked me with making basic Hylder tinctures—though none I concocted in the lab had yet to compare to the potency of the one I'd brought from home, and we couldn't determine why. She'd had me switch to practicing adding different alchemical knots to the basic tincture, but the experimentation hadn't resulted in much beyond making me feel cross-eyed.

Hylder. Gildium. Phina might not have been willing—or able—to elucidate the full purpose of the study, but the implication wasn't lost on me. The figure in the alley *had* to have been suffering from a monster bite. My tincture was medicinal, but even I knew it couldn't cure evil on its own. It was logical to assume the program's purpose was a true cure—but that meant monsters weren't simply *creatures* with innate wickedness; it meant they were *afflicted* in some way. *Cursed*.

Mariana's recurring presence had to be another clue. I didn't know her Order, but I knew she dealt with abominable things. Monsters becoming a threat to Fenrir would explain Lord Haron's stake in the study, too, though why he wanted to keep the problem a secret from the public was puzzling. Even Anya and Idris had told me not to speak of what I'd seen. So, was Sani onto something when she suggested there was a political component to this as well?

And where did Noble fit in? We'd been following our rules, but that meant I had no concept of the true nature of his involvement.

I was in over my head. I *knew* it was dangerous—for numerous reasons—but my curiosity paired with my reverent excitement at being here *at all* kept me engaged.

"No matter," Phina said with a smile. "*Most* of our research here is about ruling things out. Inconclusive is still...conclusive, as it were." Phina laced her tattooed fingers together and set them on the table. "That said, I'm hoping that you're about to enjoy your time here even more, as I've come with a new request."

I straightened in my seat. "What is it?"

"Noble has been working through the various alchemical knots, same as you, just with Gildium. I need you to organize his notes and cross-reference his findings with your own."

I sagged. *So much for our rules.*

Though we'd managed to avoid interaction, I still *saw* Noble almost daily. I was powerless to the draw of his presence; every time I passed the archway of his workshop, I couldn't help but gawk. His shirts were always filthy, sweat-soaked, clinging to the masculine ridges of his shoulders, biceps, and abs. Rolled-up sleeves showed off ropy forearms that glistened in the firelight of the forge.

These passing glances created a collage of his days in my mind, details forming into a clearer picture of the man he had become: highly skilled and focused, but also permanently tense. When we were kids, he'd possessed a similar tension, but it'd been tempered by an almost rakish playfulness. Funny, inquisitive, unruly. It seemed that at some point over the past ten years, Noble had lost that counterbalance.

Whatever fond memory you still have of me, he'd said in Waldron, *that boy is gone.*

Most days, I did not allow myself to stop as I walked past the forge. But occasionally, I couldn't help but give into the urge, pausing briefly to watch the way his hands worked. When I did, I could almost feel them on my waist again, the back of my head; I could almost feel the strength of his embrace.

Fates, that first night in the lab had been a mere moment of weakness, but after nine years of trying to be strong, that weakness had been a relief. How was I supposed to forget him holding me like that? Even after a month of tense avoidance, the feeling hadn't faded. My heart was a wound, cauterized by his gruffness—only to be reopened by the remembrance of his kindness.

"I know it's more organizing." Phina must've misread my disappointment toward having to interact with Noble for the tedious work itself. "But as we blend herbology and metal alchemy, cataloguing the parallels in the research will prove essential."

I forced a smile. "Yes. Of course. You're right."

Phina patted my shoulder and stood. "I understand he was stingy when he visited your establishment in Waldron," she whispered, "but he's really not so bad."

I know, I thought as she walked away. *That's the problem.*

17

You Like It

Hattie

A rainstorm rattled the windowpanes of my childhood bedroom, thunder rumbling in short intervals—but shrouded by the cloth canopy of my bed, tucked safely under the covers, Raina and I were giggling.

We were talking about boys: Noble, Brendan, and some of the sons of servants and soldiers who lived in cottages within the castle walls. At fourteen and fifteen, boys were one of our favorite topics.

"I *know* you fancy him," Raina teased. "And I *know* he fancies you."

"No, he doesn't," I said. "Noble's just nice, that's all."

"I think Brendan fancies you, too," Raina continued, pushing up onto an elbow. "He's always trying to impress you."

"I despise Brendan."

"He's not so bad."

"That's because he's not trying to impress *you*." I turned onto an elbow, too, facing her. "What about Ren?"

The hour was late, and in the inky blackness, I couldn't see much more than Raina's silhouette—but I could still hear the blush in her voice. "What about him?"

"Half the reason you visit the stables is for him," I accused.

She shoved my shoulder. "That's not true!"

Raina's parents had *just* publicly announced her arranged marriage to the heir of Lothgaim. She hadn't even met Archer Loth yet, and probably wouldn't for another few years. The idea of her one day being sent off to live with a strange man in a strange territory disturbed me, but she'd taken the news in stride—an arranged marriage had always been in her future.

Ren, on the other hand, worked in the stables. He had his sights set on becoming a soldier one day. Raina was not *allowed* to fancy him—or really even speak to him—but I knew she did.

Raina flopped back against my pillows with a sigh. "I wish..."

She didn't need to finish the thought. "I know."

A gust of wind sent rain pattering against the window, rattling the hinges.

I sat up. "I'm hungry. Want to raid the pantry?"

Ten minutes later, Raina and I were downstairs. The kitchens were dark, empty—spooky on a stormy autumn night. I lifted my candle holder a little higher, creeping deeper into the cavernous space—only to halt when I heard rustling up ahead. Raina gripped my arm, wide-eyed.

"Hello?" I whispered into the dimness.

A figure emerged from the pantry, a mischievous grin on his face. "Hattie?"

Raina's grip on my arm tightened, a high-pitched, teasing little squeal coming from her throat.

"And Raina," Noble said, sounding amused.

Mildly panicked, I glanced down at my frilly, floral nightdress; had I known we'd run into him, I would've worn something a little less...matronly.

I padded farther into the kitchen and set my candle holder on one of the butcher block tables. "Noble? What are you doing down here?"

"Same thing as you, I reckon," he said, holding up a peach.

My shoulders relaxed. When it came to snacks, Noble and I already had a rapport. "What are we having?"

"Dessert," he said.

"Wonderful!" Raina exclaimed, clapping her hands.

While I found bowls, Noble got to work slicing the peaches and sprinkling them with sugar, cinnamon, and clove. When our treats were prepared, I hopped onto the table, sitting with my feet dangling. Raina did the same, though she required some assistance from Noble, her legs kicking out as he helped her up. He'd always been that way with my cousin—brotherly—and it warmed my heart the way he looked after her.

He looked after me, too, sometimes—holding my hand when we traversed the fallen log on the way to our secluded picnic spot by the river or giving me a leg up when we rode horses with Raina—but the way he treated me was different somehow. A little less doting and a little more...something else.

He fancies you.

I might not have had an arranged marriage to an heir of a territory, but I knew there was an *expectation* about the sort of man I'd marry one day. Noble and I were of different social classes, and while *I* didn't care, Loreena had scolded me a time or two: *Don't give him the wrong impression. A dalliance with the wrong boy could ruin your prospects.* I wasn't concerned about my prospects, but Loreena's wrath was enough to make me think twice—not to mention the threat of negatively impacting my family's reputation with a scandal.

With Raina and I situated, we dug into our treats. Noble stayed standing, facing us, his green eyes occasionally darting to mine.

"Couldn't sleep?" he asked after a while.

"I can never sleep when it's stormy," Raina complained.

I maneuvered a peach slice onto my spoon and bit it in half. The fruit was perfectly ripe, tasting of sunshine and sweet nectar, its flesh soft on my tongue. Juice dribbled down my chin as the other half fell back into my bowl.

Noble's keen eyes tracked every clumsy movement. "What about you, Peach?"

My stomach flipped. He'd never called me Peach before, and it sounded...I didn't know how it sounded.

Raina poked me in the ribs. "Yeah, *Peach*, what about you?"

Oh, she was going to bring this up later. *Relentlessly*.

I swallowed hard. "What about me?"

"Can you sleep in this weather?" Noble asked.

"I *could*, if Raina didn't keep me up," I said, feigning annoyance. Then I met his eyes. "What about you?"

"I'm a sound sleeper."

And *now* I was picturing him in his bed. Hair rumpled. Face open, lips parted in slumber—

"Cute nightdress, by the way," he said. "Did Loreena pick it out for you?"

Raina barked a laugh, then clapped a hand over her mouth, shoulders shaking.

I flushed—furiously. "*Ugh*, you're insufferable," I said to him.

He smirked. "You like it."

"She does, she definitely does," Raina said.

I elbowed her in the side, and she descended into a fit of laughter.

"*Shhh*," I urged. "Someone will hear us!"

No sooner than I'd said it did we hear footsteps approaching from down the hall. When the butler arrived, he didn't look surprised, but he *did* break up our midnight soiree and send us all back to our respective rooms. The moment he was gone, Raina snuck back into my bed, nestling close.

"He *definitely* fancies you," she said on a yawn.

"Even if he did, it wouldn't be allowed," I whispered. "Your aunt will insist I marry someone of status."

"Maybe you can come to Lothgaim with me," Raina said. "Meet a southern man."

"Maybe," I mumbled, but as I dozed off it was Noble's face I saw, his lips curving over the nickname, *Peach*.

Standing in the archway of the Noble's workshop, I watched as he used a pair of pliers to remove a molten-orange rod from the forge and plunge it into a vat of water with a spitting hiss of steam. When he removed it, the metal glimmered, its slate-gray surface oddly luminescent. Compared to the delicate work of herbology, metal alchemy was a hazardous blend of fire and force. In such close proximity to the forge, my face flamed—but it wasn't just the heat. It was *him*.

The expert strike of his hammer.

The molten metal just inches from his capable hands.

The focused crease in his brow.

The confidence. The power. The rugged—

"You know I have sight magic, right?"

I cleared my throat, eyes darting from Noble's hands to his stubbly jawline to his prying gaze. "Excuse me?"

He cocked his head. "I can see you standing there, staring."

"I didn't want to startle you."

A short laugh.

Exasperated, I lifted my eyes briefly to the ceiling.

Noble set the metal rod on his anvil with a clatter, wiped his hands on a rag, and walked over to me. His voice was low when he spoke again. "Is there a reason you're standing here, breaking rules one and two?"

I met those stunning green eyes and pretended they had no effect on me. "We have a problem."

He inclined his head, waiting for me to continue.

"Phina has instructed me to assist you with your notes. She wants me to cross-reference them with mine."

"Ah." Noble jutted his chin in the direction of a small table to my right. It was heaped with loose papers. "Feel free." He turned away, about to return to the forge—

"*Noble.*"

He faced me again, expectant.

I pointed at the mess, incredulous. "What is *that?*"

"My notes?"

The papers weren't even in stacks—they overlapped in a giant mountain at least two feet high. I strode over to the mound and lifted one off the top. When I did, a couple other loose pages slid sideways, and I had to catch them before they fell. With my hands still planted on the stack, preventing an avalanche, I glared at Noble. "Your organization is atrocious."

He walked up behind me and shifted the pile into a steadier position. As he did, his chest brushed against my shoulder blade, his breath tickled my neck. I glanced toward the doorway, afraid someone might see our closeness, but we were hidden from view.

"What are you doing?" I whispered.

"Helping."

I slid out from the shelter of his frame, my whole body tingling and on high alert. Clearing my throat, I craned my neck to read the page on the top of the pile. "This one is just a column of numbers with X's and question marks."

"Alchemical knot numbers. X's mean *no*, question marks mean *maybe.*"

"Why aren't you using proper notation?" His system—if we could even call it that—would've given my Notation Basics professor a headache.

Noble just shrugged.

"This is a disaster, Noble," I said, gesturing at the pile.

"Good thing you're here to fix it."

Irate. I was *irate*. "*Ughhh*," I groaned. "At least help me carry all this to the reading alcove."

Noble hissed through his teeth. "Not sure that's a good idea. You better work here."

I arched a brow at him.

His expression remained impassive.

Which only made me angrier.

This would take *days* to get through. Days of sharing space with him. Days of listening to the strike of his hammer and the hiss of steam and the steady thudding of my traitorous heart. How could I focus with him so near?

"Won't I be in your way?" I asked.

"No."

"What about our rules?"

"This is research related. We aren't breaking any rules." A meaningful pause. "Except rule number three."

Court faces. "What are you talking about?"

"You're blushing."

"I'm angry."

His smirk turned patronizing. "I have sight magic, remember? You can't fool me."

I groaned again. "You're insufferable."

Our exchange from fourteen years earlier seemed to echo in the space between us.

You like it, he'd replied back then. But now, he stiffened, his expression icing over. "Good luck with the notes," he said, turning his back to me—returning to the forge.

I touched the corner of a page. "I'm not sure the Fates themselves would know what to do with these."

———— ✦ ————

Two hours later, I was seated on the floor of Noble's workshop, surrounded by papers, with my head in my hands. Noble had left a while ago, not bothering to say goodbye—which was for the best, as speaking with him usually proved...insufferable.

You like it.

I *used* to like his goading—when we were adolescents, and there was a playful fondness to it. But here, his quips carried an edge, and the constant reminders of the connection we *used* to have weren't amusing—just painful.

I let out a long, aggravated, grumbly sigh.

"Everything all right?"

My hands dropped from my face. An apprentice stood in the archway. She wore an apron over a butter-yellow tunic that complimented her olive skin and black hair.

"Yes? No? I don't know." I gestured at the papers surrounding me. "Is it possible to perish from confusion?"

She walked closer, chuckling. "I see Phina has tasked you with organizing Noble's notes."

"Generous of you to call them 'notes.'"

To my surprise, the apprentice lowered herself to the floor, sitting on her heels. She picked up one of the papers and gave it a once-over. "Fates, I'm not sure we *can* call these notes."

I laughed.

She frowned, still staring at the page. "This is practically meaningless."

"Apparently he has a system, though I can't figure it out." I lifted the page I'd been trying to make sense of. "What do you think this symbol means?"

She leaned forward to look. "Oh, that's for iron." She pointed. "And that's Gildium. It looks like he's using metal alchemy shorthand in some places, but the rest is..." She trailed off with a *humph*.

"My Notation Basics class hasn't covered shorthand yet."

"That's because it's advanced notation—and rather antiquated."

I tipped my head back, facing the ceiling. "*Great.*"

"I can write up a key, if you'd like?" she offered. "Won't help with the rest of it"—she waved at the mess on the floor—"but at least you'll be able to discern the legible symbols."

"That would be incredible, thank you."

"Happy to help."

She rose to her feet, and I followed suit, feeling done for the day.

"My name's Viren, by the way. I'm a third-year apprentice."

"Hattie," I replied. "I've been here a month."

Viren's lips twisted into a small, charming smile. "How is it so far?"

I gestured at the papers littered on the ground around our feet.

She laughed.

"I've seen you around," I said. "Are you a metal alchemist, too?"

She tipped her head from side to side—not a *yes*, not a *no*—her glossy hair brushing against her shoulders. "I'm a healing apprentice. My specialty is blood."

My forehead creased. What did blood have to do with Hylder and Gildium? Was she studying *monster* blood?

I opened my mouth to ask, but she cut me off.

"That's all I can say." She gave me a weighted look; her Oath must've prevented her from divulging more to a first-year apprentice about her role.

But maybe she could clarify something else for me. "Do you know much about Noble's work here?"

"Beyond Gildium? No." Viren cast his notes a meaningful glance. "I'd say you probably know more about his work than I do, but...perhaps not."

"His notes make me wonder if I even know how to read at all."

We both chuckled as we walked together out of his workshop.

Then my mind began churning with more questions. "Does blood mean—"

Viren turned to me, her expression kind and patient. "Apologies for interrupting, Hattie, but can I give you some advice?"

"Sure."

"Keep to your assignment," Viren said. "I know that sounds harsh, but trust me, it's for the best." She leaned closer, dropping her voice to a whisper. As she did, the sounds in the lab seemed to soften. "Around here, it's dangerous to know too much."

18

BREAKTHROUGH

HATTIE

Can you think of *any* differences between the tinctures you make here versus in Waldron?" Phina asked.

We were standing side by side at a small workstation in the center of the lab, surrounded by flower beds and buzzing bees. On the table were Hylder flowers and berries; a jar of dried thistle; a pitcher of clear spirit; as well as various utensils, including a quartz stirring spoon much like the one in Phina's classroom.

I spread my palms in a shrug. "Healing tinctures are pretty simple. For Hylder, I grind the flowers and berries into a paste, incorporate—"

"How young are the flowers?" Phina cut in.

"Depends on what I can find"—I picked up a sprig—"but I prefer half-budded, half-open. Seems more potent that way."

"*Hm.*"

"What?"

"It's just that...well, that's exactly how I make *my* Hylder tinctures."

She probably hadn't meant it as a compliment, but I took it as one. The fact that I made a healing tincture the same way as *Phina Farkept* thrilled me. Granted, I'd learned most of what I knew about tinctures from her books, but the validation was still meaningful.

"Can you not think of *anything* you might do differently from common methods?" Phina pressed.

I shook my head. "It's not a complicated mixture."

"Demonstrate, would you?"

I'd made countless Hylder tinctures for Phina since I joined her program five weeks ago, trying to recreate the effectiveness of the one I'd brought from home—but I'd never made one *in front* of her. Just the idea made my hands clammy—but at least I wasn't stuck sorting Noble's notes. After a week of organizing his mess of papers, it felt like a mercy to be out in the garden.

"Pretend I'm not here," Phina prompted.

I reached for the Hylder sprigs and berries, selecting them as I would normally—that is, rather haphazardly—and began grinding them with a mortar and pestle. When the mashed berries, buds, and tiny petals were the right consistency, I dropped them into a clean pitcher, added a sprinkle of dried thistle leaves for added protection, and a splash of the spirit to suspend the ingredients. Then I lifted the spoon—

"Wait," Phina said. "Do you use a quartz spoon at home?"

I pinched my lips and shook my head. A quartz spoon was a neutral material that limited contamination; at the Collegium, it was considered the superior utensil—but in Waldron, I made do with simpler methods.

"What do you usually stir your tinctures with?"

"I don't," I replied. "I shake them."

"With or without a lid?"

I picked up the pitcher and gave it a swirl, sloshing the dark purple liquid around until it was thoroughly mixed. When it was ready by my usual standards, I held it out to Phina. She dipped a clean spoon into the liquid, observing it with her magic. I waited expectantly, hoping beyond hope that *this* batch would please her.

When she frowned, I did, too. "I'm sorry," I said. "I don't know what I'm doing differently."

"Perhaps it's not the method, but the ingredients. Take me through your sourcing again."

I rested my palms on the table, thinking. "I gather the ingredients myself. The thistle comes from the western hill in Waldron—the south-east-facing slope, all-day sun—and the Hylder grows a bit south of town, along the Wend. I usually get my clear spirit from distillers in Waldron or from merchants from neighboring towns."

"Do you remember which distillery the spirit came from?"

I shook my head. "It was likely a few sources—I often consolidate clear spirit into one jug to save space. I pay more attention to the alcohol content."

Phina winced and ran a tired hand through her short hair, as if this practice were utterly inexcusable.

"Sorry," I said again. "You're probably horrified."

"Don't be sorry. You're scrappy, remember?" Phina bumped my shoulder with hers, and though we were failing to solve the mystery, her playful encouragement buoyed me.

"Are there *any* differences at all between these ingredients and the ones back home, aside from where they're grown?" my professor asked.

I looked down at table. The clusters of miniature white flowers, the black berries that looked like the beady eyes of rodents, the dull green powder of the thistle. Everything looked the same, except...

I picked up a flower stalk, observing the bundles of tiny buds and blooms. "I guess the petals are a little paler than the ones I usually use?"

Phina took the stalk from me, studying it closely. "What *varietal* of Hylder did you say you use?"

My brow furrowed. "I use a blend. Usually Common Hylder, but sometimes Golden Hylder, and Waldron has a lot of Black Lace Hylder."

Phina beamed at me.

"What?" I asked, sensing her excitement but dubious of the pride swelling in my sternum.

"Remember this feeling, Hattie," Phina exclaimed. "It's your first breakthrough."

19

VICTIM

HATTIE

A nd *then* I said, 'Why would I take advice from someone who doesn't understand the difference between the early Sharmidian period and the late Sharmidian period?'" Sani said, gesturing so vigorously that a droplet of juniper concoctail sloshed out of her cup.

"You. Told. *Him*," Uriel deadpanned.

We were sitting on the woven rug in the small living area of our dorm, pillows scattered about. After my modest success in the lab this afternoon, I'd wanted to celebrate with something tasty, and Sani and Uriel—though not privy to the details of my breakthrough—were more than happy to join me.

"He turned *carnelian*," Sani exclaimed, clearly proud of the effectiveness of her insult—even if Uriel and I didn't quite follow. "Xier has been tormenting me with snide comments and corrections for *months*; he deserved a retort."

"Have you considered the possibility that he wishes to *court* you," Uriel asked, "and that is why he insults you?"

"Have you considered the possibility that unkind courtship methods are repulsive?" Sani replied.

"I was not suggesting it was a *mature* method."

Sani turned to me. "What do you think, Hattie?"

Their discourse reminded me of when Raina and I debated whether or not Brendan liked me. After I was sent to Poe, I was forbidden from sending Raina letters, in case our correspondence was intercepted. I'd

cried nightly for *months*, wracked with the pain of missing her. The
only balm to my broken heart had been Anya's compassionate presence,
her cups of tea and quiet solidarity for the weepy young woman she'd
brought into her inn.

"He sounds tiring," I replied, taking a swig of my drink. The balance
of juniper and syrup was *just right*—at once botanical and sweet.

"I do appreciate crushing the spirits of lesser apprentices," Uriel said.
"Especially those who deign to act superior when they are not."

"If we weren't friends, you'd scare me," Sani said.

Uriel's grin was all teeth.

I stretched my legs out, leaning against the base of the reading chair at
my back. Between the alcohol, the cheeriness of my friends, and our cozy
nest of pillows on the plush rug, I felt more relaxed than I had in *weeks*.
Even the torment of Noble's presence felt faraway.

I closed my eyes, listening to the flow of conversation, which had
pivoted away from Sani's nemesis to Sani making fun of Uriel's rather
intense crush on the professor's assistant in her writing class. "You're in
love with a poet!" Sani was insisting, while Uriel denied such sentimen-
talities with terse grunts and halfhearted deflections.

Anya liked to call me a romantic, but my romanticism came more
from longing than optimism. After my escape from Poe-on-Wend, I'd
dared to hope that true love existed. I'd entertained a few dalliances
in Waldron—with long walks along the river, nights spent dancing at
festivals, lazy mornings in my bed—but none had felt *right*. They either
didn't get my humor, or found my reading habits tiresome, or we simply
lacked connection.

And what did it matter, anyway, when I couldn't offer them my whole
self?

There were times I felt envious of Anya and Idris's relationship. They
respected each other, doted on each other, lusted after each other, and
felt safe with each other. Even when they bickered over chores at the

Possum and around town—Idris always insisting he take care of *all of it*, Anya always demanding she help, too—it was still clear that they were on the same side.

Joyful. Loyal. Honest. *That's* what I wanted.

In adolescence, I'd experienced stolen moments with Noble that felt like that—moments that seemed *headier* than friendship—but he'd been consistent in his refusals. Firm. And now...now, he was downright chilly—for good reason.

Perhaps it was time I let go of my long-unrequited infatuation.

I took another sip of my concoctail, finding the taste suddenly bitter.

"Hattie?"

I blinked, coming out of my melancholic reverie. "I'm sorry?"

"Want to come with me to the dining hall?" Sani asked. "I need bread to soak up all this alcohol."

Uriel grunted. "Yes, please go before you insult me further."

Sani smirked as she wobbled to her feet.

"Bread sounds great." I stood, too, high stepping over the pillows and the empty concoctail bottle toward the door. "Want anything, Uriel?" I called over my shoulder.

Reclining against the pillows, Uriel grunted. "Silence. And perhaps more cheese."

I flashed her a grin as I closed the door.

Sani looped her arm through mine as we started down the corridor. "What about you, Hattie? Have anyone you fancy?"

I pressed my lips together, hoping she mistook my blush for the effects of the alcohol instead of the mixture of longing and embarrassment I experienced any time I thought of Noble. "No," I squeaked. "No one."

"Probably for the best, what with the demands of Phina's study." Sani waggled her eyebrows. "You're too busy making alchemical break-throughs, aren't you?"

I chuckled. "Exactly."

We came upon the wide stone staircase that led to the ground floor, where the dining hall was located. A gaggle of students were making their way up the stairs at the same time, a mass of unrecognizable faces. I offered them a polite, close-lipped smile of acknowledgement as Sani and I shuffled past. But when we reached the landing halfway down, someone from the group called out.

"Hattie?"

I halted, turned. A dark-haired apprentice had paused on the upper steps, while the rest of her group continued to the floor above.

"Viren, hello," I said. "Do you live in Inver, too?"

"Room 205," she said. "You?"

"201," I replied. "I'm surprised we haven't crossed paths here before."

She shrugged. "I stay at my partner's place most nights. But it's nice to know I have another friend in the building."

Friend. After she'd helped me with Noble's atrocious notes, we'd developed a rapport, but the word still caught me off guard—in a pleasant way. "Me, too."

Sani cleared her throat.

"Oh—this is my roommate, Sani," I said. "Sani, this is Viren, she's an apprentice from—*agh.*" An awful taste filled my mouth, cutting me off. The flavor was both sour and rancid, and I stuck my tongue out with a groan, trying not to gag.

Viren descended onto the landing. "Are you all right, Hattie?" she asked, raising a dark brow as she touched my wrist.

Tapped it twice.

I looked down—at my Oath tattoo.

That's what that was? The taste of Oath magic?

All Oaths were woven from extremely powerful arcane magic and were known to sting, ring in one's ears, or emit a bad taste when an Oath-taker veered too far from their tenets. I had yet to encounter the limits of my Oath of Allegiance, but given the context, the warning must've been to not divulge too much about how we knew each other.

But did it have to taste so terrible? Saliva pooled in my mouth. I swallowed, shivered, swallowed again. *Bleh.*

"I think the alcohol is giving her acid hiccups," Sani said to Viren. "We're on a trek for some bread."

"Good idea." Viren's gaze cut to mine and held for one beat, two, before she regarded Sani again. "Nice to meet you, Sani. Hattie, I'll see you around."

We split up, Viren heading upstairs and Sani and I continuing down.

When we reached the ground floor and were far out of hearing range from Viren—whom I was pretty certain possessed sound magic—I piped up. "Viren is—"

"On the research team," Sani finished. "I figured."

"I was going to say 'nice.'" I lowered my voice, choosing my words carefully so that I didn't upset my Oath again. "How did you know?"

"Only an Oath would make you choke on your own words like that."

"I've never had that happen before."

"She must be a specialist."

I cast a sidelong glance at Sani, surprised by the accuracy of her observation.

"Secret research programs don't divulge their specialists," Sani explained. "It's too revealing."

"What if folks already knew about her specialty before she took her Oath?" I asked.

"Specialties evolve; her current work can't be proven." A shrug. "It's not a perfect system," Sani added. "And I'm not sure of the exact rules of your Oath, but your inability to talk about Viren's role means that something about it is...sensitive."

I study blood, she'd told me.

According to my Oath, that *mattered*.

"You're astute, you know that?" I said, poking Sani with my elbow.

She gave me a coy shrug and looped our arms again. "I'm an apprentice of the Archives, remember? We love context."

Silvery moonlight slanted through the high windows that lined one side of the ground floor walkway. Students loitered in the hall, some sitting on the windowsills, others leaning lackadaisically against the wall, chatting and flirting. It was well after suppertime, but it seemed half the student body at the Collegium was nocturnal.

"Your hiccups excuse..." I said slowly, thinking aloud. "You did that on purpose. Why did you not want Viren to know you caught on to my Oath's interference? Why feign ignorance?"

Sani's voice barely rose above the echo of our footsteps on the marble tile. "At the Collegium, knowing more than you ought can be dangerous."

Knowing too much almost got me killed, Hattie, Anya had said.

I didn't like the similarity in their sentiments.

"Are you still worried about me being murdered?" I teased. "You know, not all research programs hold political significance."

"The secret ones do, though."

Something about her tone made me stiffen. Fear spread in my belly like an ink-drop in water, a black wisp of dread. With my arm still looped through hers, I pulled her off to the side, stopping in the relative shelter of a recessed doorway.

"What do you know, Sani?" I whispered.

She lifted her chin, a world of mystery in her dark eyes. "People forget that history isn't simply the documentation of the past—it's a study of behavior. The observations I make? They're shaded by the context of what I've learned."

Sani paused, waiting for a gaggle of oblivious half-drunk students to walk past. Once they'd disappeared down the hallway, she continued. "There's a reason history repeats itself: it's because people don't learn from their mistakes—not even when mistakes are spelled out by the Mirrors of Fate. The future isn't a placid lake, untouched by what surrounds it—it's a river that flows from the past, with a strong and erosive current. Knowledge, politics, Fate—they all have momentum. Inertia."

"But do you know—"

"I don't *know* anything," Sani interrupted. "But I see patterns, Hattie. And the patterns I'm seeing lately... Time and time again, they've proven to be deadly."

A LETTER

POSTED FROM: ANYA ALVARA, PRETTY POSSUM
INN & PUB, WALDRON-ON-WEND, FENRIR T.

Dear Hattie,

*I say: You deserve to feel proud and excited about such a rare opportunity.
I am also not surprised that Phina noticed your talent; it's hard to miss!*

*But I must add: be careful. There are many secrets in Fenrir
and—speaking from personal experience—it's best not to learn them. Idris
would also like me to remind you that Phina's brother Oderin is a safe
resource should you need one.*

*As for Illian and Alden's wedding, it was splendid: the parade, the food,
the flowers, all lovely. I have a bit of news for you, as well, but I'd rather tell
you in person—I hope you'll forgive me for making you wait! (Although,
reading that back, I suspect you've already guessed; when I tell you this fall,
please pretend you're surprised?).*

Wicker says Woof Woof!

Love and hugs,

Anya

*P.S. Richold said Noble went to Fenrir for some mysterious errand. You
haven't run into him, have you? Wouldn't that be funny!*

20

INERTIA

NOBLE

He watched her from behind tall foliage, the vantage of a predator stalking prey.

Again, she wore the white dress—*always* the white dress—light shining through thin fabric to reveal the outline of her legs. She was deadheading herbs, humming to herself. Noble felt a tingling sensation in his teeth, a desire to tear flesh. His whole body was taut; he was both a crossbow and its bolt, aiming to strike.

But he also knew this was a dream—knew he was teetering on the edge of a nightmare. Unlike in past dreams, Noble was *aware* that he was not actually a predator. He was just a man, crouched behind the fragrant stalks of sage and mint, observing a woman whom the vile part of him wanted to consume, but whom the *male* part of him wanted to—

Noble sat up abruptly.

Gray light streamed through dusty curtains; dawn was breaking, and the sky was overcast with the threat of rain. Blinking, he noticed he'd kicked his blankets onto the floor, exposing his arousal—a symptom of morning, but also...

He clenched his teeth and looked away, shame and guilt twisting around his lungs like poisonous vines. He raked his hair back with rough fingers, scrubbed a palm over his stubbled jaw. When he caught sight of the Oath of Allegiance tattoo on his wrist, a tired exhale gusted out of him, collapsing his chest.

He'd been staying at the Royal Inn of Fenrir—the name a gimmick, not a true connection to royalty—for five weeks, and only *now* were the urges of his curse returning. Based on his progression, Hattie's tincture from Waldron could be as much as twice as effective as the tinctures Phina had given him.

He'd overhead Phina and Hattie working in the garden together yesterday afternoon; he'd been on his way out of the lab when Hattie squealed with excitement. Whatever they'd uncovered, Phina would have thoughts to report to him today. A cure would be too good to be true, but hopefully, it was a longer-term solution.

The Fates might've punished him at times, but he was lucky to have met Phina. Two years ago, when his former Order had been retired, his fellow knights had slowly, gruesomely succumbed to the affliction. It was Phina who'd discovered a temporary remedy—a tincture to curb the transformation. It'd been too late for the others, but with her medicine, Phina had saved Noble's life—and launched herself into the Lord's esteem.

When her research at the Ocs began, she'd insisted Noble take an Oath of Allegiance to join her team—not just because her research had a direct impact on his future, but because his passion for metal alchemy was useful. Thus began his study of Gildium. His journey to Waldron.

Phina might've had a better workshop, but fancy tools could never replace a well-timed suggestion from an expert in the material. Lately, Noble found himself missing Richold's soft-spoken guidance and camaraderie. The blacksmith came from a long line of Gildium artisans, his lineage leading all the way back to the golden age of metal alchemy in Kelebraim-on-Gray. The once-magnificent metropolis—renowned for the skill of its craftspeople—had crumbled to ruin centuries ago, but remnants of its legacy remained in folks like Richold.

In fact, it was for that legacy that Richold had agreed to teach Noble in the first place. Without children of his own, Richold saw Noble as a son of sorts—someone to whom he could pass his knowledge. Noble didn't deserve the honor—he'd already disappointed *one* father—but he was determined to make the most of Richold's faith and kindness. He was determined to continue his role in Phina's research from afar. And with any luck, Hattie's breakthrough yesterday had moved his departure closer.

Because he *needed* to get out of Fenrir City.

Over the past month, it had become painfully obvious that Hattie was harmed by his presence—and none of their rules could fix that. He'd seen the way she looked at him in the lab: anger, fondness, desire. The emotions on her face conveyed everything he felt in his heart, and Noble hated seeing his own misery reflected back to him.

Just because he was *good* at pretending he didn't care about her didn't mean she made it easy.

The Mirrors of Fate showed Noble nothing of his future, yet time and circumstance continually brought him back to *her*. No matter how hard he tried to live his life in darkness, she was the sun around which his entire world seemed to revolve; though Noble fought her gravity, he felt constantly pulled in her direction, powerless to the inertia.

But they were meant to be apart.

They always had been.

After all, it was *his* fault she was sent away all those years ago, *his* presence that seemed to endanger her at every turn; Noble had long-ago accepted that she was better off without him. It was time Noble took that seriously—no matter how much he wished otherwise. And with a better tincture, perhaps he could escape Fenrir City, finish his studies with Richold, and leave Waldron before Hattie returned.

With a shiver, Noble climbed out of bed and went to the small wash basin in the corner to shave. By the time he was done, a spitting rain was tapping on the window. He dressed in all black, swung his well-worn cloak over his shoulders, and exited the inn, lifting his hood as he strode into the downpour.

The Collegium campus was nearly a straight shot down Rose Street. A silvery haze of rain streaked across Noble's vision, obscuring the ornate spires up ahead, the towers becoming dark shapes in the deluge. Rivulets of water streamed across the cobblestones, emitting a mineral scent. Bells tolled in the foggy distance, their echoes drowned out by the weather. Droplets hissed on accumulating puddles, splattering Noble's pant-legs. He ducked under awnings when he could, lest his clothes get completely soaked on his way to the lab.

Usually, at this time of morning, the streets in this part of Fenrir were fairly empty. But when Noble finally turned onto Adept's Walk, he came upon a crowd. A shadowy mass of loitering bodies congregated just outside one of the colleges, huddled under the wide archway that led into the interior courtyard.

Inver, Noble realized as he neared. Hattie's building.

Noble spotted professors already dressed for a day of teaching, apprentices still wearing their sleeping clothes underneath their cloaks, busybody shopkeepers from nearby establishments craning their necks at the commotion. Noble's superior vision caught the jerky gestures of people who were afraid: quivering wrists, darting glances, shoulders that swiveled and sagged. Gold and silver flashes of armor confirmed the presence of both Mighty and Lawful Knights.

The bells. They were an alarm.

Fear clamped a hand around Noble's throat as he picked up his pace toward the crowd. He caught snippets of conversation, but nothing conclusive: *break-in* and *blood* and *attempt* and *assassin*. The more he heard, the tighter his windpipe clenched. He pushed through the throng, shoving bodies aside, searching for familiar faces, for answers.

Finally, he spotted Phina beyond the archway, just inside the courtyard, talking to a golden-haired Mighty Knight with a double-edged battle-axe strapped to his back. Relief spread through Noble's limbs, and he elbowed his way through the crowd, cutting between a pair of conversing students, slipping past a professor talking to a guard, and—

An arm snapped out, barring him from going any farther. He looked down. The wrist was clad in silver-studded leather vambraces.

Noble removed his hood, glaring at the Lawful Knight who blocked him. Pulling up his sleeve, he revealed his Oath tattoo. "I'm a researcher here. Let me in."

"'Fraid I can't allow—"

"Noble! Thank the Fates," Phina called, beckoning him over.

Noble shoved past the Lawful Knight, striding across the grass toward Phina. She broke from her conversation and jogged in his direction, colliding with him in a hearty embrace. It lasted a mere moment before Phina pulled back, turned, and extended a hand toward the Mighty Knight with whom she'd been speaking.

"Oderin, this is Noble, my lead metalworker," Phina said. "Noble, this is Oderin, my brother."

Noble didn't need an introduction to know that they were related. In addition to their matching blond hair and brown eyes, they also had identical jawlines and the same quality in their gestures. Having grown up among nobility, Noble knew the mark of etiquette training, of actions refined not just by tutors, but by bloodline.

"Your reputation precedes you, Major Farkept," Noble said.

"Does it now?" Oderin perused Noble like a menu, his lips pressing into a pout. "Phina, you didn't tell me your metalworker was so *handsome*."

"Fucking Fates, Oderin," Phina whispered harshly, "this is not the time to make advances on my researcher."

Noble couldn't help but chuckle. "It's nice to meet you, Major—"

"*Oderin*, please."

"Oderin," Noble amended. "I've heard great things."

"No, you haven't," Phina countered, resting her fists on her hips, the perfect picture of a little sister (though her sass was slightly diminished by the fact that her clothes were soaked-through, her hair plastered to her head).

Oderin gave Noble a firm, if slightly lingering handshake. "You aren't Noble *Asheren*, are you?"

"How do you know that?" Phina asked.

"I'm not the only one with a reputation. His father is *General Kalden Asheren*."

Phina stared blankly at her brother.

"Mighty Knight of Marona?" Oderin went on. "He serves as personal guard to the *king*. He's a walking legend, Phi."

"Maybe among the gold brutes," Phina replied tartly.

Oderin shot his sister a glare, then regarded Noble again, his gold breastplate glimmering with raindrops. "How'd you end up in metal-work?" he asked. "I'd've guessed a man like Kalden Asheren would've wanted his son to follow in his footsteps as a knight."

In a few short moments, Oderin had managed to flirt with Noble *and* find his most tender nerve. He felt a little dizzy from the other man's attention. "Wasn't in my Fate," Noble replied stiffly.

Noble glanced around. The rain was letting up, the air turning humid. Knights of various Orders meandered throughout the courtyard, managing the crowd and talking to sopping, shivering apprentices. The bells no longer rang, but there was a hum of agitation in the air. Of barely contained panic.

Oderin's rather chaotic first impression had distracted Noble, but now he thought of Hattie again, his anxiety stirring anew. "What's going on?" Noble asked.

Phina's expression turned grave. "An assassin broke into Inver last night."

21

History Repeats Itself

Hattie

C an you describe what they looked like?" the Lawful Knight asked me, his blue eyes darting between my face and the notebook he held.

"I didn't see much," I answered. "Long brunette hair, short stature."

We were standing under the shelter of a tunnel-like archway that led from the courtyard to the southern wing of Inver College. I was still wearing the chemise I'd slept in, a knee-length scrap of fabric. Thankfully, Lawful Knights had handed out spare cloaks, otherwise, my thin dress would've gotten entirely soaked through. I was already cold enough with my bare legs and feet.

"Clothing?"

"Nothing distinct." I glanced at the crowd congregating by Inver's front gate. "Black shirt and trousers. Boots."

"Weapons?"

"A sword sheathed at her hip," I answered. "A dagger in her hand."

"Blood on the blade?"

The rain was letting up, sun beams breaking through gaps in the clouds. I watched a pair of pigeons drop from their perch on an upstairs windowsill, wings clapping as they flew over the roof and out of sight.

How quickly things could change.

One minute, I had been writing a letter to Anya by candlelight—assuring her that I was being safe—and the next, a horrifying scream tore through the building.

Between Uriel, Sani, and myself, I'd been the first to make it to our door. To see the attacker fleeing down the corridor and the blood soaking into the hallway rug just a few doors down from ours.

Room 205.

Images flashed through my mind: Viren, slumped against the wall just inside her dorm, her face pale with shock. The crimson leaking between her fingers from where she clutched her side. My own voice, shrill in my ears, calling for help. A blur of other students arriving on the scene. The odd calm in Viren's voice as she talked me through how to staunch the flow of blood. The way her words had trailed off when she'd passed out.

"Did you see blood on the dagger?" the Lawful Knight repeated.

I wrapped my arms around my middle. "I don't know."

"The person who ran away—you're sure they were the attacker?"

Are you still worried about me being murdered? I'd teased Sani just last night.

I feel like I prophesied this into being, she'd whispered to me, tearfully, as we clung to each other in the courtyard early this morning.

You are too smart for your own good, Uriel had added, wrapping her arms around us both.

Bile rose in my throat, and I blinked back to the knight. "Why else would they run away?"

"To get help?" he supplied.

"They were not a student." Of that, I was certain. If anything, the attacker's brunette hair and short, athletic build had looked strangely like... I shook my head, dismissing the thought.

"We're done for now," the knight said. He lifted a hand as if he were about to pat my shoulder but let it fall before he made contact. "The Order of the Lawful will contact you if we need more information."

"That's fine."

The shock and adrenaline were beginning to wear off, replaced by a cold dread that made me shiver. As I watched the knight walk away, I leaned against the stone tunnel wall, trying to get ahold of myself. Trying *not* to think about how hot Viren's blood had felt on my hands, how much of it had pooled on the floor. Trying to ignore the burgundy splotches that soiled the lower half of my chemise. A pair of knights had carried Viren's unconscious body off on a wood plank, with healers walking alongside her to administer treatment.

I had yet to hear whether she'd woken up.

Sani had been right: the future was a swift river. And right now, I felt like the current was pushing me somewhere I didn't want to go, toward a drop I hadn't seen coming. Had I known how perilous this opportunity would become, I might not have agreed to Phina's offer.

Then again, had Phina really given me a choice?

I covered my face with my cold hands, sobbing silently. I felt so alone. So far from home. I was being swept toward a waterfall with no one and nothing to cling to.

Sani and Uriel had walked off a while ago, allowing the Lawful Knight to interview me about the incident. And as much as I cared for them, my new friends didn't bring me the sense of safety I craved. I wished I was in Waldron. Safe at the Pretty Possum. Sitting by the hearth with Anya, Idris, and Wicker, drinking concoctails, playing cards, and enduring Anya's jokes about my nonexistent love life, my crush on the mysterious metalworker.

Hot tears tracked down my chilled cheeks; I was shaken to my core by what I'd seen.

An intruder.

A blade.

Blood on the woven rug.

It was all too similar to nearly ten years earlier: the swirl of rumors, the attempt on *my* life. Everyone had blamed Noble for the rumors, but he'd only done what he thought was right; in fact, had he not been honest with my aunt about what he overheard—had the castle guards not been put on alert—I might not've lived past that dreadful night.

It's why I never blamed him for how things unfolded after that. Had I stayed at Castle Wynhaim, Raina's arranged marriage, title, and safety would've been threatened. I couldn't fault my aunt and uncle's decision to send me away, even if it stung—in fact, I agreed with them. Raina might've been my cousin by blood, but in my heart, she was my *sister*, and I would've done anything to protect her.

Including live a lie.

An audible sob escaped me, and I bit my lips together.

"Hattie, what the fuck?"

Noble's imposing form filled the mouth of the archway, haloed by the hazy daylight that cut through the misting rain. His cloak clung to the mountainous ridges of his shoulders, gaping to reveal the undone laces of a black shirt soaked with rain.

Home, my heart sang at the sight of him. *Home, home, home.*

My logical mind tried to fight that instinct, but after last night, I was too rattled. Noble had always been a place of safety and comfort. Even though he was forbidden. Even when he was pushing me away. Even now, after all this time: *Home.*

Wild green eyes roved over my chemise, tactile as an actual touch as he took in my rumpled state, the blood stains.

His clean-shaven jaw *clenched*.

Then he was moving, long legs eating up the distance between us. Disheveled, furious, frantic. For a moment, it looked like he would pull me into an embrace—but he halted a respectable distance away, arms at his sides, hands fisted with restraint.

His voice was strained and demanding when he spoke. "Is it yours?"

I looked down at the blood on my dress. "No."

He closed his eyes with visible relief. When he opened them again, they pinned me in place. "Are you hurt?"

I shook my head.

He wiped a hand over his face, the front of his neck, his palm pausing over his heart. "*Fates*, Hattie, when Phina said an assassin broke into your building, I—" He broke off. Took a step closer. His movements were jerky and agitated. "Tell me what you're feeling."

The question surprised me. What did my feelings matter when Viren had been *stabbed*? "I'm afraid for Viren's life. I saw the wound, it was..." I shuddered, squeezing my eyes closed.

"Look at me." Noble's voice was quiet but firm.

When I met his verdant gaze, my breath caught halfway through an inhale. The usual ice in his expression had fissured, revealing an unreadable rawness underneath. His brow was furrowed, jaw set. The knot in his throat bobbed, like a fist dragging under a silk sheet. The sight of it made my own throat ache with a nameless tension.

"What *else* are you feeling?" he asked impatiently.

"I'm just glad I—"

His irritated grumble cut me off. He tipped his head back in what appeared to be...annoyance? Restlessness? "Stop trying to be brave. Tell me how you truly feel."

He knew that the trauma of last night wasn't singular; that it compounded the terror I'd faced a decade before. His acknowledgement of how the attack on Viren would bring up those old memories broke something inside me that I'd been trying desperately to hold together.

"I'm frightened," I admitted, voice wobbly and small. "It was so scary, Noble. I saw the...the...*assassin* fleeing. I had to staunch Viren's blood. I—"

Noble stepped into my personal space.

"What are you doing?"

"I'm comforting you," he said, wrapping his strong arms around my quivering body, crushing me against his rain-soaked chest.

"But our rules," I protested, even as I snaked my arms around his back, holding on tight.

Home, my heart said. *Home, home, home.*

Yet.

He *wasn't* home, was he? Not when I could never be in his arms without fear of being caught, without *heartache*. Without knowing that his warmth was brief, and as soon as he let go, the cold would return.

Noble's lips brushed against my temple. "Rules don't apply in an emergency, remember?" he murmured. "Besides, we're hidden. The knights are clearing the courtyard, everyone is heading to either class or a pub. It's just us. You and me, Peach."

The sound of my nickname had me pulling away, *tearing* myself free of his embrace. I took a step back—then another for good measure.

I felt afraid, yes—but I also felt *ragged* by the constant push and pull between us. It was one thing to pretend we didn't have a history, pretend I didn't want him—but it was another thing for Noble to pretend he wasn't breaking my heart day after day.

He couldn't be both a stranger and a comfort.

"This isn't fair," I said.

A line formed between his brows. "I know, you shouldn't have to fear for your life everywhere you—"

"No." I gestured between us. "*This*, Noble. You and me. We ignore each other, comfort each other. Back and forth, back and forth. It's—" I hiccupped. "It's emotional whiplash. It has to stop."

He flinched. Chuckled joylessly—like he *agreed* with me.

But then his eyes dipped to my blood-soaked dress. "Hattie, I was worried about you. *Terrified*. I—I'm trying to be there for you."

Rage rose in my chest. Compared to the fear coursing through my veins all morning, it felt *good*—powerful. "Be *there* for me?" A harsh, defiant laugh. "You aren't *allowed* to be there for me, remember? We're supposed to be strangers. If you really wanted to support me, Noble, you would *leave me alone*."

His throat bobbed—not out of concern this time, but frustration. I expected his icy expression to return. Instead, it cracked wide open. Underneath, he was all fever and fury.

He crowded my personal space again, walking me backward until I was trapped between him and the wall. He spread his scarred fingers wide, flattening his palms against the stone on either side of my head, caging me in. I felt so small compared to his hard and imposing presence. Given everything I'd just said, I hated how much it thrilled me.

"You think this is easy for me, Hattie?" Noble rasped. "Seeing you all the time? Missing what we had? Knowing that because of who we are, you are forbidden to me?"

Forbidden?

"Why would you care?" I challenged. "We aren't the same people we once were, and even back then, you didn't—" I broke off, too embarrassed to say it.

But he wasn't about to let me off the hook. "Finish the sentence."

"You know what I meant."

His breaths came in short pants. "Finish. The. Sentence."

"Even back then, you didn't want me like I wanted you," I said, head held high. "So why would that matter now? What about leaving me alone is hard for you, Noble? It's been a decade since we were actual friends."

"You're right, it *has* been a decade," Noble said, inching close enough that when he inhaled again, his chest grazed mine. "It's been an entire fucking *decade*, and I still miss you. Haven't stopped thinking about you."

I shook my head. "Don't." I didn't want to hear about how he missed my friendship. It made my stupid heart *hope*, and that was just too painful.

"Don't what?" Noble pushed. "Don't tell you that I miss you?"

"I don't want to hear it," I said. "We already agreed that it was safer to pretend we don't know each other."

"You're right, we did," Noble replied. "And you can continue to blame me for your heartache over our situation, Hattie—I'm happy to take the blame for you, if it makes you feel better—but just because we're better off apart doesn't mean I relish the idea."

The air between us had grown humid, pulsing with energy. When at one time his hyper-observant stare would've steadied me, the look he was giving me now made me feel exposed. "Noble, I..."

"You're wrong," he said. "About how I felt back then. About how I feel now."

He paused, and—confusingly—his eyes dipped to my mouth. With his heightened eyesight, his attention was never not intentional; when Noble gave something his focus, there was no detail that went unnoticed. And right now, he was staring at my bottom lip like—*Fates*—like it was a cliff's edge, and he was holding on for dear life.

Squirming under his intense stare, I sunk my right canine into that lip. His jaw ticked again, a quick clench that I felt low in my belly. My thoughts scattered like sparks into a night sky, twisting and flaring and turning to ash.

"I don't understand," I said.

"Yes, you do."

I went still. "What are you saying?"

"I'm saying that I'm tired of you believing that our arrangement doesn't bother me," Noble said. "I'm tired of you thinking that the rules, the limitations, the constant *carefulness* have *ever* been easy for me—because they haven't. Not back then. Not now. And I know I should just leave you alone, but..." He removed one hand from the wall and touched my cheek, dragging his fingers—slow, reverent, featherlight—down my neck.

Heat followed in the wake of that touch, burning with a different sort of adrenaline.

He flattened his palm over my sternum, my heart. "I care," he said, voice quavering with an intensity I'd never heard before. "I care more than you know, more than what's allowed, more than I should. And there's nothing to be done about it, but...I'm tired of you believing I don't."

22

CURSE
CONSPIRACY

HATTIE

I'm glad you're all right," I said to Viren the next morning.

The Collegium's private hospital was located in the center of campus, attached to Medica College, where healers studied. My apothecary training meant that I took multiple classes there, but I'd never had a need to visit the infirmary.

It was a long rectangular space with high ceilings and lots of light. Rows of beds were partitioned off with gauzy curtains, and healing supplies—linens, metal tools, bottles of tinctures and potions—were stocked on wheeled carts throughout the room. A fountain in one corner trickled musically, emanating calm. Healers and assistants walked back and forth across the tile floor, their footsteps echoing, voices kept at a whisper.

"Without your ministrations, I might not be here," Viren rasped. She was pallid, feeble—but *alive*.

Thank the Fates.

"Anyone could've followed your instructions." I was seated in a wooden chair beside her sickbed, the two of us concealed by the shroud of her privacy curtain; I kept my voice low, too, not wanting to disturb neighboring patients. "Did the healers give you a sense of when you could return to the lab?"

"It'll be a few weeks, at least." The attacker's blade had skimmed along her rib; thankfully, the wound was wide and shallow, but the healers were concerned about infection. "Any strain could prolong my healing, so they've advised me to be patient."

"They haven't allowed us back into the lab yet," I said. "Sounds like the Orders of the Mighty and Lawful are going to send more knights to guard the dorms and labs, but none of it has been sorted yet."

Viren shook her head. "I knew it was a dangerous project, but I had no idea it would be so..." She shook her head again.

"Volatile?" I supplied.

Her eyes lifted to mine. "Exactly."

I leaned closer, dropping my voice to a whisper that was mostly breath. "Do you know why you were targeted?"

"What are you, a knight?" Viren joked.

I opened my mouth to protest, but then the tapping of footsteps outside Viren's curtain faded, until no sound permeated the fabric. I immediately recognized the silence as an effect of sound magic. Anya did the same thing sometimes, shrouding us in a bubble of silence so we could discuss private matters without eavesdroppers.

"Look, I know you're a curious person, Hattie, and a skilled Hylder alchemist, too, so for the sake of your own safety, I'm going to be frank," Viren said, speaking at normal volume within the insulation of her magic. "I believe I was targeted by the Order of the Valiant."

"The Order of...who?"

"The Valiant," Viren repeated. "They're a secret Order of Fenrir, tasked to eradicate the realm of cursed beings—abominations, they call them. Monsters."

I swallowed hard, thinking of when Idris showed up at the Possum with black sludge on his hand, demanding an herb traditionally used for purging evil. Idris, a knight of an unknown Order. The same Order, I presumed, as Mariana's.

Phina hadn't confirmed it, but I was *certain* that monsters were the ultimate focus of this study. To know that Viren had come to a similar conclusion...after what'd happened, I didn't want either of our theories to be correct.

"Monsters," I whispered, "are a thing of myth." They were empty words—said for comfort, not truth.

"Monsters are a weapon of war," Viren countered, undeterred. "At least, that's my hunch. Even third-year students don't know much about the programs we assist. Limiting information stunts research, but it also keeps secrets contained." She stared at me a moment, assessing. "You already knew they existed."

"Why do you say that?"

Viren smirked. "You didn't question the notion."

"Here's a question," I said, leaning forward. "You're telling me that there's a secret Order of knights charged with fighting monsters, and they targeted *you* because of your connection to Phina's research?" I asked. "Are we not working to *cure* curses? Wouldn't that put us and the Valiant on the same side?"

Viren's small mouth twisted into a tiny, knowing grin; apparently my question was proof enough of what I'd already uncovered. "No more monsters, no more Valiant Knights," she said.

"You think they tried to kill you because our research would put them out of a *job*?" That *did* sound far-fetched.

"Not a job," Viren said. "A sentence. Valiant Knights don't take their Oaths voluntarily—it's a punishment."

I waved my hand as if to clear away that idea. There was no way Idris was a reformed *criminal*—he was one of the kindest men I'd ever met.

Mariana, on the other hand... She fit the description. In more ways than one.

Yet Mariana had been there in the alley with Phina, demanding Hylder for the hooded figure. Why endeavor to help Phina's mysterious friend, only to turn around and target one of her students? It didn't make sense. Something was missing.

"Think about it, Hattie," Viren continued. "Imagine you're a criminal. You have a choice between dungeon or Oath. You choose Oath. Your Oath is dissolved...you go back to the dungeon. If we cure the curse, their Order becomes obsolete."

My skin itched with anxiety, a slow march of horror swarming my senses like soldier ants. "But why would they target *you*, specifically? Why not another researcher? Why not Phina?"

Viren shifted against the pillows at her back, scooting more upright with a wince.

"The curse is in the blood," I realized. "And your expertise is blood."

She nodded weakly. "More specifically, I study the intersection of herbal alchemy and metal alchemy in healing. Weaving herbal magic into blood by binding it to iron."

"Phina wants to alchemize monster blood with Hylder?"

"Precisely."

I'd assumed we were merely making tinctures and potions with the herb, trying to refine Hylder's potency for consumption. This was...*far* more sordid. Blood alchemy wasn't outright illegal, but it *was* highly regulated—and though what Viren was describing wasn't *quite* blood alchemy, it was close. No wonder my Oath of Allegiance prevented me from revealing anything about Viren's role in the research.

"Wait," I said. "I thought Gildium was central to Phina's research, not iron?"

"That's because monster blood contains Gildium."

I covered my mouth with trembling fingers.

Noble was the lead Gildium metalworker on the project. As far as I knew, he'd been a member of Phina's research team since the beginning. And he'd been in Waldron studying under Richold's tutelage. *Fates*, if

Richold knew what his teachings were being applied toward, his gentle heart might've given out.

Mine certainly wasn't doing so well at the moment.

"How many researchers on the project know all this?" I asked.

"Few," Viren said. "Let's just say I overheard something I shouldn't have."

"There's a lot of that going on," I remarked. "Why are you telling *me* all this?"

Viren reached out and gripped my hand with clammy fingers. "Your breakthrough the other day progressed the research in a way we didn't expect," she said. "Common Hylder can be bound to iron, but as far as I can tell, not Gildium; Black Lace Hylder, on the other hand, appears to have more potential for binding. It could be the missing piece."

I let out a soft gasp.

"I suspect Phina will bring you deeper into the research as a result—but Hattie, once she does, you'll become a target, too." She squeezed my hand, voice going high. "I would regret it forever if something happened to you and I hadn't warned you."

My heart was thunder in my ears. "How certain of all this are you?"

"Not very," she said, "but enough to be here in the infirmary. Enough to be afraid."

"Have you told the knights investigating the incident?" I asked. "They questioned me, but this—"

"I haven't," Viren interrupted, "and neither should you."

"Why not?"

"Because if the Valiant are truly behind this, then who knows how many other Orders are tied up in it, too? They can't be trusted. Not now. Not yet." Viren released my fingers, picked up a cup of water from the side table near the bed, and drank thirstily. She looked pale and tired. She needed rest.

"I should let you sleep."

Viren offered me a wan smile. "Look, I don't want to frighten you—"

"Too late."

"—I just want to offer you a warning. Watch your back, Hattie. This program isn't for the weak of spirit."

23

CHANGING
COURSE

HATTIE

I know we're all rattled by the events of two nights ago," Phina lectured the following afternoon, "but I want us to remain focused. After all, we don't know for certain why she was targeted."

Phina spoke from atop the shallow steps leading from the entrance of her lab into the gardens; the entire research team—eight of us, without Viren—stood in a half-moon around her, everyone in various states of nervousness.

"I've been assured by the Order of the Mighty that they are investigating the incident," she continued. "Your Oaths will allow you to speak freely with them, should they ask to question you. They're also providing more guards to the Ocs. I'm sure you saw them when you came in today."

I did. Six golden-armored Mighty Knights stationed at the door, with more pacing the atrium floor just past the entryway; I heard Willa acknowledge countless others as she led me to the lab, my blindfold fitted tightly over my eyes. Even Willa had not been her normal, chatty self; when I'd tried to make conversation, her answers had been brief, distracted.

"I've been ordered not to bring on any additional apprentices until the motive of Viren's attacker has been uncovered, so we'll all have to stretch outside our comfort zones. Kent, that means you'll be..."

A butterfly crossed my vision, its brown and teal wings fluttering haphazardly, distracting me from Phina's words as she reassigned roles across the team.

I hadn't slept in two nights—not since before Viren was harmed. Her warning in the infirmary hadn't helped the seeds of paranoia that Sani had already sown; watered by my own experiences nearly ten years ago, they'd taken root, unfurling in the night. Whenever I dipped into sleep, horrible dreams abounded, filled with assassins lurking in long dark hallways, hallways that only became longer the faster I ran.

I had spent the past couple nights tossing and turning, only to give up on sleep entirely and study by candlelight instead. For the first time since my studies began, I was *ahead* on my schoolwork—but I couldn't avoid sleep forever. I was half asleep now, swaying on my feet in the gauzy warmth of the greenhouse lab. The rain persisted outside the windows, tapping on the glass, but in here, the garden was lush and peaceful.

Noble was standing at the opposite end of the half-circle, slightly apart from the rest of the research team. He wore a green shirt today, the color of his eyes. He was looking at Phina, nodding along, but his hips and shoulders were angled in my direction, and I couldn't help but wonder if he was aware that even though he was listening to someone else, his body was pointed right at me.

I care more than you know, more than what's allowed, more than I should.

Fates, how long had I waited for him to say such things to me?

Alone with him in that tunnel, I had been vibrating, speechless, dizzy. He hadn't given me a chance to respond before storming off—which was probably for the best. There had been a very real chance of me throwing myself at him—rules be damned—but this was clearly not the time for impulsive behavior.

Unfortunately, it was *never* the time for impulsive behavior.

Still, his admission had caused me to see our history in a new light.

When we were teenagers, I'd thought it was Noble's feelings that kept us apart, but what if it had *only* been propriety? He had grown up around royals, lived on our castle grounds, endeavored to one day serve my family as his father did—but he had not been *one of us*. Noble's father might've thought him undisciplined at times, but even as a boy, Noble had possessed a strong sense of self-awareness; he'd been a rule-breaker, but never reckless. And while I could afford to be careless with my heart, Noble didn't have that luxury.

I could see now how he had led me to assume that the thing keeping him from getting closer to me was his own preference—but even when I'd professed my love for him at seventeen, he hadn't told me he didn't love me back. He'd said that I *shouldn't* love him. I *couldn't*. Feeling rejected, it had never occurred to me that he might not have been *allowed* to reciprocate. That the burden of keeping us apart had fallen to him by default, because of his station.

I'm happy to take the blame for you, if it makes you feel better—but just because we're better off apart doesn't mean I relish the idea.

How had I been so clueless?

But that had been *my* role to play, hadn't it? An oblivious, high-born girl.

Well, I was certainly no longer that girl.

Where did that leave us now, though? We didn't have guardians or court decorum keeping us apart any longer, but we did have my secret. We'd both acted like it was this huge mountain between us, blocking our view of each other, but what were the actual chances of someone uncovering who I was if I stopped avoiding Noble? It's not like associating with him immediately gave anything away; in fact, as far as Phina was concerned, we knew each other from *Waldron*, not Marona.

So why was I still resisting him? Why was he resisting *me*? There had to be more to it than muscle memory from childhood—or perhaps nothing to it at all. Maybe my sleepless mind and intense feelings were clouding my recollection of our conversation. He hadn't told me he wanted me romantically; he'd said he cared. There was a chasm of difference between those two words.

You're wrong, he'd said. *About how I felt back then. About how I feel now.*

What *did* he feel, exactly?

I glanced in Noble's direction again, breath catching when I found him already looking at me. Ever since our conversation, my stomach had felt like it was attached to Noble by a tether. Even now, I felt a firm tug in his direction, like I was an anchor and he was a ship reeling me in. My spine straightened, and his gaze flicked over my throat and collarbones. When he met my eyes again, he raised a quizzical eyebrow.

"Hattie?"

I flinched, realizing Phina had been speaking to me.

"Are you listening?" my professor asked, resting her tattooed hands on her hips.

I rubbed my tired eyes. "I'm sorry, Professor Farkept," I said, "I haven't been sleeping. Do you mind repeating?"

"You are to review Viren's research," Phina enunciated, "see where she left off."

"I...what?"

"Did you not hear me that time, either?"

"No, I heard you, I just..." It was as Viren predicted: Phina, bringing me deeper into the fold. My thoughts fluttered as chaotically as a swarm of butterflies. I felt like I had no choice but to nod. "I'll do my best."

"Good." Phina clapped her hands once. "Let's get to work."

The group began to break up, apprentices whispering to one another as they went to their respective stations throughout the lab. I stood still, watching everyone scatter. Noble was still looking at me; he hesitated for a moment, as if he was considering coming over—then he frowned and headed in the direction of his workshop. Back to ignoring me, apparently.

As he walked away, I felt that tug in my stomach again. But I was not in a place to face him or this strange connection between us. I needed to focus on my studies.

I walked over to Phina, who was just finishing a conversation with another apprentice. When she turned to me, I smiled sheepishly.

"Sorry again, Phina, I'm not feeling like myself."

"You went through something traumatic, Hattie, it's alright," she replied kindly. "Just try to get some rest, alright? I need you sharp."

I nodded. "What's my first assignment? Aside from reviewing Viren's notes?"

"I'd like for you to make some Black Lace tinctures. Ten of them. We'll start running experiments on them the day after next."

"I will."

"Actually, make twelve and set two aside." She gave me a knowing look, and even in my insomnia-addled brain, it was obvious she intended to give two to her friend from the alley. "You should also read up on Gildium. Discuss its properties with Noble if you haven't already."

Monster blood contains Gildium, Viren had said.

The thought of working with a metal that was present in cursed beings made my pulse quicken. The thought of working with *Noble* also made my pulse quicken, but for entirely different reasons. The frantic beating of my heart made me jittery, uncoordinated—or maybe that was just the lack of sleep.

"I'll get reading," I promised Phina, turning away with a yawn.

With my eyelids already this heavy, I couldn't imagine spending all afternoon in the library. I really needed to get past my nightmares. A sleep tincture, perhaps? Valerian was easy to come by, but it sometimes made my dreams more vivid—which might do more harm than good. I had the sense that as long as I felt unsafe in my own dorm, the sleep problems wouldn't change.

Which meant that I needed to feel safe again.

"Phina," I called out, turning back around.

My professor—who'd been walking off in the direction of Noble's workshop—paused. "Yes, Hattie?"

"Your brother is a Mighty Knight, right?" I asked. "Could you put me in touch with him?"

24

DANGERS BE DAMNED

HATTIE

A blade swung at my head, sunlight glinting on steel. I twisted sideways, feeling a whoosh of air as the sword's tip passed by my ear. I raised my own sword, blocking the second attempted blow. The strike jolted up through my weapon and into my arm in a way that made my teeth chatter.

"Remember your core," Oderin said, lowering his practice blade and stepping back. "You're still absorbing the strikes with your arms instead of your torso. You're not bracing enough."

When I'd asked Phina to ask her brother about sparring lessons, I hadn't expected the Major Knight of the Order of the Mighty to train me *himself*—I'd thought he'd introduce me to a subordinate with some free time or allow me to attend training with new recruits. But apparently, Phina had told Oderin about my friendship with Anya and Idris.

"Any friend of Idris's is a friend of mine," Oderin had told me when we met in the Castle Might training yard on our first day.

"Seeing as he fell in love with my best friend, I'd say Idris is a solid judge of character," I'd replied.

"I said he was my *friend*, I didn't say he liked my *character*," Oderin had joked, and so our regular sparring sessions had begun.

That was two weeks ago, and now, my entire body hurt.

I was no stranger to sword wielding. When I was a girl, self-defense and weapon training had been mandatory among all the children at Castle Wynhaim—a long-standing tradition that had begun out of necessity during Wynhaim City's war-torn beginning and had endured as a hypo-thetically practical custom. I had never been good with a blade, mostly because I hadn't cared about the skill back then, but under Oderin's patient tutelage, I'd come to look forward to our sessions in the training yard.

I still had a long way to go before I was capable enough to defend myself, but the sore muscles and whole-body exhaustion *had* helped me get over my insomnia in the nights following Viren's stabbing.

Oderin reset his stance and lifted his training sword. I mirrored his pose, crossing my dull blade with his. Together, we recited the words of the Order of the Mighty—a phrase I'd heard Noble and his father utter to one another when they sparred: "Fate, Fortune, Death."

We began again. Me, clumsily striking and blocking; Oderin, match-ing my turtle-pace with a patient smile on his face. Occasionally, he made a suggestion about my body's positioning—my hips, my core, my elbows.

It was midday, the sun intense on my brow; sweat beaded along my hairline, pooled inside my sleeveless tunic, chafed in the waistband of my trousers. But because I spent the rest of my days pouring over books that detailed complex concepts about disturbing subject matter, it felt good to move and sweat in the sunshine. The stretch and flex of my muscles reminded me that I was more than a brain absorbing information like a bar rag; I was a body, fluid and powerful.

Or at least, I was getting there.

"Good," Oderin said, wiping his brow with his rolled-up sleeve. He was wearing a loose-fitting white shirt and tight-fitting black trousers, his skin and hair so golden he seemed to glow. "Let's end the session with a speed sequence, shall we?"

That's when we performed a combination of moves together on repeat, practicing accuracy and quickness until I collapsed. He'd phrased
it like a question, but this was how Oderin liked to end all his sparring
sessions.

My arms and legs were already shaking from the exertion of the past
hour, but over the past couple weeks, I had begun to crave this kind of
punishment. For every tremor of exhaustion, I could feel my body becoming stronger. I could already jog twice as long during our warm-ups
than I had when we'd started.

"Yes?" the Mighty Knight prompted.

"Yes," I agreed.

After Oderin relayed the combination of moves, we reset our stances,
said the words, and began again. Lunge, high strike, block, duck, low
strike, evade—and repeat. I performed the sequence slowly at first, finding my rhythm; Oderin matched my moves with his own counters,
blocking when I struck, swinging when I was supposed to duck. Then
we picked up speed, flowing through our deadly dance.

Fighting with Oderin reminded me of watching Noble spar with his
father. I'd hated hearing the way Kalden shouted at him and had done
my best to avoid the training yard. But now, as I moved through my own
blocks and strikes, I found myself imaging Noble's dark features before
me instead of Oderin's. Black hair instead of gold. Lean muscle instead
of bulk.

Once, a few months after we'd turned eighteen, I'd happened upon
Noble training alone. I'd been on my way to the gardens with a handled
basket hooked over one arm and had paused on the balcony overlooking
the dusty yard. I had been immobilized by the sight of him. Shirtless
in the muggy midsummer morning. His rich skin sweat-slicked and
glistening. He'd been repeating rounds of sprints and strength training,
racing across the yard, only to halt and burst through a set of sit-ups,
push-ups, or lunges.

I was no stranger to Noble's body—I had watched it grow from weedy prepubescence to sturdy new adulthood—but most of my interactions with him were reading together, walking alongside one another, the occasional summer swim. I rarely saw him *move* like that. Graceful, decisive brawn. Pure vigor.

"Faster!" Oderin encouraged, startling me back into the present.

But with the distraction of memory, I'd lost track of where we were in our sequence. I lunged—realizing in the midst of pitching my body forward that I had been supposed to duck. The mistake put my torso directly in line with Oderin's swing. His dull sword collided with the cap of my shoulder, and I went down, landing hard.

Dust swirled and settled. The taste of stone and ash coated my tongue. Pain pulsed where I'd been struck, radiating down through my arm and up into my neck, making me wince.

Oderin dropped his sword with a clatter and sank to his knees in the dirt beside me, placing a strong hand on my leg—a respectable, comforting touch. "*Fates*, are you alright?"

I sat up with a groan. An angry red line was already forming on my shoulder, tingling with hurt, but otherwise: "Fine, I think," I said.

"Dizzy?"

I shook my head and was relieved when the movement didn't send my equilibrium spinning.

"Do you remember your name?"

"Yes."

"That's not your name."

I rolled my eyes.

"You're cogent enough to be irritated by me, so you must be alright." Oderin rose to his feet and held out a hand.

I grasped his forearm, allowing him to haul me up. I swayed a little, but the moment passed quickly. Letting go of Oderin, I dusted off my trousers. Pain lanced through my upper arm, but the ache was dull and tolerable.

"I think we're done for the day," Oderin declared.

I chuckled. "And here I thought you were going easy on me."

His obscenely plush mouth pulled into a rather haughty smirk. "I was."

I placed a hand on his chest and shoved, laughing.

He laughed too, but sobered when his eyes snagged on where he'd struck me. "I am terribly sorry, Hattie. I saw you were changing the sequence but didn't adjust in time."

"I would've expected more control from a Mighty Knight," I teased, walking with him over to a refreshment table.

He poured two cups of water and handed one to me. "Why do you think I opted to train with you? I need the practice, myself."

I tilted the cup to my lips, drinking the water in three thirsty gulps. It tasted of mountain snow and granite—refreshing. When I'd first moved to Fenrir, I'd been surprised by how much *better* the water tasted. "Is that so?"

"It's the curse of a high-raking knight," Oderin said, raking his hair back with his fingers. "I spend most of my days either at a desk or ordering people around."

"Sounds dreadful," I deadpanned.

Oderin's features scrunched in a sassy pout. "It really is."

I set down my cup. "I think you just wanted to train with someone against whom you were guaranteed to win," I joked. "It's shameful, really, knocking down small and bookish apprentices just to feel superior."

"*Fates*, and I thought Anya was mouthy," Oderin said on a chuckle.

Together we walked over to a patch of lawn at the opposite end of the yard, where we liked to do our cool-down stretches. Sitting cross-legged in the grass, I started with a few spinal twists, keeping my movements slow.

When I glanced over at Oderin again, he was watching me—clearly waiting to see if I grew woozy. "Still fine," I assured him.

"Phina will never let me hear the end of it, injuring one of her researchers like this."

I chuckled at the image of Phina—petite, but strong-willed—standing up to her hulking Mighty Knight of a brother. "Are you two close?"

"We are now," Oderin said. "When we were children, however..." He trailed off, snorted, shook his head. "We were in constant battle. It was ugly."

I extended one leg and leaned forward, relishing the deep stretch in my hamstring. "What changed?"

"We aged," Oderin said with a shrug. "Took on more responsibilities. Got serious about our respective Orders. My friendship with Idris mellowed me, too."

"*This* is you mellow?"

"You should've seen me in my early twenties. I was *unstoppable*."

I giggled and switched my position, stretching the other leg. "You know, Idris didn't mention how funny you are."

"Didn't he?"

I shook my head.

"What *did* Idris say?"

"He said you were soft."

Oderin's laugh was immediate, harsh, and loud. "Of course, he did."

"He also said you were loyal," I went on. "Anya told me you were kind to her, when she went on her..." I trailed off, remembering that Anya and Idris were not supposed to speak of their journey to the Well of Fate, and that I ought not divulge how much I knew. "On her quest to clear her name," I finished.

Oderin nodded slowly, but he didn't seem concerned by what I knew; in fact, it seemed to relax him.

"And how is Anya?"

Just the thought of my friend had me grinning. "She's wonderful."

Oderin's return smile was doting—then shifted into that haughty smirk I was beginning to recognize as his default. "Did she speak of my gallant deeds?"

"She said that in spite of the grim circumstances, you spoke mostly of your romantic trysts."

Another loud laugh. "Gallant *conquests*, then," he said, bouncing his eyebrows. I must've made a face because he went on defensively. "I had to lighten the mood *somehow*, didn't I?"

In truth, I'd thought Anya had been exaggerating when she first told me about how—while escorting her to her possible death—Oderin had gone on and on and *on* about his lust-life. As he was a Major of the Order of the Mighty, I hadn't quite believed her tales, but over the past couple weeks, I'd found her descriptions of Oderin to be quite accurate. He was boisterous, warm, impossibly charming. I could see how easy it must've been for him to sweet-talk men into his bed.

"You know Idris shackled me to a tree so he could go after Anya?" Oderin asked.

"He did?"

"He was a smug ass about it."

They hadn't mentioned that part of their story. "That makes me love Idris even more," I quipped, touching my shoulder. The skin was hot and stretched with swelling from Oderin's strike.

"You ought to ice that when you get back to your dorm."

"I will," I promised.

"So, what about you?" Oderin asked, leaning back on his hands and lifting his chest, stretching his pecs.

"What about me?"

"Do you have a special someone in your life?"

I pressed my lips together, wondering how much to say.

"You *do*," Oderin intuited immediately. "Tell me about them."

"What do you want to know about him?"

"What is he like?"

I rolled my wrists, thinking. "He's thoughtful and loyal. Funny, once you break through his more serious exterior. And he's always trying to do the right thing. His actions speak louder than his words, and—" I broke off, hearing what I'd just said.

I know I should just leave you alone, but...

But his actions had said something else entirely, hadn't they?

"You *really* care for him, don't you?" Oderin teased.

I bit my lips together, *knowing* I was blushing. Rather than answering, I pulled one arm across my chest, then the other, stretching my shoulder muscles—and wincing at the new bruise.

"What of his appearance?" Oderin asked. "At least paint me a picture."

I rolled my eyes again, but gave in. "He's tall with dark features. Muscular, but lean."

Oderin appeared wrapt. "What of his jawline?"

"Sharp."

"Eyes?"

"Greener than you've ever seen."

"*Mmm,*" Oderin grunted appreciatively. "You have good taste."

"I *am* a taste magician."

Oderin laughed heartily, then grew theatrically serious. "So, is he yours, or have you not claimed him yet?"

"Not mine," I said, not bothering to hide my woe.

"Don't tell me it's unrequited."

"I thought it was," I admitted, "but now I'm not so sure."

"So, there's hope?"

"I don't know about that," I hedged.

"Why don't you slip him a love potion?"

A shocked chortle spilled out of me. "Without him knowing? That's *incredibly* unethical."

"Only kidding," Oderin conceded. "But *if* you gave him one, do you think..." He circled his wrist, leading me to the unspoken conclusion.

Do you think it would work? Or, in more alchemically technical terms: *Do you think he possesses enough feeling for you that a love potion would bring it to fruition?* After all, love potions didn't *create* love, they only elevated existing affection.

My face heated even further.

The truth was, *yes*, I did think Noble possessed enough affection for me that a potion of that sort could be effective. But that was the thing about free will: just because an emotion existed didn't mean the person intended to act upon it.

"Phina would be horrified by this conversation," I said instead.

Oderin *beamed*, causing me to break into a fit of giggles.

I'd missed these kinds of gossipy conversations. While Sani, Uriel, and I had bonded over schoolwork and our respective pursuits, we rarely spoke about our personal lives. Back in Waldron, gossip—for better or worse, usually better—was a cherished form of social currency. Never catty or cruel, just humorous and doting, if a tad nosy (though *real*, sensitive topics were treated with the utmost respect).

Though I couldn't tell Anya *everything* about my past without putting her at risk, I *did* share all my feelings with her—the yearning, the fluttery attraction, the heartache. Even more inclined to speaking about crushes and interpersonal dynamics was Idris, who liked to brew tea and snack on pastries while we chatted.

Everything at the Collegium had been so *heavy* lately. I hadn't realized how much I'd been craving a conversation like this until now.

"So...what's his name?"

"Why?" I asked, feigning suspicion. "So you can steal him away from me?"

Oderin clutched his chest. "I wouldn't do that to a friend."

"We're friends?"

"With the way I struck you this afternoon? We're either friends or enemies."

"Friends, then."

Oderin smiled. "You know, Hattie, I think you should pursue this fellow. What do you have to lose?"

Everything, I thought miserably. "It's complicated," I said.

Oderin brightened. "Forbidden love? That's my *favorite* kind. Sneaking around, stolen glances, clandestine meetings."

"It's not that simple."

"Oh, but it is." He arched a brow, his brown eyes sparkling. "In my experience, attraction can't be denied forever."

"In *my* experience, it can," I said, but something about my last conversation with Noble—the shift in his demeanor after he saw the blood on my dress—made me wonder if Oderin had a point. Dangers be damned.

Oderin smiled again, this time with an encouraging, almost boyish tilt. His deep voice was lilting when he said, "We'll see."

A Letter

Posted from: Hattie Mund, Collegium, Fenrir City, Fenrir T.

Dear Anya,

Rest assured, I'm being careful.

In fact, your suggestion for me to get in touch with Oderin has resulted in him teaching me how to wield a sword! I'm sure you're cringing at the idea (remember the carving knife incident two Astrophels back?), but it's helping me feel more confident and capable. I can't say much here, but things have proven rather...perilous...and the sword training helps. Don't worry, though, I'm being my usual nosy self, so what could go wrong? (Ha!).

As for the wedding, I'm sorry to have missed the festivities—but I'm happy for Illian and Alden! And if I'm guessing correctly, I'm happy for you, too?! Can I lead your parade?!

I'm so grateful we're friends, Anya.

Hattie

P.S. Oderin sends his best—to both of you.

25

BLACK LACE

NOBLE

With a frustrated growl, Noble set down his hammer and tongs.

When he'd last looked up from his task, the sun had still been climbing, weak beams of light streaming through gaps in the clouds to the east; now, the sun sat low in the west, casting long shadows across his worktable. The forge was well-made, his materials pure, his tools finely crafted—yet in spite of the resources and endless days, Noble *still* wasn't making any progress.

Weaving magic around Gildium involved precise tempering, attentiveness, and sheer force of will—exhausting not just for the body, but the mind. And when the stakes were this high—when failure meant he'd eventually *die*, along with countless innocent victims caught in the crosshairs of the curse's spread—it was hard not to become frustrated by his ongoing failure.

Noble cleaned his filthy hands with a damp rag and stormed out of the workshop, needing fresh air away from the hot coals and molten metal—away from his dark thoughts. Perhaps a lap around the circumference of the dome would clear his head enough for him to push through another hour or two of work.

Ever since Viren's incident over two weeks ago, Phina's researchers had been coming and going in pairs, with no one lingering after dark. As he meandered through the empty gardens, Noble imagined them off supping or studying in the safety of a pub or dorm. Laughing. Relaxing. Unburdened. *Free.*

Noble was grateful to be a part of Phina's research, but he still felt *bound*. By his affliction, by his past, by the expectations that had ruled his entire life. If Noble could figure out the key to alchemizing Gildium and Hylder, perhaps *true* freedom would be within reach. Perhaps he could prove to himself that he wasn't destined to fail at everything he set his mind to.

A breeze wafted over Noble's face, cooling the sweat on his brow and ruffling his hair. He extended a hand over a raised bed, running his fingers lightly over the fuzzy leaves of a lemon balm plant. Out here in the gardens, the lab was an explosion of green in all shades: vibrant lime, pale sage, deep emerald, chartreuse. The verdancy strained his eyes, the colors almost oversaturated in the harsh late-afternoon light. When he inhaled indulgently, he smelled mint, roses, apple blossoms.

The herbaceous scent reminded him of Hattie. *Was there anything that didn't?*

She hadn't spoken to Noble in sixteen days—not since their conversation in the aftermath of Viren's attack. In that time, he'd mentally scolded himself a million different ways. For what he'd *admitted*, but also for his selfishness.

Emotional whiplash, she'd called it. *This isn't fair.*

In adolescence, he'd thought of their friendship as a waltz of flirtation and gentle rejection. Of closeness and distance. But maybe it was really a wound, healing halfway, only to be reopened. Maybe her flirtatiousness hadn't been a sign of openness, but a form of armor to protect the truth underneath.

It'd been cruel of him to throw her feelings in her face in Waldron. Cruel of him to hold her in his arms—for nostalgia's sake, or comfort—and *know* her heart would ache when he let go. Cruel of him to tell her he cared when he knew the truth would only complicate matters.

But he'd been so frightened and furious when he saw the blood on her thin little chemise that the words had poured out of him, unbidden.

Words he'd wanted to say the first time she'd had a run-in with an assassin; words he'd wanted to say when her aunt and uncle sent her away. Words he'd held back for the sake of decorum. For the sake of them both. A burden he'd been willing to bear—until that morning, apparently.

Now that he'd admitted he wasn't as cold-hearted as he'd led her to believe since they were seventeen...well, he wasn't sure what to do. He felt as if he'd stepped up to the edge of a cliff. As long as he didn't take that final step, everything would be fine—yet still, he teetered every time he saw her.

Leave her alone, he'd reminded himself day after day in Phina's lab. *Do nothing*.

She deserved a man who didn't lie to her. He couldn't, in good conscience, pursue a closer relationship with her while bearing the massive secret of his affliction. And he couldn't *tell* her about his altered state when his retired Oath prevented him from talking about it. When Phina forbid it, too. When Hattie was who she was, and Noble was who he was, and *both* their identities—the monster blood in his veins and the scandalous mix of royal blood in hers—were at risk.

There were simply too many reasons why giving into their urges was a bad idea.

Unfortunately, her forbidden-ness just made him want her even more.

Thankfully, they hadn't encountered each other much since his admission. And with the Collegium abuzz with gossip, new procedures, and extra guards and knights of various Orders loitering about, all of Phina's apprentices had been in a state of edgy, determined focus. There hadn't been many opportunities to acknowledge Hattie, let alone speak privately.

Noble sighed. His muscles were beginning to slacken, his strides longer and looser. He'd reached the outer edge of the dome, where large shrubs and fruit trees spread their arms welcomingly toward the waning sun. The windows were cracked, magnifying the warmth even as a cool breeze slipped inside.

Noble turned down a flagstone path to his left, wandering aimlessly—only to come to a particularly striking shrub.

Its lacy leaves were the color of currants: a black that blushed dark purple. It stood well over Noble's head and bore tiny, pink-tinged buds in clusters the size of his palm. The Hattie of his youth had once shown him a diagram in one of her books of the various types of grouped flowers. These, Noble knew, were arranged in an umbel—a round cluster that resembled an upside-down bowl. They were edible, as were the shrub's dark berries, which would form in autumn.

Black Lace Hylder.

It was aptly named, its leaves delicate and dark. Noble ran his fingers over the fringe of one of its stems, and a thrill raced up his arm, skin tingling with a feverish heat—as if the plant sensed his disease and wanted to burn it out of him.

This was the varietal that Hattie had used in the tincture that had proven so effective against his affliction. Something about the magical structure of its cells being more open than common Hylder, with more threads for magical binding. *It's unique, like Gildium,* Phina had explained to him shortly after Hattie's breakthrough. *A match made by the Fates themselves.*

To investigate its properties further, Phina had instructed Hattie to make large batches of the tincture over the past couple weeks, but, puzzlingly, the tinctures she'd mixed in the lab hadn't felt quite as effective as the one she'd brought from Waldron. He knew he ought to mention that to Hattie—combine their alchemical efforts—but for obvious reasons, he'd been putting that off.

"Beautiful, isn't it?"

Noble turned and—*yes,* he thought indulgently. *Beautiful.*

Hattie stood on the path about six feet away. She wore a plain dress of rich yellow ochre, the cinched waist accentuating the modest flare of her hips. The thin straps were made of silk ribbons, barely clinging to her shoulders. She watched him with crystalline blue eyes, her pert nose scrunching. Her dark freckles were proof that even the sun wished to shower her in kisses, to mark her with adoration. As always, the soft pile of curls atop her head begged to be unbound.

But what truly caught Noble's attention was Hattie's warmth. Her smarts. Her vibrancy, even in the midst of hardship and uncertainty. The fact that she could still stand before him with a smile on her flower-petal lips, after he'd befriended her and broken her heart, abandoned her and then haunted her steps, confessed his care for her only to ignore her for weeks on end—it was a testament to her shine. Noble was both awed by Hattie's resilience and ashamed of his role in necessitating it.

Beautiful, isn't it? she'd asked.

Yes, he wanted to say. *You're the most beautiful thing in the kingdom, inside and out. I'm pretty sure the Fates created you out of pure sunshine.*

Noble allowed himself one more moment to appreciate her unexpected presence before he cleared his throat and turned toward the Hylder again. "Phina said you've been working with it quite diligently."

Hattie stalked closer, until they stood side by side, facing the mass of black lacy leaves and pink flowers.

"Diligent is one word for it," Hattie said with a self-deprecating but ebullient laugh. "Fumbling around in frustration is more like it."

Noble glanced sidelong at her profile. "Anything I can help with?"

"I've seen your notes—*no thank you.*"

He snorted.

"They *are* impressive though," she went on, surprising him. "Messy, but insightful."

In a life defined by his shortcomings, he rarely felt *proud*, but...the compliment made him proud. "Thank you."

Hattie swiveled, facing him squarely. "What are you doing here, Noble?"

He mirrored her position, facing her head-on. "Went for a walk to clear my head."

"I meant at the Collegium."

"I'm helping Phina."

"But how did you—"

He tapped his collarbone, where the faded tattoo of his former Order ringed the base of his neck. "We met through this," he said, tasting the vague warning of his retired Oath on the back of his tongue.

Hattie lifted her chin, appraising him. "When we were kids, I wouldn't have expected you to one day become a metal alchemist. When did that happen?"

"It was a long nine years," Noble said, and he wasn't planning on saying more, until he met her eyes and saw the pleading there. The desire for truth. "After you...left," he continued delicately, "I spent a lot of time in the library."

Her upper lip curled slightly, a flash of joy, followed by a stab of sorrow. He'd missed her. Of course, he had. It made him sad to think she'd ever doubted that fact.

The library had been their happy place. Snacking on bread and cheese, lounging on velvet-upholstered chaises, cracking jokes in between long stretches of amiable quiet. It was where he told her his deepest fears; where he'd discovered how ticklish the tender spots just above her collarbones could be. They had teased each other about their taste in books, Hattie deeming him fanciful for reading adventure novels while he claimed she was too clever for her own good after reading so much science.

But tucked within their silly jokes was something more profound: an unconditional fondness. He'd cherished their friendship, while also yearning for more, and duty had kept him caught in between, with no choice but to relish only the *now*, and not the fantasy of what could be.

After Hattie disappeared, the library had felt so empty—but it had also been his last connection to her. A reminder of how lucky he'd been just to read side by side with someone so incandescently funny, intelligent, and kind. And as long as he didn't look up from his book, he could pretend she was there in the chair opposite his.

Noble shrugged lightly, hoping the casual gesture would ease some of the pain of recollection between them. "One day, I picked up one of your alchemy books, just out of curiosity."

That familiar vertical line formed on her brow. "You mean to tell me that I spent my entire adolescence trying to get you to read about alchemy—only for you to read it the moment I was gone?"

"You know I love to exasperate you."

"It's a true talent of yours."

He took a single step closer, unable to resist. "My point is, when I started reading about alchemy, I found that it was actually...*interesting*."

Hattie laughed. "No shit," she said, shoving his arm.

And for a brief moment, they were sixteen again, a playful ease between them.

Then the unexpected contact morphed into painful *awareness*, time stopping for an entirely different reason. Her fingers lingered on his bicep; his muscle tensed reflexively under her touch. Sometimes, Noble hated having sight magic; it meant that he could see *everything*. The thudding in the pulse-point of her throat, the slow drag of her eyes over where her fingers grazed his shirtsleeve, the flush creeping up the side of her neck.

Her hand fell. "How is *your* research going?"

"Frustrating." Noble glanced in the direction of his workshop, finding his vision obscured by foliage. This far into the jungle of Phina's lab, he felt like they were in another world entirely. "I thought I was the only one here."

"I was engrossed in reading, as usual." Her voice was breathy.

"That happens," Noble said.

Hattie shrugged as if it couldn't be helped. The movement caused one of her ribbon-sleeves to sag off her left shoulder, drawing his attention to—

Noble reached out, gripping Hattie's upper arm, stilling her. An angry purple bruise streaked across the cap of her shoulder. This was not the pale discoloration of an accidental fall or collision—this was the mark of a strike. Whomever had landed this blow had been wielding a blunt, uniformly shaped object. Hard wood or metal.

The thought of someone striking Hattie had rage searing through Noble's chest like molten metal. Whatever careful amiability they'd been cultivating out here in the gardens burned away to ash, replaced by a sudden, overprotective, white-hot fury.

He clenched his teeth, nostrils flaring. "Who?" he ground out.

26

SATIATION

HATTIE

O h, *please*," I said, wrenching myself free of his grip. As much as his clenched jaw, bunched muscles, and growly tone felt like a wet finger sliding across my lower belly, I didn't want to encourage that kind of behavior.

Who knew where it would lead?

"It was an accident," I enunciated, pretending to be annoyed.

"*That* was no accident," Noble said, practically vibrating with rage. "That is the mark of a blunt weapon intended for you."

"If you *must* know, I've been practicing sword training."

"With whom?"

"I'm not sure I should say."

"I beg you do," Noble rasped, those green eyes cataloguing every part of my expression.

Feeling utterly exposed, I turned my back to him. "No."

"Hattie," Noble said softly, approaching me from behind. His fingers hooked under the fallen strap of my dress and slid the silky fabric onto my shoulder again, grazing the bruise in the process. "Please tell me."

Goosebumps scattered across my skin like sparks, lighting up at Noble's gentle touch. Three fingertips. That was our only point of contact, but I could feel him looming behind me, feel the heat of his breath on the back of my neck, feel him *noticing* those goosebumps. It took everything in me not to lean back against his strong chest and tug his arms around my middle.

This isn't fair, I'd told him under the archway at Inver—but the blame wasn't entirely his.

I *could* walk away.

I just chose not to.

"It was an accident," I repeated to the flagstone path ahead of me.

"You don't even like sword training."

"I've actually been having fun," I admitted.

"With whom?" he tried again.

"Not important."

"You didn't think to ask me?"

"Are you *jealous*?" I glanced over my shoulder at him, my amusement dying when I saw the way he'd been staring at my bare shoulder: not with anger, but hunger.

He smoothed the expression quickly—but not quickly enough.

I turned away again. The sun was setting, splashing the glass panels of the dome with periwinkle and pink. The evening air was fresh, cool, and herbaceous on my tongue. "Oderin's been training me."

"Phina's brother?"

"I asked her to see if he knew anyone who had time to train with me, and he offered to do it himself. It's been a nice way to take my mind off things. Make me feel less..." I trailed off.

Noble's fingers slid across my shoulder blade, following the edge of my strap, up and down. The contact was both soothing and mind-scrambling.

"Less what?" he prompted.

"Exposed," I answered, wincing at my choice of words. "It's eased my anxiety."

"At night," he concluded. "Your sleeplessness."

"Yes."

"So, it's for self-defense."

"Yes."

Calloused fingers slid over the bruise, featherlight. "Does it"—he cleared his throat—"hurt?"

"I'm *fine*, Noble," I assured him.

I wanted to turn around, to look into his eyes again, but an intensity had entered this conversation that I wasn't sure I could face head-on. He was so much easier to talk to when I wasn't looking at his handsome face and the expressions that broke through his carefully blank features.

"Just fine," I repeated more softly.

"Good." His voice was a satisfied rumble in my ear. "Good."

Except—I *wasn't* fine.

I might've been fine physically, but inside I felt like a tangled skein of yarn. Over the past two weeks, I had thrown myself into my studies and the unique mindlessness of sparring, but no amount of busyness had truly distracted me from the knots in my heart. The constant questioning of what exactly Noble had meant under that archway.

I had intended to let it go, but who I was I kidding? Even Oderin hadn't believed my denial. I was sick of burying my curiosity—my urge to have an honest conversation with Noble—under the guise of practicality and safety. Expressing parts of our history in mixed company *could* prove dangerous—but out here in the gardens, just the two of us, what was the harm in getting it all out in the open?

"Actually," I blurted, and his fingers paused their slow perusal of my upper arm. "I'm not fine."

"You're not," he repeated flatly. "Why?"

I spun around, suddenly needing to see him, needing to look up into those captivating eyes when I asked—*begged*—"What did you mean when you said I was wrong about how you felt back then? How you feel *now*?"

His eyes widened slightly. With his arms at his sides, he looked...*caught*.

"How do you feel, Noble?"

He placed his big hands on my shoulders, and for a moment I thought he'd lean closer—but then he turned me around again, so that I faced away.

"What are you—?"

"I can't..." His voice was strangled. "I can't stand you looking at me like that."

"Like what?"

"Like you want to break all the rules."

I tilted my head, stealing another glance at him. He clicked his tongue, pinched my chin in his thumb and index finger, and guided my head forward again.

"Do *you* want to break the rules?" I asked.

Without answering, he released my chin, trailing his fingertips along my jaw, under my earlobe, to my nape. He stroked the top of my spine, sending a shiver all the way down.

My bodice felt too tight; I found it hard to breathe.

If he wasn't going to talk, I would. "What *are* the rules, anyway? Other than a feeble attempt to maintain the distance that our guardians imposed upon us over a decade ago?" I asked. "We aren't kids anymore. Neither of us have to worry about our former stations. In Fenrir Territory, we can be whomever we want."

He huffed a joyless exhale. "*Hattie.*" He sounded patient, like he was humoring me. *Be serious*, that tone said.

I balled my fists. "You're infuriating, you know that? You can't just say you care about me, storm off, and never elaborate."

Noble's fingers paused briefly, then continued their slow, tantalizing perusal of my neck and shoulders. Innocent touches that made my mind go to more intimate places. My thighs tensed; my lower abdominals squeezed.

Oderin had been wrong about forbidden desire. This wasn't exciting, this was *excruciating*.

But then Noble stepped closer, his chest grazing my back as he lowered his lips to my ear. "You want me to elaborate on how I feel about you?"

"That's what I've been asking."

His breath was hot. "You want to know how I feel, even if it makes everything about this worse? Unfair?"

I swallowed thickly. "Yes, Noble."

"*Hmm*," he rumbled, as if considering the notion. "How do I feel?"

The hand that had been toying with the edge of my strap slid sideways, pushing the fabric off my left shoulder again, exposing my skin from earlobe to upper arm. I went motionless, breath caught somewhere between my mouth and lungs, waiting for...for I didn't know what. For him to do whatever he'd do next.

The anticipation did not prepare me.

Noble lowered his head, gliding the tip of his nose along the edge of my ear, behind my jaw. Awareness sizzled under my skin, burning me with a furious flush. His other hand—his right hand—found my hip, fingers digging in with a deliciously possessive pressure. He inhaled against the side of my neck like he wanted to breathe me into his lungs, then something wet—*fucking Fates*, his *tongue*—glided along my pulse-point and down, until he buried his mouth against the crook of my neck.

A soft, pleasure-filled, confused little moan escaped me. It was my most ticklish spot—as he knew—but also one of my most sensitive.

My mind couldn't keep up with what was happening, didn't know how to make sense of it, especially not with Noble's ardent mouth sliding over my skin, kissing my neck. All I could do was tilt my head, giving him better access, and he chuckled faintly at my transparent bid for *more*.

His lips were soft, *reverent*, the perfect contrast to the rough scrape of his stubble. Another moan—louder this time—rose out of my chest. It was answered by one of his own, shockingly low and feral. Hearing a sound like that come from cool, collected Noble made my heart tumble into my belly and pulse there, needy and desperate.

I leaned back into him, thoroughly enjoying...*whatever this was.*

Fates, I wasn't sure I wanted to know. *Knowing* would probably just sully it.

"How do I feel?" Noble mused against my skin, the deepness of his voice vibrating from his chest into my back. "I feel like I'm starving, Hattie. I feel like I'm freezing. I feel like I'm blindfolded. I feel like I've been living in a cold dark cave, hungry and hollow, and the only time I feel satiated or see the sun is when I'm with you."

I choked on another moan, stilling under his touch. My heart was beating wildly, frantically, like a bird trapped on the wrong side of a window, desperate to fly free. What was he even *saying* to me right now?

Everything I'd ever wanted.

"You sure hid it well," I joked shakily, but it wasn't very funny.

"I see you," Noble went on, undeterred, "and I feel full and warm, and the world around me appears brighter and more colorful." He pressed the statement against my shoulder with a kiss. "You are a sunrise." Kiss. "You are a rich meal." Kiss. "You are river water evaporating off my skin on a hot summer's day. You are the summer itself. You are—"

I couldn't take it anymore. I turned in his hold, gripped the back of his head with both hands, and brought Noble's mouth to mine.

27

TASTE

HATTIE

He tasted like dew on mint leaves. Like hushed conversation, or laughter on a shaded riverbank. Fresh as mist rising off a perilously high waterfall. Nectar-sweet as a summertime orchard. His flavor was stronger than any potion; he tasted like he *wanted* me, heady with unbidden desire.

With his tongue sliding against mine, my whole body was flooded with sensation. I felt weak, weightless, buoyant. Over the years, I had imagined what kissing him might've felt like. I'd clung to the quick peck we'd shared as kids on Raina's dare, conjuring up that fleeting taste in my mind and imagining his flavor in excess, his touch strong, passionate, claiming.

But not like *this*.

Never like this.

This went beyond my paltry imagining.

Kissing Noble was a full-body experience of hands squeezing, arms tugging, soft groans, and slippery sounds. He cupped my jaw, tilting my head *just so* while he licked and sucked, his kiss both filthy and adoring. Reverent and wild. His other hand gripped my waist with a pressure that bordered on pain, hard enough that I knew it would leave a mark. I had the sense that he *wanted* to leave a mark, as proof that this happened. I wanted that, too.

Afraid I might wake up at any moment from the best dream of my life, I threaded my fingers in his soft waves, clawed at his shoulders, pressed as much of myself against his frame as I could, until I was crawling up his body into his arms. He clutched my thighs as I wrapped my legs around his waist. He returned to kissing my neck, my throat, my collarbones. Then he hoisted me higher in his arms so he could slide his teeth across the top of my dress.

"*Fates*," I breathed appreciatively, tipping my head back. My whole body felt stretched taut.

"Have I made myself clear?" Noble asked against my cleavage.

"Abundantly," I gasped.

He paused, green eyes finding mine. His pupils were blown wide, his gaze black with need. When he smiled, it was open and boyish. *Real*. His hair was tousled from my fingers threading through it, with strands sticking out at odd angles.

I laughed.

He laughed.

Then the moment popped like a soap bubble. His palms shifted on my thighs, allowing me to slide down his body in a long, slow scrape. When my feet hit the ground, I wobbled, dizzy from what we'd just done; his palms lingered on my waist, waiting for me to find my balance before falling away.

Without his hands on me, I felt cold and unsteady. Noble flexed his fingers at his sides: open, closed, open. The veins in his forearms were overly pronounced, dark. His chest rose and fell with panted breaths.

I knew what he was going to say before he said it: "We can't."

"Can't—or shouldn't?"

"Both."

"You really think it matters, after all this time?"

His frown—genuine, unguarded, a little wry—was devastating. "Yes, *princess*."

I scoffed, even as an ancient wellspring of emotion flooded my chest. "I am *not* a princess, and you know it."

Noble tipped his head. Kind, but frank. "Heiress, then."

I knew what he was doing. Bringing up my identity was the best way to remind me what was at stake if we were caught.

My heart felt suddenly waterlogged, heavy. "Nobody wants that," I said tightly.

"Doesn't change the fact that you are an heir with lawful claim of Lothgaim."

"*Was*," I corrected. "I *was* heir. Then, if you recall, I was married off."

"I remember," Noble murmured. "I hate myself for it."

"You shouldn't."

"But I *do*," he said roughly.

I shrugged like it didn't matter, like the loss of my name—the erasure of my existence from the Census Ledgers of Marona—was an old scar instead of an unhealed wound. "Yes, well. I didn't want my claim, anyway."

"What you wanted didn't matter, though," Noble pointed out. Not to taunt me, but because it was true.

The Arcane Law of the Seven Territories could not be rejected; it's why I'd been forced into hiding before the general populous heard the rumors Noble had accidentally spread. Because if the people of Lothgaim learned that I—mixed-born Maronan—had rightful claim of their territory, there would be a revolt. The peace and unity the king and queen strived for with Raina's arranged marriage would be ruined. And I would be forced into a role I did not want. All because the law was sacred, and to publicly denounce it could shatter the sanctity of the kingdom.

"I wish that what I wanted mattered," I whispered, meeting Noble's eyes.

"Me, too."

Noble was right. This *was* dangerous.

I was a threat to the kingdom whether I accepted my claim or not. Even *after* Raina married the current heir of Lothgaim next year, my scandalous existence would still threaten her title, her safety, and the political unity her marriage was intended to foster. If anyone uncovered who I was—through my connection to Noble, or otherwise—*many* lives would be ruined.

Nearly ten years might've passed, but nothing had changed. The *only* way to avoid the unrest was to pretend I didn't exist.

But Marona and Lothgaim were a long way from here. While Noble's family was well-known, my connection to him wasn't. Of the people who'd seen us interact—mostly just Phina and her team—nobody seemed to care how long ago we'd met.

"What if we—"

"*Hattie*," Noble said, reading my mind. "Sneaking around never ends well. You of all people should know that."

I wasn't ashamed to be a product of *sneaking around*, but the reminder that my very existence was an example of it *not ending well* still stung.

He was right, though.

Noble softened, stepped closer, and fixed the silky sleeve of my dress, his fingers lingering on the fabric. The intimate touch was entirely new, but also natural. Because we were *us*, and the connection we shared...it had always been this fond, hadn't it? Even back then. Even when I felt it but didn't *know* for sure.

"How can everything be different," I whispered, voice watery, "and still be exactly the same?"

His fingertips fell away from my dress. "Nothing has changed." I got the sense that he meant emotionally *and* in the way we ought to move forward.

I touched my fingertips to my tingling lips. Noble's eyes tracked the movement. I wondered how red they looked to him, how swollen. When a faint smirk formed, I knew my mouth must've looked raw.

But then he frowned. "Maybe I shouldn't have divulged all that."

"*Divulged* is an interesting way to describe what just happened."

With a faint chuckle, he tilted his head to the dome above, as if he couldn't bear to look at me. The windows were alight with shades of tangerine and plum now, the sun's spectacular descent—a beautiful death.

"Noble."

He met my eyes again.

"I'm glad you told me."

"I'm not certain you are."

My forehead wrinkled. "Why not?"

"Because you look sad."

"So do you."

"Back in the cave."

The only time I see the sun is when I'm with you.

I shook my head. "All I want, all I've *ever* wanted, was to feel *free* to be who I am. To be with—"

"*Please* don't finish that thought," Noble said, throat bobbing. "I'm hanging on by a thread here."

I bit my lip, shook my head, frustrated—no, *furious*—at the idea of never kissing him again. Never feeling him against me like that again. Never knowing the sensation of his bare skin sliding against mine, filling me—

"Whatever you're thinking about, stop."

I lifted my chin. "That obvious?"

"Painfully."

"And what if I don't stop thinking about it?"

Noble ran a palm over his face with a grumble. "Your identity isn't the only thing that makes this dangerous, Hattie."

He meant the research program, no doubt. Viren. I hadn't been willing to admit it since the attack, but I'd found myself at the middle of *another* political conspiracy of some sort, and of all people, I knew the risk of not treading lightly.

I sighed, relenting. "You're right."

"I'm sorry."

"It's a relief," I said, "to feel like I'm not completely alone in this agony."

"You are not alone in the agony," he confirmed, a small smile quirking those lips—lips I now knew the *feeling* of. "You're doing it again."

"Doing what?"

"Staring at me like I'm a meal."

I cocked my head, assuming a haughty expression. "Yes, well, you're doing the same thing to me."

"Hard not to."

"You did a good job of pretending not to for most of our lives."

"I was just trying to spare you the burden." A sad smile. "But I was bound to break eventually."

"It wasn't *just* your burden to bear."

A nod. "I should go."

The backs of my eyes stung. "Alright."

"Hattie," Noble murmured, stepping into my personal space again. "Peach."

He pinched my chin between his thumb and index finger, lifting it so he could ghost a kiss across my lips. Again, I tasted the delicious, indescribable essence of *him*, and...Hylder? No, that must've been the scent of the Black Lace beside us, mingling with my sense of taste.

The thought was there and gone in a flash as Noble leaned into me. The kiss deepened for one hypnotic moment, a slick drag, and then we were breaking apart.

When he looked into my eyes again, he wasn't masking his expression with cool neutrality; his features were plain, apologetic. It felt like a gift to get the real him.

"Can we agree on one thing, moving forward?" I asked.

He inclined his head in a wordless *go on*.

"Can we forget the lab rules?" He opened his mouth to protest, but I spoke over him. "We don't have to be best friends, or even talk all that much, I just...don't want it to feel so cold."

He nodded. "I can do that."

"I'm supposed to be working with you on Gildium, anyway. It's against Phina's wishes for us to ignore each other."

"True."

I gave him a single nod, then stepped back.

"Do you want me to walk you out?" he asked, seeming to remember the new protocol of researchers coming and going in twos.

"I think I'll harvest some Hylder while I'm here," I said. "Willa can escort me out later."

"You're sure?"

"Yes."

"Alright." He regarded me a moment longer, eyes flicking over my features like he wanted to memorize every detail of this moment. Then his jaw ticked, and he said, "I'll see you around, Peach," before walking down the garden path and disappearing around the bend.

Earlier, I'd wondered what the harm was in getting our feelings out in the open. Well, now I knew. My heart felt like it had been cleaved open, an axe splitting wood with a swift crack. To learn that my feelings were not unrequited was both a relief and utter torture.

28

WEAPON PLAY

HATTIE

When I arrived at Castle Might for sword practice a couple days later, there were two figures already in the training yard: one huge and golden, the other dark, chiseled, and forbidden.

I was already moving slow after a series of sleepless nights of tossing and turning and fantasizing and *dreaming* about Noble—so acute that even self-pleasure did me no good—but when I saw Oderin and Noble sparring, I halted in my tracks.

They were dressed similarly in dark trousers and white shirts, their foreheads already glistening with sweat. The day was muggy from all the recent rain, hot with the hint of impending summer. Out in the intense midday sun, I was already roasting in my tight pants and sleeveless tunic. My temperature kicked up further as I watched the two men train.

It was embarrassing to realize how *easy* Oderin had been going on me during our sessions, because this was...something else. They both wielded dull practice swords, the metal glinting in the bright sunlight. The clash of steel rang out in the empty yard, echoing off the surrounding stone buildings. Their movements were quick, accurate, graceful—a deadly dance of aggression.

Noble was a force, lunging and striking with brutal precision. He wielded his hefty blade with two hands, swiveling from a solid core, his strength coming from his center the same way Oderin was always lecturing me about. I had thought Oderin was nimble on his feet, but compared to Noble, he lagged, fumbling his footsteps to keep up. The way Noble *moved*—it was a study in bodily control. Masculine power.

Though he hadn't become a Mighty Knight, Noble must've kept up with his training. It explained how utterly *solid* he'd felt against me in the gardens.

Fucking Fates. We'd managed to work rather amiably over the past few days, sharing jokes and frustrated grumbles as we experimented with binding Gildium and Hylder, the materials smoking, bubbling, repelling like oil and water. But seeing him like *this*? This wouldn't help our congeniality in the lab—this would only fan the sparks of attraction still sizzling between us.

And why *was* he here?

I thought back to our conversation that night—his fury over my bruise. Was that it? Overprotective male ego?

My lust morphed into anger, and I stomped up to the edge of the training area. "What are you doing here, Noble?"

Noble's eyes cut to me, and his flow faltered.

Oderin's did, too. "How do you know—?" He broke off, clearly making the connection. He raised a knowing eyebrow at me, evidently thrilled by the unexpected development that *Noble* was the man I'd told him about.

Noble, meanwhile, had lowered his sword. His eyes swept over my body—the pants that hugged my long legs and modest hips, the cut of my tunic accentuating my waist—with the same hunger I'd seen two nights ago. My body woke up, nerves firing throughout my core and between my legs—but it was my heart that felt his stare the most.

Because his gaze was unguarded. *Honest.*

For days I'd been wondering if it'd been a mistake to share what we had, knowing we ought to never touch each other like that again—but right now, I was grateful.

Misery really did love company.

Noble had come to a complete halt to look at me, but with the two men still technically in the middle of sparring, Oderin—clearly hoping to use Noble's diverted attention to his advantage—hefted his sword and swung. My eyes tracked the movement, and Noble—with his superior vision—must've seen it on my face. He swiveled, lightning fast, and blocked Oderin's blow.

Then he was walking into Oderin's space with a series of relentless strikes, forcing the esteemed Major of the Order of the Mighty of Fenrir backward across the yard until Oderin stumbled, landing on his ass in the dirt.

"Why do I feel like that was personal?" Oderin asked with a laugh.

Noble held out a hand, helping the knight up. "Because it was."

Oderin's raised his eyebrow at me again. He mouthed an amused, *Well done.*

I frowned, feigning mild confusion. *Whatever do you mean?* the look said.

Noble glanced between us, seeing through our silent exchange.

I remembered to be annoyed. "You haven't answered my question," I said. "What. Are. You. Doing. Here?"

Noble spread his arms, white shirt billowing away from his frame, the fabric see-through enough for me to glimpse the outline of his cut torso. "I'm sparring."

"Why?"

"Same reason as you, I reckon."

I regarded Oderin, expectant.

"He asked if I wanted to spar," Oderin said with a shrug. "Who am I to deny an Asheren?"

I groaned. We'd might've agreed to eschew our rules, but Noble's presence here was still a huge overstep.

"I'm not doing this," I said, turning to walk away.

"Afraid I'll hurt you?" Noble taunted.

Yes, I thought. *Just looking at you hurts.*

But my irritation got the better of me.

I halted, boots grinding in the dirt as I swiveled back around. "Everyone knows that the son of Kalden Asheren has been training with a sword since birth," I pointed out. "Why would you want to spar with your uncoordinated alchemy apprentice lab mate?"

Noble shot me a winning smile, all teeth. "For fun."

Standing beside Noble, Oderin appeared thoroughly entertained. I could only hope that whatever Oderin deduced about us, he'd be as amenable to keeping quiet about it as he seemed to be with Anya and Idris's secrets.

I approached the two men again, glaring at Noble. "This is serious. I want to *learn* so I can keep myself safe."

Noble's eyes dropped to my bruised shoulder, then back up to my face. "Safe?"

"Ah, *that's* why it's personal," Oderin remarked.

I shot Noble a wide-eyed glare. One that said, *Do you really want Oderin inferring any more than he already has?*

Noble appeared amused.

"I don't want any distractions," I said tightly.

"You're saying I'm a distraction?"

I pressed my lips together. Noble had joked with me when we were young, but I'd never allowed myself to assume he was flirting—at least, not for *real*. But now... now, I wondered how I'd never seen through his act. The veiled sincerity in everything he said and did.

All that time, Noble had cared about me, too, and led me to believe otherwise.

Suddenly, I didn't care that he'd done it out of duty, or out of respect for my station, or even to protect me. Nor did I care that Oderin was observing us. Fury raged inside me like river rapids, powerful and unforgiving.

I let the anger wash over me as I lifted my chin, meeting his eyes. "Fine. Let's spar."

Oderin chuckled. "Very well." He left us in the center of the ring, heading for the weapons rack.

"I love the look of you angry," Noble whispered.

"Don't push me."

His chest puffed with a silent laugh.

"Are you truly so blinded by a minor bruise that you'd risk Oderin figuring out our history?"

"You're the one making a fuss."

I growled through my teeth, then clenched them tighter, trying to get ahold of my emotions.

Oderin returned carrying two shortswords. The greatswords they'd been sparring with were far too big for me to use, and apparently, my instructor wanted to give me a fighting chance. He handed Noble a dull practice blade before carefully extending the hilt of my weapon in my direction.

Only...this sword was fancier than the one I was used to training with. Its grip was wrapped in braided leather, worn smooth from use. The pommel was gold-plated and set with a ruby the size of a grape. The cross guard was wide and also gold, the metal tooled with an intricate spiral pattern. It was almost *decorative* in its finery—if it weren't for the very real and very sharp blade.

"That's not fair," Noble said, pointing at the deadly edge.

"I have to agree," I said to Oderin. I didn't trust myself with a *real* weapon. I didn't have the spatial awareness or control to guarantee I wouldn't actually land a hit.

"As you said, Hattie, he's been training since birth," Oderin said. "I'm just giving you an edge."

Noble snorted at the pun.

"But I don't want to hurt him," I protested.

With an air of smug confidence, Noble assured me, "You won't."

Then he was tugging the hem of his shirt up his torso and off.

My mouth went dry. I was instantly *dying* of thirst, and he was a crystalline lake. I had to physically resist the urge to lap him up, because...

Fates, he was perfect. Annoyingly so. While most knights were bulky, Noble was *lean*. From his broad pectorals to his carved abdominals, every muscle stood out in stark prominence underneath an endless expanse of smooth brown skin. Wide shoulders tapered into a narrow waist, with an etched *V* bracketing the trail of black hair beneath his belly button. His body was a hard landscape, and I wanted to *crawl* across his terrain.

This was entirely unfair.

My gaze licked up the defined ridges of his body all the way back to his face, about to protest the blatant attempt at distraction—but the words died on my tongue because...he wasn't smirking anymore. He looked as hungry as I felt. More so, if that was possible.

I feel like I'm starving, Hattie.

When he arched an eyebrow, his expression echoed what he'd said the other night: *Whatever you're thinking about, stop.*

I tightened my hand on the grip of my fancy sword, suddenly ready to release some of this pent-up tension with a little violence.

Oderin clapped, startling us both. "Hattie, let's have you practice some defense," he said, walking backward out of the training circle to stand on the sidelines. "We'll have Noble take an offensive strategy, and you'll focus on blocking him."

I nodded and lifted my blade.

Noble's mouth pressed into a serious line, and he crossed the tip of his sword with mine. Together, we said the words, "Fate, Fortune, Death."

Even though I knew it was coming, Noble's first strike surprised me. I wasn't used to feeling defensive in his presence; the contrast was strange. I blocked jerkily at first, but eventually found a rhythm, angling my sword horizontally, vertically, deflecting each one of Noble's slow but persistent blows.

I did *not* look any farther than his dull practice weapon—even seeing his abs in my periphery was enough to make my heart race far faster than it ought to with this amount of exertion.

"Mind your feet!" Oderin called out to me, and I shuffled sideways, remembering what he'd taught me. "Good, Hattie!"

"Good, Hattie," Noble repeated softly, and it made me misstep.

I threw out my sword, causing Noble's blade to slide across mine; I deflected it to the dirt.

"Nicely done!" Oderin called. "Reset."

We did as we were told. Said the words. Started again.

"You're better than I expected," Noble said. The words might've sounded patronizing if it weren't for his utterly sincere, slightly amused tone.

"Really? You're worse than I expected."

In response, his blows became a little harder, quaking up the metal of my sword and into my biceps and my shoulder. Meanwhile, he held his non-sword-wielding hand behind his back like this was a pleasant walk along the river.

I put some effort into my blocks, deflecting him with more force, channeling my frustration into my training.

"Remember your core!" Oderin demanded from the sidelines.

I flexed my abdominal muscles, trying not to think about how they'd flexed last night with my hand between my legs as I imagined—

I felt a tap on my thigh: Noble's sword.

"Reset," Oderin said.

Noble bounced his eyebrows. "Distracted?"

"Absolutely not."

We started again, the clack of his strikes and my blocks filling the empty yard.

"Now switch!" Oderin ordered.

Noble stopped his attack at once. It was my turn to take the offensive, but when I looked down at my sword, I hesitated. As much as I wanted to make him sweat, I didn't want to make him *bleed*.

"Don't fear your power, Hattie," Oderin called. "Trust he can defend himself."

I shuffled forward, going for my first strike. Noble blocked it, an encouraging smile on his face. "Keep going," he said softly.

My body heard the words in a different context. I saw it in a flash: that hard, bare torso between my thighs, those scarred hands gripping my hips, rolling me against—

Sword brandished, I lunged at him, striking in quick succession, desperate to dispel the desire, to exhaust myself until my body stopped feeling so *awake*. Noble chuckled like he didn't quite believe my viciousness, which only spurred me on, raining blow after blow upon his sword.

"Pause!" Oderin ordered.

I stopped, weapon still aloft, panting.

Noble appeared out of breath, too. Sweat slicked his chest; a single bead slid between the ridges of his abdomen, and I glanced away before I saw it reach his waistband.

Oderin came over to me, gripped my elbow, and shifted it into a different angle. I felt my back muscles turn on, my grip become steadier. "Feel that?"

With my eyes still trained on Noble, I felt *everything*.

"Yes," I said.

Oderin glanced over his shoulder at Noble, and I saw the flash of appreciation in his eyes, too. At least I wasn't the only one embarrassingly bewitched by Noble's physique.

"If you're concerned that I'd tell my sister about an affair between her apprentices," Oderin whispered, "I assure you, I wouldn't."

"There's nothing to tell."

The Major chuckled, then stepped out of the circle, allowing Noble and I to begin again. This time, Oderin had us swap blocks and blows back and forth. I kept my elbow more aligned, and I *did* feel more powerful. A delicious soreness began to radiate out through my shoulder blade and arm, the exertion taking over. I became faster and more focused, eliciting more calls of encouragement from Oderin on the sidelines.

"You look good with a blade," Noble panted, swinging his dull sword with a flourish.

"Show-off," I replied.

"I'm serious," he said, speaking between strikes. "Your brow furrows, and your lips press into a pout, and you're flushed"—his voice went hoarse on that last word, as if it took his breath away—"and yet your eyes glitter like you enjoy taking your frustration out in this way."

"Stop"—I swung at him—"talking."

"Why? Is it making you angry?" he taunted, but I realized something: I wasn't the only one distracted by how my opponent looked.

As he spoke, he wasn't looking at my face or even my weapon—he was looking at my sternum, where I felt a prickle of heat underneath my skin. That must've been the flush he was going on about. I shuffled closer, enduring the clamor of his sword against mine, hefting my blade a little higher, biding my time.

"It's not just the exertion," he went on. "You get flushed when you're angry, too. And the other night, I noticed you *also* get flushed when you're—"

With a groan, I thrust my sword out. As I'd hoped, I caught him by surprise, nicking him on the forearm.

"Well done, Hattie!" Oderin called, clapping his hands.

I beamed, pride swelling in my chest. Noble had been distracted—halfhearted, even—but I'd still managed to land a blow on an incredibly well-practiced fighter. And knowing that I hadn't truly hurt him—it was barely a scratch—I felt only accomplishment as I lowered my weapon.

"You're not going to be a sore loser, are you?" I taunted.

The adrenaline of our sparring session was beginning to fade, my muscles turning to jelly. I let the tip of my sword fall to the ground with a *tap*, waiting for Noble's sassy rebuke, his witty retort—*Fates*, even a withering glance—but he was too busy staring at his arm. Blood was beading where I'd slashed his skin, except—

I blinked. Took one step closer. Narrowed my eyes to focus.

—his blood wasn't red.

It was *black*.

Oderin was approaching us from the sidelines, still clapping amusedly. The sound had Noble clamping a palm over the small cut. Green eyes found mine, and in them was a fathomless shame I'd only seen one other time: on the night he'd stood in the courtyard of Castle Wynhaim, beneath the weeping willow, and had watched the nondescript carriage take me away.

That was the same night I'd learned it was his fault the rumors about my father had spread, escalating into an attempt on my life. His fault I had to go into hiding. I'd never found it in myself to be angry with him, though; even then, I knew Noble would never willfully hurt me.

Noble dropped his blade and stormed off, his injured arm still clutched in his opposite hand.

"How badly did you wound him?" Oderin asked, sidling up beside me while we watched Noble go. "Didn't look that deep from outside the ring."

"I think it was worse than it looked," I mumbled. "I should apologize."

I spared Oderin only a glance before I dropped my own weapon on the ground and hurried after Noble.

The sunlight was bright, washing out the pale dirt of the training yard. Maybe that's why his blood had looked so dark, I told myself. Maybe it was just my eyes playing tricks on me. I was determined not to panic, not yet, but I broke into a run as I passed through a narrow alley between barracks and out into a part of Castle Might I'd never been before: the bailey.

There was a huge statue in its center—a seven-foot-high knight on bended knee, holding the hilt of a massive sword that was speared into the ground. Noble was up ahead, still holding his arm, *fleeing*.

"Noble!" I called after him. "Noble, wait!"

He turned, and the look of absolute humiliation on his face—it crushed me.

I stopped beside the statue. "Let's talk," I offered. "Please?"

He hesitated only a moment, then turned his back on me, disappearing through the barbican gate, back out into the hubbub of Fenrir City.

I didn't go after him this time. I sagged, placing a palm on the smooth base of the statue. My fingertips found writing, and with my mind still reeling, I glanced down, reading the inscription.

Noble the Mighty, the First Order Knight of Fenrir.

It was a statue of Noble's namesake.

A mirthless laugh quaked my chest. Noble's parents really set him up for failure, naming him after a legend and not a real person. It made me irrationally angry, *heartbroken*, that he should grow up with that kind of pressure. To feel constantly like he was falling short.

In spite of what I'd just seen—the implications still not fully permeating my consciousness just yet—an overwhelming sense of protectiveness swept over me. I didn't care about rules, or duty, or assassins, or even black monster blood. *Cursed* blood.

I cared only for the boy I'd met when I was just eleven years old, a boy already sagging under the weight of expectation. That sense of protectiveness roused me—set me on a path not after Noble, but after answers.

My Noble, that protective part of me said. *Mine*.

29

SHAME

NOBLE

The air was humid on the day Noble sought to take the Oath of the Order of the Mighty.

In the parade grounds of Castle Wynhaim, he stood among a hundred other prospective Oath-takers, all lined up in neat rows in the searing late-summer sun. A grand stone dais overlooked the field, backdropped by the western wing of the fortress; a magnificent white tent had been erected to shade the numerous witnesses—individuals Noble knew from growing up within the castle walls.

At the back were members of court—siblings and cousins of the royal family, mostly, along with Noble's mother and other prominent wives—lounging on silk chaises, sipping chilled wine, and snacking on cured meats. Attendants swung massive paper fans back and forth, back and forth, cooling those privileged enough to sit in the shade, while twelve royal guards encircled the tent, on patrol.

In front of the more relaxed congregation were the raised royal thrones. There, King Cassius Braven and Queen Yvira Wynhaim sat, wearing delicate golden circlets atop their heads. To the left of the thrones was the podium that held the Ledger of the Mighty: the magical tome that recorded knights' names and tethered their Oaths. A ledger-master—an esteemed Adept of the Order of the Arcane, tasked with overseeing the ledger's magic—stood behind the podium wearing the customary dusky brown and gold robes, the cowl hood obscuring their face.

And finally, stationed directly to the king's right, was Noble's father: Kalden Asheren, General of the Order of the Mighty, leader of the king's personal guard and Marona's Mighty legion. His golden armor was splendid, finely tooled around the edges and polished to a high shine; the ornate sword that hung at his hip was as much a part of Kalden as his own right hand. He nodded at each prospective Oath-taker who climbed the stairs of the dais—his acknowledgement an honor in and of itself.

As the most esteemed Order in the Seven Territories, few were admitted into the Mighty—especially the branch that served Marona. Those who'd made it to the parade grounds were of the small percentage that had passed the rigorous physical trials and mental tests. But the Ledger's magic did not accept just anyone; the Oath itself was the final obstacle.

One by one, the Oath-takers approached the podium and attempted their Oath before Kalden, the ledgermaster, and the rulers. Noble moved with the crowd, sweating profusely in the damp heat. Up ahead, he heard snippets of men and women reciting the Oath that Noble had known by heart since he was a boy.

—*I pledge my life to the protection of the realm*—

—*I will not falter from the Mighty path*—

—*I vow to hold nothing in higher regard than the sacred honor of my Oath and Order*—

That last statement was where most hopefuls failed. If one did not believe deep in their heart that they could adhere to the extreme loyalty the Oath required, the ledger would reject them.

Indeed, Noble heard more rejections than acceptances; pained grunts and sorrowful cries far outweighed the shouts of triumph. He winced at each spurned would-be knight, fearing the possibility of his own dismissal. And he was almost to the front of the line, now—only two hopefuls ahead of him.

He watched as both failed their Oaths.

Then it was Noble's turn.

He ascended the stairs slowly, keeping his head held high. He reached the king and queen first and sank to a knee, bowing deeply at the couple whose table he'd supped at countless times, whose daughter he loved like a little sister. King Braven offered Noble the smallest of nods, along with a minute tightening of his bearded cheek—the closest he'd get to familiarity in such a formal setting. The queen, on the other hand, was more forthright in her encouragement; her blue eyes seemed to glimmer as she offered him a warm smile.

Their kindness only made Noble more nervous.

As Noble rose from his bow, he saw his mother watching him from her chaise. The pair of women she'd been conversing with were still talking, gesturing with their wine chalices, but Helena didn't seem to hear them as she stared at her son with irises the same shade of green as his own. The tawny skin around her eyes was tight with tension and seeing her anxiousness...it only worsened his own.

Noble turned toward his father next, bowing quickly at the waist as was customary when greeting a general. Kalden remained stone-still, staring down his strong nose, his square jaw set. His gaze was as heavy as a mountain on Noble's shoulders, more oppressive than the day's heat.

Until it lifted over Noble's shoulder to land on another face in the crowd.

Noble couldn't help but look back to see where his father's attention had gone. An acrid, jealous anguish seared through his veins when he spotted Brendan Harrow not far behind him in the procession. Brendan had continued to train with Kalden into young adulthood, taking pleasure in always being one step ahead of Noble in skill, loyalty, and bootlicking.

Under Kalden's gaze, Brendan's expression was confident, smug—but when he noticed Noble staring, the fucker *grinned*.

Noble faced ahead again, waiting for his father's nod to proceed.

When it came, he didn't linger; he swiveled to face the podium.

The Ledger of the Mighty was bound in faded umber leather. Splayed open atop the podium, it was thick as a mattress, the paper old and brittle. Noble could see the arcane writing on the fresh page, only nine names out of forty men and women who'd recited the Oath this afternoon.

Noble offered the ledgermaster an acknowledging nod, then lowered himself to his knees and tucked his chin. Sweat trailed down his temple, slid along his jaw, and dripped from his chin onto the stone—yet in spite of the heat, he shivered. Since the moment Noble was born—perhaps even before—Kalden had dreamed of his son following in his Mighty footsteps. This was the culminating moment. Noble's chance to prove that he was worthy of his father's pride.

And he was as ready for the commitment as he'd ever be.

Hattie had been gone for ten months, and in that time, Noble had done nothing but read and train—*anything* to keep his mind off her absence. He was faster, stronger, and more determined than ever. It was high time Noble step into the future his father always intended for him.

Noble cleared his throat and began: "I, Noble Asheren, hereby offer myself to the Oath of the Order of the Mighty, the King, and Kingdom of Marona." Noble spoke slowly and clearly, allowing his voice to carry through the grounds. "I pledge my life to the protection of the realm and the safe keeping its citizens, secrets, and sovereignty. I will not stray from my duty; I will not falter from the Mighty path. I bear my charge with honor, compliance, and bravery. For the good of the realm, I am bound."

Noble paused. The next part of the Oath was the vow that would seal his future: his promise that he'd hold nothing in higher regard than his duty. If he was false in that claim—if in the deepest part of his heart, he knew he *couldn't* favor the Mighty over all else he loved—the ledger would reject Noble's bid.

When you make your vow, clear your mind of all but the sacred honor of serving your kingdom, Kalden had advised Noble the night before. *Think only of your love for the realm.*

Staring at the gritty stone beneath his knees, freckled with his sweat, Noble breathed deeply, filling his chest. He willed his voice not to quaver as he continued: "I vow to hold nothing in higher regard than the sacred honor of my Oath and Order. By the Fates and the arcane power of this Oath, I swear fealty to the great realm of the Seven Territories of the Kingdom of Marona, never to forsake my duty except in the honorable retirement of my Oath or death."

As he spoke the words, he envisioned the entire continent, from the eastern shores of Orhal to the Western Wood of Fenrir. He imagined the majestic rolling hills of the central territory of Marona and the colorful sprawl of its capital. He imagined the three-hundred-foot plateau overlooking the city, and the castle built into the stone. He imagined the river that gushed past the fortress into a magnificent waterfall, and the bridge that spanned the waters that led to its perilous drop.

Fate's Landing.

The moment the bridge entered his mind, so, too, did a memory.

Hattie stood by the marble railing in a scarlet dress, its hem fluttering against her shins. She was laughing at a joke he'd made, the sound lost to the roar of the falls. They were shrouded in a haze of mist, delirious with the exhilaration of such close proximity to the water's force. But the thing that thrilled Noble most was the way she'd abruptly sobered, stared into his eyes, and said, *I'm in love with you.*

Deep down, Noble's unavoidable truth was this: nothing in the world made his heart feel as full as Hattie's presence—not even the realm.

So, when Noble—kneeling before the ledger, his father, and the king—tasted the bitter rejection of the Oath in the back of his throat...he wasn't even surprised.

But he *was* ashamed.

The magnitude of it came on slowly, like the cracking of ice on a distant mountainside. Kalden Asheren's son, *failing* the Oath of the Order of the Mighty. For a moment, Noble forgot to breathe. As a shocked silence swept across the grounds, he was *buried* by the avalanche of his father's crumbling expectations.

His mother's delayed gasp shook him from his stupor. Whispers swept through the crowd. Noble looked up, directly into the eyes of his father. Kalden appeared neither pained nor angry; his face was hard and blank as granite. *Crushing.*

What happened after that was a blur.

Noble rose to his feet and left the dais, lingering only long enough to watch Brendan's triumphant bid and Kalden's proud grin—a grin Noble had never seen on his father's face before. Then, after the ceremony, the argument: his father's fury, his mother's tearful pleas for Kalden to have compassion, and the ringing in Noble's ears as he packed up his things and left Castle Wynhaim for good.

Not knowing where else to go, Noble had traveled west into Fenrir Territory. He'd considered seeking Hattie out in Poe-on-Wend, desperate to know how her new life was treating her—but Noble had already put her in enough danger. The king himself had demanded no one contact her.

He went to Fenrir City instead. In the days following, he met an Adept of the Order of the Arcane who was in search of would-be knights for an experimental Order under the Lord of Fenrir's banner. There were promises of superior strength and glory, and Noble hadn't *thought*—he'd simply joined.

Becoming a Knight of the Order of the Morta was just one mistake in a long series of failures.

Failing Hattie by breaking her heart on that bridge.

Failing to contain the rumors about her father that ultimately forced her away.

Failing his father and the Mighty.

Failing the mission of his Order.

Failing Phina with his inability to alchemize a cure.

But seeing the cold shock on Hattie's face in the training yard with Oderin today—fear and betrayal and disbelief—*that* was his worst failure yet.

He knew he shouldn't have showed up at Hattie's sparring session. Knew it was a bad idea when he contacted Oderin, arrived at the training yard, when Hattie had picked up her sword. The problem wasn't *knowing better*. It was the fact that apparently, he no longer had any Fates-damned self-control. Not when it came to *her*.

All his life, he'd tried to do the right thing by keeping his true feelings from her, but no amount of logic or self-loathing could dull his desire. In the gardens two nights ago, he'd tried to keep his hands off her, but her skin had looked so soft. At the sight of Hattie's goosebumps, her blush, her arousal...his resolve had simply snapped.

He'd given her a chance to change her mind, to ask him *not* to share how he truly felt, but she'd demanded his truth anyhow. He'd found he could no longer deny her, so he'd been honest with Hattie for the first time in their lives.

And today, she'd learned just how wretched he truly was.

An actual monster.

Just the sight of the black blood welling on his skin had been enough to awaken the cruel, awful curse inside of him. He'd had to leave immediately—not just to protect his secret and spare himself a little humiliation, but to keep the curse from taking over, as it did in his nightmares.

Even now, as Noble wove his way through the streets of Fenrir—following the quickest path back to the Royal Inn—his fingertips ached with the threat of claws. But not once did he remove his hand from the shameful blood beneath his palm.

When he burst through the door of his room, he quickly closed himself inside, rushing over to the newest vials Phina had given him. Hattie's Black Lace tincture. He ripped the cork out of the bottle with his teeth and drank the purple liquid in three gulps. Then he gritted his molars, waiting for the Hylder's influence to take hold. He counted to twenty, thirty.

Finally, the abomination in him slackened, falling again into slumber.

Noble wasted no time. Still shaking with adrenaline, he went to the small wash basin in the corner, and—doing his best not to look too closely—rinsed the beads of coagulating black blood off his arm. Then he swiftly wrapped a bandage around the cut, biting one end of the cloth to tighten the knot.

When he was done, he sank to his knees on the floor, buried his face in his hands, and growled into his palms.

30

BLOOD AND ORDERS

HATTIE

Y ou said there's Gildium in cursed blood. How does that happen?"

Viren looked up from her bench in the enclosed infirmary courtyard, eyes widening slightly as I stormed toward her, still in my sparring clothes. All at once, the sounds of the peaceful garden—birds chirping, bees buzzing, the distant clamor of the city beyond the surrounding buildings—faded until all I heard was my own panting.

It'd been a hot, exasperating walk from the Castle Might training yard to the Collegium campus.

"What have you heard?" Viren asked.

It wasn't what I'd heard, but what I'd *seen*: Noble's blood, *cursed*. I wasn't afraid; I was fuming. I wanted to know *how*. I wanted to fix it. I wanted to protect him from—*Fates*, from what? Himself?

Your identity isn't the only thing that makes this dangerous, Hattie.

I'd assumed he'd been referring to the research program and the attempt on Viren's life, but now...

I buried my face in my hands. "Fuck," I groaned.

Viren's infirmary slippers scuffed against the gravel path as she slowly made her way to standing. "Hattie. What do you know?"

"I'm not sure," I said into my hands. "I think I know even *less* than I did before."

"Before what?"

I lowered my hands and met her worried brown eyes. "I don't think I should say."

Viren pressed her thin lips together and nodded. "Fine. Probably better that you don't."

I sank to the stone bench, and she slowly sat back down beside me. Her skin had more color than the last time I'd seen her—more olive now than sickly gray—but she was still wearing a patient robe. It was pale blue and patterned with polka dots. Rather cheerful, considering the reason she was wearing it—but maybe that was the point.

"Phina has me going over your notes," I told her.

Viren's smile was wan. "Told you she'd bring you deeper into the fold."

"I've been reading up on Gildium, too."

"Have you asked Noble about it? He's a great resource."

I kept my face carefully blank as I said, "I haven't gotten around to asking him yet."

"He can be a bit aloof," Viren remarked.

Have I made myself clear? he'd asked against my cleavage.

Abundantly, I'd said.

"Easy on the eyes, though," Viren added, oblivious to my inner turmoil.

"I'll ask him," I promised, "but what I need to know right now is *how* do curses happen?" I'd been wracking my brain on the way here—the Gildium, the Hylder, Noble's blank Fate—but couldn't put all the pieces together.

Viren frowned. "I don't know, exactly. I wasn't made privy to that information."

"Truly?"

She shrugged. "Like I said before, no one is allowed to know everything. Well, except Phina."

I shot to my feet. "Any idea where she is?"

"In class, probably?"

I swore. I'd forgotten all about my afternoon class.

"Hattie." Viren let out a long, wheezing sigh. "Whatever you're hoping to learn, Phina's not going to tell you."

"We'll see about that," I said, marching back down the path.

"No, Hattie. She *can't* tell you."

I halted. Turned. Our voices were still muffled by her magic, no sound permeating our bubble.

"She has an Oath, remember?"

Right. I groaned through my teeth, feeling edgy and agitated by the dead-ends. The non-answers. The man I loved was caught up in...whatever this was...and I couldn't *help* him. I couldn't be there for him. Judging by the look of shame on his face and the way he'd run off, he wasn't interested in my help, either; I had no doubt in my mind that in addition to the limits of his Oaths, he'd kept this from me because he wanted to protect me.

I returned to Viren. "Phina's program is about binding Hylder to the Gildium in cursed blood, right?"

"That's what they tell us."

"Do you think Phina's lying about the purpose of her research?"

"No, but I don't trust that Lord Haron isn't using our findings for other purposes, too."

"Such as?"

"I don't know, Hattie." Viren's eyes took on a sheen, tears glittering at their inner corners. "All I know is that I was brought on to bind Hylder to the iron in regular blood. But every time I tried, the iron wasn't receptive. I eventually got frustrated, and—knowing that Gildium was part of Phina's research somehow, given Noble's presence—I tried adding Gildium into the mix, just to see if a magically potent metal would help with the alchemical weaving. When I did, the blood turned black."

"You think adding Gildium *caused* the curse?"

"I don't think it's that simple, but"—Viren shook her head, causing a tear to track down her cheek—"I'm just an apprentice, Hattie. I asked Phina about it and she started coughing like her Oath was keeping her from speaking." Viren visibly shivered. "I started digging, trying to find an explanation, *any* reference to black blood that I could. Books and old research records didn't clarify much, so I went looking for answers beyond the Collegium. One night, I overheard knights talking outside the Ire about the Order of the Valiant fighting cursed things—*abominations*—with black blood. That's how I put it all together."

I lifted my fingers to my lips and shook my head. "Do you think it's possible that black blood isn't *always* a sign of a curse? That it could mean something else?" Perhaps the color of Noble's blood was simply from contamination due to his metalworking. The thought gave me hope.

"To my knowledge, cursed blood is black, but I don't know if *all* black blood is cursed," Viren said. "What I do know is that when you add Hylder, it *repels* the Gildium, like trying to bind oil and water. It doesn't *work*."

My eyes lifted to the sky above, the sun shattering through the clouds. "Hylder repels evil," I murmured.

Viren's eyes were wide.

"No." I shook my head. "*No*. I'd be hard-pressed to believe that the metal that framed the Mirrors of Fate is a source of evil." And there was no way that Noble had evil in his veins. I wouldn't accept it. "This doesn't add up."

"None of it does."

A thought occurred. "When you added Hylder to the black blood, did it turn red again?"

Viren shook her head, and my heart sank. "I only started trying a few weeks ago, though. All of this has happened so fast."

"Did you experiment with Black Lace Hylder?"

"No, just the common varietal."

That gave me at least a *little* hope. A place to start, in Viren's absence. "Where can I learn more about the Order of the Valiant?"

"You can't," Viren said with a sniffle. "I went to the library to research them, but there was nothing—it was like the Order didn't exist. Next thing I know, I'm here—" She choked back a startled sob.

I knelt in front of her, taking her quivering hands in mine. I was reeling, but Viren—usually quite stoic—was openly weeping now, completely shaken up. It was alarming to see her this way. "I'm sorry," I said. "I shouldn't have stormed in here like this. You shouldn't be thinking about these things. You should be resting."

She let out an unsteady sigh. "It's all right. In fact, I'm glad you're asking these questions. It's dangerous, but it's the only way we can get to the bottom of this and learn how to protect ourselves. The longer we're in the dark, the easier it becomes for threats to sneak up on us."

I squeezed her hands. "Where did you leave off?"

"The archives. I didn't have enough clearance to view the classified section, but my gut tells me something's there. Something about the Orders we haven't learned yet. Maybe you can sneak in?"

I squeezed her hands one more time, then hurried for the door. "Not if I go to the source!" I called over my shoulder.

31

IRE OF THE VALIANT

HATTIE

Armed with one of Uriel's daggers and wearing my most inconspicuous dress—a plain, dark indigo—I tipped my mug toward my lips and drank. I was seated at a corner table in Fenrir's Ire, the tavern popular among knights. It was a raucous place, filled to the brim with drunk brutes of all shapes and sizes. Like Fenrir's Charm, the patrons in the Ire all seemed to know one another. Most appeared to be either Knights of the Order of the Mighty or Knights of the Order of the Lawful; as such, this was by no means a seedy place, but I still felt painfully *other* and somewhat vulnerable surrounded by so many highly trained fighters.

I probably ought to have asked Oderin for his advice before coming here, but there hadn't been time to waste.

Then again, maybe rushing into this was a bad idea.

I slumped forward, resting my elbows on worn wood of my table, and took another sip of my dark ale. It tasted of oats and malt, with a smoky hint of peat—I was almost certain it'd been brewed in Tuul, the territory to the north. The alcohol certainly wasn't helping my wit, but it was the only way I could convince myself to be brave. To not think too hard about what I was doing.

Following in Viren's investigative footsteps—the same footsteps that had gotten her *stabbed*—was obviously dangerous, but that didn't matter when Noble was in trouble.

I *had* tried to see him in the lab first. But after Willa delivered me to the gardens, I'd removed the blindfold to find his workshop empty.

"Feeling better?" Phina had asked when she found me in the doorway. "Sani said you were feeling poorly earlier."

Fates bless Sani for excusing my absence from class. "Better," I'd lied.

"Any idea where he is?" Phina asked, nodding in the direction of the forge.

"No," I said. "Do you know where he's staying? I have a question about Gildium and would rather not wait."

Phina had arched a brow, but whether or not she believed my excuse for asking for the location of Noble's lodgings, she hadn't let on. All she'd said was that he was staying at the Royal Inn of Fenrir, just a few blocks from the Walk.

When I'd tried his door just after suppertime, he hadn't been in.

Perhaps I should've waited for him to return, but after storming out of our training session and avoiding the lab, Noble apparently wasn't too keen about providing me with answers—so here I was instead. Finding answers for myself.

I smiled against the rim of my mug, thinking about how much Noble must've hated the gimmicky name of his inn. The expression fell when I thought about him staying there for the past few *months*. Was it all he could find in the city? Or had he not been expecting to stay in Fenrir as long as he had? Phina had made it sound like he was a permanent researcher on her project, but what had made him leave Richold's tutelage to travel all the way here from Waldron? Certainly, he couldn't have just been following me? Had there been a new development in the study? I'd been so offended to see him at the Collegium that I hadn't really considered his timing—until now.

I was still circling the topic in my mind when the door of the Ire banged open, letting in a gust of cold air and three Mighty Knights. They must've just finished a shift, as they were still dressed in their golden armor and adorned with their glorious weapons. There was a woman—tall, athletic, terrifying, stunning—and two men who looked vaguely familiar.

No, *very* familiar.

They were from the night in the alley with Phina and the mysterious hooded figure. I couldn't recall if I'd learned the name of the one with the longbow, but the man with the twin shortswords who'd argued with Mariana was named Faren. As the trio strode up to the bar and ordered their drinks, I watched them over the rim of my dwindling mug of ale, tracking every animated gesture, every loose-limbed shrug and fulsome laugh.

They found a table not far from mine and seated themselves with a clamor of scraping chair legs and the noisy clacking of all that metal strapped to their bodies. My stomach clenched with anticipation as I casually shifted sideways in my corner, pretending to relax into my seat as I strained to listen to their conversation. I hadn't been looking for Faren, but perhaps he could point me in the direction of the actual knight I sought.

Hopefully Faren was a *keep your rivals close* sort of fellow.

"Everyone is so quick to assume a conspiracy," the woman was saying, her voice deep and confident. "Do they forget that burglaries happen? Not every criminal can be an assassin."

"Penniless Collegium students hardly make good marks," Faren said, leaning back in his chair. "What would a burglar expect to find? Valuable books?" His tone was all sarcasm.

The woman scoffed. "Oh, but a trained assassin targeting—and then failing—to murder a student makes more sense?"

"A research student," Faren emphasized.

"What research could be so valuable?"

"Do you not read history?" the other knight—the quiet one with the longbow—asked.

"Too busy kicking your ass in the training ring, Lee," the woman said. Faren laughed into his ale.

I glanced around, wondering if anyone else was listening. The fact that three Mighty Knights were speculating about Viren's incident so openly—and with such a lack of actual *information*—was rather disconcerting. I would've expected them to have uncovered more intelligence by now.

Viren was still convinced that the Valiant had targeted her and judging by the glimpse I'd gotten—wavy dark hair, short stature, very Mariana-like—I was not disinclined to believe her. Then again, it seemed unlikely that the Mighty would not know that another Order was targeting students; they *had* to be privy to the Valiant's machinations, right?

Inclining my ear in their direction, I was somewhat dismayed to hear that they'd dropped the topic of Viren's attack and were now arguing about the relative importance of knowing one's history for tactical and political purposes. Lee had become rather vehement, while the woman had crossed her arms over her gold breastplate and was scowling at the ceiling. Faren was laughing good-naturedly, clearly enjoying the conflict.

A loud crash drew everyone's attention—including mine. A fight was breaking out on the opposite side of the Ire, with lots of shouting and a broken chair. Knights rushed to intervene, including Lee and the woman, leaving Faren alone at their table. He glanced over his shoulder at the building melee, obviously wondering if he should get involved or stay put. Eventually, he must've thought better of it, because he leaned back in his seat and crossed one ankle over his opposite knee.

This was my chance.

I tossed back the rest of my ale for fortification, then stood and strode over to Faren's table. He was a rather handsome man, with a delicate bone structure and light brown hair that shined golden in the light of the cast-iron chandelier overhead. He was fiddling with a small carved figurine. The wood was worn smooth from handling, and with his thumbs brushing over its surface—back and forth, back and forth—I couldn't quite tell what it was. A fox, perhaps?

He didn't look up until I was looming over him.

"Faren, right?" I rested my fists on my hips, hoping I looked confident.

Faren appeared almost amused to see me. "You're Phina's nosy apprentice," he said smoothly. "I didn't catch your name that night."

"It's Hattie."

Faren gestured to the empty chair his fellow knight had occupied; across the pub, she was standing between two arguing brutes, a palm on each of their chests, keeping them apart.

"Don't worry, I'll protect you from Shae," Faren quipped.

I dragged the chair closer to Faren and sat. "I'm not looking for protection, I'm looking for Mariana."

"Looking for trouble, then," he said. "Why would an apprentice seek out Mariana?"

"Because she tried to murder my friend."

Faren choked on his surprise, eyes rounding. "That's...quite the accusation."

"I saw her."

Faren collected himself quickly, his features smoothing into mild indifference again. "Look, I despise Mariana and her Order as much as the next—"

"And what Order is that?"

He smirked like I already knew he couldn't answer that question. "But she doesn't go around trying to murder students."

"And how do you know that?"

"It's beneath her."

I snorted, insulted.

He tapped his breastplate with his knuckles. "Killing innocents goes against the tenants of her knighthood. Mariana couldn't be behind the attempt. It's not how the Lord of Fenrir operates," Faren said, and I got the sense that there was *much* more he wasn't saying. "Besides, if she wanted to murder a student, do you really think she'd fail to finish the job?"

He had a point.

"Look, Hattie, you seem like a nice, albeit troublesome girl." He waved his hand with a casual flourish. "Don't be a fool, too. It'll get you killed."

"I thought you said killing innocents was beneath her?" I challenged.

"It is so long as you butt out." Faren tucked the fox figurine back into his pocket. "Innocence is subjective, Hattie," he warned, "and Mariana isn't afraid to make a judgement."

I gulped around the sudden knot in my throat. Is that what'd happened with Viren? She'd gotten too close to the Valiant's secrets, and Mariana deemed her a threat? Faren didn't seem to think so, but Faren didn't know how much Viren had uncovered.

My fingers began to itch and tingle with adrenaline. This was *definitely* a bad idea.

And yet: I was finally getting somewhere.

"Being foolish shouldn't have such extreme consequences," I said, challenging Faren to say more.

But he was a Mighty Knight. They were trained to keep the kingdom's secrets. "I agree, but that's not the world we live in." He glanced toward the other end of the pub, where the scuffle was getting louder. "You better go. Shae just drew her daggers."

Indeed, she had—two wicked blades, each the length of my forearm.

What had I been thinking, strapping Uriel's dagger to a belt at my hip and trying to track down Viren's maybe-attempted-murderer, a vicious Valiant Knight that even Idris—burly, trained fighter that he was—seemed wary of? Who was I to singlehandedly solve the mystery of cursed blood and secret Orders and the clandestine politics pulling the strings of Phina's studies when Phina herself—who knew far more than I did on all counts—had not? I was an apothecary student, not an adept, knight, or spy. I had my own secrets to keep; digging into others would only draw attention to mine.

But Noble, I thought with an agonizing twist of my stomach. My desire to help him had eclipsed my sense of caution—but even recognizing that fact wasn't enough to make me want to stop.

Then again, maybe I was going about this all wrong. Maybe I should've tried harder to confront Phina or Noble in the lab, rather than rushing to the Ire.

I stood. "Thanks for your time, Faren. No offense, but I hope we never speak again."

He laughed. "That's probably for the best, Hattie." But then his eyes narrowed and swept over my features more shrewdly. "Wait, what did you say your last name was?"

A wooden chair flew through the air and crashed into the wall with a sharp crack.

Faren was on his feet in a heartbeat, reaching up over his shoulder for one of the shortswords strapped to his back. Not wanting to stick around long enough for him to question my family name again—or see how the brawl unfolded—I hurried toward the front door, tossing the barkeep an extra coin on my way out.

Compared to the ruckus inside the Ire, this part of the city was quite peaceful. The night sky was clear, the half-moon shining without obstruction. The air was fresh, chilly. A thin fog slithered along the street, clinging to the base of the buildings; I tasted snowmelt in its vapors as I walked purposefully in the direction of the Royal Inn of Fenrir.

As my head cleared, I became more and more grateful that I hadn't found Mariana tonight—and more and more stupid for trying. There were other loose threads to follow, though—plenty that didn't involve a potentially murderous knight.

I'd thought that if Noble didn't want to talk to me, maybe I could help him from afar—but that was silly. He was the *only* person I truly wanted to talk to about what was going on—and perhaps the only person who'd be honest with me, at least within his capability.

Not to mention the fact that I couldn't stop thinking about our *kiss*; I felt raw just thinking about his hands on my hips, his tongue in my mouth, his intoxicating taste. The revelations of the past couple days had been dizzying, but curse or no, I wanted him. *Badly.*

Did that make me a hopeless romantic—or simply hopeless?

I picked up my pace, boots echoing on the cobblestones. Perhaps by now, Noble would've returned to his room, and—

My vision went dark, fabric smothering my head. A burlap sack, judging by the flashes of moonlight I managed to see through the open weave. I shrieked, and a hand closed over my mouth on top of the fabric. I tasted the grass-like fibers, along with soil and potato skins, and the faintest bit of salt from my captor's sweaty palm. An arm came around my middle, dragging me sideways. I tried to recall what Oderin had taught me about escaping holds like this, but instinct overpowered all else. I thrashed and kicked wildly, screaming, but my assailant's grip was unyielding.

"Stop. Struggling," a female voice growled into my ear.

I fumbled for Uriel's blade at my hip, but my attacker noticed and got to it first, deftly angling the dagger against my throat.

Suddenly I wasn't in Fenrir, but back in Marona, my nightgown tangled around my legs and my bare heels kicking against the rug in the hallway. A different blade against my neck, scraping the delicate skin under my jaw. Distant shouts echoing through the keep, the clash of steel too far away to give me hope.

The memory made me go slack, my libs weak and shaky.

"Please don't kill me, please don't kill me," I begged into her palm, fear lancing through me like a blade itself. "Please, please, please."

"Shut the fuck up and perhaps I'll spare you," she hissed.

I whimpered, doing as I was told as she wrenched me down the street. Not long after that, she shifted her hold from my mouth to grip the burlap at my crown, catching some of my hair in the process. In one swift move, she yanked the sack off my head and shoved me to the ground.

I fell on my hands and knees on the rough cobblestones, my scalp stinging. There was a stone building in front of me, some wood crates off to my left. I was in an alley—one that looked frustratingly familiar.

With effort, I rolled to the side, sitting with my back propped up against the wall. I blew a frizzy coil of hair out of my eyes, feeling roughed-up and afraid, but also deeply annoyed. When I looked up, I couldn't help but scowl.

Mariana loomed over me wearing all black, her legs braced in a cocky stance, arms folded across her black breastplate, a half-snarl-half-smirk causing her scarred upper lip to curl. She tipped her head as she regarded me, her expression gradually morphing into amusement.

Apparently, my irritation was funny to her.

"I heard you were looking for me." Mariana spread her arms invitingly, Uriel's dagger still gripped in her hand. "How can I be of service?"

32

YOU ASKED FOR THIS

HATTIE

You asked for this, Hattie, I told myself, mustering up the courage to speak. It was hard to find courage when Mariana was staring down at me so menacingly. I reminded myself that she might've been threatening, but in all the instances we'd crossed paths, she hadn't actually *done* anything. It was a comfort to think that perhaps—as Faren had said—I wasn't worth the effort of harming.

Then again, I hadn't opened my mouth yet. If she decided I knew too much, perhaps she *would* find me worthy of silencing.

I decided to start with the most compelling reason for seeking her out—certainly she wouldn't immediately kill me if I intrigued her, right?

"I need a favor," I said.

"I'm not sure you have sufficient leverage to ask for favors, *Hattie*." With practiced flare, Mariana twisted her fingers, spinning Uriel's dagger across the back of her hand. "I'm doing *you* a favor just by letting you speak without this sad little knife lodged in your thigh."

I gulped.

She smiled, all teeth.

"I need blood," I managed.

She took a step toward me, lifting Uriel's dagger a little higher. "That can be arranged."

"Monster blood."

She paused, big brown eyes narrowing. If she were anyone else, those eyes would be considered doe-like and quite pretty, but staring into them from my vantage, I could see how haunted they were. How troubled. How angry.

Mariana brushed a lock of her hair over her shoulder and lowered herself into a crouch, elbows on knees, facing me at eye level. "You have my attention."

Great, because that's not terrifying.

I lifted my chin. "I need cursed blood for an experiment."

She let out a long sigh. "Right. You work with Phina." She seemed vaguely disappointed by that, as if it meant she couldn't rough me up.

Thank the Fates.

"Don't look so relieved, you're still approximately one revelation away from bleeding out in this alley."

I bit my lips together.

Her smirk returned, and for a moment she simply watched me squirm. Then she tossed Uriel's dagger up, caught it by the flat of the blade, and tucked it up her sleeve.

Mariana rose from her crouch and held out her hand. "Come on, then," she said, as if dragging me into an alley and threatening me was a major inconvenience, and me sitting on my ass in the filth was more of a tantrum than obedient fear.

I stood up on my own, brushing my grimy palms on my skirts. The skin was scraped up, but not bloody; my knees, however, stung underneath my dress, and I felt a trickle of blood slide down my shin.

Though Mariana was shorter than me, her watchful gaze and intimidating presence made her seem bigger. Her apparent prowess reminded me of a wildcat, her body in a state of constant, deadly grace, forever tense and ready to pounce, shred, kill.

"Speak," she demanded.

"You're...friends with Phina?" I ventured.

"I wouldn't go that far."

"But you know about her research."

"Her charge occasionally intersects with mine," Mariana said delicately, in the way most knights did when skirting around topics controlled by their Oaths.

"Curses and Hylder," I clarified.

Her expression remained unreadable, if slightly amused; she was probably unable to give any indication about those subjects.

"Blank Fates, too?"

Her lip twitched. "What do you know?"

For a moment, I considered asking her about Noble's Fate—but I didn't want to call attention to him if she didn't already know. *Especially* if her charge was to kill cursed beings. "I'm not answering that."

She took a step forward—feline, predatory.

It took every ounce of self-control not to cow to her threatening posture, to keep my feet rooted in place. "Would you say that Phina's research creates conflict within your Order?"

"Orders are never without conflict." Her tone was patronizing, but it was the non-answer that I found most frustrating. Clearly, Mariana's Oath prevented her from saying much of anything.

I folded my arms. "Can you get me the monster blood?"

"Those don't exist," she said coolly.

"Did your Oath make you say that?"

She hummed low in her throat.

"Will you help me or not?"

"What do *you* think?"

"I don't doubt your capabilities," I said, jerking my chin in the direction of her shortsword. "Only your willingness—and the limits of your Oath."

"You're clever," she said, as if that were unexpected.

I tried not to feel insulted.

Mariana rested a casual palm on the hilt of her weapon. "What's in it for me?"

"The pleasure of assisting an apprentice in need?"

She chuckled menacingly and took another step closer. "And what is it you actually need?"

I clenched my teeth, willing my jaw not to quiver. *This is it*, I told myself. *This is your chance to lay it all out.* I was walking the same path Viren had started down, and when I spoke next, I knew I was venturing past the point of no return.

"There's Gildium in monster blood," I began, holding Mariana's withering gaze. "What I can't figure out is *why*. How did it get there? And does the metal create the curse, or is it related in some other way?" I rolled my shoulders back, relieved that my Oath had not yet limited my questioning; Mariana no-doubt knew far more than I did and was therefore safe to speak with plainly. "I need to know the cause of curses so that I can undo them."

"You're bold, I'll give you that." Mariana's demeanor softened. "But you know I can't speak of—" She broke off and glanced down the length of the alley.

"Is this knowledge you possess?" I asked.

When she met my eyes again, she shook her head.

"Is it knowledge you're actively seeking?"

"I am not an alchemist; I am a sword."

For some reason, I didn't think she meant *no* by that statement.

"Are you working *with* Phina?

"I already said I wasn't an alchemist."

"That's not what I asked."

"All I know is that it burns," she said tightly.

I perked up. "The blood?"

She made a disgusted face, and I realized she must've tasted the warning of her Oath. Clearly, that nugget of information was all I was going to get on the topic.

"Has anyone ever requested blood from you or someone you know before?" I asked.

Mariana glanced down the alley again, lips pursed. When she met my eyes again, her expression was hard. Guarded. "I'm getting bored of this conversation. You don't want me to get bored."

"You haven't killed me yet, so it must be somewhat interesting," I joked, even though adrenaline hummed in my veins. "When you came to the Possum, you asked about blank Fates."

She perked up, interested again. "Do you know—"

I held up a hand to silence her. She broke off, but her expression was dark and hostile, and I lowered my hand with a cringe.

She didn't continue, though. She waited.

I balled my fists at my sides, trying to muster the bravery to ask the question I'd been building toward this whole time. "Do monsters have blank Fates?"

She snorted a laugh. "Fucking Fates, Hattie, you're in over your head."

Thinking only of Noble, I pressed, "Is that a yes?"

Her smile was small, mocking. "How do you imagine someone would investigate such a thing, *hmm?*"

I felt my cheeks heat, but I persisted. "I already know they can *warp* Fate, but—"

"We're done here."

I shifted uncomfortably. "Fine. But if I continue to research this topic, will the Valiant...come for me?"

She scoffed. "When I'm sent to kill, I *kill*."

Just as Faren had indicated. "So Viren...?"

"Don't insult me."

"The attacker *did* look like you."

"Brown hair? Short stature?" she mocked. "Rather common description, don't you think?"

"You sound defensive."

"I am *annoyed*."

That, I didn't doubt. "Do you have any idea who, then?"

Mariana stepped closer, until we were almost chest to chest. She procured Uriel's blade from her sleeve and angled the tip against my cheekbone. "No more questions." With a flick, she removed the blade from my cheek, gripped my belt, and slid the dagger back into its sheath.

Then she turned on a heel and started down the alley.

Fear held my lungs hostage; it took me a moment to recover my breath. With a gasping inhale, I called out, "Are you going to get me what I requested?"

Mariana didn't bother to reply as she strode down the length of the alley and disappeared around the corner—but something about the way she'd softened on the topic of researching monsters made me hopeful she'd deliver.

And even if she didn't, our conversation had been enlightening. In fact, considering I was still standing and did not have a knife in my thigh, this night had gone spectacularly well.

Sparing one last glance in the direction Mariana had gone, I turned the opposite way, coming out of the alley onto Rose Street.

Perfect, I thought. I was only a few blocks away from my next destination.

33

Disgrace of the Order of the Morta

Noble

R *AAAAA!*" Noble growled, a guttural sound that came from deep in his chest.

He was chained to a stone prison wall by his wrists and ankles, panting and snarling through his teeth. With his body strung up in an *X*, he couldn't move more than a few inches, but that didn't stop him from thrashing against his constraints. His skin was rubbed raw from the iron cuffs, black blood weeping down his forearms, pooling under his feet. But the monstrous instinct inside him was stronger than the stinging pain of open wounds.

It wanted freedom. It wanted flesh.

Adepts of the Order of the Arcane crowded in his cell, staring at him with various shades of cold curiosity and disgust. New faces had joined them: a knight of some sort, a squire of the Lord, and a man wearing the shimmery brown and gold robes of a ledgermaster. Noble hadn't seen them down here before. It was clear in all their expressions that he was not a man to them, but an experiment—an abomination.

Noble snarled, the sound rumbling through the dungeon. It was met by similar growls and cries in the depthless black beyond the bars of his cell. He hated the monster inside him, hated what it had done to his mind and body. The antlers threatening to push through the skin in his temples, the claws forming at his fingertips, the way his saliva tasted like acid—*venom*. When he took the Oath of the Order of the Morta, Noble had been promised inhuman strength; he'd thought that this opportunity would bring him glory.

Maybe even make his father proud.

Chained in this dungeon, Noble doubted he'd ever see his father again. It seemed that the only way he'd escape this miserable place—and the misery inside him—would be through death.

"As you can see," the lead adept said, turning toward the ledgermaster, "it cannot be contained. I am not proud to admit this failure, but there are plenty more experiments we can—"

"We should've terminated this Order and all its so-called knights a long time ago, what with the havoc it has already wreaked," the knight interrupted, resting his palm on the pommel of the sword at his hip.

It wasn't the threat of death but the label of *failure* that had Noble sagging in his chains.

"This is the cost of research," the lead adept said simply. As if toying with nature and killing innocent test subjects was just a means to the end they sought. "Do not let one malformed iteration turn us off the path to greatness."

"*One?*" the knight exclaimed. "The Western Wood is overrun because of this program."

"The Valiant have it well in hand," the lead adept said dismissively, waving a tattooed hand. "*When* we succeed in our venture, it will all prove worthwhile."

"This Order and its vile experiments have existed for generations," the knight argued. "Your promises are as empty as the adepts who came before you."

"Lord Haron won't be pleased to hear this," the squire put in. "Is there not a way to cure..." He gestured vaguely in Noble's direction, not quite looking directly at him.

The lead adept scoffed. "We were not charged with finding *cures*, Squire. Cures move us backward. My duty is to move humanity *forward*."

"You call this humanity?" the knight said, pointing at Noble. "This is a disgrace. *This* should never see the light of day."

Noble was beginning to shake all over, not from the humiliating conversation, but from the monster's urge inside him. He wanted to peel off his skin just to let it out. He tensed against his cuffs, squirming with the horrible discomfort of living in this body, aching to tear himself apart just to escape the agony.

They were right about him. He *was* an abomination.

"You could retire the Order," the ledgermaster suggested. "Start fresh."

"What of our test subjects?" one of the other researchers asked. She was short in stature, with dark curly hair. Though Noble knew none of the adepts' names—they were careful to remain anonymous down here—he knew this one to be compassionate. "Would it not be inhumane to abandon them?"

"Their very existence is inhumane," the knight said. "Terminating them would be a mercy. Hence the Lord's investment in the Valiant."

Still panting through his teeth, his nude body slicked with sweat, Noble agreed with the knight. Death would be a mercy.

"I know an Adept of the Order of Alchemy," the researcher insisted, "whose studies in water align with the gaps in our efforts. Perhaps she could—"

The lead adept snorted. "Alchemists no know nothing of Arcane magic."

"But maybe she could help them?" the kind researcher pressed, gesturing at Noble.

"Don't be soft-hearted," the lead researcher scolded.

"I'm not," she said. "Passing the burden to an alchemist would make this program look more successful on the whole. While she addresses previous experiments, we can forge ahead."

She was appealing to the lead adept's practical side, his grandiose ambition, and it was working. She spared a single glance in Noble's direction, a small smile forming.

All he could do was snarl back at her.

"What of him?" the knight asked. "Do you really think alchemical magic can undo an arcane mistake?"

"Retire his Order," the lead adept decided. "Let the alchemist work on our past subjects. In the meantime, we'll be free to break new ground."

Everyone looked to the squire for confirmation. He frowned for a moment, pondering the plan, then gave a single nod. "The Lord will be pleased to see the research continue under a new Order."

Without additional prompting, the ledgermaster hefted the book he carried, cradling it in one arm. The foiled title—*Ledger of the Order of the Morta*—caught the light of the lone torch as he cracked the book open. "This will take a quarter hour," he told the group.

"Let us all retire to more a civilized setting," the lead adept said, extending a palm toward the open door of Noble's cell.

Footsteps echoed on stone as everyone filed out, leaving only the ledgermaster and the kind researcher behind. More howls roused in the darkness as other subjects in other cells called out to the visitors.

"Will it hurt them?" the researcher asked the ledgermaster once the rest of the group had gone.

"It shouldn't," the ledgermaster replied, dragging a fingernail down the page of the magical book to which Noble's Oath was bound. When the ledgermaster spoke next, it was in the language of the arcane, a rhythmic chant that would unravel the magic that had woven the Order of the Morta together and tie off the threads that could not be severed completely.

Noble's head began to pound with the rhythm of those words, an odd tearing sensation pulling through his chest like an overextended muscle. It *did* hurt. It felt like the very fabric of his soul was being shredded apart. The monster inside him began to thrash.

"*RAAAAA!*" he screamed again, shaking in his constraints.

Other test subjects in the dungeon answered his call, pounding on their bars and shrieking. Their agonized cries were proof that the unbinding of the Order of the Morta pained them, too. As magic seared through Noble's veins, he wondered if his cursed brethren in the Western Wood felt this; he wondered what it would do to them.

As the ledgermaster worked, the remaining researcher watched on in silence, her brown eyes trained on Noble, wobbling with tears. Her pity made him feel small. It made him think about all the ways he'd let his loved ones down.

The ledgermaster's chant became faster, more forceful. Noble's heart slammed against his chest like a prisoner trying to break through a locked door. *Thump, thump, thump.* Noble screamed again as pain lanced through his temples.

Thump, thump, thump.

Thump, thump, thump.

Noble woke with a snarl.

His room at the Royal Inn of Fenrir was dark. The moon was high, shining blueish light through his window. Midnight. His naked body was slicked with sweat, heart frantic, breaths coming quick. It'd been a long time since his nightmares coalesced into true memory—in fact, he hadn't dreamt of the research dungeon since before he'd traveled to Waldron.

Forcing a long sigh through his lungs, Noble rubbed his forehead. In his sleep, he'd kicked off the blankets. The heat of his panic was beginning to cool. His heart rate was dropping back to normal. He was alright.

So why did he still hear thumping?

Thump, thump, thump.

Thump, thump, thump.

Noble sat up, frowning. The thumping wasn't his head or heart, it was coming from a fist on wood.

Someone was knocking on his door.

Over the past few months, Noble had encountered plenty of drunk travelers in the halls of the Royal Inn of Fenrir. Yelling, banging, cries of pleasure. It was hard enough getting a good night's rest in his own mind, let alone the annoyances of other guests.

This thumping was making his head ache anew. Irritation rose. Noble flung himself out of bed and stomped to the door. With a quick twist of the knob, he yanked the door open, ready to confront the person inconsiderately waking him in the middle of the night.

His anger dissolved at the sight of her.

Hattie, on his threshold, all flushed cheeks and messy hair.

She paused with her fist in the air, eyes widening. Her attention dropped to his groin, then darted quickly back up to his face, her flush deepening from mauve to crimson. She cleared her throat, her forehead creasing as if it took great effort not to look down again.

Caught up in his irritation—with his mind still hazy from troubled sleep—Noble had forgotten to cover himself before answering the door. Yet he couldn't bring himself to move, not when Hattie's flush was now creeping down her neck to color her chest. She stared up at him with those oceanic eyes, and Noble felt as if he were caught in a net as she slid her tongue along her bottom lip, then bit down with visible restraint.

She *knew* he was a monster, and still, she was here. Blushing.

His head couldn't make sense of it, but his heart and groin didn't care. Desire hit him with a force.

He smirked like he wasn't clay in her hands, hers to shape. "May I help you?"

His voice seemed to break the spell between them.

Hattie held out a hand, blocking her view of his cock. Her gaze flew to crown molding. "*Why* are you naked?" Her voice was shrill, agonized.

Noble chuckled. "You're cute when you're flustered."

"*Noble*," Hattie said to the ceiling.

"I sleep naked," he answered. "I was *asleep*. What are *you* doing here in the middle of the night?" He considered his own question, and concern swept through him. He gripped the doorjamb, knuckles paling. "What's wrong?"

Hattie's arm was still extended, shielding her from his body, her head turned away as if his nakedness would bring her peril. Which, come to think of it, if they gave in to their urges, it probably would. "I came to *talk*," she enunciated.

Of course, she had.

After the incident in the training yard earlier today, he'd skipped the lab and instead taken a walk to clear his head. Avoiding Hattie wasn't the most mature way to handle the situation, but the shock and hurt on her face had pained him—cut him to the bone. He'd wanted to give himself time to come up with a plan for how to circumvent the verbal limits of his Oath enough to at least offer her a *scrap* of honesty. A satisfactory answer. The problem was, there was nothing honest or satisfactory about the secrets of the Orders. And there was nothing he could *do*.

A part of him still wondered if the greatest mercy he could offer Hattie would be to disappear from her life. At least if he was far away, he couldn't disappoint her any more than he already had. More than anything, Noble wanted to minimize Hattie's hurt. He couldn't stand to see any more pain on her pretty face.

But she didn't look pained now. Her bun was coming undone, curls frizzing; her dress was filthy, palms scraped; she was still blushing furiously—but she looked *determined*. Fierce.

What had she done? Where had she been tonight? Why wasn't she afraid of him?

Noble opened the door wider and stepped aside, allowing Hattie entry into his room. She brushed by without looking at him, her attention flicking over the four-poster bed and the tangle of blankets on the floor.

"I take it you weren't sleeping peacefully," she said. "Maybe it's a good thing I woke you."

Noble closed the door with a soft *click* and turned the lock. "What did you do?" he asked, his voice rough with concern.

Hattie turned. "Pants first, then we talk."

34

NOT AFRAID

HATTIE

I stood at Noble's window with my back to him, listening to him dress.

My thoughts had been swirling on the way here, trying to make sense of what I'd learned over the past twelve hours, but the moment he opened his door—bare and obscenely, *unfairly* perfect—the chaos in my mind had ceased. It was hard to think about anything with Noble standing naked in front of me.

After about a minute of rustling fabric, I asked, "Are you decent yet?"

"No," Noble said, an edge of humor in his tone.

I turned around. He was wearing pants, but he was right, he wasn't decent. Not with his lean torso on display, broad shoulders tapering into a narrow waist that—I now knew—led to a lower half that the famed sculptors of Lothgaim would probably pay a fortune to study and commit to marble.

When we were adolescents, Noble and I had spent our summers swimming and lazing on the banks of the Wynhaim River, but most of my glimpses of his physique had been stolen and brief. Our bodies had changed since then. My curves had softened, while his lanky frame had filled out with hard muscle.

But we were still *us*.

As I regarded him in the dimly lit room, that was what struck me the most. My attraction to him wasn't simply about the endless smooth skin and brawn—it was the heart that beat inside his chest. Strong. Loyal.

Kind. He was always trying to do the right thing for others—even if it meant hurting himself.

The man before me didn't look like a monster; he just looked like *Noble*. Best friend. Forbidden love. *Home.*

He took a seat on the edge of a small writing desk opposite the bed. "You came to talk?" he prompted. With his hands flat on its worn surface, I noticed a bandage wrapped around his forearm. The white fabric was stained black. When Noble clocked my observation, his jaw ticked.

I cleared my throat, suddenly unprepared to discuss his condition. "Not yet."

When he met my eyes again, he wore a confident grin. "Too stunned by my beauty to speak?" he asked, bouncing his eyebrows. He always knew when I needed levity.

I chuckled halfheartedly. "Something like that."

"Why don't we talk about something easy, first?" he suggested. "How are your classes?"

I let out a long sigh. "Fascinating. Overwhelming. Sometimes I feel like the weight of all the new information is crushing me like a toppled bookcase, but in an exhilarating way."

"You always wanted to be an alchemist." He sounded happy for me, proud.

"I almost didn't apply," I admitted, "for fear it would draw unnecessary attention to myself. Risk being identified."

"Understandable. But you deserve to chase your dream. I'm glad you took the risk."

In spite of the tenuousness of Phina's research, I had to agree. "Me, too."

Noble pushed off the desk. "Tell me more."

So, I did. While Noble made himself busy lighting candles and building a fire in the hearth, I told him about my professors, my studies, the interesting concepts I'd been learning. As I did, I felt my shoulders relaxing, my nerves softening; it was like old times, when I used to ramble on and on about alchemy, with Noble listening contentedly.

But as I settled into the comforting topics, Noble's movements remained reserved, stiff. He knew why I was here. Once the fire was crackling merrily, he hung a kettle on a hook over the flame for tea. Then he faced me again, a good five feet separating us.

I trailed off, trying to spot a sign of wretchedness and seeing none. His hair was rumpled from tossing and turning. His green eyes were soft and searching. His evasive smirk was gone; in its place was a tilted, apologetic frown.

A heavy silence spread between us.

When I spoke again, my tone was light. I *needed* lightness if we were going to get through this conversation. "So, you're cursed. Were you *ever* going to tell me?"

He smiled sadly at my misplaced sass. "Oath."

I nodded, accepting that his deception hadn't been willful. But the fact that his Oath limited his ability to speak of his condition implied... "Your curse is a part of your former knighthood?"

He couldn't answer, of course, but when a tense crease bracketed his mouth, I knew I'd guessed right.

"Is it a Fenriran Order?" It *must've* been. "*Fates*, that means that the Lord of Fenrir..." I wiped a hand over my face, shook my head, not believing my own line of thinking but also seeing no other explanation. "The Lord of Fenrir *created* the curse." Or, rather, one of his ledgermasters had.

The crease beside Noble's mouth deepened.

"But *why*?"

"Power."

Out of all the Seven Territories of the Kingdom of Marona, Fenrir had always been the most disgruntled and resistant to unity. *A weapon of war*, Viren had guessed—and she'd been right. "He wants to create a weapon," I said, my voice barely a whisper. "To—*what*—oppose the king?"

Noble didn't answer.

"*Fuck*." I began to pace the rug in front of the hearth, feeling sick with dread.

If the Lord of Fenrir's adepts created the curse—only to find that they were unable to control the monsters—that meant they must've also created the Order of the Valiant to clean up the mess. No wonder there were assassins lurking around the Collegium, suspicion rising. If other territories confirmed that Lord Haron was responsible for monsters...a conflict would be inevitable.

I couldn't imagine what sort of magic had been used on the knights of Noble's former Order, but it must've been dark and twisted. All at once, I was absolutely *certain* that this wasn't just about Gildium in the blood. There had to be more to his affliction.

I halted and faced Noble again. "How long did you serve your Order?"

"Seven years."

I stifled a gasp. "Did you know what you were getting into?"

"No."

I rested a palm over my heart, as if to contain the thunderous pounding in my chest.

Noble took a step toward me—just one. "Hattie..." he began, and the shame in his tone—I wouldn't allow it.

"No apologizing."

"A thousand apologies still wouldn't make right the ways I've deceived you," Noble said. "You should be angry with me. Or fearful. Probably both."

"The primary thing I'm feeling toward you right now is concern."

"You shouldn't concern yourself with me."

I scoffed. "You sound like my aunt."

He cracked a true smile, but it was brief.

"How do you contain it?" I asked—but maybe I already knew.

Wordlessly, Noble went to the desk and opened the small drawer, retrieving an empty glass vial from inside. He held it out to me. Our fingers brushed as I took it from his grasp. Something low in my belly fluttered at the contact. I tried to ignore it as I sniffed the mouth of the bottle, then brought the glass rim to the tip of my tongue, tasting the residue of what it had once contained.

The flavor was unmistakable because it was mine: a Black Lace Hylder tincture. I'd tasted it on his tongue when we kissed in the gardens and had written it off as the scent of the nearby shrub confusing my senses; I hadn't *wanted* to taste it on him, hadn't wanted to face the possibility...

"That was you in the alley," I realized.

Noble's lips pressed into a tense line. "Angry with me yet?"

"No, although I'm a little angry with Phina for keeping so much hidden."

The kettle over the fire began to whistle, drawing our attention. Noble turned, removing it from the heat. For about sixty seconds, he busied himself with making our tea, and I was relieved to have a temporary respite from this conversation.

When Noble finished preparing our tea, he set my mug on the small desk, pulled out the single wooden chair, and gestured for me to sit. Settling into the seat, I cradled the mug in my hands and sagged with all the tension I'd been carrying.

"I know it's no excuse," Noble said, sitting on the edge of the bed, across from me, "but I wanted to tell you. I just—"

"Couldn't," I finished for him. "I know." I blew on my tea, took a sip, smiled at the comforting flavor. "Chamomile."

"It's your favorite," Noble said. "Or, at least, it was."

"Still is."

He nodded, as if he was committing that updated information to memory.

"If Hylder suppresses your...affliction," I began delicately, "then what's the purpose of Phina's research?"

"Hylder is not a long-term solution," Noble replied. "It barely contains—" He broke off, clenching his teeth—his Oath must've been limiting him. "The efficacy is worsening."

"Phina told me the Black Lace tincture is more potent."

"It is," Noble said, and he sounded almost pleased that I had been the one to discover the better varietal. "It's not as effective as your tincture from Waldron, though," he added.

"Any idea why?"

He shook his head. "It's half the reason Phina brought you in, but..."

"But my experiments have been inconclusive." I set my tea aside. "What happens when it stops working?"

"I turn."

...*into a monster* remained unsaid.

When I'd seen that hooded figure in the alley, the violent shaking and moaning—knights arguing and the urgency to provide Hylder—it had all seemed so *alarming*. But as I regarded Noble now, with the light of the candles splashing gold across his handsome, masculine features, I was not alarmed.

I felt protective—angry.

A cold, icy fury swept through me like a winter wind. I stood and began to pace again. "How did they do it?"

Noble's throat bobbed, drawing my attention to the thin line of his Oath tattoo that ringed his neck. "I don't know much, Hattie, but the little I do know, I am not permitted to say."

"How much does Phina know?"

Noble shrugged. "Probably more than I do, but not enough to undo it."

All the secrets really *did* get in the way of research—safety be damned.

I thought back to that night in the alley and who exactly was present. "The Order of the Mighty knows about you. As does the Order of the Valiant?"

"How do you—?"

"I spoke to Mariana."

Noble stood, tea sloshing out of his mug. "You *what*? When?"

I waved vaguely in the direction of the Ire. "Tonight. Just before I came here."

"Did she harm you?"

I rested my fists on my hips. "Do I look hurt?"

Taking the question seriously, he appraised me, his attention homing in on the dark splotches of blood on the front of my dress. "Your knees." He looked like he was moments away from making this all about my minor scrapes, so I held up a hand, trying to keep us on track. Trying to think.

In the alley, Faren had wanted to kill Noble for his affliction—but Mariana had stopped him. "Why did Mariana defend you that night? Isn't it her duty to kill cursed beings?"

"Only the ones who are—" He broke off, but I got his meaning.

"Does she already know about your blank Fate?"

A nod.

I thought back to the night Mariana had come to the Possum. *Don't trust anyone who doesn't show a future.* "Then why did Mariana warn Anya, Idris, and I about others with blank Fates?"

"She—?" Noble shook his head; he must not have known she visited. "I have no idea. She came to me in Waldron, too, asking about my research progress, but that was it."

"Could she have been warning us about you?" That had been my original hunch. "A scare-tactic to keep us from asking you questions?"

"If so, she really underestimated your curiosity." A pause. "She also could've been looking for information but didn't want to give it away."

That *did* seem more likely than her warning us simply out of the goodness of her heart.

"Do you know why she's helping Phina?"

"Do you think *anyone* knows why Mariana does what she does?"

He had a point.

"What does a blank Fate have to do with being cursed?" I asked.

"Altered blood means altered—" he broke off, choking on the warning of his Oath.

Altered blood. That explained why Anya and Idris had blank Fates but weren't cursed like Noble was; their dip in the Well of Fate must've altered their blood in another way.

Noble's scarred knuckles paled as he gripped his mug tighter. "Is this why you sought Mariana out? To ask her about me?"

I went to him, easing the mug out of his hand before he shattered it with sheer force. I set it on the desk next to mine, then faced him again. "She wasn't very helpful."

"Why didn't you come to me first?"

"I tried. You clearly weren't interested in talking, and I didn't want to force you," I said. "Besides, I had another request for her."

"Which was?"

"Monster blood."

"*Fuck*, Hattie. Why didn't you ask *me*?"

It *had* crossed my mind, but: "You aren't a test subject, Noble."

He stiffened. "Actually..."

Test subject. Fucking Fates. "They called you a knight, but they ran experiments on you? That's how they cursed you." My icy fury returned; with the hearth blazing nearby, heating the entire left half of my body, I felt like I was moments away from steaming.

What I knew of Order magic was basic: an Oath was like a magical rope that tethered the Oath-taker to the Ledger that tracked them; the Order of the Arcane braided the rope. "Obviously the Adepts of the

Order of the Arcane created your Order," I said, "so why did they task *Phina*—an alchemist—with finding a cure?"

"Containment, not cure," Noble amended.

Gildium might've turned blood black, but it also possessed strong containment properties. "You don't think a cure is possible?"

Noble didn't answer, and this time I couldn't tell if it was due to his Oath or a lack of hope.

"There are no Arcane apprentices or adepts in our study," I continued, fists clenching, "yet they're the ones who did this to you?"

Noble turned his face toward the fire, watching the flames.

"Unless..." I continued, inching toward him as I thought aloud. "Unless the Adepts of the Arcane couldn't figure out how to undo what they'd done."

Noble's fists tightened at his sides. "Your revelations are not going to distract me from the fact that you tracked down a vicious knight *on your own* to ask her for cursed blood," he said. "It's my turn to be angry."

I scoffed. "She's not that vicious," I said, "seeing as she let me live."

Noble blanched. "*Hattie*—"

"Have you and Phina studied your blood? Viren didn't give any indication."

"We have—extensively. Inconclusive."

I nodded. "Your blood might be black, but *you* are not a monster," I said. "Pure monster blood is the better place to continue our research."

"'Our research.'" He shook his head ruefully. "I shouldn't have let you get wrapped up in this mess." His chin dropped to his chest, wavy hair falling across his face.

At the sight of his regret, my concerns about our research, the conspiracies of the Orders, and even his monstrousness disappeared. Suddenly the only thing that mattered was that Noble was torn-up. Hurting not over his condition—but over its impact on *me*.

His selflessness astounded me.

I approached him slowly, halting with a foot of space between us. This close, I had to tilt my chin up to meet his gaze. Flickering firelight blazed across the right side of his face, igniting the green in his irises; the left side was shaded, his straight nose and angular cheekbones splashed with shadow. Half light, half darkness.

Even now, his soft lips were pressed tight with tension. How many times had I yearned to melt the sharpness of his expression with my touch? How many times had I stopped myself?

No more, I thought. With everything out in the open, there were no remaining secrets that could dissuade me. I knew all of who he was—the blessing of his being and the curse trapped within him—and I was done holding back.

I brushed my fingers across his forehead, raking the hair out of his face. He leaned into my touch, eyes falling closed as I slid my hand down the smooth skin of his neck, across the ridge of his collarbone. When I rested my palm over his heart, his returning gaze was heavy.

"What are you doing, Peach?" His voice was leather and steel—soft, but with a cautionary edge. The sound of my nickname in that deep tone made everything in me clench.

I rolled my eyes playfully, smoothing my hand indulgently across his pecs. They were so *firm*. "What does it look like I'm doing?" I asked innocently. "I'm comforting you." This close, I could smell his scent: soap and cedar and *him*.

He gripped my wrist, halting my hand's slow journey across his bare chest. "This doesn't feel like *just* comforting."

I stared into his eyes. "It's not."

He removed my hand from his skin, but it wasn't a rejection—it was disbelief. "Aren't you afraid of me?" he asked. "Repulsed? You don't even know why I'm like this. What it means."

"You don't fully understand it, either." I glanced at the faded Oath tattoo that banded the base of his throat. "And even if you did, you couldn't tell me."

He turned his face toward the hearth, giving me a clear view of his strained neck and clenched jaw.

"Noble," I said, prompting him to meet my eyes again. "I am not afraid. I am not repulsed. I don't have to know what it means because I know *you*. And you would never hurt me."

"I've hurt you plenty."

I rested my palm on his pec again. "Circumstances hurt me, not you."

His gaze dropped to my mouth, and his throat bobbed. "Hattie," he warned.

"I. Am. Not. Afraid," I stated. "Do you believe me?"

"I *want* to believe you."

"But you don't yet. Is this why you're still holding back?"

He laughed a little. "You're a force, you know that?"

I beamed. "I try." I slid my fingers back up into his hair, curling them at his nape, nails scratching. I felt his skin pebble with goosebumps beneath my fingertips.

One firm hand gripped my waist. "You know what I am and you still...want?"

"I still want," I confirmed. "I want and want and *want*."

A rough exhale gusted out of him. "There's still the matter of *your* identity."

My hand stilled in his hair. "My identity has stolen so many things from me," I said. "My home. My relationship with Raina. My autonomy. My dreams of becoming an alchemist. *You*." I pressed my lips together. "When I came to the Collegium, I told myself I would no longer let *who I am* steal all the light from my life. I am not letting it get between us—not anymore."

For a moment, he stared down at me; I expected him to pull away, to argue, to point out all the ways that a relationship between us could lead to our history being uncovered, and declare it too risky. Feeling as if I were standing atop Fate's Landing all over again, I braced for another rejection, but then—

"Come here," he rasped. The hand on my waist gripped harder, tugging me closer.

But when our lips were mere inches from touching, I drew back—just a little.

"What?" he asked, sounding amused now.

"I'm just surprised," I teased. "Seemed like you'd take more convincing."

The smirk returned, but it was genuine this time. "You've been wearing down my willpower for years. And besides, you've made it abundantly clear that you aren't going to let anything stand between us."

"You're right," I replied, lifting my chin. "I'm not."

"Good," he whispered, ghosting his lips across mine, "because I'm done trying to talk you out of this."

35

WANT AND WANT AND WANT

HATTIE

His first kiss was slow, but not chaste. It was a wet, drugging drag of soft lips and tongue. He tasted the same as he had in the gardens: sweet like Hylder and also complexly, indescribably, *deliciously* like himself.

His body was a wall of heat, arms crushing me against his rigid torso. I snaked my arms around him, scraping my nails across the hard planes of his muscular back until he groaned into my mouth. When I did it again, the groan turned into a growl.

"Too good," he murmured against my mouth.

I smoothed my palms against his sides, resisting the urge to dig in *more*—to scrape red trails into his skin and mark him as mine. Instead, I pressed my chest against his, rocking with each sucking kiss and stolen breath. My nipples ached to feel his skin, to have nothing between us.

As if sensing my urgency, Noble's hands went to the back of my dress. He tugged roughly at the laces that crisscrossed my spine, his movements practiced and quick. "Okay?" he asked as he unraveled the ties, loosening the dress's hold on me.

"Want and want and want," I murmured.

His chest jerked with a soft laugh, then he hooked his fingers under the lacing loops and tugged the back of my dress open. I wiggled my shoulders, shrugging out of the sleeves so that Noble could yank it down my hips. When the fabric caught on my necklace, I removed that, too. Stripped down to my chemise with my outer layers pooled at my feet, I felt lighter and slightly chilly, desperate for his heat.

Noble ran his palms over my bare arms and shoulders, smoothing out the goosebumps. He stared down at the low neckline of my chemise, the peaks of my breasts showing through the thin white cotton. Abruptly, he swiveled us, seating me on the writing desk. Then he bent, closing his mouth around one nipple through the fabric and biting until pleasure edged into pain. Stars twinkled across my vision, and I gripped the back of his head, holding him there.

Desire pooled in my stomach like warm honey, slick between my legs.

When he moved to the other nipple, the air cooled the wet circle he left behind. I tipped my head back, enjoying his slow worship of my chest. His fingers fisted in the fabric at my hips as he pressed kisses into the bare skin of my cleavage, my collarbone, the sensitive hollow of my neck. He was neither rushed nor hesitant; he exuded control as he cupped my breast with a firm hand and bit down.

The fact that *he* was doing this to me made my heart pound with wild angst. The sight and sensation of him touching me—I could barely comprehend it. *This is Noble*, my frazzled mind kept repeating. *Noble, Noble, Noble.* For so long, I had been denied; it was overwhelming to finally give myself over to the pent-up need.

He must've sensed the shift in my thoughts, my distractedness. "What's on your mind?" he asked.

"Us," I answered honestly.

He stood straight again, regarding me squarely. "It's a lot, isn't it?"

I nodded, grateful I didn't have to elaborate. "You seem a lot calmer than I am," I added on a laugh.

"I'm not." He cupped my face in his hands. "But we can go as quickly or as slowly as—"

"Want and want and want," I repeated.

His observant eyes zigzagged across my face, no doubt taking in the contradictions: the tension beside my eyes and the soft, eager parting of my tingling lips. I realized I was panting a little when his attention dropped to my chest again. He brought a hand to one of the wet spots on the front of my chemise and grazed it with his knuckle.

"I can't believe I get to do this," he murmured, staring at the tiny point of contact.

It felt like my fluttering heart was about to break out of my ribs and fly free. "I can't believe you're doing this," I said. "*Finally.*"

Noble's gaze shifted to my neck. He cradled my jaw—possessively firm but reverently gentle—and pressed his thumb into my pulse point. "Your heart is racing."

I flattened my hand on his chest and felt a rapid thudding. "So's yours."

"But you want my touch, don't you?" It wasn't a question so much as an observation. His eyes were tactile, sweeping over my flushed skin and tight nipples.

"Yes," I replied anyway.

"I can tell," he murmured.

Then he was trailing his fingertips into my hair. He found the pins that held my bun in place, pulled them loose, and let my curls unravel. All the while, he watched, observing my tresses. When my hair was loose and flowing down my back, he sank his fingers into it and gave it a sensuous tug, tilting my chin up to accept his kiss.

"I've always wanted to do that."

"Had I known, I would've worn my hair down more often."

"That's why I never told you," he said. "You're a tease."

He wasn't wrong.

With his fingers still tangled in my hair, Noble grazed my bottom lip with his teeth. I felt the scrape all the way down in my belly and moaned against his mouth.

"*Mhmm*," he mumbled, like he agreed with me.

Then he pulled back, taking me in, about to say more, but—

He noticed my scuffed knees again, the dried smudges of crimson on my white chemise.

Then a different expression passed over his hungry features, clouding his desire and cooling it like tempered steel. He took one of my hands, observing the scraped skin of my palm before planting a kiss in its center.

"Don't move," he commanded, leaving me seated on the desk as he went to the small wash basin in the corner.

"What are you doing?"

"I can't make love to you when you're bleeding."

His phrasing made my breath catch. "Oh."

Noble returned with a damp rag and a bowl of water and lowered to the floor in front of me, sinking back on his heels. Gently, he ran a calloused hand up my leg, dragging the hem of my chemise with it to reveal my scraped knees. His eyes narrowed when he saw the blood, but my mind couldn't have been farther from my injuries. Seeing the strength and power of him kneeling before me, *caring* for me like this...I was on fire.

He cleaned me up slowly, carefully dabbing at the scrapes, rinsing the rag every so often. The wounds were shallow, minor, already coagulated, but Noble was tense as he worked.

"I'm going to kill her for doing this to you," he grumbled.

"No, you're not," I said. "Besides, she just wanted to scare me."

He shot me a dark look. "Exactly. I won't allow it."

I giggled.

"What?"

"I know I shouldn't encourage it," I said, "but your overprotectiveness is sexy."

He set the rag and bowl aside. "Noted."

Craving his mouth on mine again, I threaded my fingers into his hair. "Are you going to stand back up?"

"I'd rather stay right here."

He slid his hand over my bunched chemise to trace his thumb over my hip bone. When he planted a kiss on its point, the brief pressure felt like a stone dropped into a lake—sensation rippled outward. He was so close yet so far from where I wanted him, the barrier of my remaining clothing far too constraining. My belly filled with liquid heat again, tensing with desire. It was a mere flutter, but even through the fabric of my chemise, he noticed the movement.

His eyes dragged up my body to my face. "Would you like that?" he asked.

"You don't have to stay on your knees," I replied thickly.

"You deserve nothing less than a man on his knees for you," he said. "But that's not what I asked."

"Yes," I answered breathlessly. "Yes, I would like that."

"*Fates*, I love how low your voice gets when you're turned on."

Something sweet and slippery spread through my core. I was so, *so* wet already.

He slid his palms up my calves, over the tender backs of my knees, pushing my hem higher up my thighs—but not high enough. Still seated on the edge of the desk, I swayed, lost to his touch.

"Pretty sure you're the tease," I muttered.

"Is that your way of asking for more?"

"Yes," I breathed, widening my legs.

He dragged a calloused hand up the inside of my thigh. His lips parted with a knowing, unfocused smile when he found my slickness—then his brow furrowed, serious, as he began to touch me. I held onto his shoulder, fingers digging into the muscle as he toyed with me, drawing a line up and down, circling the place I wanted him most, only to slide away, leaving me aching.

Good. It was so *good*, and we hadn't even made it to the bed yet.

"Noble."

"*Hm*?"

"Kiss me."

He met my eyes. "Where?"

You know where, my gaze said.

"Here?" One finger pushed into me.

I let out a strangled gasp.

But instead of giving me what I wanted—*more, more, more*—Noble removed his finger and stood. His hands found my waist and he guided me to my feet, too. Slowly, he slid the thin straps of my chemise off my shoulders. The seam of the neckline caught on the tips of my breasts, and Noble's pupils swallowed up his irises as he tugged the fabric down my waist to the floor, revealing me.

"Look at you," he murmured. "Even more perfect than I imagined." He bent, kissing me on the mouth, hard and slow, stubble scraping my cheeks. Then, he said, "Let's get you on your back."

Before I could react, he lifted me up and carried me to the bed, laying me down with my legs hanging off the side of the mattress.

Standing over me, he dragged his hand from my sternum to my belly, then slid his thumb across my clit. My body jerked, sensitive but craving.

"Please," I breathed.

"*Anything*," he answered.

Then he was on his knees on the floor again, hooking one of my legs over his shoulder as he brought his mouth to my center. He was gentle at first, testing my responses. He slid his tongue in the same manner as he had his thumb, gliding across my clit. A soft gasp escaped me, and he did it again.

"More," I begged.

He picked up his pace, licking and sucking in the same path. In all the many ways I'd fantasized about Noble, getting feasted upon like this had never crossed my mind. His kiss was controlled but messy, precise but insatiable. While one hand trailed up my ribs, cupping a breast, the other slid between my thighs. Two fingers pushed inside, stretching me, curling upward to stroke the sweetest inner spot.

My back arched.

"Yes," Noble encouraged.

He was circling my clit with his tongue, working me with his fingers. The muscles in my core clenched with a needy pulse. The leg that was hooked over his shoulder tensed, my heel digging into his back as I grew taut. I lifted my head, glancing down to see his mouth between my legs, eyes closed, forehead creased with devoted focus. The sight brought me even closer.

I let my head fall back again, losing myself to the pleasure. That warm honey sensation was filling me, filling me, filling me...

...and then it spilled over, flooding me with golden heat.

I threaded my fingers into his hair, holding on, gasping, and shaking with release. Noble continued on, slowing as I became more sensitive, only to speed up again, demanding more pleasure from me. I moaned, riding a wave of pure light, liquid gold, the orgasm gilding me from the inside out.

Noble slowed, then stopped altogether. With his face framed by my thighs, he smiled up at me with wicked triumph.

I unhooked my leg from his shoulder and sat up to taste myself on his lips.

"More?" he asked against my mouth.

I nodded enthusiastically.

Noble rose to his full height and got to work unbuttoning his trousers. "Do you...?"

"I take an anti-pregnancy tincture."

A quick nod as he stepped out of his clothes.

My mouth went dry.

I'd seen him naked earlier, but this was...different. He hadn't been hard when he opened his door. *Now...* I looked at the ceiling, feeling overwhelmed again. He was too perfect. *This* was too perfect. My mind couldn't keep up. My skin tingled all over, charged like a summer storm, lighting threatening the air.

A calloused hand on the side of my neck brought me back down to earth, to the moment. "Hey, Peach."

"Hi."

"Tell me why your forehead is creased."

A breathy laugh. "I'm a little overwhelmed." I'd wanted this for so long, but now that he was stripped down and standing in front of me, I felt everything all at once: a lifetime of affection marred by restraint, danger, distance.

He nodded like he understood. "Should I stop?"

I stared into his eyes, finding in them the same things I was feeling. The hardships that had led us here, but also affection, hope, relief, desire. And suddenly, I wasn't overwhelmed anymore.

My answer came out hoarse with urgency. "Don't stop."

36

PERFECT ALCHEMY

HATTIE

Noble guided me back against the pillows and climbed over me, settling between my thighs with a few inches of space between our bodies, his cock heavy on my hip. "Alright?"

Instead of answering, I trailed my fingers down his hard abdominals, following the *V* of muscle leading to his erection. I took him in my hand, stroking up and down. In response to my touch, Noble's forehead dropped to my shoulder, and he groaned into my neck. Just the feel of his soft skin and rigid desire had my body flooding with pleasure all over again.

No more waiting. I angled him toward my entrance, sliding him over my wetness.

With another groan, he calmly closed a fist around my wrist, halting my progress.

A disgruntled sound escaped me.

"Not yet," he said, a bit of mischief in his eyes.

Reluctantly, I released my hold. With one palm still planted on the mattress, caging me in, he reached down and took himself in his other hand. He brought the tip of his cock to my wetness again, sliding against me, but not *in*. Teasing my body with his.

The sensation was excruciating. Spectacular.

I wanted it to last forever. I wanted him to put me out of my misery.

I rolled my hips impatiently. "*Noble.*"

"Shhh." He dipped in, just an inch, then back out. "I feel like I've waited my whole life for this," he whispered. "Let me savor you."

He repeated the motion, in a little, then out again. Each time, he went a little deeper, stretching me with a delicious sting, but withholding what I wanted most: all of him.

I lifted my head, watching the almost joining of our bodies with rapt attention.

"It's so good," he rasped, sliding deeper, then back out.

I was beginning to sweat. So was he; it shimmered on the broad expanse of his chest, catching in the chiseled lines of muscle. The high points of his cheekbones took on a russet hue as he continued his exquisite torment.

"I want you," I pleaded. "*Please*, Noble."

Green eyes snapped to mine. "You know I can't hear you plead like that and not give it to you."

"Thank the Fates."

He jerked his hips forward, seating himself all the way in.

A blaze of sunlight streaked across my vision, and I moaned with relief. Noble silenced it with a messy kiss, thrusting into me with slow, torturous strokes. I scraped my nails over his back again, and he growled into the crook of my neck, picking up his pace. I hooked my legs around his waist, matching his rhythm.

We were raw, unbidden. *Free.*

With another scorching kiss, Noble put some space between our chests, dragging a palm across my breasts, my belly. His thumb found my clit again, spinning perfect alchemy.

"Yes," I mumbled, arching against the pillows.

"Yes," he agreed, snapping his hips in a steady rhythm.

All at once, my pleasure built and spilled—a vessel overflowing. I cried out, shaking, clenching, grinding against him.

"You're so fucking flushed." His voice was gravely. "Do you always blush when you come?"

Without answer, I reached for him, kissing him with tongue and bumping teeth. He lowered himself to his elbow, chest scraping against mine as he moved. His rhythm changed, becoming frantic and uneven. He cupped my cheek, smoothed my hair, his keen eyes going uncharacteristically distant. Knowing he was close, I scratched my nails over his shoulders and back.

A groan tore out of him as he found his own release, pulsing heat inside me.

Our movements slowed, then stilled. His body became heavy on top of mine, a delicious weight.

He dropped his forehead to my shoulder, breathing quickly, chest quaking with—

—was he laughing?

Happy. He was *happy*, I realized. So was I. Still clinging to him, I let out a bemused chuckle of my own.

"That was...intense," I said.

He kissed me on the lips in a series of slow, soft presses. "Unreal."

When he pulled back to look at me again, I saw familiar green eyes framed with smile lines. Wavy hair ruffled from my touch. Dark stubble that I now knew felt so good scraping my inner thighs. A chest I'd seen in stolen glances on a distant riverbank, now slicked with sweat from the exertion of loving me. A jaw I'd always wanted to trace—one I traced now, unhesitating.

In the sum of all these details, I saw Noble: childhood best friend, object of all my yearning. *Here*, nestled between my legs. Still inside me.

He was looking at me with the same sense of history I felt, the same passionate devotion.

"What are you thinking?" I asked.

His mouth twisted into a coy, boyish smile. "Let's clean you up."

He planted a kiss on my temple, then pulled away, leaving the bed. After quickly cleaning himself, he returned to me with a fresh damp rag and wiped away the remnants of our sex with devout attention.

Then he rearranged me under the covers, piling the pillows against the headboard, and guiding me to recline against the cushioning.

Once I was cozy, he left again to retrieve...something. With my limbs this relaxed, I wasn't really paying attention. I stared unfocused at the crossbeams of the ceiling. My body felt luxuriously *spent*. Like all the threads of my being had been unraveled and woven back together into something new.

I nestled deeper into the bed, pulling the quilt up over my chest.

Noble returned with a jar and two spoons and settled beside me against the headboard. I curled against his solid body, tucking myself under his arm and snuggling close. Everywhere we touched, I felt warm and tingly, my nerve endings still sparking with his contact. I drew tiny circles on his chest while he opened the jar, distracted by his nearness and the almost-painful come-down of so much pleasure.

I stilled when he handed me a spoon. "What's this?"

Noble held out the jar so I could see.

Inside were the glistening half-moons of sliced, spiced, sugared peaches. Nostalgia spread through my chest like dye into fabric, coloring me with shades of happy yellow and wistful periwinkle.

A surprised laugh burst out of me. "Where did you find these?"

A soft, encouraging smile. "Try one."

I sat up a little taller, using Noble's chest as a pillow, and dipped a spoon into the syrupy orange treat, scooping out a peach. It tasted like sunshine, warm summer evenings, a balmy breeze ruffling my hair.

After that first dessert in the kitchens, Raina, Noble, and I had been scolded for improper behavior. Two nights later, Noble had shown up below my bedroom window with a mischievous grin and more peaches; we hadn't told Raina, but Noble and I continued the tradition, ren-

dezvousing on countless nights over the years to eat peaches on my
balcony. I could almost hear our laughter now, the way the wisteria trellis
under my window groaned as he climbed up to deliver our dessert.

Now that I knew how he felt about me, I saw the memory—and my
nickname—from an entirely new angle: not the rule-breaking, lighthearted *fun* of youth, but an excuse for a young man to make a young
lady smile. To spend time together.

Back then, those shared, stolen moments were all either of us
had—but they were everything.

"I haven't eaten these in years," I said, already scooping out a second.

Noble tried his own, humming with satisfaction at the taste. A dribble
of juice slid down his chin, and I twisted around, stretching up to lick it
off.

He laughed, kissed me.

"You taste like peaches and sex," I commented. "I think it's my new
favorite flavor."

"You're my favorite flavor."

The image of his head between my legs sent a jolt of awareness through
me.

"You're blushing again...or maybe *still*."

"Just thinking about all the ways we should make up for lost time."

"I have a few ideas, myself."

I ate another peach, my tastebuds flooded with sweetness. "I *must*
know where you found these. I'm going to need a crate."

His chuckle rocked us both. "The night we kissed, I wandered the
streets a while afterward. I found them at a little shop just off the Walk,
on Petunia Street. Couldn't help myself. Since then, I think I've gone
through eight jars."

"Will you take me there?"

The question hung for a moment, then Noble answered softly.
"Sure."

We ate in silence for a while, our spoons clacking against the glass until the only remaining evidence of our treat were the pale orange streaks in the bottom of the jar. When we were done, Noble set the dishes aside and we resettled under the covers, him on his back, me draped halfway on top of him. I couldn't get enough of all that smooth warm skin against mine, no barriers.

"We should come up with new rules," Noble said after a while, "to keep your secret safe. Us, in public. It's still too risky."

He was stroking my hair, lulling me toward the edge of sleep. It was late. The sky outside his window was already purpling at the edges with the coming dawn.

"No rules right now," I murmured against his chest, smoothing my hand across the firm plane of his oblique. "Let me bask."

He brushed a curl from my forehead. "We should keep this a secret from the other researchers, too. I hate to sneak around, but—"

I lifted my head. "According to Oderin, sneaking around is exciting."

"You talked to him about me?"

"Not with names," I said. "He asked about my love life, and I told him in vague terms about wanting someone forbidden. He swooned over the notion."

"*Forbidden* does sound rather..." Noble hummed low.

I stretched against him, sleepiness warring with my lust. Staring up at him with my chin resting on his chest, I tried to maintain the thread of conversation. "I think Oderin figured it out when you showed up to sparring practice."

Noble seemed amused by that; he must not've been too concerned about Oderin making assumptions about us. I wondered how long Noble had been acquainted with the Farkept siblings. Knowing that Idris trusted them, too, was an added comfort.

"What else did he say?" Noble asked.

"He suggested I slip you a love potion. I told him that was unethical."

A laugh. "Wouldn't have worked, anyway."

I frowned. The only time a love potion didn't work was when there was no love there at all, or...when love was already present, making the potion moot.

I met his eyes. "It wouldn't?"

He gave me an easy smile. "Nope," he said, bending down to kiss me.

My forehead creased. "What kind of declaration is that?"

"You want a declaration?" He poked my nose playfully.

I assumed an air of annoyance. "Would be nice."

"What exactly would you like to hear?"

"Oh, I don't know." I pretended to consider the question. "Something about how I'm everything you always wanted."

"Did I not express that in the gardens?"

Just the thought of what he'd said in the gardens made my head swim. "I suppose," I said, still feigning discontentment. "But that was *so* long ago, and—"

Noble rolled me onto my back, swiveled to his side, and propped himself up on one elbow so that he hovered over me. He cupped my cheek in his big, capable hand, green eyes finding mine in the dark. "Hattie, you are everything I've ever wanted. You are the sun toward which everything inside me grows."

He was being playful, lighthearted, but to hear those words from him—words I'd dreamed about, yearned for, doubted I'd ever hear out loud—made my throat squeeze. I turned my head, eyes pricking with tears. A shaky sigh slipped out of me.

"Keep going," I managed.

He turned my face toward him, his expression sincere. "Hattie." A soft smile. "I love you. I have always loved you. I've loved you since the moment I saw you, and I have not stopped loving you since. I am so sorry I denied you that truth for so long."

A tear slid down my face, past my ear, and landed on the pillow. The next one was caught by Noble's thumb.

"Do you love me?" he prompted.

Emotion blurred my vision, but I still saw it: the uncertainty that carved a line between his brows, the fear that made his nostrils flare. *You still love me*, he'd taunted me in Waldron over a year ago, yet now he seemed...unsure?

"You know I do," I said.

A frown pulled at his lovely mouth. "Even now? Even considering...?" His gaze fell to his bandage.

Oh.

I swiveled, facing him in the dark. "Noble, I've loved you for fifteen years. I'm certainly not going to stop now."

The green in his eyes shimmered. "I can't guarantee that I won't turn someday—that I won't...*hurt* you."

"Noble..." I protested.

"I have dreams sometimes. *Nightmares*." He stared at the door across the room, his gaze distant. "You're in them, and I'm half-turned...stalking you."

I tried not to stiffen. "Me?"

"Always you."

"Do you think it's because you want me?"

He seemed surprised by that question. "I'm not sure."

"Do you harm me in your nightmares?"

"No," he said thickly. "I always stop myself and wake up before..." He swallowed. "The nightmares increase in frequency when I haven't taken Hylder."

I breathed deeply, nodded. "I'm still not afraid."

"Hattie, if I turn, I won't be able to control—"

"I'm not going to let that happen," I said firmly, touching his cheek.

"How?"

"I'm the Hylder Queen, remember?"

That made him laugh, though it was weak and doubtful.

"You, me, Phina, the research team—we're going to solve it," I said.

"How are you so sure?"

"Because I only just got you," I said, shimmying closer. "Not even the Fates could stand between us now."

37

NOT IF, BUT WHEN

NOBLE

Hattie fell asleep in Noble's arms, her body boneless and heavy. Noble held her close, filling his lungs with her rosemary and citrus scent, rocking them both with his deep breaths. Not wanting to miss a single moment, he willed himself to stay awake.

The room was dark, but with his heightened vision, he was able to count every freckle on her face: one hundred and thirty-seven. His favorite was the one on her upper lip, right in the center of the bow. He stroked her hair gently, eliciting a soft sigh from her parted mouth. With her body stretched against him, he felt like he was holding the entire universe in his arms.

Perfect.

She was perfect. This night was perfect.

I've loved you since we were children. I'm certainly not going to stop now.

He'd known that she cared about him but hearing her declaration—wholehearted and without hesitation—had been the single most winning moment of his life. A part of him had always feared that one day, Hattie would see all his flaws and change her mind about how she felt. For her to *still* want him now that she knew who and what he was—it was staggering.

He wanted to talk her out of it. That would be the right thing to do. But after tonight, he doubted he could summon the willpower—and he doubted she'd listen.

So, he simply held her, feeling the fear and gratitude and everything in between. He thought about all the ways he wanted to make love to her, but more importantly, the ways he wanted to *love* her: reading together, holding hands on long walks, telling her all the qualities he admired about her that he'd held back from saying aloud before. Her openness, her humor, her curiosity, her kindness. How brilliantly she shined.

It was in the listing of these qualities that he, too, fell into slumber.

He dreamt of Hattie in a garden: white dress, bare feet, gathering flowers in her arms. And he remained himself. A man with red blood pumping through his heart. A man without worry. A man in love.

He awoke again to gauzy morning light slanting through the window, the sounds of the city muffled. Hattie stirred, pressing closer. He planted a kiss on her temple, her nose, that freckle.

She barely opened her eyes before she was traveling down his body, whispering naughty things about wanting to taste him. With her magic, it was the most intimate thing imaginable for her to take him in her mouth, to lick and suck until he forgot his own name.

He was moments from coming when he stopped her, wanting to prolong it, to feel her cunt again. She turned onto her belly, hips up, and it was better than any dream or desperate fantasy when he entered her from behind, murmuring into her ear just how much he loved her while he moved inside her slowly and indulgently.

Afterward, they dozed with their bodies tangled together. Woke ravenous and sent for breakfast. Ate pastries in bed, reminiscing. About their summer afternoons in the secret grove by the river, and Raina's lilting laugh, the stunning Maronan winters, and climbing to the top of the willow tree in the courtyard at Castle Wynhaim.

And it was *good*.

So good he wondered if he was still dreaming.

So good it scared him.

He dreaded the day this dream turned into a nightmare. Because with his affliction, he feared it wasn't a matter of *if*, but *when*.

38

ARCANE INKLING

HATTIE

A ten-foot-tall *creature*—with stag horns, sharp wooden teeth, and a mane of ribbons—staggered past me on stilts. I shuffled out of the way, laughing as a splash of spiced milk sloshed out of my mug and onto the cobblestones.

Sani, Uriel, and I were strolling through Fenrir's Night Market, a summer occurrence that drew folks from all corners of the city to Rose Street. For the span of six blocks, vendors offered grilled meats, hand-pies, and baked goods; jewelers, leatherworkers, and potters hawked their wares from covered tents; and performers abounded: strange and colorful puppet-creatures roamed on stilts, musicians drummed and strummed, and dancers in scant costumes drew the attention of the market's patrons.

For the past fortnight, when I wasn't in class or Noble's bed, I'd spent all my waking hours with him at the Ocs, reading, researching, and running experiments. After our first night together, we'd reinstated our rules—at least, in the lab—agreeing to maintain as much chilly professionalism as possible while we worked. In an abundance of caution, we'd also decided not to tell Phina what I'd learned about Noble, nor about the blood I'd requested from Mariana (which I was beginning to doubt would ever be delivered).

Progress had been slow. Every time we tried binding Gildium with my Black Lace Hylder tincture, the magical herb repelled the metal with a range of results—bubbling, smoking, even explosive, depending on the alchemical knots we used. It didn't help that my emotions were scattered—at turns frustrated, discouraged, hopeful—no doubt tainting any alchemy I performed with overarching worry.

Attempting to solve a curse with limited understanding of the materials used to create it felt like trying to read a novel backward. The fact that Noble's Fate depended on our research made the lack of progress all the more frustrating. Tonight was *meant* to be a break from all that, but...

"—no territory *wants* to be under Marona's thumb," Sani said, sliding a charred piece of chicken off a skewer with her teeth.

"I disagree." Uriel waved her hand-pie back and forth dismissively, a few potatoes tumbling out of the pastry. "The realm has more resources when it's united."

My friends were in the middle of another debate about Oaths, research, and politics. Hearing them speculate about the Lord of Fenrir's machinations—when I knew the *truth*—had my shoulders creeping up toward my ears.

"I should rephrase," Sani said. "No *lord* wants to be under the *king's* thumb. The citizens of Fenrir are all at the mercy of Lord Haron's ego."

"On that, we agree," Uriel stated.

"Me, too," I said weakly.

I knew better than anyone the lengths King Braven went to maintain unity among the territories; I wondered if he was aware of the extent of Lord Haron's scheming. Lord Haron's intentions with Noble's former Order were twisted, but unsurprising. He had a reputation for being volatile, and Anya's tales from meeting him only confirmed his boredom, cruelty, and selfishness. Fenrir's resources were plentiful—talented artisans, esteemed Collegium, fertile land—so why *wouldn't* an egotistical lord wish to rule it all without King Braven's interference?

"Even so, we are in a time of political peace," Uriel countered. "The secrecy of current research programs hardly seems necessary when—"

"'Political peace,'" Sani interrupted, "or a pause to gather forces?"

"You and your warmongering," Uriel chided—but there was amusement in her tone.

Guilt and resolve warred in my chest, a clash of spears and shields that made my heart clamor. Regardless of my Oath, knowing that what they spoke of was *true*—yet being unable to confirm it—still felt like a betrayal. I took a long sip of my spiced milk—cinnamon, clove, and cardamom, exquisitely unique—hoping it might soothe the battle behind my ribs.

"Speaking of Oaths and politics," Sani continued, "Hattie, how is Viren?"

I swallowed, cleared my throat. "I visited with her yesterday. She's much improved."

Uriel frowned. "What does Viren's incident have to do with politics?"

Sani rolled her eyes, twirling her half-eaten skewer of chicken. "Do you really believe the attacker was a burglar?"

"Do not suggest a conspiracy."

The conversation momentarily paused as all three of us sidestepped another performer stalking past us on stilts, this one dressed like a giant humanoid tree.

"*Not* that I blame Viren for what happened," Sani said once the tree had passed, "but I did hear that she was conducting research beyond her station. Oaths and hierarchies exist for that express purpose, and—"

Sani and Uriel began their debate anew; meanwhile, a sigh deflated my posture.

My whole life had been dictated by that same logic—secrecy equals safety—but to what end? Forcibly marrying a vile man, lying to my best friend and chosen community, denying myself of love? Was all that truly worth this so-called minimization of risk? Would I ever truly be allowed to embrace all facets of myself in the light of day, without fear?

Eventually, Sani and Uriel's conversation pivoted to lighter topics—but as we wandered through the tents, shopping and chatting, the shadow it cast on my heart remained. Because while I wanted to live *free* of secrecy someday, I was right to be afraid.

We all were.

"Oooh!" Sani squealed, breaking through my miserable thoughts. "Look how pretty!"

She led us over to a weaver's stall, where colorful silk scarves were draped over lines strung up between the tent poles, billowing in the warm nighttime breeze. While Sani fawned over a particularly vibrant pattern, I held her half-eaten skewer and stood with Uriel by the mouth of the tent.

"Still pining after the poet in your writing class?" I asked, nudging Uriel with my elbow.

"As much as I find her...pleasant..." Uriel scrunched her nose, the metal hoop in her left nostril twinkling. "My heart belongs to my studies at this time."

I thought of the past two weeks studying alongside Noble. "Romance and dedication to our disciplines *can* coexist."

"*Can it*, now?" Sani teased, tucking her new purchase into her satchel and taking her skewer back from me. "Could *that* be the reason you've been sleeping elsewhere for the past two weeks?"

I pinched my lips together with my teeth, hoping the colored lanterns of the market obscured my blush. "I've been studying late."

"Studying *what*, exactly?" Sani prodded.

Noble's wicked mouth. Noble's toned stomach. The taste of his sweat as I—

Now I was *definitely* blushing.

Sani giggled and clapped her hands.

"I *believe* we were talking about Uriel's studies," I squeaked, shouldering my way into the center of Rose Street again to keep pace with the steady flow of the crowd. "Have you decided on a mentor?"

Uriel's face brightened. "I delivered a formal request for Professor Gour, the instructor of my Arcane Materials class, this morning."

"What's their area of expertise?" Sani asked.

"He studies water," Uriel said.

A flash of yellow flame gusted toward us as a fire dancer blew a mouthful of alcohol across a lit torch. I stopped short, watching the flames arc over the performer's head in a rainbow of fire.

But it wasn't the display that caught my attention—it was Uriel's statement.

Phina studied water, too. I thought back to my first day in her lab, all those jars of blue and green liquids on the shelf in the mezzanine...

I gripped Uriel's wrist, skirting the outside of a gathering circle of onlookers. Sani trailed after us as I dragged Uriel away from the cheers, gasps, and rhythmic drumming of the fire dancer's performance. Up ahead, along the market's fringes, there was a gap in the endless stalls where a cross-street bisected Rose.

I paused there and whirled on Uriel. "What about water, specifically?"

Uriel rubbed her wrist where I'd gripped it. "Why are you...intense?"

I opened my mouth, faltered.

Sani narrowed her eyes at me. "I don't think Hattie can say why."

"Water?" I prompted.

Uriel folded her arms. "Have you not taken *any* Arcane classes?"

"I'm studying to be an apothecary," I said impatiently. "You know I haven't."

Uriel lifted her gaze to the stars above. "Alchemists," she muttered. When she looked at me again, her expression was patient—if a little patronizing. "Alchemists work with the magical threads in materials, either weaving their magic *around* or *into* said material—yes?"

"*Yes*," I said impatiently.

"Arcane magic comes solely from within and requires a neutral material that magic is woven *onto*, like a scribe writing on paper." Uriel mimed holding a quill, scribbling words into the air. "There are three neutral materials onto which we traditionally weave: stone, wood, or skin."

Sani visibly shuddered. "*Skin?*"

"Like our Oaths?" I asked, lifting my wrist to show off my Allegiance tattoo.

"Oath tattoos—including the finger tattoos on adepts—are an example of arcane magic written onto paper, with a secondary manifestation on the skin," Uriel said. "Weaving arcane magic *directly* onto skin is a darker practice. Bloody. Involves carving arcane symbols into the skin with a knife. It is potent and not easy to undo. Rare and highly regulated."

My stomach twisted. I thought of all the tiny marks on Noble's hands—similar to the tattoos of adepts, but *scars* instead of *ink*—and wondered if they were not the marks of metalwork, but *magic*.

"Wood—including paper—is the most agreeable material," Uriel continued, "which is why we have the Oath Ledgers."

Feeling disturbed, I finished the rest of my spiced milk, clutching the small wooden mug as I wrapped my free arm around my torso in a makeshift hug. "What does any of that have to do with water?"

"Water is a common ingredient in balancing arcane magic."

I stiffened. "Truly?"

Uriel spread her palms as if to say, *Why would I lie?*

It was just that...*water* seemed far too simple.

"*Any* water?" I asked.

"I have not learned that yet, though I'm sure the source alters the result," Uriel said. "There is a reason the ancient city of Kelebraim-on-Gray was the birthplace of arcane magic."

Kelebraim-on-Gray was also where Gildium was discovered. Where the Mirrors were created. The site of numerous magical pools that bubbled up from the earth.

"For the sake of sourcing the water," Sani cut in, "I hope arcane adepts have other options than Kelebraim. The surrounding woods are treacherous—not to mention the geothermal pools themselves, which are famous for their strange and adverse effects. No one has gone to the ruins and returned in generations."

Anya and Idris had. *Barely*.

In fact...

My breath hitched.

Anya and Idris had bathed in the Well of Fate, and—in spite of Idris's knighthood and the Oath of Proving the Lord had forced Anya to take for her trial—they'd returned to Waldron free of all Oath-related obligation. Could it be that the magical water in the Well of Fate had altered the arcane magic in their Oaths?

"There *are* theories that the magical pools are why Fenrir is so fertile," Sani added, tapping her chin. "Most of Fenrir's fresh water—the River Gray, River Wend—originate in springs not far from the pools."

That *had* to be why Phina was studying water.

"Sani, how much do you know about the history of the Mirrors?" I asked.

"You're thinking of the Well of Fate," she said, easily catching on. "The water *is* magical; there's a long history of nobility who visited the pool to alter their foreseen futures. But I've never read anything that suggested the water undid arcane magic—otherwise, we would have recorded accounts of folks visiting the pool to nullify their Oaths."

"It *is* possible there are recorded accounts that you have not read," Uriel pointed out.

"Unlikely," Sani said—and I couldn't tell if she was joking or not.

I could see Sani's logic—but that left out what'd happened with Anya and Idris. Not to mention the fact that nobility visited the pool to *change* their Fates, not make their Fates blank. Perhaps something else had happened when Anya and Idris had visited the pool? Another unknown factor, like an added ingredient? Maybe Idris had been carrying my Hylder salve, and that had interacted with the water? *No*, that didn't seem right.

Maybe the Well of Fate simply possessed its own magical qualities, separate from its interaction with arcane magic.

"Water balancing arcane magic," I said, facing Uriel again. "Does it happen by touch, or is there a specific process?"

"I hope to learn that from Professor Gour."

"Right," I muttered. "And I suppose that after you join, an Oath will prevent you from telling me."

"Probably so," Sani cut in.

I pinched the bridge of my nose and shook my head. I was so close yet so far from any tangible answers. "Fucking *Fates*."

"Enjoyable as it is for you to ask cryptic questions," Uriel said, pointing a thumb toward the market, "there is a blade smith's stall that I would like to visit. Seeing as you *still* have not returned my dagger."

It was perhaps midnight, now, and the Night Market was packed with laughing, dancing, and meandering bodies. Knowing I wouldn't solve the curse tonight in the chaos of Rose Street, I smiled at Uriel. "Why don't I purchase you a new one?"

"Better yet," she said, leading Sani and I back into the throng, "return mine and purchase one for yourself."

It was after one in the morning when we returned to our dorm. While Sani and Uriel retired bed, I lingered in the common area of our quarters, my mind still *awake*. I felt akin to Anya's wolfhound Wicker when he caught onto the scent of a dropped morsel in the bar room, his nose skimming the ground as he sought it out, singular in his focus. Dissatisfied until he uncovered his prize.

Once I'd stripped off my dusty outer clothes and donned a chemise to sleep in, I cracked the window by the writing desk, set my new six-inch dagger on the worn surface, lit a small taper candle, and plopped down in the hard wooden chair. Inside the desk drawer were a quill, ink, and paper—I pulled out two sheets and started writing.

> *Dear Anya,*
>
> *I highly doubt you are willing to expand upon the experience that altered your Fate—especially not in writing—but I must ask anyhow. Something has come up in my research program here*

My Oath stung the back of my throat, warning me not to put too many details on paper.

> *that has me curious about the exact sequence of events and the materials involved. Did you or Idris use your magic when in contact with the water? Did either of you have any Hylder or Gildium on your person? If you can share any details, I'd be grateful.*
>
> *I wish I could say more about what's happening here. I promise I'm taking care.*
>
> *Hattie*

P.S. I had a rather fabulous, warmed milk concoction here in the city that I think our regulars at the Possum would love, perhaps when craving something a little more decadent than tea. I've included my best guess at the recipe on the second page.

P.P.S. Burn this missive upon receipt; we can't be too careful.

I folded the letter and recipe, dribbled the candle over the outer pleat, and pressed a heart-shaped seal into the warm wax. As I scrawled the Pretty Possum's address across the front, my heart squeezed. If I thought hard enough, I could smell the savory scent of the pub—ale, woodsmoke, and the sage-and-sausage aroma of supper—and hear the jovial music and laughter of the evening rush. I imagined our regulars seated at the bar: Martha's rosy cheeks and riveting stories, Vera's nose wrinkling with her usual wryness, Hugh's scandalized coughs and grunts as the women gossiped.

When I closed my eyes, I could *feel* Anya's presence beside me. Chopping potatoes and kneading dough in the kitchen after the regulars all went home for the night, our preparations for breakfast like a practiced dance. In the time Idris had been living at the Possum, he'd lent a hand in the kitchen also, following my instructions with precision. He'd even shared his maple syrup with me for new recipes.

I had planned to return to Waldron once I received my apothecary license, but now that I was entangled in Phina's program—with Noble's life hinging on our studies—I wasn't sure *when*. The thought made my stomach sink with worry, homesickness.

In all the years I'd lived in Waldron, I had never felt unwelcome. The town had embraced me from the moment I arrived, showing me unconditional kindness even before I'd earned my keep. And while I relished the life I'd created there, not a day went by in which I didn't feel guilty about deceiving folks who had shown me such openheartedness. I only hoped that *when* I returned—hopefully with Noble, *healed*—I could tell them all the truth, and they'd find it in their hearts to forgive me.

Once Anya's letter was sealed and dry, I tucked it into my satchel, so I'd remember to take it to the messenger service tomorrow. Then, with a sleepy sigh, I closed and locked the window, blew out the candle, and retired to bed.

Early the next morning, I stirred awake with a grumble. Having spent so many nights with Noble, I'd grown accustomed to being woken up by his lips on my neck, filthy whispers in my ear, his hot and solid body curling behind me.

Fates bless him for cultivating the habit of sleeping naked.

But this morning, the emptiness of my bed had me rising in spite of how few hours I'd slept. Out in the common area, I stoked the hearth and prepared a kettle for tea, while soft snores came from Sani and Uriel's shared bedroom. While the water boiled, I turned toward the window, stifling a yawn.

Our quarters overlooked a narrow strip of lawn that cut between our dormitory building and the twenty-foot wall that separated it from the neighboring street. We were on the third floor, which gave us an excellent view over the barrier. Golden sunlight splashed the faces of the buildings opposite us. I could hear pigeons cooing in the eaves of our roof.

Blinking the sleep from my eyes, my vision sank to the writing desk—and landed on a new object resting there.

A vial.

Paper had been curled around its exterior and bound with twine, leaving the corked top poking out. I snatched it quickly off the desk and slid off its paper shroud. I knew what it was—knew what to expect—but my breath still caught when I saw the viscous black liquid inside the clear glass.

My gaze flicked the window. It was closed and locked, just as I had left it. I swiveled toward the door, finding that still locked, too. Leaning over the desk, I observed the ledge outside our window, and—*there*: a smudge in the speckling of pigeon poop. The only evidence that Mariana had snuck into our dorm.

My lungs tensed, air wheezing out of me as I imagined Mariana creeping inside while we all slept. No doubt, the violation was meant to intimidate—remind me of her skill and mercy. But disturbed as I was, I was also impressed by her ability to deliver the monster blood *at all*; I tried not to think of what she'd had to do to retrieve it.

Without sparing the cursed liquid another glance, I slid the vial into my satchel—only to discover that my letter to Anya torn open, with only the recipe remaining.

Fists clenching, I returned to the desk, finding the paper Mariana had used to cover the vial. There was writing on it, her scrawl surprisingly delicate.

Letters like that will get you killed.

39

ALCHEMIZE

NOBLE

W hat if we tried water as a solvent instead of alcohol?" Hattie asked.

Noble glanced down at her, his thoughts fracturing. They were standing side-by-side at the table in his metal workshop, giving him the perfect view of her delicate profile and the necklace that disappeared down the front of her dress. A tiny purple bruise marked her neck from a biting kiss he'd given her that morning.

Distracting. She was altogether distracting.

"Noble?"

He cleared his throat. "Yes?"

Hattie cast a meaningful glance in the direction of the archway, through which they had a clear view of Phina and Kent discussing something with furrowed brows and questioning gestures.

"Court faces, remember?" Hattie whispered under her breath. "You can't look at me like that. It makes me want to..." She trailed off, raised her eyebrows.

"Go on."

She laughed throatily and poked his bicep. "Later."

She was right, of course, but *Fates*, it felt incredible to flirt with her for real, to talk to her for real, with no veiled meanings or withheld truths. Beyond what he could see, it was how he felt when he was with her: strong, determined, optimistic for the first time in ages.

And in spite of the harrowing purpose of their research, it had been thrilling to see Hattie work up close. She had a quick mind, easily pin-pointing details that Noble would've missed, asking all the right questions about Gildium, referring back to patterns she'd observed in his notes. Day after day, failed experiment after failed experiment, Noble was still amazed by her prowess with herbal alchemy.

Hattie rested her fists on her hips. "You didn't even hear my suggestion, did you?"

"I am capable of admiring you *and* hearing your words," Noble said. "You were talking about water."

Hattie appeared unimpressed but continued her line of thinking. "Ever since Uriel told me about water and Arcane magic last week, I've been racking my mind as to how to incorporate it into our research."

"Haven't you been adding water to your experiments all week?"

"Yes, but I realized this morning that I've never tried a Hylder tincture with water as the *base*—I've been using my usual alcohol-based tinctures and incorporating water as an addition." Her blue eyes seemed to sparkle with possibility. "But since Hylder and Gildium won't bind to each other, perhaps they could be bound to water directly, *then* mixed? Do you think Gildium could be alchemized that way?"

Noble thought back to Richold's teachings. "It could be even simpler than that," he replied. "I might be able to dissolve Gildium powder in water, no alchemy required."

"Can we try both?"

Noble smiled.

"What?"

"Nothing. It's just fun to share alchemy with you."

"It is."

"Fun sharing other things, too."

Her lips pressed into a curt little line as she stared up at him, clearly holding back from saying something flirtatious or familiar. Without another word, she turned, making to leave.

"Wait." Phina and Kent had disappeared from view, and Noble took the opportunity to catch Hattie's fingertips with his.

Her attention darted to the contact—then his face.

"How are your studies with the...?" He didn't bother finishing the question.

Noble had been holding a thin rod of Gildium when Hattie came into the lab a week ago with Mariana's *delivery*. He'd bent the rod in half when he heard about *how* it'd been delivered. While Mariana had served as an ally to Phina (and himself)—providing insight into the cursed creatures to propel their progress—her sneaking into Hattie's dorm was third on his list of reasons to dislike her.

First and second on his list were making Hattie's knees bleed and threatening her with a knife.

"I cross-referenced the sample with the notes you gave me on..." Hattie trailed off, eyes tracing his forearm where the scratch was now healed. *Your blood* was what she left unsaid. "So far, the only discernible difference is that the cells in the new sample seem more...jagged? Almost like they've morphed over time."

"That makes sense."

"Blood is mostly water," Hattie went on, that familiar vertical line of concentration forming on her brow. "But the water in both samples is different, somehow. It has its own open threads. I think that's why the arcane adepts thought Phina could contain the curse—bind Hylder to it, maybe?—but with Gildium and Hylder repelling each other, I just don't know. I've arranged a conversation with Viren to discuss it in more detail."

Noble nodded, feeling vaguely disappointed. The more they learned, the farther he felt from real answers. Meanwhile, the Black Lace Hylder

tinctures Hattie had made in the lab were waning in effectiveness—not
as much as the Common Hylder tinctures Phina had been giving him,
but still worse than what Hattie had brought with her from Waldron.
And Noble couldn't help with her experiments on the blood out of fear
that seeing it would trigger the monster inside him, as his own blood had
in the training ring. The culmination of all those dead ends was hard to
take.

Hattie squeezed his fingers. "We'll get there."

Noble grunted and let go of her hand.

From there, the day passed by in a blur that seemed both endless
and immediate. Noble prepared a few mixtures for Hattie in that time,
including Gildium alchemically bound to water, as well as tempered and
untempered Gildium dissolved in water.

It was dusk when Noble found Hattie in the library. She was standing
on her toes, struggling to reach a book on a particularly high shelf. Phina
and the other apprentices had all left for the day, and without the threat
of witnesses, Noble set his vials on the study table and walked up behind
Hattie, caging her against the bookcase. With his chest pressed into her
back, he tucked a kiss behind her ear, then slid the book she needed off
the high shelf.

With a soft laugh, she turned to face him. Their gazes locked as he
handed her the book.

"Thank you," she whispered.

"You're welcome."

She clutched the book against her chest. "I assume everyone else has
gone?"

"*Mhmm*," Noble hummed, cradling her jaw loosely in his palm.

Hattie pierced her smile with a canine. "Oh."

He wanted to suck that lower lip into his mouth, but instead he asked,
"Have you had a productive day, Hylder Queen?"

"Yes. You?"

He pointed a thumb behind him. "Brought you Gildium, as request-ed."

Her attention flicked to the vials on the table. "Excellent." Her eyes glazed, becoming unfocused past his shoulder.

"Hattie?" Noble murmured, amused.

Her blue stare slid back to his face. "Noble?"

"What are you thinking?"

"I'm not sure yet," she mused.

"A theory?"

"A...thought," she answered cryptically. "Are you finished for today?"

He nodded. "I was going to suggest you put on your blindfold and let me lead you back to the Royal Inn"—they hadn't entered or exited the lab together before, but the idea of Hattie blindfolded and entirely in his care made it seem worth the risk of being seen—"but I have a feeling you're not quite ready to leave."

Her cheeks puckered. "No, I'm sorry."

"Need help?"

Hattie slid her palm up Noble's chest, blazing a path of heat that made his pec flex.

"I need quiet, I think," she said regretfully. "How about I stay another hour, then bring my blindfold to the inn?"

Noble bent, brushing a few featherlight kisses across her soft lips. "Yes. Do that."

Hattie giggled against his mouth, deepening the kiss to slide her tongue behind his teeth for three, four, five delicious seconds. He was gripping her hips, about to push her firmly against the bookcase, when she pulled back and tsked.

"You're insatiable," she said, but based on her dilated pupils, so was she.

"Making up for lost time, remember?"

Hattie's lustful expression faltered. "I'm afraid we're losing time ahead of us, too."

"I thought you were staying late to follow a thought?"

"I am," Hattie said, sliding her fingertips up into his hair. She curled them against his nape, sending a shiver down his spine. "I just..." She rested her head back against the bookshelf behind her, staring up at him with love and pain and pleading. "I want to *savor* you."

He thought back to how he'd savored her on their first night together. "I *do* know," he purred.

A short, breathy chuckle. "I *mean*...I want to go swimming in the river together. Hold hands as we walk down the street. Be honest about who we *were* and who we are now, without fear, without secrecy, without..." The oceanic blue of her eyes took on a crystalline quality, shimmering like water. Her voice was throaty when she spoke again. "I don't want to feel like all our moments have to be stolen."

Noble swallowed thickly and brushed a few frizzy hairs out of her face. "Me, too."

Tears wobbled on her lower lashes. "Do you think we'll ever get that?"

Her sorrow made him want to rage against the Fates for doing this to her. Birthing her into a life of secrets and shame. Letting her fall in love with a man whose own existence was a series of failures and hurtful mistakes—a man who perhaps couldn't be cured of his wickedness. Who would one day *succumb* to it, leaving Hattie all alone.

Noble knew she loved him with eyes wide open—and he respected her choice, he *basked* in it—but he wouldn't have chosen any of this for Hattie. For her, he would've chosen sunshine, laughter, freedom, *joy*. The love of a normal man, not a monster.

Noble forced a deep breath. He couldn't change their past, but with their Fates not yet fixed until next year, he was determined to create the future she desired.

"I don't know what the Fates have in store for us," he answered honestly. "But I'm going to do everything in my power to give you the life you deserve."

Hattie nodded, shaking a tear loose. Noble bent to kiss it, and she laughed wetly, her voice throaty in his ear. "I know I seem weak right now, but—"

"I would never think of you as weak."

"—but I'm determined, too," she finished. Then, more firmly, "I'm determined."

40

IDENTITY

HATTIE

For the past hour and a half, a theory had been forming in my mind. Seated at the table in the library with a single candle flickering before me, I stared at the book Noble had retrieved for me—*Arcane Basics*—and reread the passage I'd found.

> *When balancing or neutralizing arcane symbols, it is recommended to boil or filter water to remove undesirable contaminates—otherwise effects can vary greatly. The source of water is also significant.*

I stared at the crude formulas I'd scrawled in my notebook:

> *Gildium + Arcane magic + water = cursed blood*
> *Gildium + Hylder + water? = containment or cure?*

Under that, I added a simple question and underlined it three times:

> *Water = source???*

Perhaps that's what I kept getting wrong—not the method of alchemy, but the source of the ingredients.

After Noble had left the lab this afternoon, I'd run a few preliminary experiments with the monster blood and various types of water-based tinctures. They had not gone well. Not only had the Hylder repelled the Gildium in the blood as usual, the mixture had bubbled like boiling honey, only to harden, candy-like and sticky. The stench had made me want to gag. Mariana had told me that monster blood burned when it touched the skin, but I hadn't expected it to stink like rotting flesh, either. Something about the water had only made the rancid liquid worse.

Discouraged, I'd returned to the library alcove to reread the notes I'd compiled. Thankfully, the report on Noble's blood hadn't indicated a scent or sting, which meant something about the jagged cells in the monster blood were responsible for its vileness. At least Noble's condition wasn't *that* bad. *Not yet.* But his blood still had Gildium in it, and that...that I couldn't seem to solve.

Just the thought of losing him to his affliction made me feel like I was suspended above a vast chasm, the fall inevitable.

Don't think like that, Hattie.

I refocused on my notebook.

The water I'd used this afternoon had been from a well—and I hadn't boiled it. Perhaps that was my problem? In the name of honest research, I probably ought to try water from as many sources as possible, but the idea was overwhelming.

I stared harder at my notebook, only for the words to blur. My mind felt like porridge. Perhaps I ought to return to this when I was fresh, maybe ask Uriel more vague questions. I was already late to meet Noble; he'd be worried if I delayed any longer.

Stifling a yawn, I snapped my notebook shut and tucked it into my satchel, along with *Arcane Basics*. After blowing out the candle, I pulled the cord for Willa.

Ten minutes later, she delivered me to the entryway of the Ocs. The heavy wooden doors were locked and secured with an iron bar at this hour, the foyer crowded with extra guards. I exited to a chorus of jangling keys and groaning hinges, offering Willa a wave as I slipped the blindfold into my pocket and stepped out onto the wide street.

Outside in the balmy dusk, I made my way south along the Walk, my footsteps echoing on the cobblestones. Fenrir was *finally* warming with the season, the temperature quite pleasant considering the hour. I breathed deeply, the air tasting of mineral grit and the meat-scented smoke pouring out of a nearby tavern's chimney.

The Walk was by no means empty at this time of night, but it wasn't crowded, either. People mostly congregated in pubs and restaurants, music and jovial chatter spilling outside whenever someone opened a door. Meanwhile, shopkeepers swept their stoops and locked up for the night, offering curt nods as I passed.

Fenrir was not an unfriendly city, but it was still a city. There was an air of selfishness and survival here that the small towns along the Wend did not possess. If I were Waldron right now, the curt nods of shopkeepers would be welcoming waves instead. And I wouldn't be listening to scraps of music and voices from the street—I'd be right in the thick of it, delivering pints to the delight of the Pretty Possum's patrons, holding ten conversations at once, flitting between tables to take orders and chit-chat, hearing the same story from every point of view. I'd be blushing at compliments about my concoctails, leaning in close to hear over the bard's stomping tune. I'd be making my neighbors feel full and happy and welcomed with my cheer.

I would also be fielding questions about my love life. Anya would be teasing me about the way I looked at Noble, and I'd be lying to her about just how deeply I cared for him. Martha and Hugh would be badgering me about when I wanted to "settle down with a nice man," and Vera would tsk and remind them that "settling" was the wrong word to use when trying to convince a lovely young woman to go on a date with someone's son, brother, or nephew. Anya would ask what I was looking for, exactly, and I'd wax poetic for their enjoyment and my own: a man who was kind, a man who was humorous, a man who loved reading, a man who took the time to learn what I liked, and who encouraged me to indulge my passions. Anya would beam at my display of romanticism, Martha would tell me a man like that didn't exist, Hugh would take offense at Martha's statement, Vera would chuckle at the ensuing argument, and all the while I'd be thinking about Noble—alone in Richold's guest house on the edge of town—and wondering if I'd ever find a man like him who actually loved me back.

I wanted to hug the version of myself who didn't know just how much Noble cared. I wanted to introduce her to the version of me now, who felt his affection in every lingering look, attentive touch, and easy laugh. And I wanted to rescue this current version of me—*of us*—from the prison of our hidden identities. I wanted to take us back to Waldron and introduce the entire town to the Hattie and Noble who were *free*.

As much as I loved studying alchemy at the Collegium, there was nothing as sweet as the sense of *belonging* I felt in Waldron. To have that along with an apothecary license and the man I loved by my side—cured, *healed*—would be a true Fortune.

As I hurried down a narrow side street that connected the Walk to Rose Street—a shortcut to the Royal Inn—I imagined bringing Noble fully into my life in Waldron. Picnics on Stone Hill. Swimming in the Wend. Purchasing peaches from southern merchants and experimenting in the kitchen to get the spices *just right*. The town had welcomed Idris—Anya's once-Fated killer—with open arms. Perhaps they would soften to Noble once they saw the side of him that wasn't quite so reclusive.

A smile broke across my face at the thought. There were still plenty of obstacles standing between us and that future, but perhaps my developing theory would get us closer to—

My vision went black as a burlap bag was shoved over my head. Arms closed around my torso, hauling me sideways. I let out a little yelp as my heels skidded across the cobblestones, the strap of my satchel digging into my neck.

"Very funny, Mariana," I called out, laughing nervously as she wrenched me backward. "Is this really necessary?"

Her arms tightened, forcing the air from my lungs. Instinctually, I twisted my body, struggling to break free. The movement sent both of us into the alley wall, my shoulder slamming into the stone, followed quickly by my temple, a sharp *smack* that made my head spin.

"I thought we were past roughhousing?" I complained with a pained grunt. "And the burlap sack is quite demeaning. Couldn't you have just snuck into my room again like a dignified—"

"Quiet, you."

My blood went cold.

That was *not* Mariana's voice.

The voice was female, but rough and raspy, her accent...*eastern.*

Animalistic panic charged through my bloodstream like a bull. I thrashed in my assailant's hold, jerking my shoulders and bucking my hips, but the arm banded across my middle held firm. With my arms pinned at my sides, the new dagger in my satchel was out of reach of my desperate fingertips. I shrieked, and a hand closed over my mouth, the burlap and palm muffling the sound.

"I am under no obligation to spare you," my assailant growled. "You will cooperate."

Fear stopped me short. My attacker took the opportunity to replace the hand on my mouth with a blade under my chin. She pressed hard, the sharp metal scraping against my throat.

"Give me a reason not to slit your throat, Alchemist."

Alchemist.

I began to tremble. "What do you want to know?"

The blade cut a superficial but punishing line of pain along the underside of my chin, a dribble of hot blood sliding down my chest. "You know what."

"I don't." I'd never heard my own voice sound so reedy and terrified. Tears slid down my cheeks, my mind going blank with fear that was at once fresh and familiar. "I don't know what you want."

The blade pressed harder, blood beading. "Guess."

With the way she'd snuck up on me, she could've killed me outright—which meant she must've thought I was valuable enough to interrogate before murdering.

"The c—," I tried. "The c—" I shivered, gagging on the vile taste that flooded my mouth when I attempted to say *curse*. I tried another angle. "Gildium," I blurted through another horrible tang of Oath magic. "Hylder."

"You're fucking useless."

I swallowed hard. I was getting close to breaking my Oath, but even if I did, what useful information did I truly have? All my experiments had failed, there was plenty I was not privy to, and if these assassins were *here*, they probably already knew about Lord Haron's plot.

I needed to get ahold of myself. To try another angle. To *think*.

Licking my lips, I stretched my magic past the rancidness of my Oath, tasting tears and burlap. The bag didn't carry the memory of potatoes, as Mariana's had—it tasted like turnips. *Maronan* turnips. I would know that flavor anywhere, because my aunt used to refuse to let me leave the dining hall until I finished eating mine; I'd slip them to the dogs under the table when she wasn't looking.

The blade bit deeper, blood trickling from my chin now. It would take barely a slight re-angling of its edge to drag across my jugular, to bleed me out in this random alley.

Memories of my last days in Marona rumbled through my body like thunder. A blade on my neck. A body holding me firm. Powerless. Fearful. *Vulnerable.* It was a twist of Fate that defied the peaceful end that the Mirror of Death had shown me, and I had been terrified knowing my future was not yet fixed.

Now, for the second time in my life, I felt the fragility of my existence hanging on by the temporary mercy of someone who obviously wanted me dead.

Except...

Well, except this time, my attacker's ire wasn't about who I *was*, but who I *wasn't*.

Fucking useless.

Pain lanced across jawbone, poked against my pulse-point. I moaned, tasting the damned turnips again, like a cruel joke from the past.

Useless.

What if I *wasn't* useless, though? What if who I *was*...was useful?

"Marona," I panted. "You're from Marona."

Her grip stilled but didn't soften. It was a clue; it was enough.

"How did—?"

"I hate turnips," I said, teeth chattering with adrenaline. "Marona might be famous for them, but I think they taste like ass."

A mirthless chuckle. "A distraction. Nice try."

The knife pressed harder; each beat of my heart throbbed against the metal point.

Footsteps were approaching, the strides jaunty. "Thought you'd be done by now, Corla," a gruff male voice called.

"She not done yet?" another asked.

"Last chance to plead your case, Alchemist," Corla purred in my ear. "Give me one good reason to keep you alive."

Don't fear your power, Hattie, Oderin had told me. He'd been talking about sword fighting, but the advice was sound.

My bloodline was powerful. Dangerous, but consequential.

It was the flip of a coin, a fifty-fifty chance. Either my identity would save me in this moment or end me.

I took the chance. "I'm Hattie Wynhaim," I said breathlessly.

"The fuck?" the man behind us said, footsteps stopping short.

"Not possible," the other murmured.

Corla ripped the turnip bag from my head, but nobody came within view. All I saw were the walls of stone narrowing toward Rose Street, the dirty cobblestones, and the diamond-like stars above. Past the curve of my cheek, I caught a glimpse of ruby red and steel—and beyond that, my captor's shoulder, her wavy brunette hair.

My shallow wounds throbbed with the pounding of my pulse; sticky heat soaked the neckline of my dress.

Corla's grip tightened around me, but her breaths came short and shocked in my ear. Someone entered my periphery, but I didn't dare move with the blade against my neck. All I could hope was that they took in my curly blonde hair, blue eyes, and dark freckles and decided to believe me. Because while it was unlikely for someone from Fenrir to recognize me outright, most Maronans knew the unmistakable features of my bloodline.

And they *all* knew my name.

"Your Grace..." one of Corla's co-conspirators said, while another muttered, "She's full of shit."

"I *am* Hattie Wynhaim," I said, more firmly this time.

And in spite of the icy fear of death in my veins, the words felt incredible to say out loud. Exhilarating as the surge of Wynhaim Falls; refreshing as the spray that hazed around Wynhaim Castle. Expansive as the sprawl of Wynhaim City, the capital of our kingdom. Empowering as the knowledge that even King Braven was a guest in the home of my ancestors, his *wife's* family. My aunt, Queen Yvira Wynhaim of Marona.

"I'm Hattie Fucking Wynhaim!" I screamed into the night.

My assailants began arguing, panicked by my claim. The blade against my throat dropped to the ground with a clatter. Then I was shoved—hard—against the stone wall, stars bursting across my vision. I fell, but the world went black before I landed.

41

Don't Threaten the Messenger

Noble

In anticipation of Hattie's visit, Noble had bought more peaches.

He set the jar on the nightstand on Hattie's side of his bed—the left side, which was closer to the hearth. His hair was still wet from bathing, dripping onto the shoulders of his loose shirt—a shirt he knew Hattie liked on him, a little tight across his chest. He'd refrained from shaving his face for her, too, knowing her appreciation for the roughness of his stubble on her inner thighs.

Some nights, when Hattie was asleep in Noble's arms, he imagined they were in Waldron. Instead of city noise floating in from the window—drunken singing, clanging bells, yipping dogs, near-constant shouting—he imagined more pastoral sounds. Bleating sheep. Wind sighing through maple leaves and pine boughs. The early morning songs of robins and the trickle of the Wend.

Hattie might've *escaped* to Waldron, but he could see why she'd stayed. The festivals, the tight-knit community, the care with which everyone looked after each other—Waldron's indulgence in simple pleasures was the exact opposite of her upbringing in Marona. As much as Noble had tried to refrain from being a part of the town while studying with

Richold, he'd been powerless to its charm and jealous of the folks who were blessed enough to call it *home*.

Noble had always wanted to settle down in a place like that. One that was joyful, welcoming, and peaceful. One that had Hattie in it.

Noble raked his hair out of his face and surveyed his room. He had hot water boiling in a kettle on the hook above the fire. A spread of meats, cheeses, and bread waited on the desk, along with two cups for tea. He'd already fluffed the pillows on the bed, lit a half dozen candles. He'd taken his time bathing and tidying and readying the space for her arrival—but she *still* hadn't come.

He sat on the edge of the bed and stared out the window, watching the pale wisps of clouds float across the deep indigo sky like fingers dragging across velvet, imagining all the ways he'd love her when she got here—trying his best not to worry. She'd stayed late at the lab—later than she promised—but when Hattie had an idea, she followed it relentlessly. Who was Noble to interrupt her brilliance? In their youth, he'd learned to respect her intellectual momentum. And seeing as she was studying *for him*, he ought to be grateful, not impatient.

Knuckles rapped softly on his door, and Noble sprung to his feet, relieved. He remembered their conversation about the blindfold, and an anticipatory smirk played across his lips as he opened the door, eager to draw her into his arms.

"Happy to see me?" Mariana asked, bumping Noble's shoulder with her own as she barged into his room.

Noble closed the door and folded his arms across his chest, resisting the urge to punch Mariana in the nose for the ways she'd roughed-up Hattie. His tone was a blade brandished for violence. "What are you doing here?"

She plucked a piece of cheese from the plate he'd prepared and popped it into her mouth. "I know you were anticipating a bubbly blonde, but don't look so disappointed to see me," Mariana said. "I'm a delicate flower, sensitive to scorn."

Noble scoffed—then stiffened. "Who do you think I was expecting?"

"Oh, please." Mariana went to the kettle next, lifting it off the fire and pouring the hot water into one of the two waiting cups of chamomile leaves. "You two have been fucking for weeks."

"I don't know who or what you're talking about."

Mariana leaned back against the edge of the desk, crossed one ankle over the other, and blew on her tea. "Sure, you don't."

She wore armor tonight: a black breastplate and matching vambraces over a black short-sleeved tunic. Black leather straps crisscrossed her hips and thighs over black trousers, with numerous blades sheathed in convenient locations. The silver pommel of her sword—the weapon imbued with magic by her Order—jutted awkwardly out from her hip.

"I'll admit, I was impressed by her ability to keep the bigger secret," Mariana continued in a taunting drawl. "The illegitimate daughter of the queen's dead sister? *That's* a reveal."

Noble was on Mariana in a heartbeat, the serrated bread knife under her jaw.

But she merely chuckled, glancing down at the dagger she had aimed at his oblique. She hadn't even spilled her tea; it was still cradled in her other hand, held aloft and out of the way.

"Use your head, Noble," Mariana tutted. "Don't threaten the messenger. I'm doing you a favor."

Noble lowered the bread knife an inch. "What's going on?"

Mariana made a show of sipping her tea, then set it aside. "Move."

His concern for Hattie barely outweighed his anger. He stepped back, allowing Mariana to push off the edge of the desk. She opened the drawer, pulled out one of his Hylder vials, and tossed it to him.

Questioningly, he held the glass aloft, the purple liquid sloshing.

"Just in case," Mariana said.

"In case of what?"

"Your princess has been taken."

Noble saw *white*, a flash of fear and rage so potent that he felt the abomination in his veins awaken. He took a single step toward Mariana, not knowing where to direct his fury. A growl rumbled up from his chest, rattled through his clenched teeth. His temples ached, his fingertips pulsed, and suddenly he wasn't sure he wanted to hold the monster back.

He wanted to set it loose on whoever the fuck had kidnapped Hattie and shred them to pieces.

"Drink your juice, Noble," Mariana said. "Your lady won't like you showing up turned."

White dress in a forest; the urge to shred flesh. His nightmares always ended with the desire to tear *her* apart, and Noble—Noble the man, the Noble who loved her—would *never* let that happen.

With shaking hands, he removed the vial's cork and drank.

"Breathe," Mariana said.

"Fuck you," Noble retorted, but he did. He breathed.

With the Hylder spreading through him, the monstrous rage subsided—leaving behind a wasteland of worry, all harsh wind and cold terror.

"Speak," Noble demanded.

Using her dagger like a fork, Mariana popped another piece of cheese into her mouth, chewing slowly. "I'll admit, it took me a while to put it all together."

Her calm demeanor was an insult. Unable to bear the sight of it any longer, Noble turned away from the Valiant Knight and began shoving clothes and random provisions into his pack—anything that might prove useful. The thought of Hattie in peril, harmed and frightened, *taken*...he sucked a deep breath in through his mouth and forced it out through his nose, trying not to lose control. "Speak faster," he ground out.

"I think I'm the only one who knows, so far," Mariana mused. "Even the Mighty Knights haven't solved the mystery, although"—a chuckle—"their swords tend to be sharper than their wits."

I love you, Hattie had whispered against his shoulder just this morning. And now...

Noble shoved his arms through the straps of his pack. "Mariana, I know we both work for Phina, but I am not above—"

"I wouldn't say I work *for* her," Mariana interrupted, sipping her tea. "My allegiance is to my *cause*. Phina and I have a mutual interest, is all."

Noble retrieved his dagger from under the bed and pointed it at her. "*Fates help you,* Mariana," he snarled, "if you do not tell me what happened to Hattie—"

"I'll explain on the way. You ready?" Mariana pinched out the lit candles, then dumped the kettle on the fire in the hearth, extinguishing it with a cloud of hissing steam.

"On the way?" Noble slid his dagger into the holster at his belt. "You're coming?"

Mariana retrieved the other two vials from the drawer and handed them to him. "Don't need you losing your shit before we get there."

42

TREACHEROUS NIGHT

HATTIE

I landed on damp grass and hard gnarled roots.

My head throbbed. My shoulder and hip were sorely bruised. My muscles ached with the long-held tension of being strapped to the back of a horse like a saddle bag and jostled for a night and a day of hard riding with few breaks. It was a relief to rest on solid ground, even if I did feel like the land was still juddering underneath me at a gallop.

With my hands bound behind my back and my ankles tied, all I could do was roll awkwardly onto my side, then shimmy into an upright position to lean against the trunk of a tree. The night was inky black, the forest at my back a depthless mass of shadow. We were on the upper edge of a shallow valley, a plain unfurling before me like a moonlit sheet, meadow grass rippling in the soft breeze.

I had awoken from the blow to my head already strapped to the horse, so it'd been difficult to get my bearings at first. As my captors rode through thin stands of trees and open meadows, I'd craned my neck for landmarks and watched the trajectory of the moon and sun. Had I been taken west, I would've spotted the Western Wood on the horizon by now; had my captors headed south, we would've encountered the Wend. But *no*. The Axe Mountains carved a rough line above the treetops to the left—which meant we were traveling east.

Toward Marona.

My captors bustled around, making camp with gruff efficiency. They wore black clothing and cruel scowls, all armed to the teeth. If it weren't for their fine saddles and healthy-looking horses, they could've been bandits, but Marona was known for its horsemanship—wild herds still roamed the territory's wide plains—and the quality of their mounts was another clue that they were of higher Maronan station.

As was the fact that I was still alive.

My parentage—specifically, the identity of my father—might've been a secret to the citizens of the kingdom, but *I* was not. For once, being Hattie Wynhaim—at least, the *Wynhaim* half—hadn't endangered me, but saved me.

For once, I felt lucky to be who I was.

I didn't trust my captors not to change their minds about killing me, though. Earlier, when I'd finally glimpsed my assailant from the alley—Corla—I'd immediately recognized her as the brunette who'd stabbed Viren. These were clearly the miscreants tasked to murder Collegium alchemists. While I had royal blood in my veins, I was also complicit in the research that my kidnappers were clearly sent to uncover and end.

But who'd sent them?

They wore no uniform, and I hadn't gotten a good enough look at any of their throats to notice if they bore Oath tattoos. I couldn't imagine King Braven—my kind-hearted uncle—sending spies out to murder academics in another territory. Then again, given what I'd learned about Lord Haron's schemes, perhaps drastic measures were justified (too bad they were targeting the researchers tasked to *fix* the problem, instead of the Arcane magicians who caused it). An association with the crown *would* explain why my captors hadn't killed me yet—but if they *weren't* associated with the crown, harboring the king's niece was excellent leverage for all manner of nefarious aims.

Essentially, I had only half an idea of what was going on—and I had *no* desire to stick around long enough to uncover the rest. I was still close enough to Fenrir City to return on foot if I could escape.

Slumping against the rough bark of my tree, I rolled my neck, wincing at the way the muscles twinged. My hair was a loose tangle, frizzy tendrils tickling my cheeks and nose; the pins that'd held my bun had fallen out long ago. The cuts under my jaw stretched uncomfortably when I yawned, scabs reopening for the thousandth time. My whole sternum was crusted in dried blood; the neckline of my blue dress was stained crimson. Miraculously, I still wore my vial necklace, though I wasn't sure what good the sentimental keepsake would do, aside from reminding me of how far away I was from everyone I loved.

I smelled like horse. I wanted a hot bath. I wanted a *bed*. I wanted Noble. I wanted...

Fates, I wanted to wallow in self-pity while someone else worried about getting me out of this quagmire. But no one was coming to save me. No one knew where I was. At some point, Noble would've realized something had happened to me, but there was no way he'd know where I'd gone. Exhaustion threatened to pull me under—to drown me in a deep and dazed slumber, far away from the terror—but I had to come up with a plan.

I closed my eyes, trying to calm my pounding head and heart—trying to *think*.

As girls, Raina and I had been prepared for situations like this. We'd learned how to hide in the secret passages at Castle Wynhaim, how to use daggers, how to fight back, how to survive in the woods for at least a day or two. I'd used that knowledge when I escaped Poe-on-Wend, but those original lessons had happened two decades ago, and my memory was hazy. And though Oderin had gotten me more comfortable with a sword in the past few weeks, I certainly couldn't take five trained killers all on my own.

I would have to bide my time. Be clever.

A boot kicked my shin. "Wake up, Princess."

I opened my eyes. A man stood before me. He was small-boned, athletic, with a patchy beard and scraggly, shoulder-length hair. Jord, I'd overhead someone call him.

"I'm not a princess," I muttered. "You're thinking of my cousin."

He lowered into a squat so he could regard me at eye-level. "I was going to offer you a bit of food, but since you seem rather ungrateful, I've changed my mind."

I pressed my lips together, trying to ignore the acid in my stomach as he sent his boot swiftly into the side of my hip. I took the hit, biting my tongue so I didn't cry out—but he seemed satisfied by my wince, sniggering before he wandered off.

My mouth was dry. My belly hollow and sour. In the past twenty-four hours, I'd been given only a heel of bread and a few scant sips of water. But I would not beg. I didn't want to give my captors the satisfaction.

The night carried on, bringing with it a damp chill. The wind picked up, whistling through the forest, tree branches creaking and squeaking as they bobbed and rubbed together. The ground was hard underneath my bottom, the tree unyielding at my back. My cheeks stung with cold, as did my bare shoulders. The dried blood in my bodice itched. But I remained silent, stoic, allowing the group of five to forget my presence as they supped.

They'd built a fire a short way down the hill from me, just past where the horses—tethered to tree trunks on long ropes—munched on grass along the outskirts of the camp. There were three men and two women. After hours on the road, I'd managed to learn their names and voices, and pick up on their familiar but acrimonious interpersonal dynamic.

I closed my eyes again, listening.

"—still not convinced it's her," Jord was saying.

"Fits the description," another man—Sid—pointed out.

"Plenty of blond-haired, blue-eyed, freckled bitches in Marona," Jord said. "Royal or not, though, I can't say I dislike the look of her."

Corla grunted. "Pig."

"I'd rather be a pig than an assassin who can't make a kill," Jord bit out. "First the blood alchemist, now her? Are you capable of finishing a job?"

"I'll gladly prove it to you." Boots on grass, a grunt, a scuffle.

I opened my eyes to see Corla's shape silhouetted against their camp-fire, the front of Jord's shirt twisted up in her fist.

"*Fates*, you two." That was Henren, their leader on the road. He was taller than the others, with light brown hair that fell past a small, pointed chin. "Save the violence for our orders, would you?"

Corla released Jord and sat back down on her log; the shadows the flames cast on her face made a caricature of her frown.

"And what *are* our orders, Henren?" Jord snarled, rubbing his sternum. "Because I thought they were to question and kill, not kidnap."

"Her claim changes things," Henren stated.

"Just because she knows the name doesn't mean she *is* her," Jord pointed out. "Seems a stretch that the niece of the king would be in Fenrir, working as an anonymous alchemist."

"Wasn't she married off to a nobleman in Fenrir?" Corla asked.

"About ten years ago," the other woman, Breen, answered. "Who knows where her Grace could've ended up? I remember the rumors. They wanted her to disappear."

Sid snorted. "Or she was just a royal girl who got married off. Rumors aren't facts."

"*Her* rumors were damning, though," Breen said. "Worth a cover-up."

"Which means they could've killed her—not sent her away," Jord argued.

Corla grunted again. "I don't care for royal politics."

"Funny, given your charge," Henren quipped.

"That's *why* I don't care for royal politics," Corla retorted.

Their voices continued, filling the night with chatter. Aside from their bedrolls, they'd left their packs and saddlebags heaped not far from where I sat, near where the horses were tethered. My satchel was among the gear, resting atop one of the saddles.

While the five of them continued to debate the truth of my claim, I inched along the ground on my knees, using the mass of bags and tack as cover. I prayed that none of them were sound magicians, able to hear the soft scuffing of my movements—and thankfully, no one seemed to hear me. When I reached my satchel, I twisted around, facing the forest; with my hands bound behind my back, I had to rely on touch to open it. The cloth was worn and supple, making no sound as I lifted the front flap and dug my fingers into the main pocket. My heart leapt when I felt the hard leather sheath of my new dagger.

I didn't waste any time—I withdrew the blade, swiveled it in my palm, and angled the point up between my wrists. I sawed at the rope, willing myself not to shake, whimper, or rush; I forced myself to take my time, knowing that slow and quiet was better than clumsy and noisy.

When finally, the rope slackened, I quickly turned my attention to my ankles, holding my breath as I sawed through the last of my bindings. My heart was a wild beast banging against the cage of my ribs, desperate for escape.

The moment my ropes were cut, I slung my satchel over my shoulder and *ran* for the forest.

Behind me, I heard Henren's raised voice, still arguing with his subordinates: "—doesn't matter now. She looks the part, and given her claim, the captain will want to see her for himself before—"

A branch snapped under my shoe, announcing my departure. Conversation morphed into shouts as my captors scrambled to find their weapons and begin their chase.

I pumped my arms, racing through the maze of trees. Moonlight shined through the leaves overhead, lighting my path with shifting silver beams. The underbrush was brittle, branches snapping and cracking, snatching at my dress. Roots and soft patches of decay made the ground treacherous, but I maintained my reckless pace, crashing through the gloomy darkness as fast as I could.

My chest ached with each breath, my pulse throbbed in my temples, but I pressed on, knowing I had to ignore the discomfort if I wanted to escape.

The deeper I ventured, the denser the forest grew. Scraggly bushes and gnarled tree trunks hunched over me like huge, ancient beasts, curious about my frantic presence. The terrain was changing, too, mounds of half-rotted logs and large stones creating new obstacles. But my pursuers were quicker than I'd hoped, running just as carelessly as I was over the ankle-breaking ground.

I needed to find cover.

I needed to lose them.

Fates, I needed to catch my breath.

Cresting a gentle hillock, I spotted a huge boulder halfway down the opposite slope. It was at least twelve feet high, tucked within a stand of pines, and covered in shaggy moss and vegetation. I could climb it and hide above my pursuers' sightline until they passed, but—*no*, that was too risky. If they spotted me, they could encircle my perch, and I'd be trapped. Best to use it as cover, instead, and hope the sudden silence would cause them to lose track of my direction. Then I could press on at a more sustainable pace.

My shoes sank into loamy soil and soft decay as I ran downhill toward the boulder. When I reached it, I circled around the back, skidding to a halt. I placed my palm on the cool stone, lungs burning from the exertion, muscles quivering from fear and exhaustion.

But the forest did not quiet when my movements did. The snapping and cracking continued, as if I were still clambering through the under-brush. At first, I assumed it was the raucous pursuit of my captors—but the sound was closer than their shouts. And it was coming from the opposite direction, deeper in, northward—not just the snaps of twigs underfoot, but a terrible *grinding*, with sharper cracks like breaking bones.

I turned toward the sound, peering into the woods.

A shadow lurked.

It was at least the height of a man, with hind legs that bent backward at the joints. When it passed into a patch of moonlight about sixty feet away—emitting that horrible *splitting* noise—I saw claw-tipped arms. Red glowing eyes. A crown of black antlers. Its body was mangled, skin stretched in some places and nonexistent in others, with white ribs poking through tendons and sinew, and a fringe of pointed appendages lining the sides of its torso. Black veins spider-webbed across gray slabs of bare muscle.

I'd never seen anything like it. Or maybe...maybe I had.

It was a creature of *nightmares*. An abomination.

And it was coming straight for me.

43

FEARS

NOBLE

The night was too peaceful for the tempest raging in Noble's heart.

While starlight twinkled above, he was filled with wind and rain, a thunderous fury streaked with bright, brilliant fear. Yet he sat tall and stoic atop the horse Mariana had secured for him in Fenrir, keeping the storm contained, even as it threatened to tear his inner world apart.

Mariana had kept her word. As they rode out of Fenrir City, she'd explained what happened to Hattie. How Mariana had been leaving Fenrir's Ire and heard Hattie screaming her own name—her *real* name. How Mariana ran toward the shouting and saw that Hattie's assailants matched the descriptions from previous incidents. How she'd watched them carry Hattie away, Mariana opting to notify Noble instead of pursuing them on her own ("Not because I couldn't take them," Mariana had said, but she hadn't bothered to explain her true reasoning).

That had been twenty-four hours ago.

Twenty-two hours ago, they'd found the tracks of Hattie's captors on the outskirts of the city, heading east.

Eight hours ago, while resting their horses, Noble had spotted a shiny, metallic flash in the grass: one of the pins Hattie used for her hair. He'd had to take another dose of Hylder to maintain control of the monster inside him, even though a part of him wanted to let it rampage. Hunt down Hattie's captors and tear their limbs off one by one.

Now, the eastern flats of Fenrir unraveled before them like a pale ribbon, framed by the forested foothills of the Axe Mountains to the north and the jagged treetops of the Great Forest to the south. Stars twinkled, unobscured by clouds. An owl hooted, answered by the call of another.

Noble's horse—a bay mare with a quick walk—snatched at the feathery tips of the tall grass stalks, surprisingly energetic considering their almost nonstop pace. To Noble's left, Mariana whistled a jaunty tune that made him want to wring her neck. The calmness of evening and his company was not a comfort, but an insult.

How could the moon shine so brightly when Hattie was in danger?

How could the Fates continue to unspool their cosmic yarn when Noble's entire future was at stake?

In truth, Noble never had much faith in Fate; his had changed too much over the years.

Because the Mirrors of Fate belonged to Fenrir—relics of the merging of Fenrir Territory with the Kingdom of Marona some seven centuries ago—the Mirrors only toured beyond the limits of their home territory once every seven years. However, they were brought to the king and queen anytime, upon request, which gave those in the royals' inner circle the chance to look upon their Fates with more frequency than the rest of the Seven Territories.

The first time Noble had looked into the Mirrors of Fortune and Death, he'd seen the willow tree in the courtyard at Castle Wynhaim as his Fortune and the steel of a sword entering his chest as his Death. His father called it an honorable Fate—a sign he'd die serving as a knight ("For the king, no doubt," Kalden had added proudly, clapping Noble—barely thirteen at the time—on the back).

But Noble's Fate differed each time the Mirrors visited Marona. His death changed from battle scenes to old age and back again, never quite the same. Meanwhile, his Fortune had shifted from the willow to the riverbank where he and Hattie picnicked to the curve of her freckled cheek. He'd liked that last one. But that, too, had disappeared. After he joined the Order of the Morta, his Mirror visions had gone entirely blank.

Empty.

When Noble had first run into Hattie in Waldron, he'd wondered if his Fortune had changed again. He'd attended the Mirror Festival among Hattie's friends and neighbors, justifying the risk of folks witnessing his strange Fate with his hope that he'd see *something*. Yet it had remained blank—proof of his enduring wickedness. And while few folks in Waldron seemed curious about the reclusive metalworker's future—especially in the chaos of the celebration and then Anya's shocking Fate—he'd been ashamed to learn that *Hattie* had still witnessed his vacant future.

He'd thought the blankness was *because* of his monstrousness. After all, no cursed beings had a Fate—and, after fully turning, a monster's presence could warp the Fates of other beings, too. It'd been a comfort to hear the whispers in Waldron about Anya and Idris's blank futures—proof that perhaps it wasn't just curses that made the Fates uncertain about a person's outcomes. It'd given Noble hope that there was still time—before he turned thirty and his Fate became fixed—for him to find his way back to that sweet vision of Fortune.

Of Hattie.

Would Noble *ever* feel like that future wasn't slipping through his fingers?

They were twenty the year the Mirror of Fortune had shown Hattie as Noble's greatest Fortune. It'd been three years since Hattie confessed her love for him on Fate's Landing. Three years of enduring the wretched temptation of her and fearing all the ways he might ruin her life if he gave into their desires. But that year, he'd wondered. Hoped. Questioned if somehow the societal rules keeping them apart could be overcome.

Then, a different sort of Fateful day came.

Noble had been sparring with Brendan in the training yard at Castle Wynhaim—and losing, as usual. Their session had ended prematurely when a shove of Brendan's shield had dislocated Noble's middle finger; he'd gone to the barracks to see if one of the off-duty, medically trained castle guards could reset it before it got too swollen. With his finger swaddled in a makeshift splint, Noble had cut through the stables on his way back to his family's small cottage in the eastern ward.

The castle grounds were abustle with newcomers that day, as the Lord of Lothgaim and his son, Archer, Heir of Lothgaim, were visiting. Raina had been engaged to Archer since she was fourteen, their ceremony set for the day she turned thirty, as was custom among nobility (when it came to political marriages, no one wanted any surprises, so arranged marriages were not sealed until both parties' Fates were fixed). Raina claimed to have hated Archer since the moment she met him a couple years prior, which meant that Noble hated him, too, no explanation needed.

So, when Noble happened upon a pair of Lothgaimian footmen gossiping about their heir as they unloaded trunks from a carriage just outside the barn, Noble had stopped. Ducked into the small storage room at the end of the long corridor of horse stalls. Crouched behind a stack of grain bags. Listened as their voices carried just outside the double doors.

"—haps he's such a prick because he grew up with an absent mother," said the first footman flippantly—no doubt speaking of Archer. "Selfish of her to live in the country castle, away from her own son, just because of his father's dalliances."

The second man laughed, the sound gruff and raspy from years of pipe smoking. "Can't say I blame the woman, when her husband probably has bastards in every territory."

"You're such a fucking romantic."

"I believe in the sanctity of marriage, is all," the older footman said.

A trunk landed on the ground with a heavy thud.

"Even a sexless, political one?" the younger man argued. "All nobility fuck outside their vows. Keeps things interesting when they get bored staring out across their estates and ordering folks like us around. You'd do it, too."

"Not to my dear Mabel."

"You would if you were married to the Lady of Lothgaim, though. She's a cold bitch."

A snort. "That she is."

"Explains the Lord's roaming, then," the younger footman said. "Especially up this way. You ever seen portraits of the queen's sister?"

"He *didn't.*"

"Twenty-one years ago."

"Said *who?*"

"Mr. Pim," the younger footman replied. "You don't get a more trustworthy source than the Lord's long-suffering butler."

"He truly told you the Lord of Lothgaim bedded Queen Yvira's *sister?*"

"The late, lovely Lady Odella," the younger footman said, adding a respectful, "*Fates bless her in rest.*"

The wagon squeaked, and another trunk thumped on the ground.

"You know...she had an illegitimate daughter," the older footman mused. "Grew up alongside Princess Raina. You don't think...?"

"Wouldn't surprise me in the least."

"Would surprise the royals, though." A pause, a grunt, another thud. "The girl's older than Archer. She would have lawful claim over Lothgaim."

A harsh laugh. "Fuck, I didn't think of that. What a mess that would be. Would ruin the whole marriage agreement."

"Start a war, maybe," the older footman added.

"You think?"

"If Archer marries the princess, it's an amicable union that maintains peace between Marona and one of its most valuable territories. He, elder; she, higher-ranking. Balanced power." The older footman loosed a raspy chortle. "But the daughter of Queen Yvira's sister? Older than Archer *and* with royal blood? She outranks both of them; she could usurp."

"Lothgaimians wouldn't take kindly to a Maronan assuming power like that."

"*No one* would, but she'd have rightful claim. It would be against Arcane Law *and* tradition to deny her rule—or seat anyone else in her place."

Noble's pulse quickened, his injured finger throbbing painfully with each beat.

His father spoke often about court politics, but Noble never paid much attention—it all seemed so tedious. But the idea of Hattie having rightful claim to an entire *territory* according to the Arcane Law—the law that magically bound the entire kingdom—with consequences of the magnitude these footmen discussed...he didn't know what to make of it, aside from a numb sort of shock.

"Marona doesn't need another problem," the older footman went on. "To keep the peace, Archer and Raina are the smart choice—for all parties. For the realm."

Silence spread between them—not even the sound of them unloading.

Finally, the younger footman whistled a long sigh. "Good thing it's just conjecture."

"Fates help us if Mr. Pim is right."

Noble peeked out from behind the bags of grain, catching a glimpse of the green uniforms of Lothgaim. For a moment, he simply watched the footmen from his hidden vantage, not truly hearing anything more of what they said. He felt as if he'd been pushed off Fate's Landing, his thoughts tumbling in an endless pummel of water; a loud whooshing filled his ears.

Then he was walking out of the storage room and back down the long corridor of the stables, moving swiftly away from the troubling gossip. There was a chance they were wrong—but knowing how quickly Hattie's family always changed the subject whenever she asked about the identity of her absent father, he didn't think they were.

Hattie deserved to know what he'd overheard.

Noble didn't consider the repercussions, didn't entirely *realize* what he was doing until he was inside the keep, breezing past the guards stationed outside the residence, hurrying through the massive foyer toward the curved staircase that led to Hattie's room.

It was the sight of Queen Yvira herself that startled him out of his trance.

She was wearing a burgundy gown, the bodice embroidered with carnelian beads. The colors brought out the richness in her brown freckles and emphasized the flush in her pale cheeks. He saw Hattie's resemblance reflected in her aunt every time he looked upon the queen. Except where Hattie's hair was golden, Yvira's had more of a strawberry quality; the color made her look delicate, almost naive, but Noble knew the queen was just as fierce as her forebears who'd founded Marona and conquered the continent.

King Braven might've married into the family to become the headpiece of the kingdom, but Queen Yvira Wynhaim was the true ruler. As cunning as she was beloved by her people.

"Noble, what happened to your hand?" Queen Yvira asked, her velvety tone tinged with concern.

She had never been anything but kind to Noble, but in her presence, he was painfully aware of his rank relative to hers. Therefore, he was powerless to the pressure of her mere presence, his panic rising out of his throat before he had a chance to think.

"Is Hattie's father the Lord of Lothgaim?" he blurted, voice echoing through the foyer. "Is she his true heir?"

Someone at Noble's back let out a choked cough; he glanced over his shoulder to see a pair of maids scurrying away. When he turned back to the queen, awaiting her answer, her eyes were wide with shock, cheeks flushed with sunset pink.

She reached out, snatching his good arm. "Where did you hear such a thing?"

From there, the afternoon unfurled like a river's current, sweeping him away.

Queen Yvira ushered Noble up the stairs opposite those that led to Hattie's room, urging him into King Braven's private study. There, the explanation burst out of him, beginning an uncontrollable cascade of events steered by the king and queen's swift and merciless mitigation of what was, in fact, the truth.

A truth that—until that day—only they had known.

In the following months, the royals did all they could to avoid the terrible unrest that Hattie's claim could cause, squashing all hints in an effort to keep the marriage agreement between Archer and Raina intact. They refrained from informing the Lord of Lothgaim of the result of his long-ago dalliance with Odella. The Lothgaimian footmen were found—and then they disappeared. Maids and guards were questioned—a few, he heard, were paid off.

Hattie was kept in the dark; Noble was forbidden from visiting her.

Then a Maronan soldier—one of the few entrusted with the containment of the secret—broke into the keep and tried to murder Hattie in an act of misguided loyalty toward Raina. After that, the king and queen rushed an engagement between Hattie and the nephew of one of the king's advisors, a mayor in an insignificant town in southern Fenrir. Her dowry was enough that her new husband did not question her lineage, nor the reason the marriage was so rushed. And by taking the surname of a lesser-titled man in a different territory—officially recorded by Fenrir's Census Ledger instead of Marona's—Hattie Wynhaim's true identity was erased.

On the eve of Hattie's departure, Noble snuck onto her balcony one last time. To tell her the truth. To confess that it was his fault. To admit that he loved her, too. But before he could express that last part, Loreena was knocking on her door, and he was climbing back down her trellis with the image of her tear-stricken face seared into his mind like a brand. Then he was hiding behind the willow, watching the nondescript carriage steal Hattie into the night. Steal his heart from his chest. Never to return.

That night, Noble had thought he lost Hattie forever. Now that she was in his life again, he refused to give up on that long-ago glimpse of precious Fortune.

"Is the Hylder still working?"

Noble glanced sidelong as his travel companion. Mariana had her horse's reins looped around the horn of her saddle and was using both hands to carve into an apple with her dagger. She slid a thin slice into her mouth and crunched down, waiting for his answer.

Generally speaking, Noble didn't dislike Mariana. Over the past two years, they'd formed a cool but amiable rapport. She'd advocated for him more than once, and her clandestine contributions to Phina's research had been invaluable. But he was not privy to her motivations, and therefore, he didn't fully trust her. Knowing she'd harmed Hattie—*for no fucking reason*—had greatly soured his opinion.

"Yes, the Hylder is still working," Noble grumbled, returning his gaze to the open land ahead of them. No matter how hard he strained his nocturnal eyes, he'd yet to spot evidence of a camp. "Why do you ask?"

"You look murderous."

"I am."

Mariana let out a little snort of amusement. "Are you about to tell me that I should be scared? Watch my back around you?"

"Are you *capable* of fear?" Noble joked, fully expecting her to deny any and all weakness in that quippy, dismissive way of hers.

But she surprised him. "Of course, I am."

"I would've thought you abandoned fear a long time ago," he said, "what with your charge."

She leaned forward, offering the rest of her apple to her horse. The charcoal-colored gelding kept walking, but turned his neck, taking the treat gently. Mariana patted his neck, then sat tall again. "I don't fear what most people fear," she said. "Pain, Fate, death. Those are inevitable and therefore not worth my concern."

He decided to play along. "Then what *do* you fear?"

"Swans."

Noble snorted. "You fight abominations, and yet you're afraid of pretty white birds?"

"I got bit by one as a child."

Noble shook his head, bemused by her sense of humor. He'd thought he had Mariana pinned, but perhaps there was more to her than her prickly countenance. "Swans," he accepted. "Is that it?"

Mariana rubbed her forehead with the back of her wrist, staring out over the moonlit plains. "Swans, and captivity."

Noble considered that. He didn't know much about her past, but he knew some things. That she was a thief. That she was tried for her crimes and forced into an Oath at a cruelly young age. That she fought monsters as punishment. And that her sentence was for life.

"Why are you helping me?"

"What? Do I not seem like the helpful type?"

Noble scoffed.

The moonlight made her tawny skin appear pallid, the night carving deep shadows under her angular cheekbones. Her doe-eyes reflected a depthless sorrow, a vacancy that Noble knew all too well. As he waited for her to answer his question for real, the pale scar that bisected her upper lip stretched with her smirk...then softened.

Mariana broke eye contact and patted her horse's neck again. "I know what it's like to lose someone you care about," she said finally. "The powerlessness and regret. I figured if I could help prevent..."

Noble offered a quiet nod. Her sentiments were strangely tender. Who would've thought she was capable?

"Mariana," Noble teased, "are you a romantic?"

She pinned him with a dark look, but this time, he knew it was an act. "Also, if you turn, someone needs to be around to run you through."

"Comforting," Noble remarked—even though she was right. "Thank you," he added.

Her shrug was forcedly casual. "Beats spending time with my fellow knights."

Noble thought about all the things he feared: failure, the wickedness inside him, the possibility of never seeing Hattie again. In the darkest moments of his knighthood, Noble had wondered if the world would be better off without him—if he should take his Fate into his own hands. But he wanted more than an ending. He wanted a beginning, and everything in between.

"Your fear," he said. "How do you face it day in and day out?"

"I do what I can do avoid lakes and rivers."

"I'm serious."

"So am I." He thought she might leave their conversation there, but then her rich brown eyes found his and held. "I face it just as you said: day in and day out. Bit by bit." She swung her gaze ahead of them again, then up to the infinite stars above. "There's no other option, as far as I can tell. Besides death."

"You don't fear death, though," Noble pointed out.

"No," Mariana said, "but that doesn't mean I don't want to *live*."

Noble hummed in acknowledgement, finding that he agreed with her. Wholeheartedly.

"What?" Mariana prompted.

"Nothing," Noble said. "I just hate how much we have in common."

44

KNIGHTS

HATTIE

Tears blurred my vision as the abomination crept closer, its red eyes fixated on me. I swallowed a horrified cry, shaking with true terror; my limbs were weak and wobbly, as if my joints weren't my own. An animal part of my brain became certain that this was *it*, this was the end. I would die in this unknown forest, far away from everyone I loved, and no one would know what happened to me.

I would die anonymously before I got to *live* as my authentic self.

No.

Absolutely not. I would not allow it. I'd faced my fears before. I could do this. I *had* to do this. *Think, Hattie, think.*

With my captors approaching from behind and the creature stalking me from straight ahead, I had nowhere to go. Clearly, I couldn't hide or outrun what had already caught up to me—but perhaps higher ground was a good idea, after all? All I had to do was get myself out of reach of the abomination long enough for it to forget me and set its terrifying sights on my pursuers—then, in the chaos, I could escape.

I scrambled against the boulder, searching for a leg up. The face of it was steep, the moss slippery. Bracing against a nearby tree trunk, I finally found purchase, clambering between tree and stone. Small branches caught at my clothes, my hair, but it wasn't long before I hoisted myself up.

Among the ferns and lichen that crowned the boulder, I had a vantage of the surrounding forest: five kidnappers to the south, abomination to the north, a racket of sound all around. For a few moments, I caught my breath in the relative safety of my perch. Any second now, the creature would change course toward the others...

Except...as it neared, I realized I'd underestimated its height. When it wasn't hunched, it stood *well over* the height of a man. Ten feet, at least. Which meant that when it reached the boulder and stretched up on its hind legs, it was almost eye-level with me.

A cold panic clutched my throat, choking me.

The creature had a human-like face, gaunt and skinless, with gray tissue and bone showing. Veins lined the sides of its neck muscles, pulsing with black. Gnarled antlers twisted out of its skull, branching at deformed angles. When it opened its mouth, a black tongue wriggled like a leech behind pointed teeth. A guttural hiss emanated from its throat, gusting rancid breath across my face. The cloying, rotten-carcass scent was so viscerally awful that I could *taste* it; I gagged with nausea and terror.

This must've been what had infected the diseased bobcat I'd seen back at the Possum.

This was what had bitten Idris the night he first came to Waldron, what he and Anya had faced in the Western Wood.

This was what Mariana fought for her Order—and had to kill to deliver to me the black blood.

This was the curse I'd been trying to undo.

This was what Noble would become if—

Don't go there, Hattie.

It was so *close*, and I didn't even have a weapon. I'd grabbed my satchel but had dropped my dagger in the grass as soon as I'd cut myself free. Could such a simple mistake seal my Fate?

"*Nooo*," I whimpered, kicking my feet as I crab-walked backward through the tangle of ferns and moss atop the boulder. "*No, no, no.*"

Shouts pierced the night at my back, yet the abomination was singular in its focus. It raised a bony hand, the tendons stretching as it flexed its claw-tipped fingers. It snarled again, snapping its teeth, tongue lolling out hungrily. Then it struck, snatching at my legs. I *shrieked*, my scream shredding my throat as the creature caught the side of my shoe, slicing through the leather—but thankfully not my skin.

I kicked out with my other foot, clipping it in the jaw. The creature wailed, angered, but its second strike was interrupted by a commotion to the south: my pursuers arriving on the scene.

"*MORTA!!!*" someone screamed.

Fates, did these Maronans *recognize* the monster? How far east had the cursed things spread?

The abomination—the Morta—was not deterred by the arrival of my pursuers, nor the ringing of their steel as they brandished their weapons. I had no time to wonder what would compel them to *fight* the creature instead of running in the opposite direction, leaving me to die in its clutches, because—

Claws scraped against stone, emitting a metallic sound as the creature climbed up the boulder. Black saliva dripped from its maw and *sizzled* on the vegetation. *It burns*, Mariana had said, and I was going to take her word for it. I scrambled backward, feet kicking and slipping on the damp moss.

The Morta *lunged*, teeth snapping a hair's breadth from my face. A hoarse, high-pitched squeal tore out of me as I threw my hand out, bracing a palm on the creature's disgustingly slick face. Its breath reeked of venom and rot, a sour and sickening stench that stung the back of my throat. I shoved against its jagged cheekbone, but the abomination was strong. It leaned tauntingly into my hand, dribbling caustic drool onto my dress. I dug my nails into its cheek, pressing my thumb into the outer corner of one red eye. It pushed harder against my hand, snarling and biting the air, forcing me to inch backward on my bum, until—

The boulder was no longer underneath me, the Morta shrinking from view. I was tumbling backward, *falling*, the world flipping upside-down.

I landed hard on my left forearm—a sharp crack of bone with an even sharper burst of pain. White-hot shock streaked across my vision. Bile rose up my throat, but I swallowed it back down, coughing and dazed. I didn't see any blood, but there was a distinct bend between my wrist and elbow that made my vision swim.

Hands gripped me underneath my armpits, lifting me and dragging me backward.

"Stay hidden," Breen hissed in my ear, depositing me behind the wide trunk of a fallen tree.

Then she was racing into the melee, where her compatriots were—*Fates*—they were rushing toward the creature with blades engulfed in green fire. *Oath magic.*

The Morta leapt down from the boulder, landing on all fours and snarling at the circle of glowing swords and axes. In the ethereal light, its gray pallor took on a sickly hue, making it appear all the more grotesque.

It didn't hesitate. It swiped wildly at the five fighters. Henren jumped out of its reach; Corla deflected it with her sword, cutting a black streak into its forearm; Sid stumbled backward, falling on his ass. Then Jord was charging at the creature, sword blazing with otherworldly flame. He managed to sever two of the many short, insect-like appendages on the Morta's torso. It spun, snatching at him. Breen defended Jord by blocking the attack with her axe, but as she did, the creature's claws wrenched her weapon out of her hands, flinging it into the underbrush.

I knew I should run. I knew I should use the chaos to get far away from here, to escape into the night. But I couldn't force myself to stand—not when there could be more monsters lurking in this forest. I remained crouched behind the fallen log, frozen with shock, exhaustion, and terror. My broken arm dangled limply at my side, and I tried not to look at it, afraid it would make me woozy.

Five Maronan knights of some kind, barely keeping one cursed monster at bay. They came at it in waves, striking and evading, losing their footing or weapons only to regain them, relentless in their bravery—but ineffectual against the Morta's viciousness.

Sid sliced the abomination's hind leg with a spray of black blood, screaming when the poisonous ichor splattered his bare skin. Enraged, the Morta spun on him; Sid ducked, causing the monster to smack Henren with the back of its long forearm instead, flinging him into the trunk of a tree, where he landed with a hard thud and did not stir. Corla and Breen advanced—and then retreated as the Morta snapped and snarled at them.

Jord took the moment of distraction to rush the creature again, stabbing upward into the side of its body; it *screeched*, wheeling on him. Jord hung onto the hilt of his weapon, moving with it, trying frantically to yank it free of the abomination's flesh, but the blade wouldn't budge, it was *stuck*. The Morta bent, sinking its teeth into his shoulder with a wet crunch. His shout was ear-splitting, filled with so much agony and terror that I immediately knew the sound would haunt my sleep for years to come.

Sid appeared, hacking his weapon into the side of the Morta's neck. It released its bite on Jord to open Sid's stomach with a long claw. There was a gush of crimson, a spillage of gore, a gurgle in the back of Sid's throat. Both men slumped, mortally wounded.

Unable to bear the sight, I forced my eyes closed, trying not to wretch. When I opened them again, I saw the Morta turn away from a half-eaten Jord—maw dripping red—and snarl in the direction of Corla and Breen.

Fuck.

The women's weapons were still alight, glowing in the darkness. They stood shoulder to shoulder, legs braced wide, their dark clothing and leather armor encircled in a green glow.

But their weapons were no longer the only source of radiance in this clearing. Another light splashed across the underbrush—not green, but *blue*. It was coming from behind me, illuminating the log I hid behind and the surrounding vegetation.

I turned, and—

It couldn't be.

Her features were unmistakable—angular face, dark hair, a white scar on her upper lip—and yet I stared at her in disbelief. *Mariana* was traipsing out of the trees, her sword ignited with blue Oath magic.

Had my fall knocked me out? Was the terror making me hallucinate?

"There you are," Mariana said to me, like I was an unruly dog who'd run off. "I'd suggest you get the fuck out of here—now."

"Wha—what—are you—?" I stammered.

Mariana gripped my upper arm in her non-sword-wielding hand and yanked me to my feet, shoving me eastward. "*GO*," she ordered.

Then she was stomping toward the Morta.

"Out of my way," she said to the others, swinging her blade in an elegant blue flourish.

Corla and Breen didn't question her—they backed away from the Morta, faces pale. Henren was just coming to, clutching the side of his head with a disoriented frown, taking in the bloody mounds of Jord and Sid before slumping sideways to vomit.

"Go now!" Mariana yelled at me.

My legs shook, but I forced myself to lift one foot, then the other, stumbling away from the gruesome scene. The others were quick to catch up to me. Corla supported a dazed Henren on her shoulder; Breen reached out to grip my non-broken wrist and pull me along.

Behind us, the Morta's furious cry echoed through the clearing. I couldn't help but glance back at Mariana, fearing for her while also fearing *her* as she hacked into one of the creature's long arms. It had been *winning* against five Maronan Oath-takers and yet Mariana faced it on her own—and while logic told me she'd lose, no part of me doubted her ability to kill.

After all, this was her duty. This abomination was not the first she'd faced.

I hurried south with my captors, back in the direction of their camp. Though we were on opposite sides of *whatever* was going on, we all had the same present goal: to escape with our lives. Knowing Mariana was in the area was—*Fates help me*—comforting enough.

The Morta's cries and Mariana's shouts grew distant as we fled. When we made our way out of the forest, the camp appeared wholly the same. The fire smoldered, a tendril of smoke curling into the sky. Gear was heaped around the perimeter. The horses were still tied up, but they eyed the trees uneasily, testing the extent of their tethers, flaring their nostrils with low, trumpeting breaths.

Henren, Corla, and Breen swiftly gathered their things and tacked up. I found my dagger in the grass and slipped it back into my satchel. Then Corla was beside me, handing me the reins of a horse—Sid's horse.

"Get on," she said.

"My arm..."

She jutted her chin at the saddle. "Get. On."

Perhaps I should've escaped in the opposite direction when I had the chance. But they'd rescued me from the abomination—even when they didn't have to—and paired with the fact that they were knights and were therefore *somehow* affiliated with the crown, going with them seemed better than wandering off into a monster-infested wood on my own again.

"I'm more likely to kill you if you *don't*," Corla added.

That was enough to convince me.

Shoving my foot in the stirrup, I gripped the horn of the saddle and one-handedly hoisted myself up. The horse danced sideways, antsy and eager to move. I gritted my teeth as I gathered the reins in my good hand

and tugged back, urging the horse to quiet. My broken arm hung at my side, bumping against my leg. The pain was a throbbing, constant agony, but the jostling was what dizzied me—sharp, searing streaks of lightning that traveled from my wrist to my elbow and up into my shoulder and jaw.

I was barely settled in the saddle when Breen whistled sharply, urging her horse into a gallop. My head whipped back as my mount launched forward, keeping pace with the others. I gripped the pommel of the saddle, leaning forward to better absorb the jolting pace while I held my injured arm away from my body. My eyes watered from the wind and pain.

It'd been a long time since I'd ridden with such speed. The thundering hooves and undulating gait inexplicably took me back fifteen years in time: atop Sweetpea, my sorrel mare, racing Raina in the flat basin of the Marona's central plains. The memory wasn't enough to transport me from the nightmare that was this night, but it reminded me of the way I used to brace my legs in the stirrups.

I shifted my weight, focusing on my balance. Then I was simply...*flying* across the fields. My horse gathered the ground beneath its feet, propelling us eastward. And for a while, that was all I experienced: the wind, the strain in my thighs and core, the rhythmic galloping. Pale moonlight splashed across the fields. Miles passed in a blur of exertion. My captors rode on either side of me, keeping their mounts close.

Then—sometime later—we slowed to a trot, a walk. My skin buzzed. My lungs dragged air in and out, rocking me in my seat. My dazed mind began to clear, like sunlight burning off fog to reveal all the anxieties of before.

We were winding our way between two hillsides toward the crest of a third. Henren led the way, with Breen to my right and Corla close behind. As my breathing slowed, I inhaled more deeply, focusing my taste magic on the particles that caught on my tongue. My horse steamed with sweat, humid and musky. Pollen clouded the surrounding wind, hazing up from the stalks of grass. Someone smelled of urine, and I was pretty sure it was Henren, who quite possibly had wet himself when he passed out; *that* made me wrinkle my nose.

But the higher we climbed the small hillock, the more the taste of the wind changed. Maple and mountain fog. Pine resin and leather.

Smoke and charred meat.

I tasted the salt, the gristle, the blackened edges of fat. I tasted ash and charcoal and—

Henren crested the rise, and horns blared from up ahead, echoing through the surrounding hills. A metallic flicker on the rocky outcrop to my left signaled that there were archers at the ready. I stiffened—*had we entered a trap?*—but Henren merely raised a hand in greeting and continued on.

When I reached the pinnacle of the knoll, I *gasped*.

Approximately sixty white tents dotted the valley below. Campfires cast orange orbs of light, sparks zipping toward the sky. Men and women sat around warming their hands, drinking from mugs. Other soldiers crisscrossed the open field carrying supplies or leading horses, their armor glinting. Flags had been planted outside a few of the tents, and though it was still dark, I had no trouble recognizing the richness of the hue, nor the seven-pointed star stitched into the center.

A Maronan camp.

Two riders were approaching from the valley below. One held the horn I must've heard earlier, while the other carried a large and menacing spear. Henren met them halfway down the hill, bringing our party to a halt.

Corla's leg brushed mine as she sidled up to me, boxing me in between herself and Breen.

"Where are we?" I whispered. "What is this?"

"Keep your mouth shut," Corla said.

"You were tasked with *killing* alchemists, Henren, not bringing them here," the soldier with the spear said.

"I require an audience with the captain," Henren said.

"The captain is busy."

"Not for this."

I leaned out of my saddle toward Breen, whispering, "Who is your—"

Corla reached over and squeezed my broken arm, causing me to cry out.

The guards' attention flicked to me—then back to Henren.

"Who is your captive?" Spear Soldier asked.

"Hattie Wynhaim," I said, prompting another terrible squeeze from Corla that had me panting through my teeth.

Horn Soldier chuckled. "Not possible."

But Spear Soldier urged his horse closer, eyes narrowing on me as he studied me in the dark. The way he catalogued my features—I recognized that level of careful observation. He must've been a sight magician.

"That's quite the claim," he said finally.

Among Maronan soldiers, my identity had the potential to be positive *or* perilous. But I was done hiding. "Yes," I replied, "it is."

He stared at me a moment longer, and whatever he saw...it must've been enough. "Very well," he said, pivoting his horse toward camp. "This way."

Corla grabbed my horse's reins, assuming control of my mount.

"What is this?" I asked again, looking around at the camp. The weapons. The Maronan flags planted in Fenrir's soil. "Who is your captain?"

Corla snarled at me, no doubt seconds away from squeezing my broken arm a third time—but Spear Soldier turned around in his saddle, answering my question without hesitation.

"This is a war camp, sweetheart," he called back, "under orders from Mighty General Kalden Asheren, overseen by Captain Brendan Harrow."

45

MONSTER

NOBLE

Noble sat with his back to a tree. His wrists were bound behind his back, eyes covered in a blindfold, scraps of wool cloth shoved in his ears. With two of his senses limited, the world around him seemed soft, muted. He breathed deeply, smelling leaves and soil. In spite of his vulnerable position, he felt...peaceful.

Which was the intent.

He would've never allowed Mariana to tie him up like this if it weren't for the proximity of a Morta. They'd been riding in relative silence, staring out across the shadowy plains, when a monstrous, high-pitched scream had pierced the night. The sound had taken Noble back to the dungeons of his Order, back to being chained to a wall with arcane magic searing his fingers, listening to the agonized cries of other knights in other cells and trying not to let his inner monster take over.

If the sight of his own blood made him want to turn, Noble was certain that the sight of a Morta—or even an animal afflicted with the disease of a Morta's bite—would be enough to turn him, too.

It'd been his idea to have Mariana tie him up with their horses.

She had been all too happy to oblige.

Was it dangerous for him to sit here, exposed, with a Morta lurking nearby? Yes. But it was *more* dangerous to risk turning into a Morta, himself.

Noble breathed deeply, trying not to think too hard about the risk of monsters in his vicinity. He and Mariana were close on Hattie's trail now—he'd seen it in the fresh tracks of hoof-trampled earth, trails cutting through the tall grass with folded stalks that had not yet sprung back up. It had taken immeasurable strength not to go with Mariana, but he couldn't. If Hattie was in those woods, facing that monster, Noble had to stay away. He hated that his absence always seemed to be the safest thing for her—but he was more than happy to hate himself for the sake of her well-being.

So, he sat there, breathing, trying to think of happier memories with Hattie.

The way the snow had glittered in her golden hair the first time he saw her, spying on him from the upstairs window of the keep.

The way her freckles deepened from chestnut brown to a chocolaty umber in the summertime.

The way she braided daisies into her hair on parade days.

Her mischievous smile.

Her laugh.

Her earnestness, her attitude, her romanticism—

The ground tremored with footsteps, announcing Mariana's return.

Something in Noble's chest released, like a fist unclenching. He was eager to hear what Mariana had seen—if she'd spotted Hattie. If she'd faced the monster and rescued Hattie amid the chaos.

"It's about time," he called out, his teasing greeting distant to his own ears through the wool. "I'm assuming you were successful?"

"Successful, indeed," a male voice intoned.

The wool was tugged out of Noble's ears, the blindfold yanked off his head, and Noble looked up to see—

—the very *last* person he wanted to encounter.

Brendan Fucking Harrow stood in front of Noble with his fists on his hips, flanked by four subordinates carrying torches. While the soldiers were dressed plainly, Brendan's chest was fitted with the signature gold breastplate of a Knight of the Order of the Mighty. The tooling along the edges and the star in the middle was distinctly Maronan—and high-ranking.

Captain.

Noble's stomach twisted in the same way it had on the day he'd been rejected by the Mighty Oath. Just the sight of the breastplate Noble had failed to earn, on the man whom his father had once referred to as *a second son*, opened a deep well of shame in his gut.

So Noble tried not to look at Brendan's Mighty armor too closely.

Aside from the uniform, Brendan looked basically the same as nearly a decade before: dirty blond hair, cruel eyes, and a straight nose above permanently pursed lips. Though Noble stood six inches taller, Brendan had always been bulkier, and the advantage of Noble's height was useless when he was seated on the ground, bound, with Brendan looming over him.

"Surprised?" Brendan asked.

"I'm always surprised to see you standing on your own two feet instead of crawling to kiss my father's boots," Noble replied.

Brendan lowered himself into a crouch, scowling. "You've always been a jealous bastard."

"Of the two of us, I'm not the bastard. Or wait—you're an orphan, not a bastard. My mistake."

Brandan's eyes narrowed. "Do you really want to taunt your rescuer?"

Resisting the urge to spit on Brendan's face, Noble smirked. "Fancy me your damsel?"

"In my experience, damsels are more...grateful."

"Gratitude is irrelevant," Noble said, "as I am not in peril."

"Your bindings beg to differ."

Noble glanced at the soldiers who accompanied Brendan. In his disdain, he'd forgotten how illogical it was that Brendan was here. "What are you even doing in Fenrir?"

"Do you truly not know?" Brendan asked. "Why else would you be so close to my camp?"

"Your..." Noble frowned.

Brendan was not a mere adventurer, camping in the wilds for the sake of exploration—he was a Mighty Knight of Marona, camped on *Fenrir* territory.

Which could only mean one thing.

This was *bad*.

"Oh, you actually *are* surprised." Brendan clapped amusedly, then placed his palms on his bent knees and rose to his full (inferior) height. "You know, I always wondered if the rumors were true. The son of General Kalden Asheren, leaving Marona in shame to join an unknown Order under Fenrir's banner? I never quite believed you'd betray your father like that, but"—he jerked his chin, gesturing at Noble's Oath tattoo—"it seems you have."

"Fuck off, Brendan."

"I'd say the same to you, but you can't. Why is that, *hmm*? Who tied you up?"

An eerie whine echoed from far within the forest, followed by a large crash.

Mariana's killing blow.

The sound of the Morta's death call rippled through Noble like a stone tossed into a lake, disturbing his calm inner waters; something terrible began to rise from the deep, sliding through the depthless black of his being. Noble breathed through his nose, hoping that if he remained still, the monstrousness inside him would slip under the surface and return to the depths.

The soldiers shifted uncomfortably, but Brendan didn't flinch at the Morta's cry. He noticed Noble's discomfort, though, his face brightening with cruel amusement. He crouched again, appearing utterly delighted to explain the situation to Noble. "Fenrir Territory has a long his-

tory of reckless magic and sordid research, but Lord Haron has been particularly naughty with his Arcane Adepts." Brendan glanced in the direction of the Morta's dying wail. "He has insulted the Fates by endeav-
oring to alter *nature*. The results have been rather nasty, although"—he
lifted a finger—"seeing as you clearly recognized that sound just now, I
don't believe any of this is news to you." Brendan smiled, haughty and
cruel. "Your father tasked me with investigating Lord Haron's operation."

"The assassins," Noble said.

"*Knights*," Brendan clarified. "A new Order under my stead, tasked
with keeping Maronan interests secure from any and all Fenriran
threats."

"I should've known it was *you* who sent such bumbling, incapable
morons to the Collegium."

"My scouts informed me that those *morons* are returning to my camp
with a prisoner as we speak."

Noble failed to stifle his flinch.

Brendan brightened. "You know the weasel? I haven't had the pleasure
yet—but I will soon."

Brendan didn't know his morons took *Hattie*? He was even more
inept than Noble would've guessed. It took an incredible amount of
focus for Noble not give in to the monster's desire for flesh and fury. It
would feel *so good* to sink his sharp teeth into Brendan's neck.

Noble's chuckle was mocking. "You're in over your head."

Brendan didn't hesitate. The prick threw a punch, striking Noble
squarely in the mouth, splitting Noble's lip.

Noble spit out the blood.

It was black.

Three seconds passed in which they stared at it, a dark splotch in the
grass between them.

When Brendan looked at Noble again, his eyes were wide with shock and wild with anger. "*That's* the Order you joined?" Brendan snarled. "You fucking traitor."

Noble's curse was waking up, snarling and angry. "You're dead unless you get the vial from my pack," he said through gritted teeth.

Noble's rucksack and saddle were heaped at the base of a neighboring tree, his horse tied to its trunk. He had one Hylder tincture remaining, which he'd foolishly left out of reach, opting to have Mariana tie him up instead. He hadn't anticipated *this*, however. With Brendan taunting him and Hattie in danger, Noble found it hard not to *welcome* the power, the wrath, the wickedness. A hiss emanated from his chest as his temples began to throb.

The soldiers flanking Brendan shifted uneasily. "Captain?" one of them prompted.

Brendan glared at Noble a moment longer, then—with a huff—hasted to Noble's pack, procured the vial, and returned, holding the tincture in front of Noble's face.

"What happens if you *don't* take this?" he asked.

"You die," Noble snarled, straining against his binds.

"I don't believe you," Brendan said.

An involuntary growl burst out of Noble, vicious and low. "You should."

"I want to see what happens."

"Have you ever seen a M—" Noble's Oath cut him off.

"Captain?" one of the soldiers repeated, their voice going high.

Noble thrashed, the ropes around his wrists biting into his skin. He barely felt the pain as he opened his mouth, snapping his teeth. His temples *throbbed* as the grotesque horns of his curse pushed against his skin, stretching it. Red tinged his vision around the edges. He hissed again, and the sound—it wasn't *human*.

His resolve was slipping. The monster was winning. A raw, corrupted sense of power was beginning to course through him like lightning, and Noble couldn't bring himself to care when he felt like this, the power and glory the adepts had promised him, so strong and fierce and furious and—

A rough hand gripped his face, forcing his mouth open. He bit the air, trying to sink his teeth into the nearest flesh. A cold, cloying liquid was poured into his mouth, his jaw held shut with too many hands to fight against, forcing him to swallow, and then...then the monster was dissipating, his normal vision returning, the pain his head and hands easing.

Then he was just Noble again.

Disgraced son. Failed knight. Traitor.

With the monster again submerged in the lake of Hylder, Noble hung his head. His skin was clammy, muscles weak. The anger remained, but it was smothered by a sense of defeat. He knew the feeling well.

Brendan gripped Noble's jaw and forced him to meet his eyes. "You're a Knight of the Order of the Morta."

He curled his upper lip. "Now who's surprised?"

Brendan raised a hand as if he'd strike Noble again—then thought better of it.

Noble loosed a harsh, singular laugh.

"Bold of you to laugh in a moment like this." Brendan stood tall, unsheathed his sword, and rested it against the hollow of Noble's neck.

Noble lifted his chin. "We both know you won't do it."

A flicker of doubt flashed in Brendan's eyes, confirming Noble's statement, even as he said, "Oh? And why not?"

Brendan—a hearing magician—tended to forget how easily Noble saw through him.

"You could've killed me a minute ago, but you fed me the tincture instead." Noble did not mention the fact that the tincture had been his last. He prayed to the Fates he wouldn't need more Hylder in the coming hours. "Which means," Noble continued, slipping into a familiar feigned confidence, "I'm an asset to your cause."

Brendan stared at him, mouth twisted into an angry little pout. Because Noble was right. If his father had sent Brendan to Fenrir for information about the curse, they couldn't afford to kill Noble—at least, not yet.

The moment stretched, and Noble could *see* Brendan fighting the truth, an inner war evidenced by the tension in his forehead, the narrowing of his beady eyes. Brendan couldn't get around this—and he *despised* Noble for it.

Good.

Brendan lowered his sword and gestured to his soldiers. "Unbind him from the tree, but keep his hands tied. He's coming with us."

46

MEDDLING

HATTIE

*O*w!" I yelped, wincing.

Firm hands pressed on my broken arm, bone grinding as the break was realigned. The pain made my head swim, and I gripped the arm of my chair with the other hand, holding on as the healer worked.

Breen had deposited me in the captain's pavilion a half hour ago. The healer had arrived soon after, not bothering to introduce himself before he took my arm in his hands and began poking and prodding. He'd given me a tincture of white willow bark, meant to reduce pain and inflammation, but it had yet to take effect.

"Almost," he muttered to me now, pressing his thumb against the bruised skin by my wrist. He was young, soft-spoken, but overly efficient in his ministrations—which I supposed made sense for a healer in a war camp. Why learn any sense of bedside manner when it would only slow you down on the battlefield?

Not that we were on a battlefield. Yet.

"*Owww.*" I moaned as purple spots burst across my vision.

The grinding in my arm intensified, then lessened, replaced by an all-encompassing pressure as the healer fitted a splint along the underside of my forearm and wrapped it in place with a lengthy strip of cloth.

I wiggled my fingertips to test their range of motion, shuddering with discomfort as I touched forefinger to thumb. "Will it heal properly?" I asked.

He procured another, wider cloth from his supply bag, fashioned it into a sling, and fitted it over my head. "Quite likely," he said noncommittally.

"Well. Thank you for your help," I said.

"It's my duty."

Once my arm was cradled close to my chest, he wordlessly stood and made his way toward the overlapping flaps of the tent's entrance.

I stood, too, glancing down to adjust the sling against the chain of my necklace. My chest was still crusted with dried blood from the cuts Corla had carved under my chin. "What about these wounds on my neck?" I called after the healer. "Can I have a wet rag to clean them up?"

"I was instructed to fix the arm. No more is necessary."

Rude. "Surely cleanliness is necessary?" *For Fate's sake*, there was still black monster blood on my dress.

He didn't acknowledge me as he slipped through the flaps and out into the night.

I let out a frustrated sigh. At least my arm was set to heal properly—and my life wasn't presently threatened. After the past couple days of strife, these seemed like blessings.

Still, what was I supposed to do now? Simply wait for my childhood-acquaintance-turned-Mighty-Captain-of-a-secret-war-camp to arrive?

Apparently.

There was no chance of escape. I had not been bound, but guards had been stationed all around the tent's exterior; the orange glow of the surrounding campfires illuminated the white canvas, casting their shadows in stark relief against the walls like moving frescoes. All around, the sounds of soldiers and knights permeated: harsh laughter, convivial chatter, the clatter of metal on metal. Even in the dark, there would be no sneaking out of camp with this many trained fighters around.

Besides, the encounter with the Morta had shaken me. What if there were more lurking in the foothills of the Axe Mountains?

I rubbed my injured wrist, feeling terribly vulnerable and alone. The fact that I *knew* the captain of this camp wasn't a comfort. I was supposed to be the dutiful wife of a wretched man in southern Fenrir, not an apprentice of a secret research program at the Collegium. I wouldn't put it past Brendan Harrow to send me back to Poe—or worse, tell Noble's father and my family, who would no doubt invent another, more effective method of making me disappear.

Because as long as I breathed, I—as the eldest child of the Lord of Lothgaim—had rightful claim. *Peace* among the Seven Territories of the Kingdom of Marona was how King Braven kept his power secure, and I was a threat to that peace. After all, Raina's upcoming marriage was far more politically advantageous for fostering unity between Marona and Lothgaim. Archer Loth was respected by his people; Raina was beloved by hers. While Raina *or* I would have the power to sway Lothgaim's diplomacy for the Maronan crown, Raina was a gentler choice. Romantic through marriage, instead of violent through a (lawful) coup.

I hadn't fully grasped it nine years ago, but my aunt and uncle could've had me killed for who I was. I might've been *like* a daughter to the king and queen, but Raina was their *everything*, and killing me would've been the only way to guarantee their daughter's future. (This had been my attempted assassin's logic—a rogue act of loyalty from a castle soldier).

Sending me to Poe had been a kindness on their part.

Now that I'd resurfaced...I wasn't sure they'd make the same mistake twice.

With a shiver, I turned away from the tent's entrance and took in my surroundings. The pain in my arm was beginning to ease, receding enough for me observe Brendan's quarters with a more focused, calculated attention.

A large table took up the center of the tent. A map of the continent was spread across the majority of the worn wood, anchored at the corners with flickering lanterns and empty goblets that smelled of wine. All around the map were platters of food: breads, cheeses, cured meats, fruits, and even a crystal dish of Lothgaimian chocolate truffles.

There was the wooden chair I'd sat in while the healer worked, the stool upon which he'd perched, a few unmarked crates. A shaving knife rested on the lip of a wash basin in the corner. Breen had let me keep my satchel but had confiscated my dagger; I plucked the blade from the empty basin and tucked it into my pocket. *Just in case.*

The only other furniture was a luxurious-looking bed—piled with furs, quilts, and pillows—that took up the entire back wall of the tent. For a few seconds of weakness, I stared at it with a covetous need. Had it not been Brendan's, I would've been tempted to lie down—but this was *his* war camp, *his* operation, *his fault*. I hadn't had a good night's sleep in days, but the exhaustion was eclipsed by my simmering dread.

The fact that Brendan was here, following Noble's father's orders...this seemed to be about more than just targeting alchemists at the Collegium. Something bigger was going on.

And clearly, Brendan had no problem making me wait to find out.

I turned away from the bed, sweeping my attention across the spread of food. My stomach was pinched and hollow from days on the road, but when I picked up a cube of cheese, I couldn't bring myself to eat it—so I set it back down on the platter.

"It's not poisoned, if that's what you're concerned about."

I looked up and there he was. Brendan Harrow, but older, standing just inside the tent. In my youth, I'd watched countless girls swoon over his bulky arms and symmetrical face, but his conniving countenance had always set me on edge. His competitiveness, superior attitude, and distain for Noble had only added to my distrust.

I gestured at the table. "Not much of an appetite."

"Somehow I doubt that." His appraising expression softened into a tender form of bemusement. "*Fates*, it really is you."

The whole central table was positioned between us, and yet I still felt like we stood too close.

"My subordinates weren't entirely convinced, but..." Brendan looked me up and down—eyes lingering on my chest—or perhaps the crust of dried blood that his healer had refused to let me clean—before finding my eyes again. "It's unmistakably you."

"Glad someone believes me."

"You sound tense."

"It's been a tense few days," I replied, "what with the attempted murder, kidnapping, and—" I lifted my left shoulder, drawing attention to my injured arm in the sling.

"But you're safe now."

"Am I?"

"Do you not feel safe in my camp?"

"I'm your prisoner."

Brendan frowned and took another step farther inside. "We don't have to talk about that right now."

"I think we should."

"Are you sure you aren't hungry? Tired?" He gestured to the bed. "You're welcome to—"

"What am I doing here, Brendan?"

A flash of something sinister darkened his eyes for the briefest moment, then cleared. In all my years knowing him, Brendan had never threatened or harmed me, but sometimes he got this look—a harsh tension that signaled a capacity for violence, like he was simply waiting for an excuse to unleash it.

"I'm not sure what you're doing here, Hattie," Brendan said slowly, "but I'm curious to find out. Why don't we sit?"

"I'm comfortable standing."

"Very well." He plucked a grape from one of the platters at the opposite end of the table and popped it into his mouth. The crunch sent a shiver down my spine. He raised a palm in an inviting gesture. "Whenever you're ready."

I rested my good fist on my hip. After the past two days, I was in no mood for veiled conversation. "I'm here because you sent five morons to Fenrir to murder alchemists and they targeted me."

Recognition—or perhaps irony—flickered across his face, but I didn't know what to make of it. "I'm glad you outsmarted my *morons*."

"I'm sure you are," I said. "It would've been embarrassing to tell General Asheren that you accidentally murdered a Wynhaim."

"You are not just *any* Wynhaim."

I couldn't tell if that was a compliment or a threat. As evidenced by my attempted murder nine years ago, patriotism could make people do extreme things—and I'd been sent to Poe before I learned exactly where Brendan fell on that spectrum.

I set my jaw, refusing to appear afraid. *Court face, Hattie.*

"In any case," I continued, maintaining an air of sass, "I'm *here* because of you. Which brings us back to the question: what are *you* doing camped on the Fenriran side of the border?"

"It's uncommon for captains to reveal sensitive information to prisoners," Brendan replied blandly.

"So, I *am* your prisoner, then."

"Only if you don't comply."

I smirked, unamused. "My guess is that you're here because the Lord of Fenrir is plotting against Marona," I said, thoroughly enjoying the way his eyes widened. Another thing about Brendan: he always underestimated my wit. "Am I wrong?"

He bit down on another grape. When he swallowed, his Oath tattoo shifted up, then down. "Fenrir has had a long line of egotistical Lords."

"Must be in the water," I quipped.

Brendan stiffened. *Huh.*

I traced my fingers along the etched edge of the glass bowl of truffles. "So, Fenrir has been experimenting. Trying to amass power to overthrow Marona's hold," I said. "But Lord Haron made a mistake, altered nature—"

"*Hattie*," Brendan warned, clearly surprised by what I knew.

I wiggled the fingers of my injured arm, reminding him of what I'd encountered. There was no doubt in my mind that Henren had just reported to Brendan the full extent of tonight's happenings.

"My theory is that you're camped here because of an impending conflict," I said. "Perhaps also to keep the curse from spreading into Marona. And in the meantime, this is a convenient place to conduct missions into Fenrir's capital." I paused, thoroughly enjoying the dumbstruck look on his face. "How am I doing?"

"You don't know what you're meddling with, Hattie."

"Yet I'm close, aren't I?" I taunted. "Folks love telling me not to meddle. Love to underestimate me, too. But I've always been a curious person." I gave Brendan my most thoughtful frown. "Here's what I don't understand: why *kill* the alchemists who are trying to clean up Lord Haron's mess?"

Brendan paused with a grape halfway between the platter and his mouth. "Clean up?"

I waved my good hand dismissively. "Contain. Cure. Whatever you'd like to call it."

Brendan dropped the grape and braced both hands on the table; one of the nearby oil lamps illuminated the underside of his chin, cheeks, and eyes, giving his face a menacing appearance. "*Solve*," he said. "That's what I would call it."

As in: solve the mission of Noble's former Order.

But how could that be? Phina might've kept us in the dark about the origins of the study, but it'd been clear from the beginning that her research was meant to *undo* the curse, not solve the problem and succeed in the Lord's designs.

Right?

She had never explicitly *told* me the study's purpose, though, had she? I'd just assumed.

Brendan stood tall again, folding his big arms across his golden breast-plate. "Interesting," he said, easily reading my surprise. "They've kept you in the dark, then. Can't say I'm not relieved to learn that you weren't *willfully* a part of a program to create...well..." He pointed at my arm, which was apparently our code for that which he could not speak.

"Nonetheless," Brendan went on, circling around the side of the table, "you *are* complicit in the crimes of Fenrir. Sending assassins to a school isn't ideal, but we're on the verge of war, Hattie, and drastic measures must be taken to secure the future of our kingdom."

"You're lying," I said.

"I am not," he assured me, and—

—and I couldn't bring myself to doubt him.

The truth of the matter was, *I* had been looking for a cure, but who's to say that the moment I found one, it wouldn't have been used to further Lord Haron's twisted research? After all, containing the curse was likely just a step away from *controlling* it. And the moment he and his Arcane Adepts succeeded in creating a curse they could control...the Fate of the Seven Territories *would* be at risk.

Had Phina been lying to us? Or was she in the dark, too?

"You're in shock." Brendan was standing close, now. He reached up to caress my injured elbow, thumb stroking the bare skin there, and I cringed—but not out of pain. "Why don't you rest?" he murmured.

"Why kill the alchemists, though?" I asked. "Why not question them?"

"Your research isn't valuable, it's corrupt. Besides," he added dismissively, "we already know plenty."

I stepped back, and Brendan released my arm. "Are you going to kill *me*, then?" My tone betrayed my genuine concern.

Brendan frowned down at me, his expression deceivingly doting. He was shorter than Noble, but he was still taller than I was, with a menacing bulk that he knew how to use.

"There has been a new development," Brendan said after a pause. "One I hope you can help me with." He lifted a palm, gesturing toward the front of the tent.

My feet moved of their own volition, carrying me forward with hesitant curiosity. Instinctively, I lifted my satchel off the chair and slung it over my good shoulder. When we reached the entryway, Brendan swept one of the tent flaps to the side, allowing me to pass through.

Outside, the air was cool. The night lingered, its darkness freckled with firelight and the pale, ghostlike figures of the surrounding tents. A crowd of knights and soldiers stood in a half circle, ringing the clearing just outside Brendan's pavilion. In the middle of the open space, five guards held onto chains that led to a single prisoner.

My footsteps faltered. Brendan caught me, his fingers digging into the narrowest part of my waist. Everywhere his body touched mine, I recoiled—but I couldn't stand on my own. Not at the sight of Noble in the center of the crowd.

He'd been stripped down to his trousers, his feet bare. He wore shackles around his ankles and wrists, an iron collar around his throat. A chain extended from each metal cuff to one of the guards. His head hung, black wavy hair obscuring his face in a posture of defeat.

A small sound escaped me—a strangled gasp. Noble looked up, seeing *all* in a matter of moments:

The dried blood on my sternum.

The sling around my broken arm.

Brendan's fingers clutching my hip.

The filth on my dress.

Then my eyes.

He held me with his gaze for three seconds, four, and that stare was filled with *novels* worth of apologies and explanations and love and pain and promises—so many words that an entire library wouldn't be able to contain all he said to me with that look. Volumes of longing and tenderness and regret.

But it was the warning in his expression that worried me. And the way he was panting, his bare chest shining with sweat, rising and falling with rage...

He'd come for me. *With Mariana*, I was sure of it. And—*Fates*—what of the Morta? How had Noble contained himself? How had he not turned?

How had Brendan found him?

There was a black streak of blood on Noble's swollen lip. Evidence of an altercation. Which meant Brendan *knew* what Noble was—he had to.

I looked up at Brendan, still pressed against me, too close for comfort. I was afraid. Petrified.

But I was also uncontrollably, incandescently furious. How dare he chain up Noble like a war prize? How dare he think I'd want to help him when the love of my life was in shackles?

"Help with what?" I asked, my words guttural and slow—barely contained.

Before Brendan could answer, chaos erupted.

47

HUMANITY

NOBLE

If there were ever a sight to make Noble want to forsake the Fates and tear the world apart, it was this.

Hattie, adorned in a garnet-red necklace of her own dried blood.

Hattie, with dark bruises marring the bare skin of her wrist, her arm in a sling.

Hattie, cringing in Brendan's grasp, her sensuous body shrugging away from the unwanted touch.

Hattie, with black ichor on her dress—the same vileness that was awakening in his veins.

Hattie, with a bruise blooming across her perfect temple, her luscious hair tangled with leaves and twigs.

And, worst of all, Hattie: with fear and fury in her eyes, agony plain on her face. So strong, when she shouldn't have to be. So brave, when she shouldn't need to be. So good—*too good*—for a world filled with unfairness and darkness and brutality. So unbelievably beautiful inside and out, defiant of all the ways the Fates had endeavored to dim her brilliance.

It was unfair.

It was unconscionable.

It was unacceptable.

Noble was more than willing to endure the inhumanity of this world, but he would *not* allow it to *touch* his Hattie.

He had always tried to be good. He had valiantly fought against the riptides of his own inadequacy to be the man his father and society had expected him to be. He had fought against his inner wickedness, be it his inability to ever be *enough* or the literal curse the Arcane Adepts had injected into his veins. He had always tried to live up to the legend of his namesake. And though he had failed to meet those expectations, he had *tried* to do the right thing.

But Noble was done trying.

Now, he would do the wrong thing.

Now, he would welcome failure and give in to the power that simmered under the surface of his humanity.

As he felt the wretched, wicked swell of the curse surging into his veins, awakened by the blood on his lover's dress and encouraged by his rage over her peril, Noble had no problem becoming a monster.

He embraced it.

Because if there was one person worth giving up *everything* for, it was her.

48

NIGHTMARE

HATTIE

H is transformation began with the sickening breaking of bone:
gnarled antlers pushing through the skin at Noble's temples and
unfurling with a horrible *cracking* noise, like splitting wood. He growled,
seething through bared teeth that were already sharpening into points.
At his sides, his fingers splayed wide, revealing elongated claws. His bare
chest rose and fell with quick breaths, his beautiful body glistening
with sweat as his muscles became more bulbous and his legs and torso
stretched.

"*NOBLE!*" I screamed, breaking free of Brendan's grip.

He didn't hear me. His body was shaking violently with the disfig-
urement of his disease. A memory of the Morta flashed in my mind,
showing me his eventual future: skinless, gaunt, a haunted creature of
nightmares.

I stumbled forward, powerless as the man I loved gave into a curse
that wasn't *him*, that didn't *belong*, that was everything wicked and
awful—the opposite of his pure, inherent goodness.

"Noble, don't do this!" I shouted. "Noble, listen to me!"

His legs cracked, bending backward sharply. I shrieked as he pitched
onto his hands and knees, his shoulder blades rippling. The guards surrounding Noble were wide-eyed with terror, the chains rattling as they
held on to the monster he was becoming.

I wheeled toward Brendan, shouting, "Hylder! He needs Hylder!"

I expected Brendan to be pale in the face—shocked—but he was *grinning*.

The expression wasn't just rage-inducing, it was cruel. I wrenched my wrist free of his grip and shoved his chest—hard—but he stood firm, spreading his arms helplessly.

"According to our intelligence, Hylder isn't enough," Brendan said. "He needs a cure."

He gestured to our right, where the crowd of onlooking soldiers and knights had backed away, revealing a small table. A collection of bottles and jars were cluttered on the wooden surface, along with a lantern.

Help with what? I'd asked. I was afraid *this* was my answer.

"I'll be honest with you, Hattie," Brendan began, "General Asheren sent me here for the sole purpose of protecting Marona from Lord Haron's nefarious adepts and wretched creatures. The Order of knights under my purview—whom you so lovingly referred to as *morons*—have done their best to mitigate the risks, but Fenrir's rot runs deep."

A guttural snarl came from Noble, making me shudder. A tear tracked down my face as Brendan continued.

"When I found Noble lurking a few miles from my camp, on his way to rescue the apprentice my knights had captured, I wasn't exactly sure how I'd leverage his unexpected presence." His grin turned conniving. "But then *you* turned out to be that apprentice, and, well, I couldn't pass up the opportunity."

He gripped my upper arm—fingers pressing painfully into my flesh—and hauled me toward the table.

The makeshift *lab table*.

"You've always been obsessed with alchemy, haven't you? I used to think it uncouth for an otherwise *lovely* lady of court, but seeing as my knights have been so ineffective, I thought—with your help—I'd try a different tactic to protect Marona," Brendan explained. "Instead of working for Fenrir, why don't you lend your talents to *us*, your home territory? I had my men prepare this table with everything you might need. Heal General Asheren's son, or else you both die."

Brendan wanted me to uncover the cure. He wanted to *force* it out of me.

Tears blurred my vision. "Are you *mad*?!" I boomed, shoving him again. "Researchers have been working on this for years! Noble has minutes!"

"Then you better get to work," Brendan said.

Noble was still on his hands and knees, his skin webbed with black. Dread gripped me by the windpipe, strangling all thought except for the horror of what was happening to him.

The man I loved.

My future.

My *everything*.

I would not allow the Fates to forsake Noble like this.

"Go on," Brendan taunted.

I wanted to throttle Brendan for this. Destroy him and everything he held dear, just as he was doing to me. But I didn't have the means, and there wasn't time.

I turned toward the worktable and took in the spread of ingredients. The setup was strangely familiar—similar to the research benches in Phina's lab. There were three empty, wide-mouth pitchers and a quartz stirring spoon. A jar of powdered Gildium, sprigs of Common and Black Lace Hylder flowers, a bottle of pure Hylderberry syrup, a few dried leaves of other purification herbs, a mortar and pestle. Plus, a series of half-pint bottles, clear glass, identical in shape, but filled with various shades of clear liquid.

I picked one up and examined its label: *Water, River Gray.*

I looked at another: *Water, River Wynhaim.*

Another: *Water, Geothermal Pool #16.*

Water, Geothermal Pool #39.

Water, Geothermal Pool #7.

Water, Well of Fate.

I hesitated on that last one, lifting it up to the lantern light.

It was the color of a fresh sprig of sage, a translucent blue-green. Perhaps it was the exhaustion or my frantic nerves, but the water seemed to glow faintly, like starlight reflecting on a still pond.

How in the Fates had Brendan gotten his hands on such a sample? Anya had made it sound like *no one* had visited the Well of Fate in centuries. Except...well, except she and Idris hadn't been alone in the Western Wood. A group of knights from Idris's past had helped them escape.

A deep, guttural growl spilled through the camp like a landslide, rattling the glasses on my little table. Noble was rising from his hands and knees, and he was—

A sob escaped my lips.

—he was utterly *changed.*

His height now reaching at least nine feet, his body horrifically stretched. Ribs poked out above an overly narrow, concave stomach; his knees were bent backward, his shins too long, extending from of his trousers much farther than they ought. Antlers protruded from the soft waves of his hair and twisted toward the sky. And his hands—hands that had touched every inch of me, that had cherished my body with reverence and care—were tipped with jagged black claws, meant to shred.

When he looked up, he looked right at me, and his eyes—once kind, observant, spring-green—glowed crimson.

Oh, I was going to *kill* Brendan.

That is, if Noble didn't kill him, first.

Noble's eyes slid to Brendan and narrowed. He made to lunge at the captain, but the guards still holding onto the chains on his arms, legs, and neck pulled him back, preventing his progress. He snarled at them, changing tactics. In a swift move, Noble rotated both wrists, looping the attached chains around his forearms. It took barely a tug to yank the guards holding his restraints off their feet. Noble bent, picked up the chains attached to his ankles, and pulled those guards down, too. The remaining man—who held the tether attached to Noble's neck cuff—began to pull, shouting with admirable bravery. Others jumped in to lend their strength, heaving against the remaining chain as Noble turned on them.

Then a lot of things happened in mere moments.

Claws swept out, slicing the guards with a shocking spray of blood.

All around me, soldiers and knights brandished their weapons with a chorus of ringing steel.

Noble met them with a low growl, pouncing on those nearest and taking them out with terrifying ease. Gore splattered the grass. Metal flashed in the torchlight. Men cried out in valiance, fear, and death.

I couldn't watch. I didn't have *time* to watch. If there was even a small chance that Noble could still be saved, I needed to alchemize.

And yet I sagged over my little worktable, overcome with a sickening despair.

How could Noble *possibly* come back from this?

How could tonight end with anything other than total carnage?

How could I make any difference?

Hope, I told myself. *You don't have to believe fully—you just have to* hope.

I took in my spread of ingredients, thinking of the tapestry of theories I'd been weaving over the past few months. Hurriedly, I dug into my satchel and pulled out my notebook to review where I'd left off: broken formulas, question marks, dead-ends. My many failed experiments entered my mind's eye, filling me with worry: visions of the black blood and Hylder bubbling, smoking, hardening. The thought of any of that happening *to* Noble made me feel sick. Judging by the chaos all around me, I had only one chance to administer the right potion—but what *was* it?

Men shouted, Noble snarled, the wet *crunch* of violence filled my ears, but I would not look up from my table and allow myself to be shaken. I reached for the Black Lace Hylder blossoms, mashing them with the mortar and pestle. By now, mixing Hylder tinctures was almost second nature, and in spite of being one-handed, I moved deftly. A splash of the berry syrup to the crushed flowers, dried thistle to boost the Hylder's effects. I gave the paste a brief taste, making sure the balance was right; it was sweet, botanical, purifying.

It tasted, inexplicably, like hope.

I shifted focus to the Gildium rods and powders provided. I didn't have blood to experiment with, nor did I know how to alchemize the metal, so I'd have to dissolve the powder in water as Noble had suggested, and hope he'd been right about that being a viable option.

Which left me with the water itself, the varying sources.

I braved a quick glance at clearing in front of me. Bodies were slumped all around, heaped in burgundy pools of blood. White tents were splattered with red and black, and one was collapsed and aflame. Noble was free of his chains, speckled with gore, a slash of black blood across his right pectoral. His face—pulled into an unrecognizably cruel snarl—was not his anymore, and it made me afraid. Not just *for* him, but *of* him.

Knights came at Noble with determination, breaking on his body like waves on stone. A blood-curdling *scream* vibrated my ear drums as one of Brendan's Mighty Knights—her sword brandished with the red fire of her Oath magic—fell.

"Work faster," Brendan urged.

He was hovering over my shoulder, and he looked scared now, his face pale.

"Fuck you," I spat, but I did as I was told.

I stared down at the water samples again, examining the bottles in the yellow glow of the lantern. Brendan, to his credit, had supplied me with numerous options—but which one was the answer? The samples labeled with the rivers Gray and Wynhaim, as well as the numbered geothermal pools all seemed too far off—my gut told me they weren't worth exploring.

With care, I lifted the *Well of Fate* bottle to the light. Even through the glass, I sensed its power; my magic purred in its presence, but it seemed too potent, too powerful, too volatile on its own.

I set it back down.

There was a source missing, I realized. One I should've considered long ago. Because while my tinctures from Waldron were alcohol-based, the Hylder I gathered there had absorbed into its roots a potent water: the River Wend.

Removing my birthday necklace, I placed the vial of Wend water next to the other bottles.

"*Hurry*," Brendan hissed.

"I can't think with you whispering in my ear," I bit out.

"Hattie..." This time, the warning in his voice made me look up.

Noble was stalking toward us, his red-ringed eyes fixated on me. He was predatory, focused, and I didn't want to believe it, but—

I have dreams sometimes, Noble had told me the first night we made love. *Nightmares. You're in them, and I'm half-turned...stalking you.*

Do you harm me in your nightmares? I'd asked.

No, he'd said. *I always stop myself and wake up.*

Brendan dropped to the ground, cowering behind my table.

I straightened and raised a palm. "Noble, stop."

Miraculously, he did as I asked, halting perhaps fifteen feet away from my makeshift workbench. His body was twisted and broken, his skin veined with black, diseased—but I saw a semblance of him still there.

The shape of his jaw. The waves in his hair. A flicker of green remaining in his red-ringed eyes.

He reminded me of a frightened animal, overtaken by instinct. But it wasn't *his* instinct taking over. It was his curse. It overwhelmed whatever sense of self was still inside him. His eyes narrowed, and then he was stalking closer, closer, closer—

A flash of blue caught my eye to the left.

"No!" I screamed.

Noble turned, evading Mariana's blue-blazing sword moments before she could cut him down.

She'd come to do her duty—but he wasn't a lost cause yet.

"Don't harm him!" I shrieked.

Mariana gave me a wild look, like I was deranged. "Hattie, he's gone—"

"No, he's not," I insisted—not just to Mariana, but to myself. "Hold him off. Give me time."

Her brown eyes dipped to my table of alchemy bottles, and perhaps I saw a quick nod of agreement—but then Noble was swiping at her, and her focus shifted to her charge.

No time to waste.

I stared down at my table of ingredients. The Wend water and the bottle labeled *Well of Fate* were the most viable sources, I was sure of it. I had to decide, but I felt immobilized. Ill-equipped. I didn't have my books. I didn't have a lab. I didn't have—

I blinked.

The bottles, the ingredients, the tools, my notebook—the spread wasn't just familiar because it resembled Phina's lab.

I had seen this *exact* tabletop before: in my Mirror of Fortune.

49

VISION OF
FORTUNE

HATTIE

Alchemy had been my vision of Fortune since young adulthood.

When the Mirror of Fortune had first shown me my life's greatest blessing, I'd felt encouraged—vindicated, even—to continue exploring my interests in herbal alchemy, no matter how improper Aunt Yvira insisted it might be.

After I arrived in Waldron—still rattled from the awfulness in Poe-on-Wend—I'd been eager to view my Fortune again. Seeing alchemy that time had felt like an assertion of self, a reminder of who I was. My identity had made a mess of my life, but at least my connection to herbs remained. The Mirror's vision had given me the ambition to continue my studies in Waldron, to perhaps one day become the town's licensed apothecary.

And I'd been glad, for the most part, ever since. Glad that this part of me—my passion, my Fortune—was unchanging. I might've occasionally wished that my Fortune would morph into a great romance—and when Noble arrived in Waldron, I'd wondered if that might come to fruition—but ultimately, I had been grateful for the persistent presence of alchemy in my future.

The consistency of my vision of Fortune was, in and of itself, fortunate. Because as I took in the various vials, bottles, and jars before me...I knew *exactly* what to do. I'd seen it at countless Mirror Festivals; I knew the steps by heart.

Perhaps my Fortune was about love, after all; perhaps my love of alchemy could save Noble.

The samples of water were arranged exactly as in my Mirror, an arc of various shades of blue—including the vial from Anya (familiar—I realized now—not because I saw it at the festival where Anya had acquired it, but in my vision of Fortune). Using their colors and order on the table alone, I worked from memory, moving quickly but with extreme care.

I started by arranging three pitchers in front of me in a row. In the first, I dissolved a pinch of Gildium in a splash of the blue-green Wend water from Anya. In the second pitcher, I mixed the Hylder paste with the same water to make a tincture. Next, I uncorked the bottle all the way to the right—labeled *Well of Fate*—and tipped a single drop into the third pitcher, along with the rest of my Wend vial.

The two waters mingled, changing color, the liquid shifting into an opalescent blue; I gave it a swirl with the spoon, *feeling* through the crystal the way the waters didn't just mix, but wove together. *Bonded.* Potent, yet balanced.

And it made sense, didn't it?

That the arcane magic and Gildium that had cursed Noble's blood could be neutralized by the waters of the Wend and the Well of Fate? The clue about the Wend had been in my tinctures from Waldron, where Hylder sprouted on the river's banks, drinking the Wend into its roots as it grew, its very cells *potent* with the magical water. And as for the Well—it'd healed Anya and Idris, hadn't it? Perhaps it could heal Noble, too?

I wondered if the Well of Fate had been used in the original experiments on Noble, to balance the arcane magic. That would certainly explain why adding Gildium to his blood hadn't killed him, and why he—along with Anya and Idris, who'd entered the pool with open wounds, therefore mingling the water with their blood—all possessed blank Fates. And *if* water from the Well of Fate had been used in Noble's original curse—was *already* in his veins—perhaps that meant the cure would bind more easily to his blood.

That *had* to be it.

A strangled shriek broke my mental flow. Brendan was crawling on his hands and knees toward his tent; Noble had caught him by the leg and was dragging him backward across the blood-soaked grass, stumbling over the slumped bodies of fallen soldiers and knights. Mariana came to Brendan's rescue, slicing Noble's forearm; the blow was restrained, precise. She was holding back as I'd asked, but Noble was becoming more feral by the moment; Mariana wouldn't be able to dissuade him like this forever.

I closed my eyes, calming my mind in spite of the surrounding carnage and chaos. I returned to the memory of my Fortune, the three pitchers. With the mixtures prepared, the final step was to pour the Gildium solution and the Hylder tincture into the third pitcher simultaneously, while alchemizing the mixture.

The only problem was that, in the vision, I hadn't—to my knowledge—had a broken arm. Then again, the vision never showed much above my wrists. And didn't the presence of cursed beings warp Fate? The thought gave me a jolt of panic—*what if Noble had changed my Fate? What if this was all wrong? What if this was no longer the cure?*—there was no room for doubt. I had to press on.

Gritting my teeth, I removed my sling and cast it aside. My left arm ached fiercely, but with the willow bark tincture still in my veins—not to mention the adrenaline—the pain was secondary. It had to be.

This was the moment of truth. Of *Fate*.

Rousing my magic, I recalled what Phina had taught in her herbology class all those months ago: that no matter how cleanly one wove the magic, the alchemist's emotions also had an effect on the outcome. I couldn't pour fear into this potion—I had to imbue it with *love*. Pure, unflinching love.

My wrists shook as I—with as much control and care as I could muster—picked up the Gildium solution with my left hand and the Hylder tincture with my right. Hindered by the splint, my movements were jerky; my forehead pinched as I poured the mixtures simultaneously, tangling my magic with the threads of the materials.

While I did, I pictured all the other moments of Fortune throughout my life: laughing with Noble on the riverbank, reading with him in the solarium, sneaking peaches on my balcony, finding pleasure together in his room at the Royal Inn, hearing his declaration of love.

The Gildium and Hylder hit the magical water with a swirl of blue, black, and purple, a shimmering storm cloud of liquid alchemy. With intense focus, I used my magic to coil the threads of Gildium, Hylder, and the water together, creating a loose weave. My breath caught when the water tightened its hold, binding the Hylder and Gildium together, like it was my partner in this—an alchemist in its own right. And though I put none on my tongue, I could still taste the essence of it through my magical connection: botanical, sweet, with a strange mineral quality that reminded me of...*life*. Complex and thrilling.

The potion was done—*made*.

My vision of Fortune always ended here, with a glittering potion before me, swirling of its own volition, *alive* with power.

What the Mirror didn't show was Brendan on the ground, clutching his bloody pant leg, sobbing. Nor the blue glow of Mariana's blade, cutting through shadow and darkness and the tight skin of Noble's shoulder. It didn't show what I was supposed to do next.

But I knew.

I just didn't know *how*.

Mariana's sing-songy voice cut through the clatter. "How's it coming, Hattie?"

Noble scrambled toward her on all fours, snapping his teeth and snarling. His body was twisted and broken, streaked with so much black and red I could barely make out the smooth brown skin underneath the smears of blood. The wounds.

Soldiers and knights still hovered on the sidelines, but with so many of their comrades fallen, they made no moves to assist Mariana. Their faces were pale with shock, the whites of their eyes showing; the clearing reeked of vomit and urine and death.

Noble lunged at Mariana, and she sidestepped him at the last moment, slicing his thigh.

"Anytime, Hattie!" Mariana called, dodging another attack.

"I need to get close to him," I said.

Mariana ducked and rolled out the way of Noble's onslaught, his claws just barely missing her face. "Good luck with that," she said, her words ending in a grunt as she swung her sword in an arc of blue flame.

I hugged the pitcher of potion against my body with my bad arm and came out from behind my table, scurrying along the perimeter of the clearing. "Can you lure him closer?" I shouted.

"Little busy!" Mariana leaped to the side, barely evading a wild swipe of claws.

With this latest move, Noble was now between us: me on one side of the clearing, Mariana on the other, Noble in the center. His back was to me, unaware of my presence as he crept toward the Valiant Knight.

Numerous tents were fully engulfed, now, spilling golden firelight onto the scene. Mariana had a scratch on her cheek and welts on her arms where Noble's blood had splattered and burned her. Her breastplate was dented. Her hair was mussed. She looked tired, but she also looked fierce. The living embodiment of her Order's name.

Seeing her like this—it made me feel all the more feeble and unprepared.

"*Fates, help me,*" I whispered as I approached Noble from behind.

The earth was slick with blood, the ground spongey beneath my feet. I tried not to think of it—tried not to wretch—as I carefully picked my way closer, weaving around the abandoned weapons and dismembered bodies.

As I walked, the potion sloshed in its pitcher, humming with each jostle, its power palpable. I could taste it in the air, its strange potency and potential. Memories of experiments gone wrong filled my mind's eye: smoking, separating, bubbling, boiling. There was a very real chance that this so-called "cure" could kill Noble—if he wasn't lost to his curse already.

Mariana and Noble were in a quiet sort of standoff: stances wide, arms outstretched, taking each other in, daring the other to make the first move. With Noble distracted, this might be my only chance. I was within six feet of him now, my limbs shaking, but my courage holding firm. I could do this, I could—

Mariana's attention flicked to me, her eyes widening. "Hattie, what are you—?"

I shook my head, hoping she understood that I needed her to hold her ground. But the exchange distracted me, and my foot caught on something—the arm of a fallen soldier—and I stumbled.

The ground was too slick for me to regain my footing. I skidded and toppled forward, barely catching my fall with my good arm. The potion sloshed, spilling on my dress and stinging the cuts on my neck as I went down. I landed on my knees in the blood-soaked grass, the pitcher toppling.

"No," I whispered, scrambling to set the glass upright. Only a dribble remained in the bottom. "No, no, no."

At the sound of my peril, Noble turned, red eyes zeroing in on me.

"Hey! Hey!" Mariana called, trying to capture his attention, but his focus was singular, now.

Noble crept toward me, lips curled in a snarl. There were far too many teeth crowding his gums, needle-like and razor-sharp.

My blood went cold. I struggled to stand, but the ground was too slippery.

Noble inched closer, dark drool sliding out of the side of his mouth. He barely looked like himself anymore; the monster had taken over, corrupting his features into something vicious and terrible.

"Noble," I said, scooting backward on my bum. "Noble, it's me, Hattie."

His glowing red eyes narrowed, tongue darting out to lick the points of his teeth.

I kicked my feet, but I didn't have any traction on the blood-slicked ground. My dress was soaked with mud and gore and the spilled hope of his possible cure.

"Noble," I pleaded. Hot tears streamed down my face. "Noble, please."

He took another step. Another. Ferocious. Predatory.

Then he was hovering over me on all fours, looming so close that our faces were only inches apart. Still hugging the pitcher with the remaining drops of potion to my side, I leaned back on my elbows, cowering in the face of death. My cursed lover.

A droplet of drool landed on my sternum, stinging like hot oil. I winced, but kept my eyes trained on his, searching for even a flicker of green among the glowing red.

"Noble, it's *me*. It's Hattie. It's your Peach."

At the sound of my nickname, his eyes widened slightly, a flash of recognition.

"It's Peach," I repeated, fumbling with my right hand to reach my pocket.

Noble had numerous cuts along his chest, his arms, all of them half-coagulated and contaminated with dirt and sweat.

"Remember what you told me about the nightmares?" I continued, closing my fingers around the small shaving blade I'd stolen from Brendan's tent. "Remember when you said you always woke up before anything bad happened?"

He growled, rattling the metal collar clamped around his throat.

"Can you hear me, Noble?" I whispered. "Can you wake up for me?"

For a moment, I thought he might.

For a moment, I thought the humanity inside him would prevail.

Then the monster sprung for my face with snapping teeth.

He missed me by a hair's breadth as he was yanked back by Mariana, who held the chain attached to his collar.

I did not hesitate. Flicking my wrist in a move Oderin had taught me, I sliced into Noble's forearm with the shaving knife, opening a clean wound.

Then I poured the last remaining drops of the potion into his blood.

50

CURE

HATTIE

As the potion mingled with the blood welling on Noble's arm, his body went slack, and he slumped over my lap, pinning me against the soiled ground. Then Mariana was there, rolling him off me with a groan. I went to him, cupping his blood-splattered face in my palm, running my thumb over the sharp lines of his cheekbones.

"Noble?" I murmured. "Noble?"

Tears streaked my face. My arm hurt, my skin stung, my muscles ached—but it was my heart that felt like it was tearing in half.

I slapped lightly at his cheek. "Noble? Noble! Wake up!"

Silence filled the clearing.

A warm hand touched my back. "Hattie, maybe we should—"

"No." I shrugged off Mariana's touch. "*No.* I'm not leaving him."

Footsteps squelched away from me. I was distantly aware of the whispers and murmurs of the remaining soldiers, looking on from the edge of the circle of destroyed tents. I heard Mariana say something, someone's sharp retort, then she was returning to my side with a set of keys.

She unlocked the cuff around Noble's neck. His throat was ringed red from the pinch of metal, black veins spider webbing under the surface of his skin. His eyes remained closed, his mouth slack, his body...monstrous.

Mariana felt for a pulse, frowning.

"Noble," I begged, frantic with dread. I shook his shoulder, pounded a weak fist on his sternum. "Wake *up.*"

But he remained limp.

Mariana removed her hand from his neck and shook her head, mouth pressed into a grim line.

A low wail pealed out of me, and I dropped my forehead to Noble's bare chest, ignoring the sting of his cursed blood against my skin. The world was collapsing around me, burying me in rubble. My lungs convulsed with dry sobs, heaving for air that wasn't there. Without Noble, I couldn't *breathe*.

"Hattie?" Mariana prompted.

"Leave me alone," I said, curling against Noble's lifeless chest.

"No, *Hattie*," Mariana urged.

I looked up at her through tearful eyes. "What?"

She inclined her head in Noble's direction.

I looked down at him, searching for the remnants of the man I knew. Long lashes fanned out over a gaunt face. Gnarled antlers protruded from the soft waves of his hair. The smooth skin of his neck was streaked with thin black veins.

Only...the veins weren't just black. They were *flickering* with gold, flashing like lightning beneath the surface of his skin, as if his blood were...*changing*.

I sat up a little taller, watching the scintillating light travel through his veins. Mariana reached forward again, finding his pulse point, and she flinched when she found it. I watched as his skin gradually cleared of the black webbing entirely, his sickly gray pallor returning to his usual warm brown coloring.

"That's it," I encouraged, voice breaking. "That's it, Noble, come back. Come back to me."

A startling *crack* had me jumping to my feet, stumbling backward, colliding with Mariana. She gripped me by the middle, holding me upright as I watched Noble's body begin to transform in reverse: antlers breaking off and crumbling into dust, legs shrinking down to their normal size with a series of sickening snaps, claws dulling to form regular nails again, wounds healing at a rapid pace. The Oath tattoo around his neck faded and disappeared.

Each new change in Noble's appearance was like the pierce of a needle, a timid, anticipatory relief stitching my heart back together. Breathing became a little easier. I leaned into Mariana, allowing her to take my weight as I watched Noble turn back into himself.

As silence filled the clearing once more, I heard Brendan stirring over by his tent.

"Fucking bastard," he growled.

Mariana released me. I didn't follow her path toward Brendan; I kept my eyes trained on Noble, watching as his chest jerked with a breath. Then another. When his breathing leveled out, I sank to my knees beside him again and placed my palm over his heart.

It thudded against my hand in a steady rhythm.

He hadn't opened his eyes yet, and his breaths were shallow, but his body...his body was *his* again. Familiar, perfect, *human*.

I let out another sob, this one of pure, unbridled relief.

It worked—not just containment, but a *cure*.

I had solved the curse.

A strangled, "*Hey!*" punctured the quiet, followed by a swift smack and a thud. A quick glance over my shoulder showed Mariana standing over Brendan's unconscious body, shaking out her fist.

She smirked at me.

I huffed a laugh.

Then my gaze caught on the horizon behind her.

Dawn was approaching, a soft paling in the east; washes of light blue and apricot swept across the sky, dimming the stars.

And there, on the hillside, were the silhouettes of countless horses and riders. Their armor glinted gold; bannermen brandished the Maronan flag.

General Kalden Asheren's regiment.

51

DREAM

NOBLE

Noble's life had never felt like his own.

When he was a boy, his days had revolved around preparing him for proper society—a dream of his mother's, while his father climbed the ranks in Marona's branch of the Order of the Mighty.

When he was an adolescent, and his father was promoted into King Braven's inner circle, Noble's existence had then centered on training to become a Mighty Knight, himself—a dream of his father's.

When he'd entered the Order of the Morta, of course, his existence had been all but forfeit.

There were flickers of respite, though, where Noble felt like his life was in his hands, on the tip of his tongue, in vivid color—his wants not so forbidden.

His mind went to one of those days, now: Hattie's postponed birthday picnic. Sneaking off to their secret grove by the river. Spending hours swimming in the gentle current, splashing each other, laughing. He'd tried so hard not to stare at her in her soaked underclothes, but nonetheless, his keen eyes had gravitated to those intimate places he'd wanted to touch so badly—her breasts, her bottom—and eventually he'd had to leave the water to get ahold of himself.

Hattie had called after him, chiding. "Where are you going?"

"I'm tired," he'd drawled, even though every part of him felt *awake*.

While Hattie continued to splash around in the shallows, Noble had collapsed onto the mossy ground in the shade. He crossed his arms behind his head, resting but nowhere near asleep. Dappled light danced across his eyelids, a patchwork of leaf-shaped shadows and the orange-gold quality of summer sun. Droplets of cool river water had warmed and evaporated on his skin. A gentle breeze had caressed his bare chest. And everything, *everything* felt warm and heady.

Adolescence had a way of turning sweet moments into agony.

Yet while he longed to tell Hattie how he felt and ease the tension between them, and it made his chest hurt to deny them both that relief, sixteen-year-old Noble—in the briefest of moments in that grove—had felt content with the life unfolding around him. Because in spite of it being a life that actively kept him from being with Hattie in the fullest expression of his desire, it was a life that had brought him to her doorstep, too.

Somedays he felt cursed by the limitations of his station, but that day, he'd thought to himself that *if* he was cursed, this curse was sweet. Lounging on the riverbank with the girl he loved was about as close to perfection as Noble could imagine. Even when it ached.

Eventually, Hattie had climbed out of the river, cool water sluicing down her body onto the moss beneath her bare feet. She'd padded over to him, purposefully dribbling water onto his face from the wet ends of her hair, filling their secret grove with mellifluous laughter. He'd peered up at her and known he'd never love anyone else.

In the years that followed, that memory had remained imprinted on his heart like a thumbprint pressed into clay. He could almost feel the warmth on his skin, now. Sunlight on a broken body—or maybe that sunlight was *inside* him?

His veins were alight with it—heated, blazing, burning. The ache of adolescent yearning turned into a searing, full-body torment. Shadow flickered through him like clouds covering the sun, cooling his blood with something sinister and *wrong*—but then his world was turning, sun swiveling, shade clearing.

Soon, Noble wasn't in the dark at all.

He felt warmth on his face.

He heard Hattie's voice, calling his name.

Had he fallen asleep?

Was this him waking up?

When he opened his eyes, would he see the riverbank and the bright green boughs of trees? Would he see the Hattie of his youth, tan and sopping wet, grinning at him with her plump bottom lip pinned by a playful canine?

If he woke from his slumber, could he still hold onto this dream?

He wasn't sure.

He hoped so.

But just in case, Noble decided to bask on the riverbank a little while longer.

52

NEW

HATTIE

A s dawn broke and a new day unfurled over the valley, I sat on a cot inside a freshly erected pavilion, numb with shock and exhaustion. Noble's unconscious body rested beside me. During the healer's assessment, Noble's skin had been washed, his clothing changed. Miraculously, his wounds had disappeared—all except the scars on his hands, a remnant of the arcane magic that'd first altered his being, perhaps too potent to be healed like a regular injury. His face was rosy with color, no black veins in sight.

He was *human*.

He was *alive*.

But he had yet to stir.

In the hours following the arrival of Kalden Asheren's regiment, order had been gradually restored. Flaming tents were put out. The bodies of the dead were loaded into wagons, driven a mile downwind, and burned. A series of new pavilions—including this one—had been set up on the edge of the valley, far from the gore of Noble's destruction. Four guards had been assigned to Mariana, whom General Asheren would question later. And Brendan...he had been carted off to receive medical attention, and maybe I'd enjoyed the thought of the healer's poor bedside manner as he assessed the captain's injuries; I'd certainly enjoyed overhearing the irate, scolding words Kalden had given him about his stunt, with the promise of an official punishment to come.

But now...now, I wasn't sure what would happen. All I'd been able to focus on was Noble; I hadn't let go of his hand since a pair of royal Mighty Knights had transferred him here hours ago.

"Never could keep you two apart," a gruff voice said.

I looked up to see an older, sterner version of Noble stepping through the flaps of the tent. Except Kalden Asheren had brown eyes instead of green, and a thick, silver-streaked beard that reached his mid-chest. While Noble shared his father's height, Kalden's build was bullish, with round shoulders and a barrel chest that stretched the front of his plain black tunic; though at some point he'd removed his golden breastplate, Kalden's formidable stature still seemed to diminish this makeshift room by half.

"Our families certainly tried," I replied, smoothing my thumb across Noble's temple.

Kalden moved deeper into the tent. "How is he?"

"Why do you care?"

"He's my son."

"Is that so?" I asked tartly.

Kalden's voice was weary when he said, "Yes."

In my youth, I'd been intimidated by the general; now, I couldn't decide if I despised or pitied his narrow-mindedness. He'd been incredibly blessed to have a son like Noble, and yet he'd never seemed to recognize it, always focused on what Noble *could be* instead of who he *was*.

I bent, pressing my lips to Noble's forehead, before making my way to standing. With my hair knotted, dress filthy with mud and gore, skin crusted with blood—mine, Noble's, others'—I must've been quite the sight. "Are you here to interrogate me?"

Kalden folded his arms across his chest. "Brendan explained the events of the past twenty-four hours. Noble's...affliction..." The general trailed off. It was perhaps the only time I'd ever seen him at a loss for words, and I felt my anger toward him slacken an inch.

"You know about his former Order, then," I said.

Kalden spat on the trampled grass between us. "I didn't know he belonged to that horrific excuse for an Order until today. I thought, after he failed to join the Mighty, he'd simply—"

"Left?" I supplied.

Kalden gave a single nod.

"You did not disown him?"

A vertical line formed between Kalden's eyebrows. "I was disappointed. Angry. But I would never exile my own son."

"*You* wouldn't? Or your wife wouldn't allow it?"

A surprised *pah* slipped out of him; it was harsh, as if Kalden wasn't accustomed to laughter. "You remember Helena well."

"I always admired her."

While Kalden was hard as stone, Noble's mother was much like the wisteria that grew up the side of Castle Wynhaim: stunningly beautiful, almost whimsical, but with strong and formidable roots.

"So, when your captain sent assassins to Fenrir," I said, back to the matter at hand, "you didn't know he was potentially targeting your son? Or me, for that matter?"

"I did not realize that my son was part of Lord Haron's plot to create an army of abominations, no."

A weapon of war, Viren had said, but an *army*? "It's true," I murmured. "Lord Haron plans to rise against Marona."

"Lord Haron comes from a long line of insubordinate rulers. Fenrir has never had the numbers to challenge Marona, but if it had abominations the Lord could control..." Kalden trailed off, allowing me to conclude the rest.

An icy claw trailed down my spine. "But our research was meant to *undo* what Lord Haron's Arcane Adepts had done," I said weakly.

Kalden took another step closer, brown eyes narrowing. "Do you truly believe that?"

I shifted on my feet, not liking what he was implying.

"Oh, you do," he said. "That's a relief."

I lifted my chin. "Go on."

"Phina Farkept's research was never meant to '*undo*' the curse, to use your phrasing," Kalden said. "It was meant to further the failed program. Complete its mission."

Brendan had said something similar last night, but: "Phina would've never agreed to—"

"She didn't know."

"You expect me to believe that Lord Haron would task a brilliant Collegium professor to undo his mistake, hoping she'd solve it instead?

"Would Phina Farkept have accepted the opportunity otherwise?"

"Rather convoluted of the Lord, don't you think?"

"Politics are always convoluted."

I shook my head, not seeing the logic in such an endlessly veiled endeavor. "But—"

"It was a success, wasn't it?" Kalden asked. "According to my captain, Noble was a monster, and *you*—an apprentice of Phina's—cured him."

"It was your *captain's* stunt that almost got your son killed," I shot back. "And my *Fate* that saved him."

His jaw clenched, temple pulsing. "I was not aware of the extent of Captain Harrow's..." He trailed off, lips twisting like he'd tasted something sour. "Plot."

"You were ignorant of your subordinate's overzealous dealings?" I shot back, angered all over again by what Brendan had done. How he'd used us.

"I tasked my subordinate to protect Marona's interests from Fenriran threats, namely, to infiltrate the Collegium and stop the curse from being solved," Kalden said—not without a bite in his tone. "Brendan's methods might've been misguided and—as evidenced by last night—impulsive, but we are on the brink of destruction. His motivations were pure."

I balled my good fist. "Brendan is a boot-licking ass-kisser," I said, "who cares more about your approval than the realm. He's always had a vendetta against Noble, and if you can't see that—"

"You might have royal blood, Ms. Wynhaim, but be careful how you speak to the king's Mighty General."

I rolled my eyes.

"You are complicit in a plot of treason." Kalden stepped toward me, and I instinctually stepped back. "The *only* reason you aren't in shackles is because you uncovered the cure for *my son*."

I glanced back at Noble, still unconscious on his cot. What did Kalden's accusations and threats matter when Noble hadn't woken up? "I'm afraid that remains to be seen," I whispered.

"How we proceed from here has consequence, *Ms. Wynhaim*," Kalden enunciated. "The real question is how *you* ended up at the Collegium, when you were supposed to be in Poe-on-Wend."

I refused to cower in the face of Kalden's judgements and accusations. "You know, General Asheren, I'm not really in the mood to get into it."

"My apologies, Hattie, but you don't exactly have a choice."

"Can you at least give me the courtesy of washing up?" I asked. "I'd rather not have this conversation with your son's blood all over my dress."

An hour later, I was back in the pavilion, my skin scrubbed clean.

The brief respite had allowed me a chance to assess my own state of being. The pain in my broken arm was significantly diminished—a fortnight of healing in the span of a few hours—and though I'd donned a clean sling, I wasn't sure I'd need it for long. My Oath of Allegiance tattoo was gone, too, as were the cuts under my jaw. I could only conclude this was due to the potion I'd spilled on myself in the chaos of last night, but pondering the changes was low on my current list of priorities.

A small table had been brought into Kalden's tent while I was gone; now he sat at one end, and I sat at the other. I wore a simple white tunic and a pair of borrowed trousers from one of the female soldiers. Though I hadn't slept, the fresh clothes helped me feel revived—as did the chunks of roast chicken on the plate in front of me.

It was poor etiquette for me to eat with my bare hand—shoving the greasy, delicious dark meat into my mouth with a ravenous haste—but we were far away from polite society, and I had been through far too much to care about propriety.

Kalden had better manners, though. He ate with a knife and fork, spearing bites that were comically small for a man of his size. He looked more likely to eat off the bone, but like me—like Noble, like everyone in the Fates-damned inner circle of Marona's royalty—Kalden had been trained. And unlike me, he was still entrenched in the rules of court.

No amount of politeness would apparently coax either of us to touch the plate of steamed Maronan turnips in the middle of the table, though. That, Kalden and I had in common.

"We can't avoid the conversation forever," he said finally, setting his knife and fork aside.

"'Forever' is quite the stretch, considering the fact that I haven't slept in over a day, and up until an hour ago, I was covered in blood," I quipped—but seeing as my reappearance was a threat to the king Kalden served, I understood where the general was coming from.

I didn't agree, but I understood.

And with my hunger halfway satiated, Kalden's earlier accusations weren't so frightening. I shoved more chicken into my mouth, talking over it. "You already know I'm not a traitor."

He lifted a bushy black eyebrow. "Do I?"

"Yes."

"But you're an alchemist of Fenrir?" he supplied.

I held his gaze, mustering courage. "Exactly."

"I cannot allow you to report your findings to Lord Haron," Kalden said. "You understand that, don't you?"

That was...reasonable. And certainly not part of my plan. "What is there for me to report? I rid Noble of the curse. If what you say is true, that's the opposite of what Lord Haron wants."

"And what do *you* want, Hattie?"

I dropped the chicken thigh onto my plate, wiped my fingers off on a napkin, and threw the soiled cloth on the table. "I want to be an alchemist, which should be no surprise to you or anyone else in Marona," I said. "I want to graduate from the Collegium of Fenrir with an apothecary license I can take home to Waldron. I want to live a peaceful life far away from the expectations and limitations of my former court. I want *freedom*." I gripped the edge of the table. "Do you believe me?" I pressed. "Do you believe I'm not a willful participant in Lord Haron's conspiracy?"

Kalden sat back in his chair, appraising me with a cool, calculated expression. "I believe you," he said. "However, I am afraid that's not an option."

My grip on the table slackened.

So, this was it. I was back at the beginning. Kalden could overlook my role in Phina's research, but he couldn't overlook who I was.

"What's your plan, then?" I asked flippantly. "Last time, you had me sent away, but clearly that didn't work. Do you think my uncle would agree to have me executed this time?"

"I never suggested such a thing."

"You might as well have," I said.

"Sending you to Poe was a kindness."

"Sending me to Poe was a death of a different sort," I snapped.

Kalden stiffened, catching my meaning. "So, you escaped."

"I had to."

"Was the marriage agreement broken?" Kalden asked.

"Yes. I received documentation and assurance that the divorce was reported to the Census Ledgers in Fenrir."

"Your *real* name is on the Fenriran Census Ledgers? That was a grave risk, Hattie."

"Yet it has remained a secret until now," I retorted. "Almost as if no one in Fenrir has been scouring the Census Ledgers for Maronan names."

Kalden's temple pulsed with irritation—then a new thought seemed to occur. "The crown was never notified."

"That's because the crown was sending the bastard money."

My ex-husband Corvin's greed had been a failsafe of sorts, a guarantee that my family would never learn about our separation. As the king still thought we were married, money continued to flow to Poe-on-Wend, and Corvin was more than happy to keep his mouth shut about my disappearance.

"And you ended up in...Waldron, you said?"

"That's the short version."

"And Noble?"

I glanced over my shoulder at the man I loved, still resting on the cot. While I'd been out, a healer had come to assess Noble again; Kalden had reported to me that he was stable, but asleep. The update gave me a reticent sense of hope.

"Our reunion was a coincidence," I murmured.

"An act of Fate," Kalden mused, and he sounded serious.

I met his eyes again. "You truly won't let me go?"

"Raina is not yet married."

"And next year, when she *is* married?"

"The risk—to Marona, to Lothgaim, to the realm—remains. Fenrir's treasonous dealings only makes our unity with Lothgaim more important."

"So, death, then?"

"I will escort you back to Marona," Kalden said cooly, "where we will speak with King Braven about how best to proceed."

"No."

"No?"

"No. I will not go to Marona."

"Hattie," Kalden said gently—too gently. "So long as you—"

I sprang to my feet, my chair toppling behind me. "So long as I breathe, I am seen as a threat, is that it? No matter how much I don't want my claim? No matter how many times I promise I will not come forward? No matter how vehemently I insist that I would never, *ever*, endanger Raina's future? I am *still* seen as a threat?"

"This isn't just about your potential actions," Kalden said, resting his fists on the table. "You have already been recognized. Rumors are already spreading—just as they did before."

"Rumors can be dismissed!"

"Rumors," Kalden enunciated darkly, "have a mind of their own."

"But what do they matter, this far from Marona?" I pressed. "That was part of your logic nine years ago, wasn't it? Get me so far away from Castle Wynhaim that I become invisible." Kalden opened his mouth, but I continued. "I've been living in hiding for nearly a decade, just to preserve what little freedom I found in Waldron. Why do you not trust me to continue as I did before?"

"There is the matter of your name," Kalden said.

"I use a fake name."

"Census Ledgers can't be forged, though," Kalden said—back to that gentle, pitying tone, a tone that struck genuine fear in my heart. "As long as you remain unmarried, you can be traced. No one might've been looking for you before, but according to Captain Harrow's spies, you recently announced yourself in the middle of Fenrir City. Witnesses *could* be looking, now."

"I think you're overestimating how much Fenrirans care about Maronan and Lothgaimian court politics," I argued.

"It is my duty to overestimate all potential threats to the crown."

"So, what, you'll marry me off again?" I asked, voice strangled and shrill. "Send me to a more remote territory this time? Tuul, perhaps, or Vernfal, or—" I broke off as a sob worked its way up my throat. This couldn't be happening. Not now. Not *again*.

Kalden rose from his seat and approached me, placing a huge hand on my shoulder. I didn't feel threatened, but his touch wasn't a comfort, either. Because it was pitying.

"I do not relish this, Hattie."

"Is there no other option?" I whispered.

"She could marry me."

Kalden's hand fell from my shoulder as I whirled toward the familiar voice.

Noble was sitting upright on his cot, rubbing his temple as if he were nursing the remnants of a terrible headache.

Emotion welled in my eyes, throat, chest, filling me with watery relief. A choked, jubilant cry escaped me. I wanted to fall into his arms, collide with his solid frame, but I didn't know how fragile he was—how careful I ought to be. I sank to my knees in front of him instead, cupping his cheek with my good hand. "You're awake," I said, tears pouring down my face even as I laughed with glee. "Fates, you're actually *awake*."

"Came back just for you," he murmured against my temple, pressing a kiss there.

I pulled back to look into his eyes, green eyes, so bright and keen and *open*. "How are you feeling?"

His brow furrowed with a troubled expression. "Hattie, I—"

"No apologies," I said. "How are you?"

"Groggy," he replied. "But strangely fine."

"Are you sure?"

Noble slid his hand along my neck, into my hair, gripping my nape like he might never let go. "Come here, would you?"

Then his mouth was on mine, his soft lips claiming me, making me forget about everything before and everything ahead—bringing me, blissfully, into *now*. With him. I stretched up from where I knelt, wrapping my uninjured arm around his middle, sliding my hand under the hem of his shirt to feel the warm, solid strength of his back.

He was awake.

He was alive.

He was—

I broke our kiss. "Wait, what did you say?"

53

HATTIE'S CONUNDRUM

NOBLE

Noble cupped Hattie's beautiful face in his palms. "You said you need a new last name?" he asked. "Take mine."

A tear tracked down her cheek—her *flushed* cheek. He took that as a positive sign. "You say that like it's simple."

He offered her a soft, hopeful smile. "It *is* simple, isn't it?"

Moments ago, Noble had awoken to two familiar voices arguing. He hadn't followed at first, but as consciousness had returned to him, he'd begun to catch on. After all, it wasn't a new argument—just new circumstances.

Even if his father was right about *her* name, nobody would be looking in the Census Ledgers of Fenrir for *Noble's*. And unlike nine years ago, their connection to Castle Wynhaim was diminished; unlike nine years ago, they didn't have status or his potential Mighty Knighthood standing between them.

It was not a perfect answer, but it had potential.

"But our history..." Hattie said. "We've spent the past few months trying to hide how we know each other because of what could be inferred."

"In a city, being associated with me matters," Noble reasoned. "But somewhere remote...somewhere like Waldron..." A smile teased his lips. "You saw it yourself. Nobody knew who I was. Nobody recognized my name."

Hattie placed her palm over his heart. "Are you sure you're in your right mind?"

Noble didn't know how long he'd been asleep, nor did he remember much from his rampage, but he knew he loved her. "Is that a yes?"

Her cheeks tightened with a smile, tears welling in her eyes again. Unable to help himself, he pressed another kiss to her perfect mouth, absolving her of the need to answer. *Yet.*

Love wasn't the issue at hand, of course. Love couldn't guarantee that his proposal was a viable solution to her problem.

Noble glanced at the shadow looming a few feet away. "What do you think, father?"

Noble hadn't seen General Asheren in nearly a decade—not since their argument after he failed to become a Mighty Knight. New wrinkles creased Kalden's brow, more silver threaded his beard, but otherwise, he appeared just as steely as always.

Or...perhaps not?

Noble's head hurt and his eyes ached from the brightness in the tent—the white canvas was washed-out and glaring with sunlight—but that didn't stop him from noting the slight wobble in General Asheren's bottom lip, the moisture in his eyes. It was about as much affection as Noble could expect from his father, yet seeing the relief there—the genuine tenderness—touched him deeply.

Kalden cleared his throat. "Your association with Hattie remains a hazard. It's an imperfect solution."

Leave it to Kalden to ruin a romantic moment.

Hattie rose from her position in front of Noble, allowing him to come to his feet. Vague memories of his legs breaking backward made him wince, but as he stood, his calves and thighs felt normal. Strong.

"Does a perfect solution exist?" Noble asked.

"Aside from death?" Hattie added, coming to stand at Noble's side.

Her tone was sarcastic, but there was an edge of truth in the suggestion, and Noble frowned. "Death is not an option," he all but growled.

"I didn't suggest it was," Kalden stated.

Perhaps not, but Noble wouldn't put it past his father to silently consider it. After all, it had been one of *Kalden's* soldiers who attempted to take Hattie's life the first time. Kalden might not have suggested such a ruthless thing, but he had a way of cultivating extreme loyalty in his subordinates.

Brendan was a perfect example. Noble had escaped Kalden's shadow, while Brendan had made it his home.

Fates, at what point had Noble become *glad* he never lived up to his father's wishes? It was a new feeling for him, but he liked it. It was freeing.

"Nobody wants me to exercise my claim," Hattie said, bringing Noble back to the present issue. "Even if there are rumors, no one would want to sabotage Raina and Archer's union—not when the majority of Maronans and Lothgamian's are in favor of the match."

"There are always contrarians," Kalden countered, but the argument was half-hearted.

Noble took advantage of the moment of weakness. "Let us marry. Let her take my name. Let us disappear in Fenrir. She'll be all but invisible there, and—"

"She still knows too much. We can't risk you two returning to Fenrir and exposing last night's findings to your Adept."

Last night. So, he hadn't been unconscious for long.

Noble looked down at Hattie again. "What happened last night?"

Her eyebrows pinched together. "Do you not remember?"

Noble closed his eyes for a moment, trying to see through the lingering fog in his mind.

He remembered Brendan finding him by that tree.

He remembered being fitted with chains and dragged into a war camp.

He remembered Hattie, injured, and his instant rage.

The rest was a series of vague flashes of gore and screaming, and the dazzling blue light of a sword on fire.

Then, peace. Sunlight on his face, in his veins.

Belated realization hit him square in the chest, and he turned to Hattie, overcome with pride. "You discovered the cure."

She frowned, nodded.

"How did—" he broke off. She could tell him all about her brilliance later. Right now, their future took precedent. Noble faced his father again. "You're afraid the Lord will use Hattie's discovery to further his plan—but Phina won't take part in that."

"Hattie expressed a similar sentiment," Kalden said tightly.

"If you keep us out of Fenrir, the research will continue," Noble said. "Let us return to the Collegium. Let us persuade Phina to shut down her program."

"You truly believe you can convince an ambitious Adept of Alchemy to give up—"

"Yes," Noble interrupted. "Phina endures the long days and oppressive oversight because she believes in her work, but I know for a fact that she hates the lifestyle. If we communicate to her that her program is corrupt—"

"You mustn't give her the cure," Kalden insisted. "It will advance the Lord's research in creating the weapon he seeks."

"Phina doesn't have to know," Noble said.

"She will, though," Hattie cut in. "As soon as she sees you, she'll know."

"How?"

Hattie grazed her fingertips across his collarbone, sending a shiver through him. He'd almost died, but he never felt more alive than when she was near. "Your Oath tattoos are gone."

His hand flew to his throat, as if he could feel the missing mark from the Order of the Morta. His skin was smooth—same as always—but when he turned his attention inward, the old magical tether was odd-ly...*nonexistent*. He felt like a dog whose collar had been removed, its absence more noticeable than when it had still been wrapped around his neck. When he checked his wrist, his Oath of Allegiance tattoo was also gone.

"How will Phina know that's a result of the cure?" Noble asked Hattie.

"Because Anya and Idris lost their Oaths, too—as soon as their blood mingled with the water from the Well of Fate."

A sudden clamminess swept over him. Noble stepped back from her, as if seeing her from a different angle might help him understand her words better. When that didn't work, he sank to the cot, disbelieving. "You mean to tell me..." he trailed off.

He had water from the Well of Fate in his veins? *That* was how Hattie bound Gildium to Hylder? How she altered the Arcane magic of his curse? The notion seemed to go against the Fates themselves, and yet—it made *sense*. Hadn't his monstrousness gone against the Fates, too? Why wouldn't the cure be just as *unnatural*?

Hattie sat beside him and rubbed his back. He allowed himself a moment to recover, then looked to his father again.

"Phina won't want a discovery like this to fall into the wrong hands—even if those hands are that of her Lord," Noble said. "Even if those hands are her own."

"You mean to tell me that Phina Farkept would be content with never learning the cure, purely for the sake of undermining her Lord?" Kalden asked. "Her brother is a Major of the Mighty in Fenrir."

"Their allegiance is with their territory, not the corrupt headpiece pulling their strings," Noble said. Of that, he was certain.

But Kalden shook his head. "I can't put my trust in an alchemist I've never met. Not when the Fate of the realm is at stake."

"I understand," Noble said, "but can you put your trust in your son?"

Kalden—who'd been scratching his beard—let his hand fall to his side. He regarded Noble—really, truly regarded him—and Noble felt as if he were sixteen again, standing before his father with a practice sword. Only this time, it wasn't approval he sought from his father—it was respect. *Faith.*

"I will trust you in this, Noble," Kalden began slowly.

From beside him, Hattie let out a whoosh of breath.

"But I have a duty to my king. I cannot allow my affection for my son to endanger—"

Noble chuckled. He couldn't help it. "Since when has your affection for me ever clouded your sense of duty?"

Kalden's eyes cut to Hattie, then back to Noble. It was barely a glance—a fraction of a second—but it was enough to tell Noble *everything* about how that fateful day nine years ago had gone.

Kalden—Noble's own father—*had* wanted to eliminate Hattie for the sake of Raina's safety and the security of the kingdom's future. He might not have made the call, but he'd considered it—perhaps that's why his subordinate had taken charge.

Yet Kalden Asheren had held back. He'd spared Hattie and sent her away instead. For Noble's sake. A trade of deep grief for a lesser sort. Hattie's death would've broken Noble, but never seeing her again...that had been Kalden's attempt at mercy.

Noble wasn't heartened by the realization, but knowing his father had chosen his son's feelings over the most secure outcome for the realm...it did help Noble see his father in a kinder light.

Noble stood to face his father. "What are your conditions?"

Kalden squared his shoulders. "I will have knights of *my* regiment—not Brendan's—standing by. One hint of Phina Farkept's recalcitrance, and she will be dispatched. Do you understand?"

Noble nodded. "It won't be necessary; she'll comply."

"Does Marona want the cure?" Hattie cut in, standing. "I can write down the formula."

"That will not be necessary," Kalden said. "We have no interest in cures, only eradication. Marona does not condone the use of arcane magic in the manner Fenrir has been exploring."

"The materials Brendan provided me suggest otherwise," Hattie said.

"Captain Harrow's leash is about to get shorter." Kalden inclined his head, his tone taking on a stony authority, as if Noble and Hattie were knights under his tutelage. "Concern yourself only with convincing Professor Farkept to shut down her program. Once you are successful, you will leave Fenrir and return to Waldron, where you will lie low."

"What of Hattie's conundrum?" Noble asked.

"You will be wed," Kalden said flatly. "That will at least keep her name out of the Census Ledgers."

Noble was unable to conceal his grin. His heart felt as if it'd sprouted wings; it lifted off, soaring. He spun around, ready to accept Hattie into his arms, but—

Her brows were drawn together, lips twisted into a contorted little frown. She'd wrapped her uninjured arm around her torso in a self-conscious hug, and when she met Noble's eyes...there was apology in her pretty blue stare.

Then she lowered her arm to her side, balled her fist, and shifted her attention to Kalden.

"We will not be wed," Hattie said.

Noble's heart dropped from its flight like a stone.

54

SELF

HATTIE

The smile on Noble's face broke apart, and I rushed to his side, placing a hand over his heart again. "Not because I don't want to," I assured him in a rush. "But because I don't want to marry you for the sake of keeping a secret." A crooked smile teased my lips. "*When* I marry you," I said, "it will be out of joy and celebration. Not desperation. Not to remove my identity—*again.*"

My first marriage had been about stripping me of my personhood; I didn't want my marriage to Noble to be about the same thing. I'd spent enough of my life living a lie, denying myself of being my *true* self.

No more.

Noble closed his hand over mine, pressing my palm more firmly against his chest. "That sounds like a Fortunate Fate," he said to me, then looked to Kalden again. "We will do as you wish—*unwed.*"

"Absolutely not."

"Either kill me, or let me live," I said. "I will accept no in between."

"And *I* will accept only the latter," Noble added.

"Rumors will spread, and the Census Ledgers will lead anyone with ill-intentions directly to you," Kalden insisted. "Hattie, if you truly wish to evade your lawful claim, it is in your best interest to—"

"Start new rumors, then," I said. "Or have my uncle update the Arcane Law. I don't really care, so much as I am left alone."

"I cannot allow—" A chorus of shouts interrupted Kalden's refusal.

The three of us went to the tent's entrance, stepping through the flaps into the searing midday sunshine. At least a dozen horses were loose and racing through camp, soldiers rushing around to contain them before the animals hurt themselves or ran off. Meanwhile, a charcoal-colored horse was galloping over the western hill, disappearing from sight.

So much for the four guards keeping Mariana in camp.

Kalden pushed past Noble and I, barking orders. Following Mariana would be a lost cause, but she *did* pose a threat to all that we'd discussed in Kalden's tent.

As Kalden shouted at his soldiers, trying to restore order, Noble grasped my hand and squeezed.

His lips brushed my ear as he whispered, "This might be a good opportunity to..." He pulled back, tipping his head in the direction of a gray mare prancing nervously around a nearby hitching post, yanking at her tether.

Before I could think, Noble was tugging me in the mare's direction, helping me onto the horse's back. Once I was settled, Noble untied her lead, fastened the end to her halter to create a makeshift bridle, and—with impressive agility—swung up behind me. Our horse danced sideways, riled by the high energy of the other animals running loose. It took only a tap of Noble's heels on her belly to send her launching forward.

"Stop them!" Kalden yelled.

The camp was a maze of tents, people, fire circles, supplies, and loose horses—all conspiring to slow us down. Soldiers jumped into our path, waving their arms. My head jerked to the side as we doubled back, weaving through obstacles. Kalden's hulking form came into view again; he shook his fist as we passed in the opposite direction, heading deeper into camp, only to turn around again. I threaded my hands into our mare's mane, holding on for dear life as Noble maneuvered us this way and that.

Soon, we found our opening: a gap between tents that led west, toward Fenrir. Noble angled us for the narrow path, our mare barreling forward fiercely—

—only to skid to a halt when Kalden positioned himself in the way, his greatsword raised.

"We weren't done with our conversation," he called.

"I respectfully disagree," Noble said.

Kalden lowered his blade and approached, his feet treading slowly over the trampled grass. Our mare skittered sideways, nearly bumping into one of the tents that formed this narrow chute to freedom. I glanced over my shoulder, dismayed to see a handful of soldiers and knights closing in.

We were blocked on all sides.

Kalden moved closer to our mount, lifting his non-sword-wielding hand in a placating manner, palm up. "There is still more to discuss. More options to consider."

"No," Noble replied firmly, "there isn't. We will go to Fenrir and do as you asked, and then we will disappear. In a situation with no perfect outcomes, this one suits all parties."

"Noble," Kalden said, "I don't wish to hold you captive, but—"

"Then let us go," Noble interrupted. "You might serve the king, but I don't, and neither does she. We will do as you asked, but in return, we ask for freedom."

"Son..." Kalden's palm remained lifted as he stepped sideways, nearing our mare's shoulder.

"Give my best to Mother," Noble murmured.

Kalden shook his head—then snatched forward, gripping my ankle with a firm hand. I cried out—not in pain, but in surprise. Behind me, I felt Noble's entire body stiffen.

With just as much speed as his father, Noble reached down and gripped Kalden's forearm. "Release her."

Kalden shook his head, holding my leg firm. "Come back to the tent. We can strategize."

Noble's scarred knuckles paled as he squeezed his father's arm. "Release. Her."

Kalden scowled, jaw clenched.

Then, underneath Noble's grip, something *popped*.

Kalden's eyes went wide, watering with pain. Noble flinched, releasing him abruptly. Our horse—nervous and eager to run—sidestepped, bumping into the canvas wall of a tent. I reached for her makeshift reins, tugging back, keeping her in place. Kalden was cradling his arm now, red-faced and sweating.

"You broke it!" Kalden panted, his face paling with shock. "It's broken!"

Had Noble truly just squeezed Kalden's arm so hard he crushed bone?

"Don't follow," Noble said, then kicked his feet.

Our mount barged her way through the narrow gap, blazing past soldiers with outstretched arms. We cleared the camp, then we were climbing the hill, our mare moving at a swift gallop through the meadow grass. With Noble's hands on the reins, his arms caged me in, steadying me as we rode for our escape.

Toward Fenrir.

Toward our future.

Hours later, we came upon the remnants of a small camp. Noble swung off our mare, then helped me down, holding my hips loosely—*notably* loosely—as I found my footing on exhausted, wobbly legs.

We were in the foothills of the Axe Mountains, where long tapered hills stretched down from the mountain rage like bony fingers. The camp was nestled in the slight valley between two ridges, on the edge of a stand of twiggy saplings.

Safe—at least for now.

"Rest," Noble said, kissing my cheek.

He didn't have to tell me twice; I collapsed into the grass, seating myself with my legs outstretched. Noble handed me our horse's lead, allowing her to graze without wandering too far. Then he disappeared into the trees, returning a few minutes later with his pack, which he must've been forced to abandon when Brendan found him.

"I think a raccoon got into it," Noble said, holding up the disheveled canvas, "but I found a stash of leftover jerky in the bottom." He handed me a piece, then sat beside me with a groan, snacking on his own scraps.

It was late afternoon, sunlight zinging through the grass, making the green stalks glow golden. With the warmth of the sun on my face, I wanted to lie back and nap—but the threat of Kalden's soldiers finding us kept me alert.

"He won't follow," Noble said, reading my mind—or maybe just my darting, vigilant attention. "But we ought to keep moving for another couple hours to find a more sheltered camp—preferably one with water."

"Should we look for Mariana?" I asked. "She was as much a part of last night as we were, and since she's been helping Phina...she should know what's going on."

Noble stared down at his piece of jerky, turning it over in his hands. "I suspect she already does," he said. "In any case, if she wants to be found, she will be."

"But can we trust her with *my* secret?"

Noble's nod was instant. "Yes."

I released a long sigh, content with his confidence in her—for now. "Do you think Mariana supplied the water from the Well of Fate to Brendan?" I wondered.

I'd explained the basics earlier: how Brendan had forced my hand, how the table he'd set up was the same as in my Mirror of Fortune, and how I'd uncovered the cure. I'd left out the rest—one day, we'd discuss that night in more detail, but for now, the memory of Noble's broken body was too painful to relive in full.

"I wouldn't put it past her to assist anyone seeking to uncover a cure," Noble answered. "Though she's proven an ally to both Phina and myself, her true motivations are a mystery."

"But if the Morta are cured," I said, "her Order will be dissolved—she could go back to the dungeon."

"If *Lord Haron* cures the Morta, yes," Noble said. "But if the Valiant—" He broke off, but not from Oath magic this time. He seemed surprised by what he could say without limitation.

I squeezed his arm, smiling.

"If the Valiant can beat Lord Haron to a cure..." He spread his hands. "There's more happening within Mariana's Order than we know. Much, much more."

"I wonder if Idris could tell us," I said. "Then again, he and Mariana aren't exactly *friends*. And he tends not to divulge much unless it's essential."

"It'll become essential soon enough."

"True," I mused, but the thought didn't trouble me at the moment.

I was too busy thinking about my return to Waldron—seeing Anya, serving Martha and Hugh and Vera at the bar of the Pretty Possum. Simple pleasures, but meaningful ones. Would they treat me differently when I told them who I was?

Probably not, I realized.

I'd seen travelers of all backgrounds and sorts pass through the Possum, and time and time again, Waldron's locals had based their opinions on more important things than status: a sense of humor, a kindness of spirit, and—when I, myself, had been a newcomer—my willingness to pitch in.

Not to mention the ability to mix great concoctails.

"We can certainly ask Idris when we get home," I added. "You're coming back to Waldron with me, right?"

"I want to..." Noble said, but his voice was strained. He dragged his attention from his hands to my face, green eyes searching. "Hattie, what happened earlier..."

His father's arm, *broken*.

I nodded encouragingly, waiting for him to say what I already knew.

"I'm...stronger than I was," Noble said. "*Different* than I was."

Delicately, I asked, "Is the monster still...?"

He shook his head. "No. No, it's gone. But the strength remains." He swiveled toward me, placing a careful palm on my knee. "Hattie, I don't think you cured the curse. I think you altered it. I think you succeeded in the Lord's original aim."

I bit my lip and broke eye contact, staring out over the southern hills, where a soft breeze was sending ripples through the stalks. *My* strength was still normal, which meant that it wasn't just my potion that made the difference—something about the arcane magic already in Noble's veins played a role, too. I was relieved I couldn't recreate the effect. Relieved that what I *did* know had not been passed on to Marona's adepts.

When I met Noble's eyes again, I shrugged innocently. "I don't know what you're talking about."

He quirked a brow. "Don't you?"

I shook my head, causing my curls to bounce. "Nope."

"Hmm." He wrapped an arm around my shoulders, tugging me closer. "Well, never mind, then."

A gentle gust of warm, late-spring wind rustled the leaves of the trees. I brushed a lock of Noble's hair away from his forehead, smoothing my fingers over the place where the horns had pushed through.

"So, Waldron?" I asked him.

"Do you think they'll have me?" he asked. "I'm afraid I cultivated a reputation of standoffishness. Won't they be protective of you?"

I pressed a kiss to his stubbled cheek. "Once I come clean to them about who I am, I believe you'll be the least shocking thing about my return."

Noble chuckled into my hair. "You're probably right." When he pulled back to look at me, the skin around his eyes had creased. "Are you sure you want to tell them?"

I smoothed the creases with my fingertips, smiling. "I'm willing to hide in Waldron to avoid my claim," I said, "but I'm done hiding *myself* from the people I love."

55

No Questions
Asked

Hattie

Two days later, Noble and I stood in Phina's chambers at the Collegium, dusty and smelling of horse from the hard ride back to Fenrir City. It was dark—just after midnight—and yet Phina hadn't seemed surprised by our arrival. She'd simply ushered us inside, locked her door with a *click*, and offered us wine (Noble had declined, but I'd gratefully accepted a heavy pour).

Now, she sat in one of the upholstered reading chairs by the window. "Care to sit?" she asked, crossing one leg over the other. She wore a flowing dressing gown, but in spite of the late hour, she seemed wide awake.

I was too antsy to sit, as was Noble, but I did take a fortifying sip of my wine. "Phina, the program—"

"I've already notified Lord Haron of its termination," she interrupted.

I spluttered, and Noble rubbed my back.

"Mariana paid me a similar visit a few hours ago," Phina explained, gesturing at us with her cup. "I had my suspicions that Lord Haron had ulterior motives for my research, and she confirmed."

"What else did she say?" I asked.

"Nothing," Phina said, "and I don't wish to know."

Noble shook his head. "But your research—"

"Ought not be dictated by a corrupt ruler," Phina finished for him. "My joy is in the research itself, which I can conduct independently from my cottage." She glanced meaningfully at my bare wrist, Noble's neck—our missing Oath tattoos. Having seen the effects of the Well of Fate on Anya and Idris, she *must've* known that it played a role. She had to be curious about how I'd solved the curse. I certainly would be.

I stepped toward her. "I can tell you how."

She smiled softly. "Unlike you, my curiosity does not outweigh my sense."

A laugh burst out of me.

Phina flashed us a mischievous grin. "I do have my theories, though. And my research is never over—even if the setting changes."

"What of your Adept Oath?" Noble asked. "And Oderin? Are you not obligated to divulge—"

"What, exactly? I have solved nothing. It is not against my Oath to give up," Phina said. "As for Oderin, he prefers to stay out of my affairs—and I, his."

"Can he be trusted not to speak of *our* affairs, either?" I asked her.

Phina shrugged. "What would he say? Noble is no longer afflicted, and your identity is irrelevant."

My breath caught. "You know who I am?"

"Unlike the attendance records of the Collegium, the Oath of Allegiance magic tied to my Research Ledger is too strong to record false names, Hattie *Mund*," Phina said with a smirk. "My brother made the connection after he saw you two interact. Thankfully for you, neither of us care much for titles—or endangering our friends. And with the study retired, the Ledger is unlikely to be reviewed from outside eyes."

I let out a harsh exhale, both shocked and amused that my professor had known my identity this whole time—and that she considered me a friend.

"You should be very proud of yourselves for what you accomplished." Phina's kind eyes then landed on Noble. "I'm relieved you're all right."

Noble bowed his head. "Thank you, Phina. For your help, your friendship—everything."

She smiled warmly, then tossed back her wine and stood, wandering over to a writing desk in the corner. "Speaking of accomplishments"—she retrieved a scroll and handed it to me—"congratulations are in order."

I unraveled the paper. *Apothecary License* was scrawled across the top in swooping letters. It'd been signed by Phina and the lead adept of the Collegium, and an official wax seal adorned the corner.

"Phina, I..." I trailed off, shaking my head. "I can't see how I've earned this. I didn't complete my classes."

She placed a hand on my arm and jutted her chin in Noble's direction. "He's proof enough of your skill, Hattie. You earned it."

Noble's palm nestled between my shoulder blades, rubbing gently. "She's right, Peach."

Tears sprung to the corners of my eyes. This was the culmination of *years* of obsessive reading, learning, practicing, and dreaming. Saving Noble might've been my Fated Fortune, but this validation of my passion and dedication to alchemy was a close second.

"You're a talented alchemist, Hattie Wynhaim," Phina said.

Hearing the sentiment from my idol, with my *real* name...I couldn't help myself. I stepped forward and wrapped my arms around Phina's shoulders, squeezing hard. She let out a soft *ooph*, belatedly reciprocating my embrace. Then she was laughing, and so was I, and Noble was wrapping his arms around us both, savoring our odd triumph.

The hug didn't last long, though.

When Phina pulled back, her expression had turned grave. "There is one thing I need from you—both of you."

"Anything," Noble and I replied in unison.

"When Mariana comes looking for you," Phina said, "I need you to trust her."

56

RIVERBANK

NOBLE

Noble lay with his hands behind his head, staring up into a canopy of weeping willow branches. Their long, slender leaves twirled like ribbons, pale green catching the light of the sun overhead. Beyond the treetop, wispy clouds drifted across a sky that was one shade lighter than the intense blue of Hattie's irises.

The air was hot, muggy. As water from his swim dried on his bare chest, a sheen of sweat replaced it. He turned his head to the side, where a picnic basket had already been ravaged: empty jars and sticky spoons, lemon cookie crumbs, a bottle with only a sip of citrusy concoctail remaining.

Noble sighed, feeling his body relax into the bed of cool moss beneath him. He closed his eyes, dozing.

A splash woke him.

He angled himself up on one elbow, shading his eyes with a hand.

Hattie was emerging from the river, lithe and glistening. Her naked skin was a wet, breathtaking expanse of gentle curves, freckly skin, and the beautiful mauve blush that persistently painted her cheekbones and sternum. As she approached, Noble wondered, briefly, if he was still dreaming.

While the rest of Waldron were setting up their summer solstice festival, Noble and Hattie had snuck off to a secluded bend in the River Wend. Even with the guarantee of privacy, watching the water sluice down her waist, hips, and thighs felt illicit.

Forbidden.

Call it habit, but he still sometimes forgot that she *wasn't* forbidden. Not anymore. On the contrary, she was all his—and he, hers.

She padded closer, picking her way across the soft moss with her bare feet. A smile parted her lips, hungry and suggestive, and when she reached him, she climbed up his body on her hands and knees to straddle his hips.

"Hi," she said.

"Hi," he said.

She smelled like peaches and the fresh earthiness of the river—one half of the magical water mixture that had saved him. Hattie said that someday, she intended to learn more about the Wend's magical properties—but she wasn't in a hurry.

"Were you asleep?" Hattie asked.

"Dozing," he said. "Did you enjoy your swim?"

Her skin was cool from the river, slick with moisture. He held her hips, rocking her forward against his growing erection.

"Yes," she said, her voice breathy and low. "Did you enjoy watching?"

He had—up until the blood rushed to his groin, and he'd forced himself to stop staring. He would be thirty next year, yet Hattie still made him feel like a Fates-damned adolescent. "You're beautiful," Noble said. "Inside and out."

Hattie leaned in for a kiss, her nipples—tight from the cold—brushing his chest. "Oh yeah?"

He nodded slowly. Her freckles had darkened from the summer sunshine and stood out starkly against her pale cheeks. "When you're with me, the world appears brighter and more colorful," he murmured against her lips, repeating what he'd said to her in Phina's lab, just before they'd kissed.

She nibbled on his bottom lip. "Go on."

He brushed an unruly curl off her forehead. "You are a sunrise," he said. "You are the summer itself."

"Is that so?"

"Every day, I thank the Fates that they gifted me with eyes capable of appreciating your beauty so closely. Every shade, every freckle, every expression. Nothing else compares." He paused. "Even if I were blind, your radiant character would still take my breath away."

Hattie's lower lip wobbled, and he pinned it with a kiss. "I love you, too," she whispered against his mouth.

He was still getting accustomed to his painfully perfect existence in Waldron with Hattie. Two months had passed since their return, and the events between their confrontation with his father and now had rushed by more swiftly than Wynhaim Falls, a cascade of conversations and emotions.

After escaping his father's camp, they hadn't stayed more than twelve hours in Fenrir City. Following their meeting with Phina (which had ended with Hattie insisting Phina give Oderin her best and emphasizing that they were welcome in Waldron anytime), Hattie had snuck into Inver College to collect her things. Sani and Uriel had eyed Noble with a blend of teasing and suspicion, but when it was time for Hattie to leave, they hadn't asked any questions; Hattie's vague insinuation about *knowing too much* had been enough for both her friends to understand her swift departure. After that, Hattie had written notes to Willa and Viren for Sani and Uriel to deliver, Noble had claimed the rest of his abandoned things from the Royal Inn of Fenrir, and then they'd ridden south.

To Noble's relief, Kalden had ultimately allowed their escape. With Phina's research program shut down, the general must've been satisfied enough by the neutralized threat to leave Noble and Hattie alone. He had no doubt that Kalden would be monitoring the spread of rumors from afar, but in truth, it was a comfort to know that as long as his father didn't come for them, no one else was likely to, either.

It still pained Noble to not have a closer relationship with his father, but he no longer wished to please Kalden, and that gave him a sense of freedom he'd always thought was out of reach. As far as Noble was concerned, hiding in a paradise like Waldron was the perfect solution to the concerns they'd discussed in Kalden's pavilion.

Noble *did* look forward to proposing marriage to Hattie again soon—but the next time he did, it would not be in an effort to *hide* her, but to devote himself to her out of love and *only* love. He'd heard that Waldron weddings were boisterous affairs.

Hattie had been right about Noble's reception in Waldron, too. After she'd called a town meeting to reveal her true identity, no one had questioned Noble's presence. It had been touching, really, to see how Hattie's community welcomed her truth. In spite of her protests, they'd held a festival in her honor—then vowed never to speak of the matter again. He wasn't sure a town full of gossips could be trusted on such matters, but Anya had assured him that when it came to *important* secrets, Waldron looked after their own.

And welcomed newcomers, too. Ever since folks had caught on about Noble not *actually* being a recluse, he'd been inundated with social requests. Most meaningful, however, was Richold, who'd invited Noble back into his workshop to continue passing along his knowledge of Gildium (when he wasn't spending an increasing amount of time with Kara). Noble, having cultivated a genuine passion for metal alchemy, had been honored to resume his studies—this time, for fun.

The one thing Noble and Hattie had kept to themselves, however, was his curse—specifically, his altered strength, something he and Hattie didn't yet fully understand. Some secrets were worth keeping. And aside from the occasional questioning look from Richold when Noble demonstrated too much strength at the forge or Idris when helping with chores around the Possum, that secret was easy enough to keep.

So, there they were: basking on a riverbank in a small town in southern Fenrir, far from the perils of their past—living, finally, inside the promise of their future.

"You're pensive," Hattie said, pressing her body fully against his.

The contact made him groan. "I was thinking about you."

"I'm right here," she said, poking his nose.

He laughed. "Still hard to wrap my head around that," he admitted.

Her playful demeanor shifted, becoming more serious. "I understand," she said. "Sometimes this feels..."

"Too good to be true?"

Hattie nodded.

"Go on," he urged.

Hattie slid off his body, coming to rest on her side beside to him, her head on his collarbone, her palm flat on his chest, one sensuous leg hooked over his, keeping their bodies close. "I guess I'm afraid, still," Hattie said. "Of being discovered. Of what it could mean for Raina. I don't regret living more truthfully here, but sometimes I think about your father's warnings and..."

Noble kissed her temple. "I know what you mean." His father had a way of saying things that rang in the mind like a bell, a constant, echoing clang that never truly faded. "But we can't control the future—we can't control Fate," Noble said. "All we can do is enjoy the peace while it's here."

Hattie tipped her head up, meeting his eyes. From this angle, with her body draped over him, and her brilliant attention aimed directly at him...how could he not feel like the luckiest man alive? His Fate could still be blank—they'd know for certain this fall, when the Mirrors passed through town—but as long as Hattie was by his side, Noble was certain his future would be blessed.

"Ugh, look at me, talking about myself when *you* were the pensive one," Hattie said, propping herself on an elbow to regard him more squarely. "What's troubling you?"

They might've solved his curse, but Noble never did learn what the Arcane Adepts had originally injected into his veins. He still didn't know the full extent of his strength or how else he might be altered. He'd spoken to Anya and Idris a bit about the strangeness of possessing a blank Fate, and though it was comforting not to feel so alone in the experience...he sometimes still felt *other*.

Then again, he also felt incredibly fortunate.

"No trouble," Noble said, tugging Hattie closer. "Just...loose ends occupying my thoughts, I suppose."

"Ah," Hattie said. "You mean the remnants of your curse, the Morta in the Western Wood, and Lord Haron's plot against Marona?"

He laughed. "You're astute."

"I worry about the same things you do," she said.

"There's nothing you can do."

"I could say the same to you."

Somewhere downriver, ducks quacked, their voices echoing off the surface of the calm water. It brought him back into the moment, into this perfect day, far from corrupt magic and the machinations of rulers.

"Well, there's something I can do." Noble guided Hattie onto her back and rolled on top of her. All that bare skin was a fever dream straight out of his adolescence.

She giggled, her body shuddering beneath him. Her golden hair was fanned around her face, a stunning contrast to the vibrant green moss cushioning her head. She dragged her nails across his back in the way she knew he liked, tracing the ridges with a delicious scrape. In answer, he rolled his hips, feeling his whole body wake up.

"We should probably help with the festival preparations," Hattie said, even as she arched against him, pressing close. "I have my tent to set up, and—"

Noble bent, sliding his tongue along the side of her neck. He cupped a breast, squeezing, then slid his hand between their bodies to feel her wetness. A little sigh slipped out of her, and he pulled back to see the flush climbing up her neck, painting her cheekbones.

Fates, he loved that color.

"What were you saying, Peach?" he teased.

Hattie bit her bottom lip, smiling. "You know? I don't remember."

Epilogue:
Sharpen Your
Knives and
Wits

Hattie

My sides hurt from laughing. My legs hurt from dancing. My cheeks hurt from smiling.

In all my years in Waldron, I'd never been to a Soliden Festival so joyful.

Soliden was Waldron's annual summer solstice celebration, a mirror of Astrophel in winter. Three days of music, amazing food, summery beverages, dancing with ribbon streamers, and socializing so much my voice went hoarse. Not to mention the rows upon rows of market tents selling clothing, jewelry, metalwork, crafts, snacks, and—new to town this year—a stall with tinctures and potions made by a newly licensed apothecary.

Me.

It had been the perfect opportunity to share my new wares: potions for sleep, tinctures for digestion, salves for minor cuts and burns. I'd also bottled a few town-favorite concoctails, and managed to recreate the jarred, spiced peaches that Noble had found in Fenrir. Those—along with a new Hylderberry jam—had been my bestsellers. Seeing my fellow neighbors enjoy my creations (and *pay* me for them!) had filled me with a giddy sort of contentment. A sense of true self.

Now, Anya, Idris, Noble, and I were back in the Pretty Possum Inn and Pub's cavernous, empty bar room, collapsed in the overstuffed chairs facing the cold hearth. It was after midnight, and all the windows were open, letting in the balmy summer breeze. A few lanterns flickered, but otherwise, the space was dark. Wicker snored from his pile of blankets in the corner.

The past few days had been hot, sticky, but wonderful. My head pulsed with the faintest hint of a headache from pulling three all-nighters in a row and sleeping at odd hours of the day. A sign of a successful Soliden.

"I'm beat," Noble said, running a hand over his face. "Are all Waldron festivals like that?"

We were wedged into one overly wide chair, his arm slung around my waist.

Anya—seated on Idris's lap in the chair across from us—chuckled. "If you aren't nearing total exhaustion, with ringing ears and a wicked hangover, it's not a proper Waldron festival."

"And how many festivals are there, annually?" Noble asked wearily.

Idris grunted. "Too many."

Anya shoved his chest, and he laughed, capturing her hand in his. Upon our return, Anya had informed me that they were engaged to be wed—just as I'd guessed. They were planning to hold the ceremony close to Astrophel, near Anya's birthday. The cloying sweetness that radiated off the happy couple would've bothered me, if it weren't for the fact that I knew how they felt—and knew how hard-won their love had been.

"You lived here for a year," I said to Noble, "you should know how many festivals we have."

"I did my best to avoid them, if you recall."

"Rude," Anya quipped.

"It's just because he was so smitten with me, he couldn't take it," I said, beaming.

Noble pressed a kiss to my temple. "It's true."

"Thank the Fates," Anya said, "because Hattie was also smitten."

"That wasn't as much of a secret," Noble said dotingly, sliding his fingers up the back of my neck, making me shiver.

"She had a bigger secret to keep," Anya said, offering me a soft smile.

I love you, I mouthed at her.

Who, me? Idris mouthed back.

I giggled. Anya glanced between us, one eyebrow raised.

When I'd come clean to her about my past, I'd fully expected Anya to be angry, grow cold, or lose all trust in me—perhaps all three. She would've been justified; after all, I'd spent nine years lying to her. Betraying her.

Instead, Anya had drawn me into a fierce hug, holding me so tightly the embrace had stolen my breath. "Aren't you angry?" I'd asked. To which Anya had replied, "I'm only angry that I couldn't be there for you fully. It must've been so isolating to keep such a secret from everyone." I'd subsequently burst into tears, and we spent the whole night pouring our hearts out: me, telling her everything about my upbringing, my friendship with Noble, how much I missed Raina, and the events that led me to Waldron—and her, telling me everything she knew about the Well of Fate.

When once we'd kept secrets from each other to protect each other, we'd discovered that truth was a greater form of protection against an increasingly unstable world.

"There are four major festivals—one for each season," Anya explained to Noble, back to the topic at hand, "plus the Mirror Festival every autumn. That doesn't include all the weddings, birthdays, funerals, and countless other—" she broke off, her gaze swinging toward the door.

"What do you hear?" Idris asked her, his hand falling from her hip as she climbed out of his lap.

Ever attuned to his owner, Wicker lifted his head and let out a soft *woof*.

"Don't worry, it's just me," Mariana said, sauntering in with the confidence of an old friend. And—Fates spare me—she sort of *was* a friend, considering the ways she'd helped all four of us.

Anya and I rose to meet her, Idris and Noble following close on our heels. An angry tension radiated off the men, but Anya and I weren't afraid of her.

Mariana went straight for the bar, leaning over the oak counter to pour herself a pint.

"Seriously?" Anya said. "Have you no manners?"

Mariana plopped onto a stool, her back to the bar, elbows resting on the counter behind her. She took a long sip of her ale and licked the froth off her upper lip. "Sorry to interrupt your happy congregation, but I need a favor."

"We're retired," Idris said.

Mariana raked her fingers through her unbound hair. Perhaps it was the moody lighting of the lanterns, but she looked tired. Darkness ringed her eyes, and a faint tension bracketed her casual smirk. Otherwise, she appeared much the same: black armor over black clothing, a sword sheathed at her hip.

She set her ale aside and hopped off her stool, coming closer. "Maybe I didn't make myself clear," Mariana said, meeting Idris's hard stare—then Noble's—then mine. "You owe me. I'm here to collect."

While Idris grumbled in protest, Noble and I shared a knowing look. *When Mariana comes looking for you*, Phina had told us two months ago, *I need you to trust her.*

"What do you need?" I asked.

Mariana flipped open her satchel, dug around, and procured a clear glass bottle. She set it on the bar counter with a hard *clink*, the blue-green water inside it sloshing.

"Wait," Anya whispered, pointing at the bottle, "is that what I think it is?"

Mariana kept her attention on me. "I need you to make more cure."

All eyes swung in my direction.

"You...what?" I choked.

Mariana stepped closer, until we were face to face. "You heard me." She jerked her chin at Noble. "You cured him. I need you to cure more."

"Why?" Idris asked.

"Because the Valiant are planning an uprising," I realized, "and this is their advantage."

Mariana grinned at me, a flash of wicked teeth. Her pride in my smarts was unsettling...and flattering.

"Remember when I said the war is coming?" Mariana asked, eyes flicking to Idris, before sweeping over our little group. "I'm sorry to be the bearer of bad news, but it's time to sharpen your knives and wits."

To read a bonus chapter with Hattie and Noble, receive Hattie's lemon cookie recipe and other exclusive content, and get notified about upcoming books and special editions, please join my newsletter:

nicolavictory.com/newsletter

Reviews mean a lot to independent authors like me—even a single sentence can help new readers discover my books. I can't wait to hear what you thought of *Fate's Sweetest Curse* in an online review!

Remember when Mariana put her boot on that Mighty Knight's neck? The Mirrors of Fate series will continue with Mariana and Faren's enemies-to-lovers story of clashing loyalties, brewing war, and burning attraction. Coming 2026.

ABOUT THE AUTHOR

Nicola Victory is the sword-wielding alter ego of an award-winning, bestselling, contemporary fiction writer. Nicola writes spicy romantasy books for adults about brave heroines and strong-but-kind heroes facing their fears for love.

When Nicola is not writing books, she enjoys reading, sipping coffee, and exploring the wilds of the Pacific Northwest. She spends her days with her very own romance hero and two cats named after celestial bodies.

Connect with Nicola on Instagram and TikTok @nicolavictorywrites or via her website: nicolavictory.com